Outstanding Praise for the Novels of T. Greenwood

Bodies of Water

"A complex and compelling portrait of the painful intricacies of love and loyalty. Book clubs will find much to discuss in T. Greenwood's insightful story of two women caught between their hearts and their families."
—Eleanor Brown, *New York Times* bestselling author of *The Weird Sisters*

"*Bodies of Water* is no ordinary love story, but a book of astonishing precision, lyrically told, raw in its honesty and gentle in its unfolding. What I find myself reveling in, pondering, savoring, really, is more than this book's uncommon beauty, though there is much beauty to be found within these pages. The real magic of this book is not its lingering poetry or even the striking subject matter of two families trying to survive in an era in which many men and women found themselves bound by strict constructs of "husband" and "wife," often resulting in them losing themselves and each other. The magic of this story is found in the depth and power of these relationships, as rich in texture as velvet, as fluid as water, as astonishing in their frailty as they are in their strength. Here is a complex tapestry of lives entwined, a testimony to the fact that a timeless sort of love does exist—one that sustains memory, derails oppression, and with its striking ferocity can cause human beings to relinquish love and yet also to recover it. T. Greenwood has rendered a compassionate story of people who are healed and destroyed by love, by alcoholism, by secrets and betrayal, and yet she offers us a certain shade of hope that while the barriers between people can make a narrow neighborhood street seem as wide as the ocean, soul mates can and do find each other—sometimes more than once in a lifetime. A luminous, fearless, heart-wrenching story about the power of true love."
—Ilie Ruby, author of *The Salt God's Daughter*

"T. Greenwood's *Bodies of Water* is a lyrical novel about the inexplicable nature of love, and the power a forbidden affair has to transform one woman's entire life. By turns beautiful and tragic, haunting and healing, I was captivated from the very first line. And Greenwood's moving story of love and loss, hope and redemption has stayed with me, long after I turned the last page."
—Jillian Cantor, author of *Margot*

Breathing Water

"A poignant, clear-eyed first novel . . . filled with careful poetic description . . . the story is woven skillfully."
—*The New York Times Book Review*

"A poignant debut . . . Greenwood sensitively and painstakingly unravels her protagonist's self-loathing and replaces it with a graceful dignity."
—*Publishers Weekly*

"A vivid, somberly engaging first book."
—Larry McMurtry

"With its strong characters, dramatic storytelling, and heartfelt narration, *Breathing Water* should establish T. Greenwood as an important young novelist who has the great gift of telling a serious and sometimes tragic story in an entertaining and pleasing way."
—Howard Frank Mosher, author of *Walking to Gatlinburg*

"An impressive first novel."
—*Booklist*

"*Breathing Water* is startling and fresh . . . Greenwood's novel is ripe with originality."
—The *San Diego Union-Tribune*

Grace

"*Grace* is a poetic, compelling story that glows in its subtle, yet searing examination of how we attempt to fill the potentially devastating fissures in our lives. Each character is masterfully drawn; each struggles in their own way to find peace amid tumultuous circumstance. With her always crisp imagery and fearless language, Greenwood doesn't back down from the hard issues or the darker sides of human psyche, managing to create astounding empathy and a balanced view of each player along the way. The story expertly builds to a breathtaking climax, leaving the reader with a clear understanding of how sometimes, only a moment of grace can save us."
—Amy Hatvany, author of *Best Kept Secret*

"*Grace* is at once heartbreaking, thrilling and painfully beautiful. From the opening page to the breathless conclusion, T. Greenwood again shows why she is one of our most gifted and lyrical storytellers."
—Jim Kokoris, author of *The Pursuit of Other Interests*

"Greenwood has given us a family we are all fearful of becoming—creeping toward scandal, flirting with financial disaster, and hovering on the verge of dissolution. *Grace* is a masterpiece of small-town realism that is as harrowing as it is heartfelt."
—Jim Ruland, author of *Big Lonesome*

"This novel will keep readers rapt until the very end . . . Shocking and honest, you're likely to never forget this book."
—*RT Book Reviews*

"*Grace* amazes. Harrowing, heartfelt, and ultimately so realistically human in its terror and beauty that it may haunt you for days after you finish it. T. Greenwood has another gem here. Greenwood's mastery of character and her deep empathy for the human condition make you care what happens, especially in the book's furious final 100 pages."

—*The San Diego Union-Tribune*

"Exceptionally well-observed. Readers who enjoy insightful and sensitive family drama (Lionel Shriver's *We Need to Talk About Kevin*; Rosellen Brown's *Before and After*) will appreciate discovering Greenwood."

—*Library Journal*

Nearer Than the Sky

"Greenwood is an assured guide through this strange territory; she has a lush, evocative style."

—*The New York Times Book Review*

"T. Greenwood writes with grace and compassion about loyalty and betrayal, love and redemption in this totally absorbing novel about daughters and mothers."

—Ursula Hegi, author of *Stones from the River*

"A lyrical investigation into the unreliability and elusiveness of memory centers Greenwood's second novel . . . The kaleidoscopic heart of the story is rich with evocative details about its heroine's inner life."

—*Publishers Weekly*

"Compelling . . . Highly recommended."

—*Library Journal*

"Doesn't disappoint. A complicated story of love and abuse told with a directness and intensity that packs a lightning charge."

—*Booklist*

"*Nearer Than the Sky* is a remarkable portrait of resilience. With clarity and painful precision, T. Greenwood probes the dark history of Indie's family."

—Rene Steinke, author of *The Fires* and *Holy Skirts*

"Greenwood's writing is lyrical and original. There is warmth and even humor and love. Her representation of MSBP is meticulous."

—*San Diego Union-Tribune*

"Deft handling of a difficult and painful subject . . . compelling."

—*Kirkus Reviews*

"Potent . . . Greenwood's clear-eyed prose takes the stuff of tabloid television and lends it humanity."

—*San Francisco Chronicle*

"T. Greenwood brings stunning psychological richness and authenticity to *Nearer Than the Sky*. Hers is the very first work of fiction to accurately address factitious disorders and Munchausen by proxy—the curious, complex, and dramatic phenomena in which people falsify illness to meet their own deep emotional needs."

—Marc D. Feldman, M.D., author of *Patient or Pretender* and *Playing Sick?: Untangling the Web of Munchausen Syndrome, Munchausen by Proxy, Malingering, and Factitious Disorder,* and co-author of *Sickened: The Memoir of a Munchausen by Proxy Childhood*

This Glittering World

"In *This Glittering World*, T. Greenwood demonstrates once again that she is a poet and storyteller of unique gifts, not the least of which is a wise and compassionate heart."

—Drusilla Campbell, author of *The Good Sister* and *Blood Orange*

"T. Greenwood's novel *This Glittering World* is swift, stark, calamitous. Her characters, their backs against the wall, confront those difficult moments that will define them and Greenwood paints these troubled lives with attention, compassion and hope. Through it all, we are caught on the dangerous fault lines of a culturally torn northern Arizona, where the small city of Flagstaff butts up against the expansive Navajo Reservation and the divide between the two becomes manifest. As this novel about family, friendship, and allegiance swirls toward its tumultuous climax, *This Glittering World* asks us how it is that people sometimes choose to turn toward redemption, and sometimes choose its opposite—how it is, finally, that we become the people we become."

—Jerry Gabriel, author of *Drowned Boy* and winner of the Mary McCarthy Prize in Short Fiction

"Stark, taut, and superbly written, this dark tale brims with glimpses of the Southwest and scenes of violence, gruesome but not gratuitous. This haunting look at a fractured family is certain to please readers of literary suspense."

—*Library Journal* (starred review)

"Greenwood's prose is beautiful. Her writing voice is simple but emotional."

—*RT Book Reviews*

Undressing the Moon

"This beautiful story, eloquently told, demands attention."
—*Library Journal* (starred review)

"Greenwood has skillfully managed to create a novel with unforgettable characters, finely honed descriptions, and beautiful imagery."
—*Book Street USA*

"A lyrical, delicately affecting tale."
—*Publishers Weekly*

"Rarely has a writer rendered such highly charged topics . . . to so wrenching, yet so beautifully understated, an effect . . . T. Greenwood takes on risky subject matter, handling her volatile topics with admirable restraint . . . Ultimately more about life than death, *Undressing the Moon* beautifully elucidates the human capacity to maintain grace under unrelenting fire."
—*The Los Angeles Times*

The Hungry Season

"This compelling study of a family in need of rescue is very effective, owing to Greenwood's eloquent, exquisite word artistry and her knack for developing subtle, suspenseful scenes . . . Greenwood's sensitive and gripping examination of a family in crisis is real, complex, and anything but formulaic."
—*Library Journal* (starred review)

"A deeply psychological read."
—*Publishers Weekly*

"Can there be life after tragedy? How do you live with the loss of a child, let alone the separation emotionally from all your loved ones? T. Greenwood with beautiful prose poses this question while delving into the psyches of a successful man, his wife, and his son . . . This is a wonderful story, engaging from the beginning that gets better with every chapter."
—*The Washington Times*

Two Rivers

"From the moment the train derails in the town of Two Rivers, I was hooked. Who is this mysterious young stranger named Maggie, and what is she running from? In *Two Rivers*, T. Greenwood weaves a haunting story in which the sins of the past threaten to destroy the fragile equilibrium of the present. Ripe with surprising twists and heartbreakingly real characters, *Two Rivers* is a remarkable and complex look at race and forgiveness in small-town America."
—Michelle Richmond, *New York Times* bestselling author of *The Year of Fog* and *No One You Know*

"*Two Rivers* is a convergence of tales, a reminder that the past never washes away, and yet, in T. Greenwood's delicate handling of time gone and time to come, love and forgiveness wait on the other side of what life does to us and what we do to it. This novel is a sensitive and suspenseful portrayal of family and the ties that bind."

—Lee Martin, author of *The Bright Forever* and *River of Heaven*

"The premise of *Two Rivers* is alluring: the very morning a deadly train derailment upsets the balance of a sleepy Vermont town, a mysterious girl shows up on Harper Montgomery's doorstep, forcing him to dredge up a lifetime of memories—from his blissful, indelible childhood to his lonely, contemporary existence. Most of all, he must look long and hard at that terrible night twelve years ago, when everything he held dear was taken from him, and he, in turn, took back. T. Greenwood's novel is full of love, betrayal, lost hopes, and a burning question: is it ever too late to find redemption?"

—Miranda Beverly-Whittemore, author of *The Effects of Light* and the Janet Heidinger Kafka Prize–winning *Set Me Free*

"Greenwood is a writer of subtle strength, evoking small-town life beautifully while spreading out the map of Harper's life, finding light in the darkest of stories."

—*Publishers Weekly*

"T. Greenwood's writing shimmers and sings as she braids together past, present, and the events of one desperate day. I ached for Harper in all of his longing, guilt, grief, and vast, abiding love, and I rejoiced at his final, hard-won shot at redemption."

—Marisa de los Santos, *New York Times* bestselling author of *Belong to Me* and *Love Walked In*

"*Two Rivers* is a stark, haunting story of redemption and salvation. T. Greenwood portrays a world of beauty and peace that, once disturbed, reverberates with searing pain and inescapable consequences; this is a story of a man who struggles with the deepest, darkest parts of his soul, and is able to fight his way to the surface to breathe again. But also—maybe more so—it is the story of a man who learns the true meaning of family: *When I am with you, I am home.* A memorable, powerful work."

—Garth Stein, *New York Times* bestselling author of *The Art of Racing in the Rain*

"A complex tale of guilt, remorse, revenge, and forgiveness . . . Convincing . . . Interesting . . ."

—*Library Journal*

"In the tradition of *The Adventures of Huckleberry Finn* and *To Kill a Mockingbird*, T. Greenwood's *Two Rivers* is a wonderfully distinctive American novel, abounding with memorable characters, unusual lore and history, dark family secrets, and love of life. *Two Rivers* is the story that people want to read: the one they have never read before."

—Howard Frank Mosher, author of *Walking to Gatlinburg*

"*Two Rivers* is a dark and lovely elegy, filled with heartbreak that turns itself into hope and forgiveness. I felt so moved by this luminous novel."

—Luanne Rice, *New York Times* bestselling author

"*Two Rivers* is reminiscent of Thornton Wilder, with its quiet New England town shadowed by tragedy, and of Sherwood Anderson, with its sense of desperate loneliness and regret . . . It's to Greenwood's credit that she answers her novel's mysteries in ways that are believable, that make you feel the sadness that informs her characters' lives."

—*Bookpage*

Books by T. Greenwood

Bodies of Water

Grace

This Glittering World

The Hungry Season

Two Rivers

Undressing the Moon

Nearer Than the Sky

Breathing Water

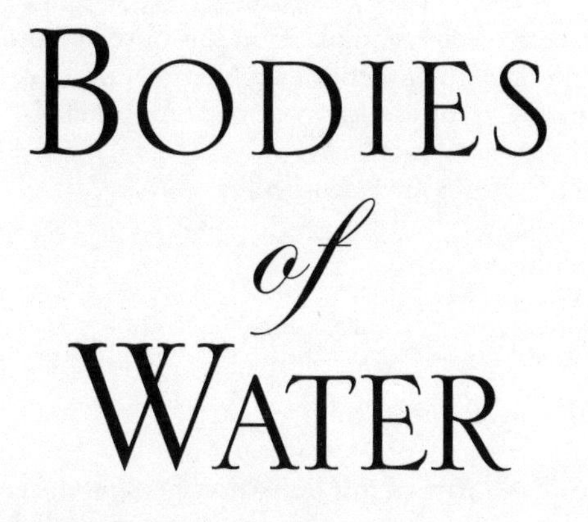

BODIES *of* WATER

T. GREENWOOD

KENSINGTON BOOKS
www.kensingtonbooks.com

KENSINGTON BOOKS are published by

Kensington Publishing Corp.
119 West 40th Street
New York, NY 10018

ISBN-13: 978-0-7582-5093-3
ISBN-10: 0-7582-5093-2
First Kensington Trade Paperback Printing: October 2013

eISBN-13: 978-0-7582-9144-8
eISBN-10: 0-7582-9144-2
First Kensington Electronic Edition: October 2013

10 9 8 7 6 5 4 3 2 1

Printed in the United States of America

For Carlene and Angela

This is what I know: memory is the same as water. It permeates and saturates. Quenches and satiates. It can hold you up or pull you under; render you weightless or drown you. It is tangible, but elusive. My memories of Eva are like this: the watery dreams of a past I can no more easily grasp than a fistful of the ocean. Some days, they buoy me. Other days, they threaten me with their dangerous draw. Memory. Water. Our bodies are made of it; it is what we are. I can no longer separate myself from my recollections. On the best days, on the *worst* days, I believe I have dissolved into them.

It was the ocean's tidal pull that brought me here to this little beach town forty years ago, and later to this battered cottage perched at the edge of the cliffs, overlooking the sea. It is what keeps me here as well. And while I may not be able to escape my memories, I have escaped the seasons here; this is what I think as summer turns seamlessly into fall, the only sign of this shift being the disappearance of the tourists. During the summer, the other rental cottages are full of families and couples, the porches littered with surfboards and beach toys, the railings draped with wet swimsuits and brightly colored beach towels. Sometimes a child will line up shells along the balustrade, a parade of treasures. At summer's end, the kindest mothers will pack these up as they pack up the rest of their things, slipping them into a little plastic bag to be stowed inside a suitcase. The other mothers toss them back toward the sand when the child is busy, hoping they will forget the care with which they were chosen. I understand both inclinations: to hold on and to let go.

But now, in September, the flip-flops and buckets and shells are gone and the children have returned home, the inevitability of fall, the certainty of autumn just another textbook fact as they sit wearily in their September classrooms. But I imagine they must keep this magical place somewhere in their memory, pulling out the recollections and examining them, marveling at them, like the shimmery inside of a shell: a place without seasons, as far away as the moon. Their mothers have returned to their kitchens or offices, their fathers to their lonely commutes. Only I remain, in my little cottage by the shore, as summer slips away soundlessly, and, without fanfare, autumn steps in.

At night, in the fall when the tourists are gone, there are no distractions. No blue glow of a television set in a window, no muffled sound of an argument or a child's cry. There are no slamming doors or moody teenagers sneaking out to a bonfire on the sand below. There is no laughter, no scratchy radio music, no soft cadence of couples making love. There is only the sound of the lapping waves, the lullaby of water. It is quiet here without them.

I don't have a landline. When someone wants to reach me, they call the manager's office and I return the call on my cell phone, its number known only to my daughters and sister. My eldest, Francesca, calls once a week on Sundays, dutifully reporting on her life in Boston, detailing the comings and goings of my grandchildren. Mouse is less predictable, more like me, calling only when the spirit moves her. She sends beautiful letters and postcards and photographs, though, that offer me glimpses into her gypsy life. The wall behind my bed tracks her travels in a cluttered collage. Only my sister, Gussy, calls every day. She relies on me more than she used to. We are both widows now, and growing old is lonely. We need each other.

I expect her call each night like I expect the sunset. "Hi,

Gus," I say. "What's the news?" Though there is never any news, not real news anyway: a broken pipe, a sale on prime rib, a silly conversation in line at the bank. More often than not she calls to read me one of the increasingly frequent obituaries of someone we used to know.

Tonight, I slip into bed for our conversation, watching the sun melt into the horizon from my window. When summer is over, I no longer bother to close the shades, modesty disappearing with the tourists.

"I got a letter today," she says. "The strangest thing."

"Who from?"

She is quiet on the other end of the line. I picture her, nestled in her husband Frank's old recliner, cradling the phone between her chin and her shoulder as she knits something for Zu-Zu or Plum.

"Gus?"

"The letter was from John Wilson. Johnny Wilson."

I feel a hollowing out in my chest, and worry for just a fraction of a second that this is it. I am waiting now, for that failure of my body that will, finally, remove me from this world. But then my heart, this old reliable heart, thumps again, a gong, and my whole body reverberates. "Why?" I ask.

"He's looking for *you*."

I take a deep breath and study the sky outside my window, looking for an answer in the confusion of colors, in the spill of orange and blue.

"He just got out of rehab or some such thing. Doesn't surprise me at all, frankly. Probably part of his twelve steps, making amends and all that."

It does not surprise me to hear that he's had these sorts of problems, though why he would want to talk to *me* is a mystery. Johnny Wilson would have nothing to apologize to me for; if anything, it should be the other way around.

"He says he wants to talk to you about his mother. But he wants to see you in person. He wants to know if I can help him find you."

My eyes sting. Suddenly the sunset is too bright. I stand and pull the curtains across the windows and sit down on the bed again. Breathless.

"*Can* I help him?" she asks. "Find you?"

"Where is he?"

"He's still in Boston. But he said he could come up to Vermont if you might be up for a visit. He must not know you're in California."

Of course he wouldn't know this. I haven't spoken to Johnny Wilson in decades.

"You *could* come for a visit, you know," she says. "Make a trip of it. Francesca could come up too, meet us at the lake?"

Lake Gormlaith. I haven't been back to the lake since 1964. Johnny was still a little boy then. A child. My heart (that swollen, weakening thing in my chest) aches for him: both the little boy he was and whatever damaged man he has now become.

"I don't know," I say. "I haven't flown in so long. Doesn't security make you take your clothes off or some such nonsense now?"

"Shoes." Gussy laughs. "You only have to take off your *shoes*. Come home, come see me. Let Johnny say what he needs to say. And you can see Effie and the girls."

Effie, my grandniece, and her family live year round now in the cabin at the lake. I haven't met the children, and the last time I saw Effie she was still a teenager. I haven't even seen Gussy for nearly two years now, and she was the last one to visit. I know it's my turn. Still, I am happy here at the edge of the world where none of the rules, even those regarding the changing of seasons, apply. Why would I leave?

"Please?" Gussy says.

"What did the letter say exactly?" I ask, wanting to hear her name, hoping she will say it.

"It just says he needs to talk to you about Eva." And there they are, the two syllables as familiar, and faint, as my own heartbeat. "He says there are some things you should know."

"What do you suppose that means?" I ask.

"I don't know, Billie. Just come home and find out."

I look around my tiny cottage, peer once again at that predictable sky. In Vermont, the leaves would be igniting in their autumnal fire, the whole landscape a pyre. There is no such thing as escaping the seasons in New England.

"Let me think about it," I say. "I'm not too wild about getting naked for just anybody who flashes a badge."

Gussy laughs again. "Think on it. I'll call you tomorrow."

"Tomorrow," I say, committing to nothing.

In the morning, I wake to the blinding reminder of daylight through the pale curtains in my bedroom. Outside, the waves quietly pat the shore as though they are only reassuring the sand. Each day begins like this; only the keening of the foghorn tells me that today it is autumn, that the sky is impenetrable.

My whole body aches, though it has for so long now that the pain no longer registers as unusual or worrisome. I rise anyway—what else can one do?—slip out of bed and into my bathing suit, which I keep hanging on a hook on the back of my door. I sleep in the nude, which makes this transition easier: no cumbersome nightgown to fuss with, no pajamas to unbutton or from which to undress. I realized long ago that I'd only ever worn nightclothes as a barrier anyway: a fortress of flannel or silk.

The bathing suit I wear these days is bright green. It complements my eyes, or it would if the cataracts hadn't rendered them this icy blue. My hair isn't the same color anymore either. Still, I wake up every single morning expecting to see the red-haired woman I used to be in the mirror, but instead I see an old lady with milky eyes and an untamed white mane. I have, on the darkest days, demanded to know who she is.

Sometimes I try to imagine what Eva would look like now, but she remains fixed in my memory the way she looked back in the summer of 1960 when I first met her. Only I have aged. Only I have watched my body slowly abandon me. I am alone in this slow decay. Nevertheless, I do imagine her here, though she appears as a ghost, and I wonder what her morning would be like. Would she also slip into her bathing suit at the break of dawn? Would she walk with me from the bungalow down the stone steps to the beach? Would she peer through the thick marine layer that hangs like a white stole on the sea's shoulders and then wink at me before tossing her hair back and running headlong into the water, disappearing into the ocean leaving me to wonder if she would resurface again? Would she leave me at the edge, fearful—an old woman with cataracts and high blood pressure—looking for her through the gauzy morning? Would she emerge from the water, riding a wave in to shore, coming home again, or would she simply vanish?

I'm never truly alone on the beach, even in autumn, even this early in the morning. The surfers come in their wet suits, carrying their boards under their arms. They paddle out to wait for the waves, bobbing and dipping like shiny black seals. The bums who sleep under the pier emerge, scavenging for food, for half-smoked cigarette butts left in the sand. Middle-aged women rise early and walk up and down the beach, purposeful in their velour tracksuits, still believing that the inevitable might be delayed, if not halted entirely. They rarely acknowledge me; I am evidence of the one thing they cannot change, the reminder of a future they aren't ready to imagine. But if they were to look, to *really* look, this is what they would see: an elderly woman in a green bathing suit walking slowly toward the water's edge. She is old and she is thin, but there are shadows of an athlete in her strong shoulders and legs underneath that ancient skin. She is a swimmer, peering out at the water as though she might be looking for someone.

But after only a moment, she disappears into the cold, her arms remembering. Her whole body remembering, her whole body *memory,* as she swims toward whatever it is, whomever it is she sees in the distance. If they were to listen, to really listen, they would hear the waves crashing on the shore behind her, beating like a pulse: *Eva. Eva.*

There were secrets before Eva. There were things I kept hidden, buried, long before Eva and Ted Wilson moved in across the street. There were a hundred things I didn't say, and a thousand more I could barely even admit to myself. But the summer of 1960, when our neighbor, old Mrs. Macadam, died and the Wilsons moved in, marks for me the moment at which all of those secrets began to rise to the surface. I think of them now, shimmering like objects underwater, coming in and out of focus, obfuscated and then revealed. Exposed and then concealed.

"Somebody's moving in!" Mouse squealed, throwing open the kitchen door.

"Don't slam the door, Mouse!" Francesca said as she followed behind her little sister, shaking her head in the disapproving way that made her father call her Miss Ninny. At eight years old, Francesca was everything I was not as a child: tidy and polite, a good student, obedient and kind. Mouse, who was six, was my secret favorite, my kindred spirit. Unruly, untidy. Feral even.

It was the first week of July, and so hot. My hair frizzed and curled at my neck, my hairline beaded with sweat. I was in the kitchen struggling to unclog the drain with a plunger, the smell of potato peels (or whatever other sludge had clogged the delicate innards of our house) making me reel with nausea.

"Mama! Mama! There's a family moving into Mrs. Macadam's house. They've got a rocking horse and bunk beds, and a bright red car!" Mouse clung to me, tugging at my apron, stepping on my feet. "Do you think they have little girls?" she asked.

"Let's go look," I said, walking with her to the bay window in our living room, where I could see a moving truck parked in front of the Macadams' house with a bright red Cadillac sedan parked behind it.

There was, indeed, a giant painted rocking horse, the kind on a metal frame with springs, as well as a crib, a set of bunk beds, and a whole stack of Hula-Hoops. "I think they might have some children," I said, nodding.

And then, as if on cue, three children came bolting out of Mrs. Macadam's house followed by a young woman, a very pregnant young woman, who stood on the front steps with both hands on her hips. Behind her loomed a tall man in a suit and a fedora.

I watched, riveted, as the smallest child, a boy of maybe four or five, wearing a cowboy hat and rubber chaps, chased down the two other children, both girls, shooting his cap gun dangerously close to their faces. I watched through the window as the mother silently voiced her objections, shaking her head but smiling. I also watched as the man circled the woman's very large waist with his arms and nuzzled her neck. I felt myself blushing as she stretched her neck to the side, as if to expose more flesh for his hungry mouth. Then she collapsed into silent giggles, hitting him with the oven mitt in her hand and shooing him out the door. He obeyed, blowing kisses and tipping his hat as he made his way to the shiny red car, into which he disappeared and drove off down the road.

When he was gone, the woman put her hand on her back in the way that enormously pregnant women do, as though she were trying to stretch a kink out. A worker emerged from the moving truck, carrying a large cardboard box. She smiled and spoke to him briefly, gesturing toward the house with her free hand.

"Whatcha looking at?" Frankie asked, coming from the bathroom smelling of Aqua Velva, still wearing his undershirt. Undressed, Frankie always looked like a boy rather than a man. At 140 pounds, he weighed just a little more than I did. His belts never fit; he used a leather hole punch to add extra holes. He was *a small man with a big personality,* he liked to say, though this was always accompanied by a slight grimace, the consequence of growing up small with a mean daddy, his bravado crafted in response to years of torment. It was one of many things that endeared me to Frankie early on. He was, in many ways, like a child himself; his joy was enormous, but so too were his disappointments and rage.

"There's a family moving in across the street," Francesca said. "And they've got a boy. He looks *naughty*."

"Looks like we lost our chance at old lady Macadam's house," Frankie said, peering out the window as he wiped a bit of shaving cream from his cheek. "Though it seems they might need the space more than we do," he said, as the brood of children emerged again, this time from the crawl space under the front porch. Each of them was grass stained and dirt smudged.

Mouse was elated. "Can I go play?" she asked, rushing toward the door. She was still wearing her pajamas.

"Go put some clothes on first," I said. "And let their mama know I'll bring over a coffee cake in an hour."

The house that Frankie and I owned in 1960 was in Hollyville, Massachusetts, only a half-hour train ride from Boston, but, in those days, still quite rural. We lived on a dead end drive with only four other houses: the Bakers, the Bouchers, and the Castillos. And across the street was the house that Mrs. Macadam lived in for fifty years before she fell asleep and didn't wake up.

Mrs. Macadam's son and his wife discovered her body a whole week after she passed away when they came to take her to the hair salon, and it made Frankie and me feel like terrible neighbors. There's a fine line though between being a good neighbor and being a busybody. I've always erred on the side of caution, keeping my nose out of other people's business. Though we shared this dead end drive and a telephone party line, we left each other alone. There were no other children on our street, the other residents much older than we, and so we had nothing but proximity in common. Frankie made much more of an effort than I, waving a hearty hello to Mr. Boucher as he mowed his lawn or to Mrs. Castillo as she tended her terminally ill roses. Offering to help Mrs. Baker carry in her groceries. But Mrs. Macadam rarely left her house. Her porch light came on only some nights. And she didn't subscribe to the *Herald* or the *Globe,* so there were no newspapers to pile up in her driveway after she died. Maybe if I'd been paying more attention, I would have noticed that by the end of that week the mailman was struggling to get her mail into the stuffed mailbox. (Though, if you ask me, perhaps he should have gone and knocked on Mrs. Macadam's door himself.) Regardless, with or without our notice, Mrs. Macadam went to bed one night that spring and didn't get out again until the coroner came a week later and carried her out. Her son and daughter-in-law spent a week emptying the house out, and then he planted a For Sale sign in the front yard next to the lilac bush, which was in full bloom by then.

Frankie had talked to Mrs. Macadam's son every time he saw him that spring, inquiring if there had been any offers made. Any bites. They stood in the driveway, the way that men do (arms folded across their chests, shuffling their feet, gesturing and nodding). But the son just shook his head sadly, probably wishing his inheritance were more than this sad old house with its sloping front porch and tired roof.

"It's got *five* bedrooms, Billie," Frankie had said one morning.

I froze, shaking my head. We'd bought this three-bedroom house more than ten years before, when we were still newlyweds, Frankie optimistic that we would fill the two extras with children by the time we celebrated our third anniversary. But three years of trying brought nothing but blood and heartache and had made those two rooms (the rooms Frankie had painstakingly painted and furnished) feel like tombs for our lost children. Finally, in 1952 we adopted Francesca and then, two years later, Mary. Without any empty rooms left, Frankie had seemed sated. He appeared to resign himself to our small family. Having a baby, or adopting another baby, would have meant starting over again. And as much as Frankie had dreamed of having a large family (he had had five sisters), I knew he didn't miss those sleepless nights, the vigilance of parenting toddlers. The constant fear.

But what he didn't know that late May morning, as he peered through the kitchen window at the FOR SALE sign leaning a little to the right, was that I was pregnant again: probably just a few weeks along as far as I could tell, which didn't mean anything except that I was just a few weeks closer to losing another child. But my plan this time had been to keep quiet about it. No need to get Frankie's hopes up; he was the most optimistic man I'd ever met, a trait that I found to be somehow both endearing and pitiable. If I told him, he'd have been out in his shop by noon building a cradle that would only remain still and empty in the garage.

"With a little spit shine, it could be a real beauty," he had said, nodding at the house across the street. That was one thing about Frankie. He was able to see the potential in things. I'm fairly certain that was the only reason why he'd wound up with me in the first place. When he'd first met me, ineptly typing a whopping forty words per minute at Simon & Monk, a large insurance firm in Cambridge, a pencil stuck in my frizzy red hair and refusing to wear a girdle, it wasn't my great beauty he'd been riveted by but rather what he might be able to turn me into. I was a fixer-upper in his eyes. A girl with some real potential.

Growing up on my parents' farm in Vermont, I'd wanted nothing but to get away as soon as I graduated from high school. I'd been accepted into Wellesley College, but my parents insisted that I turn down my spot and go to secretarial school in Boston so that I might make something *useful* of myself. What they really meant was that I should find a husband, start a family. If I'd gone to Wellesley, I'd have been surrounded by girls, with no marriage prospects in sight. My mother's dreams were not of a girl on the college swim team, an academic, a librarian (which is what I'd hoped to be). They were, instead, of grandchildren and holidays spent around an upright piano no one but my mother knew how to play, singing Christmas carols. I'd have gone to Wellesley anyway, but I had no way to pay the tuition. It didn't help that Gussy had just gotten married to her own Frank (Frank McInnes, her high school sweetheart); my mother wouldn't rest until both of her girls were safe from spinsterhood.

When *my* Frank came into the office where I was pounding at the behemoth electric typewriter with two fingers, he saw me as a project, and I saw him as a way to appease my mother. Unfortunately, he was no Frank McInnes. For one thing, he was Italian. And even worse, he was Catholic. *My* Frank couldn't be further from Gussy's Frank with his quiet intelligence, his good looks, and manners, and my mother would never let me forget that. But Frankie was vibrant and loud and funny, and I liked him. And better yet, he liked me.

That's what my thinking had been when Frankie Valentine, all five feet six of him, walked into the office where I worked pushing his mail cart and whistling "O Sole Mio." When he leaned against the desk where I was miserably typing up underwriting forms and said in his slow, sly way, "Well, if it isn't the new girl. And even prettier than they say." (I'd never once in my life been referred to as pretty.)

That was my thinking when Frankie took me out dancing and managed to make me feel graceful for the first time in my whole life, when he crooned like Vic Damone in my ear, his breath hot, both his feet and hands quick. When he walked me back to my apartment and kissed me on my doorstep. (A man had never put his hands—or *lips,* for that matter—on me before, and certainly never sang love songs in my ear.)

And that was my thinking when I told Frankie I'd marry him: that he was the first and only man who had loved me (who might ever love me enough to marry me), and as a plus, I'd be getting my mother off my back while still getting in one last jab. That had been my modus operandi for most of my life at that point. I truly didn't think beyond that moment when I walked down the aisle of St. Paul's Church, and saw her in her mother-of-the-bride dress crying tears of both relief and sorrow. It wasn't fair to Frankie of course, and it only took the first miscarriage to realize that.

We'd only been married a couple of months when I got pregnant the first time. But just a week or so after Dr. O'Malley confirmed the pregnancy, I woke up in a cold sweat in the middle of the night, bleeding so heavily I thought I might be dying. Frankie had held me and whispered, feverish in his reassurances, "We'll try again. It's okay. We'll keep trying."

And we did. Three more pregnancies, each one lasting just a few weeks longer than the first, making the agony of each loss successively more painful. Frankie mourned those lost babies intensely, insisting on giving them each a name: *Rosa, Maria, Antonia,* convinced they were all girls, though it had been too early to tell. At Sunday mass, he lit a candle for each one, whispered prayers with his eyes shut tightly, hands clenched together. And though he never said so, and would never have placed blame on me, I blamed myself. Blamed my body for failing him, for failing those little girls.

Not long afterward, Frankie arranged for the adoption of Francesca, and he offered her to me like a gift. He was what I imagined the perfect father to be, coddling and cuddling and spoiling her with his affections. My own father had been a shadow in my childhood: up before dawn, working until dusk, arriving at the dinner table exhausted and starving. His interest in us was no different than his interest in his cattle, except that unlike his prized heifer, we could offer nothing useful in return.

Frankie, on the other hand, loved being a father. He lived to make Chessy happy, singing her songs and tickling her belly, proudly showing pictures of her to anyone willing to peer into the depths of his cracked leather wallet. And when Francesca was two, I could see that hungry look in his eye, that now-familiar desperation. "She needs a sister," he'd said. "Every girl does." And so we adopted Mary, our little *Mouse,* and we were finally a family. Frankie was content with his girls, his *ladies* as he called them. And I was careful, making sure there would be no more pregnancies, and no more miscarriages.

But then that June of 1960, the June when Mrs. Macadam died in her sleep, I knew (from the tender swell of my breasts, from the familiar twinge—that death knell I knew so well) that I was pregnant yet again and that this baby, like all the others, would soon be nothing but a whispered prayed, a lit candle, a name without a face.

However, outside Mrs. Macadam's house, the lilacs bloomed and then fell to the ground, collecting in wilting violet heaps. Spring departed and summer came and, still, the baby held on. One month passed and then two, and I knew that soon it would be hard to keep the pregnancy a secret from Frank. I'd become an expert at turning him away in the bedroom, at feigning sleep. Headaches. My monthly visitor. But soon I'd have no choice but to capitulate, and he would notice the changes in my body. His fingers would remember; his hands would know.

It was terrible, but I wished that it would just happen already, knowing that after two months, while a pregnancy might be hidden, a miscarriage would not be so easy to conceal. The pain would be too much. I wouldn't be able to manage this on my own. The last one I'd had was at almost three months, and I had never felt anything so horrific in my life. I'd felt possessed by the pain, as if it were something alive, something living inside of me. I couldn't just pretend it wasn't happening.

Mornings were the hardest. From the stringent smells of aftershave and sweet bacon to the cloying scent of Frankie's Chesterfield cigarettes and the pungent Maxwell House coffee he drank, my poor stomach could barely take the assault. The very thought of baking a coffee cake for the new neighbors, of the brown sugar and cinnamon, made my stomach roil, but I knew it was what was expected, and it would also give me an excuse to go introduce myself. Like Mouse, I was wildly curious.

An hour later, after I finally managed to get the sink to drain, I pulled the hot coffee cake from the oven, burning my finger on the electric filament. I stuck my finger in my mouth and tried to suck the sting out. I seemed to burn myself every time I used the oven, and I often felt as though I were at war with the appliances in our kitchen, like they had some personal vendetta against me.

Frankie had gone into the city to work. Francesca was pouting in her room. (Francesca, who did not like change of any kind, was skeptical of this new family that had moved in across the street, and she had refused to go over and play with Mouse.) I imagined her sitting on her bed, chin resting on her bent knees, a dog-eared copy of *The Secret River* or *A Tree Grows in Brooklyn* in her hands. This might have been the only similarity we shared; when the going got tough, we both retreated into our books.

"Chessy!" I hollered from the foot of the stairs. "We're going over to meet the new neighbors." I had learned early on that the way to get what I wanted from Francesca was to simply demand it. There were no negotiations between us, only declaratives. And her adherence, while reluctant, almost always followed.

"Coming," she grumbled, and came to the top of the stairs, making clear in her heavy steps and slumped shoulders that this was one change she would resist. She had loved Mrs. Macadam, who gave her dusty mints and stale, store-bought cookies and let her pick flowers from her flowerbeds. Francesca had taken her death the hardest, asking too many questions about heaven and God. Questions Frankie took in stride but ones I avoided answering. God and I had a difficult relationship, to put things kindly.

We walked across the street together, the coffee cake so hot it burned my already-wounded hand even through the dishrag I'd used to protect it. The smell that rose up to my nostrils made my stomach quiver and my neck break out in a cold sweat, despite the summer heat.

Mouse and the youngest daughter of the new family, a little girl with black hair and pale, pale skin who looked to be roughly Mouse's age, were playing in the driveway. "Hi, Mama," Mouse said, while jumping rope, her face scrunched tightly in concentration. Her hair was curly and red like mine, as though she were really my own. I could almost imagine sometimes that she was one of those lost babies, as though she had resided inside of me instead of some other woman's womb. The other little girl looked bored, scraping at the cracked pavement with a stick, and didn't acknowledge me or Francesca as we made our way up the rickety steps of the front porch, which was covered in unopened packing boxes.

I reached for the knocker and rapped it gently against the wooden door. Francesca instinctively straightened her skirt, one of the same plaid skirts she wore to school every day during the school year: her unsanctioned uniform, regardless of the season.

"Coming!" A woman's voice came from inside. When she opened the door, she was breathless.

What I remember now was how striking her face was. I hadn't noticed as I peered across the street from inside my house; I'd been too busy taking in the entire family to dwell on anyone in particular. But hers was the kind of face that grew more startling and remarkable the closer you got to it, as though her features sharpened in direct relation to your distance from them: like an impressionist painting in reverse.

"Can I help you?" she asked. And her face came into sharp and exquisite focus. Framed by smooth, dark hair, a widow's peak at the top of her high forehead, her face was small, childlike. Dark brows, like wide brushstrokes, sat above her large, brown eyes, which were heavy lidded and long-lashed, like Mouse's baby doll's eyes: the ones that really opened and closed. Flawless skin; small, heart-shaped mouth with plump lips; and a jaw that was somehow both square and soft at the same time. Even swollen with child, she was stunning: the kind of woman Frankie might call a "knockout."

"Hi," I said, feeling suddenly even more coarse and unrefined than I usually felt. The humidity brought out the worst in my already-frizzy hair. If my hands had been free, I would have patted at it self-consciously. "I'm Billie. Billie Valentine. From across the street." I smiled as she came out onto the porch and noticed, possibly for the first time, that there was a child not her own in her yard.

"Oh!" she said, her big, dark eyes opening, her whole face opening.

"We brought a coffee cake," I said. "My mother's recipe." I still had difficulty taking credit for my own cooking. When things actually turned out well in the kitchen, I knew there were larger forces than my own skill at work: mainly my mother's carefully handwritten recipe cards she'd made for me as part of my unofficial trousseau.

"How thoughtful!" she said, clapping her hands together. "I'm Eva. Eva Wilson. Come in, come in." She took the coffee cake from me and gestured for Chessy and me to enter the house.

Inside, it was dark and cool. There were boxes everywhere and a half-dozen fans humming and stirring the still air. The furniture was pushed together in the center of the room. I'd never actually been inside this house before, or *any* of the houses on our street; I'd only stood in the doorways with the girls as they sold Girl Scout cookies or solicited donations for their school.

"So sorry, we haven't put a thing away yet," Eva said.

"Oh, please, don't apologize. We probably should have waited to come over. Given you some time to settle in."

"It may take forever if this heat keeps up. I move one box and I'm drenched in sweat. Is it always this hot here in the summertime?" she asked, fanning herself futilely with her hand. Her neck glistened with sweat. "I feel like I might combust."

"Not always," I said. "July and August can be hot though. It's the humidity that makes it so miserable. Just wait until January; you'll be missing summer."

Winter here was a beast. I'd noticed California plates on the Cadillac. Clearly, they had a big surprise coming for them.

The other girl I'd seen earlier, the tall one with dirty-blond hair and a long, horselike face, came down the stairs. Eva smiled and motioned for her to join us. "Donna, this is Mrs. Valentine from across the street and her daughter . . . ?"

"Francesca," I offered when Chessy only stared at the floor.

Donna looked Francesca up and down appraisingly and said, "Let's go to my room. I have a Barbie doll."

Francesca looked at me as if waiting for my permission, and I nodded. *"Go!"* I said. "Have fun."

They disappeared upstairs and I followed the nauseating scent of my mother's coffee cake into Mrs. Macadam's kitchen. The little boy was nowhere in sight.

The kitchen was bright: yellow walls, clean white floors and cabinets. There were boxes everywhere, including on the surface of the Formica table where another portable fan made its best attempt at fighting this ruthless heat.

"Please sit down," she said, motioning to a free chair at the table. "Would you like some coffee?"

I shook my head.

"I probably couldn't find the percolator anyway," she said, sighing, and sat across from me at the table.

"So you're from California?" I asked.

"San Francisco," she said. "But then Teddy got the job offer at

John Hancock. Ted, that's my husband, he's from here, grew up in Boston."

"And you drove all the way from San Francisco?" I asked. "With three kids?"

Frankie and I hadn't ever taken the kids farther than Vermont to Gussy and her Frank's camp at Lake Gormlaith, where the girls and I spent the whole month of August every summer, and those four hours in the car were almost more than either Frankie or I could take. We gave up on driving after one trip when we had to pull over three times for Mouse to throw up. Most summers, the girls and I took the train and Frankie drove up every other weekend to visit.

"It was terrible," she said, nodding. "And it took about twice as long as it should have because I had to stop every half hour to use the restroom. I've seen pretty much every gas station from San Francisco to Somerville."

"When are you due?" I asked.

"The doctor says late August, but I'm hoping for tomorrow. Day after at the latest." She laughed. "How about you? When are you due?"

Stunned, I caught my breath and found myself shaking my head in denial.

She looked at me, confused, and said, "You are pregnant, right?"

I wasn't *really* pregnant. A real pregnancy meant a real baby. And there never would be a real baby. And I wasn't even showing yet, never mind that the only two people in the entire world who knew about my condition were me and my doctor.

"How on earth did you know that?" I asked, feeling my throat grow thick. "I haven't told anyone. Not even my husband."

"I've got almost four of my own. I know what pregnant looks like," she said.

My eyes must have widened like a crazy person's.

"And you looked like you might vomit when you handed

me that coffee cake," she said, laughing. "I'd offer you a slice, but I have a feeling you'd say no. Am I right?"

I nodded. I felt panicky. I had just come over to deliver a coffee cake, but suddenly I felt exposed. Vulnerable. Frankie could not find out about the baby. It would kill him. And here I'd told a perfect stranger. Why hadn't I just denied it? This was none of her business. Suddenly, I just wanted to go home, to be back inside my own house where my private life was private. This was exactly why I usually kept my distance from my neighbors.

"I'm just a couple of months along." I looked toward the kitchen doorway, mapping my escape. "I've had some . . . um . . . bad luck, I guess you'd say. I'm waiting before I get everyone's hopes up."

"Of course," she said. "And I bet it's a boy. That's why you're so sick. I threw up every single day until Johnny was born. Boys are like poison."

I forced a smile and tried not to think about the poison inside of me. And then, upon hearing his name, Johnny materialized in the doorway, drawing his pistol from his holster and holding his mother at gunpoint. "Bam!" he screamed.

I felt like I might jump out of my skin; my heart pounded hard in my chest.

Eva's face flushed. "Johnny Wilson, you've got five seconds to hand over that cap gun. One . . ." And with that, cowboy Johnny ran off, out the door to the backyard, where I could see him mount that massive rocking horse, yelling "Yee-haw!"

"I'm sorry, I really should go. I've got a load of laundry in," I said.

"I'm glad you came over," she said, the color still in her otherwise pale face. "I don't know a single grown-up person in this town besides Teddy. I really could use a friend."

I grimaced.

"And don't worry," she said. "I won't tell anybody. Your secret's safe with me."

* * *

When I told Frankie about the visit with Eva Wilson, I carefully omitted our discussion about due dates and morning sickness and babies. "They have a little boy," I said. "He's a holy goddamned terror. And her husband works for John Hancock. Some sort of salesman, she says."

Frankie snickered. "That must be why he's got that showy car. *Sales. Humph.*"

He and Ted Wilson had pulled into our respective driveways at the same time that night. I'd watched Frankie looking at that car, which made our Studebaker look like a shabby brown shoe.

Frankie smacked the table. "We should invite them over for drinks. A barbeque. He drinks, doesn't he?"

"I would imagine," I said. (It turned out that drinking was one of two things Frankie and Ted had in common. The other was the Red Sox: both of them afflicted by that crazy, futile love for a team that would always, always let them down.)

But despite Frankie's interest in the Wilsons, I was not so keen on the idea of a barbeque. After that first visit with Eva, I had no desire to go back to their house. I'd left that first morning feeling like a dissected frog: splayed open, prodded, and studied. And the idea of having them over seemed downright dangerous. What if Eva slipped up? Frankie would be furious I'd kept the pregnancy from him, and even angrier that I had shared it with a total stranger. And so I made excuses and studied the Wilsons from the safety of our kitchen window. I still hadn't even met Ted Wilson yet, though I had watched as he disappeared out the front door every morning, straightening his hat and tie and getting into his car. I also heard him when he pulled in each night; he always honked three times and the children would come running from their respective perches: in bedroom windows, on the porch swing, and, for little Johnny, up in the enormous dying elm tree in their front yard. When Ted Wilson pulled up, Johnny would shimmy down from whatever branch he was clinging to and then swing, like some sort of wild monkey, to the lowest branch from which he could drop almost directly into his father's open arms. Ted was, like Eva, stunning to look at, with dark hair, a wide square face, and broad shoulders. Eva always greeted him, throwing her arms around his beefy neck, kissing him, right there on the front porch for the entire world to see. Something about this made me uncomfortable, but I still couldn't seem to turn away.

I had also watched as the boxes slowly disappeared from the porch, and curtains went up in the bare windows, as the loose boards were repaired. A young man showed up with a ladder and buckets and brushes to put a fresh coat of paint on the house. There were plumbers and repairmen of every sort in and out of the house those first couple of weeks. And, thrilled by a change of scenery, I watched them come and go from the window in the kitchen where I spent most of my day.

Despite my reluctance to start a friendship with her mother, Donna Wilson and Francesca became fast friends, disappearing together into the Wilsons' house or up into Chessy's own bedroom each day, whispering and giggling, lugging around an old red train case of mine filled with their collective doll collection. Mouse and the little dark-haired Wilson girl, Sally, also paired up. They did cartwheels in the yard and tossed their baby dolls onto the Wilsons' roof, watching them roll down again, which seemed to provide endless hours of entertainment, each plunge from the shingles causing them to erupt into explosive fits of little girl giggles. Johnny, however, was a lone wolf. With not another single little boy on our street, he was left to his own devices. You never knew where he would turn up, though he spent most of his time pretending he was some sort of sniper, shooting off his rifle from the safe camouflage of the elm tree foliage at his moving targets below.

I started to think maybe I was overreacting, that I was just being paranoid. Eva had promised to keep my secret, hadn't she? She'd given me no reason whatsoever to distrust her. And admittedly, I longed for a friend. It would also be great if Ted and Frankie hit it off, if our families could be friendly with each other. Maybe I was just being silly. And so once the traffic in and out of the Wilsons' house finally slowed, I sent Donna back to her house just before suppertime with a handwritten note, inviting her family to join us in our backyard for burgers and franks that weekend. She returned only moments later with a delicate piece of scented stationery that said, "We'd be delighted." I looked out the window then and saw Eva standing on her porch, waving at me. Embarrassed, I waved back and then wondered if I'd just made a terrible mistake.

The Wilsons arrived that following Saturday night after a family trip into the city. They'd taken the children to the Franklin Park Zoo, and Johnny was doing his best monkey imitation on our front porch, scratching his armpits and swinging from the railings.

"Settle down, fella," Ted said. His was a booming, warm voice, one that came from the gut rather than the throat. A voice that shook the floorboards under my feet as I stood there watching Johnny's primordial display.

Eva stood behind Ted, her girls like bookends on either side of her, both looking uncomfortable, as if they hadn't been playing on this very porch themselves for the past three weeks. As if I hadn't fed them a steady diet of cookies and Kool-Aid every day of July.

"You must be Ted," I said, reaching out my hand, but instead of shaking it, he bent down and gently kissed the back of it.

"*Enchanté,* as they say," he rumbled, and I felt my face grow hot.

"Oh, stop it, Teddy. You're embarrassing her," Eva said, playfully pushing Ted aside and coming toward me. She embraced me, which was difficult considering the enormity of her belly, and then kissed my cheek. I felt my skin flush, and I returned her hug awkwardly, noting the strong scent of her perfume and, surprisingly, my lack of a nauseated response to it. I actually hadn't felt my stomach perform its awful acrobatic queasy tumble in a few days; I'd even eaten eggs for breakfast, with bacon, instead of my usual favored Melba toast soaked in warm milk.

She backed up then and pushed the girls inside. "Go find Chessy and Mouse," she said, and they happily obliged, disappearing up our stairs.

"Frankie's in the backyard getting the charcoal started," I said to Ted, and he lumbered past me through my house as though he too already knew the way, and I heard the back screen door slam followed by the muffled sounds of their conversation.

"This is for dinner," she said, handing me a Jell-O mold inside which several green grapes were suspended like tiny planets. "And this is for you," she said, pushing a little vial into my palm and closing my fingers over it.

"What is it?" I asked.

"Shhh," she said, and ushered me into the house, glancing around to make sure we were alone. "It's unicorn root. An herb. I have a friend in San Francisco, an herbalist. I spoke to him after we talked, and he told me where I could find some in Boston. The Indians discovered it, used it to prevent . . . *bad luck*"—she said quietly, squeezing my arm—"with pregnancies."

"Thank you. That's very thoughtful," I said, slipping the vial into the pocket of my apron. She clearly hadn't told her husband anything, but I still felt my stomach tighten into a knot.

Outside Frankie was standing in his favorite bowling shirt and Bermuda shorts at the grill, enclosed in a cloud of smoke. Frankie's fire pit was his pride and joy. It was enormous, made of cobblestones he'd salvaged in the city when the old streets were being torn up and paved. It was a wonder of masonry, with an enormous grill he'd also made himself. You could have barbequed an entire side of beef on it if you'd wanted to.

Ted was sitting in a lawn chair next to the grill like a foreman overseeing one of his workers, as Frankie flipped and checked the meat. Ted had one of our cocktail glasses perched on the ice chest next to him. It was almost empty already. Frankie had opened a gallon jug of his favorite Chianti and poured himself a tall tumbler full. He was never one for liquor, but he liked his wine, drinking nearly half a jug every night. He'd grown up drinking wine instead of water in his house; he insisted that it was one of the major food groups, that the Surgeon General would likely make an announcement to that effect any day now. *Una cena senza vino e come un giorno senza sole,* he had said. *A meal without wine is like a day without sunshine.* I was not a wine drinker myself, especially not the sour Chianti Frankie favored, but I did like a good cold 'Gansett every now and then. A nice dirty martini on special occasions.

"Can I get you another cocktail, Ted?" I asked, gesturing to his glass.

"Brought my own." He smiled slyly and pulled a flask out of his shirt pocket. "Didn't know whether or not you might be a couple of goddamned teetotalers," he said boisterously as he sloshed some sort of amber-colored liquid on top of his melting ice.

"Well, let me at least get you some fresh ice," I offered.

By the time I spread my mother's hand-embroidered picnic cloth on the table and put that bright yellow Jell-O mold at the center like some sort of shining, jiggling sun, Ted and Frankie were both glassy eyed and half soused. Ted had drained his flask, and Frankie had finished the open jug of wine and broken into the dusty collection of bottles we kept for the entertaining we almost never did.

"So what's your line of work, Frankie?" Ted asked, adding two franks and a blackened burger to his paper plate.

"Boston Post Office. Main philatelic clerk," Frankie said proudly. He had started in the mail room of Simon & Monk, where I met him, and then took the Postal exam when I got pregnant the first time. He'd slowly worked his way up at the post office until he was in charge of all of the commemorative stamps. Now he dealt mostly with the collectors, and was involved in the "first day of issue" commemorative stamp releases. Frankie liked to know the history of things, and he researched the story behind each and every stamp he encountered so that he could share that information with his patrons. His work was something he was proud of.

"Worry about dogs much?" Ted said.

"What's that?" Frankie asked.

"Dogs! German Shepherds. Rotties." Ted slammed his drink down on the table. The Jell-O wobbled. *"Beware of dog!"*

"Not sure I understand your question," Frankie said.

"I'm asking if you ever worry about the dogs! Back in San Francisco, I heard there was a mailman got his face eat off by a Rottweiler, poor fellow just trying to deliver the electric bill."

"Oh, no, I'm not a mailman," Frankie said, stiffening. I felt my heart plummet. Frankie's shoulders tensed. He clutched his knife and fork in his fists.

"Well, what are you then?" Ted guffawed.

"Teddy," Eva said, reaching for his hand before he could grab his glass and take another drink. He shook her off like one of the many flies that had been landing on the food and on the table all afternoon.

Frankie's face was turning red, his jaw grinding. "I'll tell you what I'm not . . ."

"What's that?" Ted laughed. Eva tugged on his arm.

Suddenly, I peered at Johnny through the yellow gelatin. He was sitting directly across from me, and he'd been shoveling food into his face steadily since we sat down. He was up to four franks and two hamburgers as well as two ears of corn by my count. Through the Jell-O, he looked a little green. And just as Frankie opened his mouth to answer Ted, Johnny threw up. All over my mother's embroidered strawberries and vines. All over the plate of deviled eggs, splattering the Jell-O salad with undigested hot dog meat. All over the platter of dogs and burgers.

"Well, Jesus Christ," Ted said.

"Oh dear," I said, rising from my seat and rushing to the other side of the table. Eva was trying to get out from between the bench and the seat, no small feat given her girth. "You stay," I said to her. "I'll take care of him."

As I whisked Johnny into our downstairs bathroom to clean up, I prayed that both men would just drop the argument. Here I'd been so worried about being able to trust Eva, so concerned about whether or not to pursue a friendship with her, I hadn't thought about what would happen if Frankie and Ted didn't get along. I certainly didn't need them to be best friends, but it would have been nice to have a couple we could spend time with. Someone our own ages. And our children got along so well. I already had so few friends, so few people I could talk to. Suddenly, as I wiped Johnny's face and removed his soiled cowboy shirt, I was mad at Frankie. He *was* a mailman after all. It was wrong of Ted to make fun, but it was the truth, wasn't it? He'd only been teasing.

"How's your tummy?" I asked Johnny. His eyes were red from crying, and his breath sour. I dug around in the drawer until I found a bottle of Listerine. I rubbed his small back as he swished the mouthwash around his mouth, his eyes watering, and I thought about boys. About how terrible and primitive they are. About how violent, how dangerous. Even a little boy like this one: a little boy who would be happier living in a zoo among the other animals. What if Eva was right? What if this baby was a *boy?* And I realized that this was the first time I'd let myself imagine a baby. A living, breathing, crying, hungry being. The revelation nearly took my breath away.

I still don't know what magic Eva worked in that backyard while I was gone, but the two men had settled down into a more polite banter: Ted talking about the garden he planned to grow, and Frankie offering tips to keep aphids off the roses and deer away from the green beans. He even took Ted on a tour of the labyrinthine garden of our own that Frankie had cultivated, and I was careful to make sure they left their drinks behind.

While they were gone, I said to Eva, "Sorry about that. Looks like Ted accidentally pushed one of Frankie's buttons."

She brushed her hand dismissively, and shook her head. "You don't have to tell me about buttons. Ted's got more buttons than a telephone switchboard." Despite this kind attempt to make me feel better, I found that hard to believe. Ted and Eva had seemed like such a happy, playful couple the few times I'd seen them together. He was a drinker, that was obvious, but he also struck me as more bark than bite.

When the two men emerged from the garden, Ted was slapping Frankie on the back. "Well, it seems like they made up," I said.

Eva nodded. "Come here, Teddy," she said, and reached for his hand, pulling him to her and pressing her body against his.

Ted seemed to soften around Eva, turning from a grumbling bear into some sort of puppy. It embarrassed me to watch her flirt with him, and the way he responded to her. All afternoon I had kept thinking that there was something familiar about Eva. Something I couldn't quite put my finger on. But as she leaned into Ted's shoulder and he circled her with his arm, nuzzling his big, square face into her neck, I realized it was that she reminded me of Marie Bilodeau from back home. Marie lived down the road from me growing up, the only girl in a family with six boys. She didn't look anything like Eva, wasn't nearly as pretty, but she had the same *ease* as Eva, the same comfort in her own skin. The same way of making a man feel like he was the only one in the entire world. Of hanging on his words, and on his arm, while still clearly being the one in control. Of seeming to offer herself, pressing herself close, while somehow simultaneously rendering him powerless. Of crushing him. I had always been riveted by girls like this: girls who knew how to use their bodies, their beauty, as a way to control situations. My body had always been such a utilitarian device, something made simply to get me from one place to another. It was like the difference between our Studebaker and the Wilsons' Caddie. Girls like this, like Eva, both fascinated me and made me feel clumsy and awkward. Girls like this had no use for girls like me.

As the sun went down that night and the kids chased fireflies, Eva helped me clean up while Ted and Frankie sat by the fire pit and lamented the Red Sox season thus far, making plans to catch a game together, maybe bring Johnny along, one weekend. Then when the air grew chilly, and the children sleepy, the Wilson family said their good-byes and made their way back across the street.

I sent Frankie upstairs to bed, told him I was feeling a little under the weather (a tired excuse, worn out as the dishrag in my hand, but one I knew he had no power to refute and no choice but to accept). And as he lumbered upstairs, I lingered at the sink washing the charred remains of our dinner from the spatulas and platters, peering at the house across the street.

From the kitchen window, I watched the downstairs lights at the Wilson house click off one by one. And then Eva's and Ted's silhouettes appeared behind the closed drapes in one of the illuminated upstairs windows, their separate shadows merging into one before this last light went out. I felt my skin grow warm as I imagined them making love. Wondered if they still did with Eva's belly so very big. I could barely remember the last time I had made love to Frankie; the only reason I had any recollection of it at all was because I had racked my brain trying to figure out when it was that I got pregnant.

I clicked out our own lights and went upstairs into our bedroom, where Frankie had, thankfully, already fallen asleep. I slipped into our bathroom and studied the vial that Eva had given me. It touched me, suddenly, that she'd gone to such trouble. Inside was a brownish liquid that looked similar to whatever had been in Ted's flask. I touched my finger to the opening and then my finger to my tongue. It was bitter. But I took the prescribed dosage anyway and imagined what would happen if this one actually stuck.

I also thought about how nice it would be to have a friend to share this experience with. Someone to share my troubles with. My secrets. For the first time in a long time I thought I might not feel quite so alone.

In the morning after my swim, after a hot shower, and after my usual cup of coffee and scone at Daybreak, I head to the library where I volunteer in the children's room three days a week. I'd always dreamed of working in a library, and now I finally do. It's a small branch library, but I love it all the same. Our tiny beach community is self-sufficient; we have a post office, three banks, four churches, and this library. I never go into the city; I don't have to. Everything in the world I need is here.

There are good people in this little beach town, as all little towns, and I feel taken care of. I think about poor Mrs. Macadam sometimes, how long her dead body sat inside the house across the street from us before it was discovered. I suppose I have spent the last few years ensuring that this won't happen to me.

I live alone now, but I am not lonely.

I am a creature of habit, and each of my customs involves daily interactions with my neighbors. If I don't show up for my coffee and raspberry scone at the Daybreak Café or at the library or at Theo's, where I get a Greek salad every day for lunch, I'll be missed. If I fail to stop by the little pub where I like to have a pint of stout before going for my nightly swim, Juan Gaddis, the bartender, will miss me, maybe even send someone over to the cottages to check in. Once when I was sick with a cold and didn't appear for my nightly pint, he came over himself and knocked on my door. Since Lou died, these are my caretakers. My friends.

Each night I turn on the Christmas lights I have strung along my porch like twinkling stars, and I click them off when I wake.

It is my silent signal that all is well, that I have survived another night. And in the morning, Pete, who owns and manages the cottages, delivers my newspaper to my door while I swim. He would notice if I didn't wake up.

Of course Gussy would also know if something were amiss. As would Francesca, if I failed to answer my phone for her Sunday call. Only Mouse might not notice, at least not right away, if I disappeared off the face of the earth.

The fog is still thick, and I walk the six blocks from the coffee shop to the library, unable to see more than one block ahead at a time. I am surprised every time a fellow pedestrian comes into view. They appear suddenly, emerging from the haze like apparitions: Bob Hudson, who owns the jewelry shop; a floppy-haired teenage boy on a skateboard; a sullen homeless woman in a bathrobe and boots, clutching a battered phone book under her arm. I see her most mornings; sometimes she asks me if I have a quarter so she can make a call. I wonder who she's looking for in those tattered pages.

It's chilly without the sun, but I also know that by noon the sun will have won in this struggle with the fog. For now, I wrap my cardigan more tightly around me, knowing that for the walk home, I won't need it.

The library doesn't open for another ten minutes, but I have to walk past a half-dozen people waiting outside. When Linda unlocks the doors they'll all go straight to the computers. Like them, I don't have a computer in my cottage, though Francesca keeps trying to buy me one. She went so far once as to send me an Apple Store gift card with explicit instructions as to what to buy. I even made the trek to the store at the mall, allowed a salesman to ring all the bells and blow all the whistles for me, but I left empty-handed, leaving him red-faced at the display. I am happy to use the computers at the library. And when I'm done, the computer stays right there. I've seen how lost people get on the Internet, tapping away frantically. Teenagers lined up in a row not speaking to each other, but rather clicking away on their Facebook pages, sending e-mails, instant messaging, ignoring one another in favor of their virtual friends. Watching them makes me feel strangely lonely.

Linda waves at me through the glass and unlocks the door, ushering me in and telling those waiting outside, "Five more minutes."

"Pretty sweater," she says to me.

"Thanks," I say.

Linda's husband died last year after a boating accident in Mission Bay, but her cheer is unwavering. I know it is in part because of her son. Robert had just graduated high school when the accident happened. He's delaying college for a year now, staying at home to help out. He is inside already, flicking on all of the fluorescent lights.

"Good morning," I say, and he nods silently at me.

He is at the library all day long every day. I know Linda is trying to keep him close. But despite proximity, they rarely speak to each other. I watch them, and it makes my heart ache. I try to imagine them at home, moving around that empty house filled only with their grief, and it pains me. I felt the same way after Lou died, like a single marble rolling around inside an elaborate maze, looking for a way out.

I push the cart full of library books waiting to be returned to the shelves into the children's room. And I take my time; after nearly a decade of volunteering here, I am familiar with every single book. I have repaired hundreds of them myself. I know each of them simply by the feel of their cracked spines in my hands. After I have finished putting the books away, I settle down at the librarian's desk and wait for the computer to boot up. After last year's budget cuts, the children's librarian position was reduced to half time. I am here more than she is now, and so I have taken over some of her duties. I conduct the Wednesday morning story time, reading to a crowd of mothers and their squirming toddlers. I assist the teachers from the elementary school across the street who bring their students over once a week to pick out books. Today she has left a note asking if I can make a wish list by looking at recent award winners and starred reviews in the *Library Journal*. This is one of my favorite jobs, though we rarely have enough funds to purchase even a fraction of the books on my list.

I spend an hour or so compiling a thoughtful list of new picture books, middle-grade chapter books, and young adult novels. Robert comes in as I'm finishing up and slumps down into one of the beanbag chairs near the puppet theatre. He sighs and puts his hands behind his head. Linda told me a few months back that he hasn't cried yet, not even once, about his father. I suspect they're both trying to be brave for each other, but to what end? I can see his sorrow. I can feel it; it's palpable.

"Would you like to read to the kids today?" I ask, and he shrugs.

I have discovered that this is something he is really good at, and the children love him. While he rarely speaks to anyone else, he comes alive when he reads for the kids. He changes his voices for all of the characters, making the children laugh. For the half hour of story time he loses his sullenness. His sadness. It's all I have to offer him. And so after the mothers and their children have come in and settled down on the colorful carpet, after Robert has selected a stack full of books to read, I settle back in at the computer.

I am not even sure what I am planning to do, but it can't hurt to browse some of the travel sites Gussy mentioned. Check out the airfare specials. Now that summer is over, I imagine I could probably get a deal. If I change my mind and decide to go. It amazes me how simple it is to make such an enormous decision; a couple clicks of the mouse, a credit card number, and suddenly I could be going home.

I try to imagine leaving, returning to Vermont if even only for a couple of weeks. The possible disruption in my routine worries me a little; I tick through a checklist of all those people who might notice my absence during those two weeks, the people I would have to let know I'd be gone. I tell myself that if I were to leave, if I were to actually take Gussy up on her invitation, I would be missed.

I look up at Robert, who is impersonating a bear, his face and body and voice transformed by the story, and see that Linda is standing in the doorway watching. She smiles as she watches him, and catches my eye. "Thank you," she mouths, and I nod.

I worry that without me here Linda might fall apart. I have heard her crying in the bathroom. I have seen her sit in her car eating her lunch, her eyes wet with tears. What would she do if I were to leave?

I stare at the computer screen, and I feel short of breath, a heat spreading through my body. And so I stop. And I think about what Lou would say, if Lou (*logical Lou*) were still here to help me keep the past in the past.

I've made a life here. Why would I want to revisit this? It's not as though Eva is still alive. When I speak of Eva now, I distill things, reducing her and everything that happened into a single, aching anecdote, offering only a shadow to prove there was a sun. *I'm sorry,* was all that Lou had said when I explained what happened, as I uttered their names like sharp slivers: *Eva, Donna, Sally, Johnny*.

Johnny. His name feels like a sharp knife in my chest. I try to picture what he might look like now, what sort of man that little boy became. But every time I try to assemble the details of his face, I see only his boyish cheeks flushed pink, a coonskin cap cocked crookedly on his head, his tiny hands pulling the trigger of his Daisy rifle. *Pop, pop, pop.* What does he want with me? Why can't he let me be?

The girls and I were scheduled to leave for Vermont at the end of July. Usually, it was my favorite moment of the whole summer; climbing the steps onto the Boston & Maine as the sun rose meant that by the end of the day we'd be pulling into the station in Two Rivers, and that Gussy and Frank would be waiting to pick us up and drive us north to Lake Gormlaith. Even though I'd fled Vermont years ago, it was a place I still longed for. Ached for. Gussy and Frank's camp offered everything I loved about Vermont, but at a safe distance from my mother and father. I'd take the girls, of course, on an obligatory visit or two to see them at the farm, but they never came to the lake, and that was just fine with me. It also meant a vacation from the domestic drudgery that was my life. And a furlough from Frankie.

But this year, I wasn't just leaving Frankie behind. I was also leaving Eva. My new best friend. My *first* best friend. Since the Wilsons came over for the barbeque, Eva and I had spent nearly every afternoon together chatting and avoiding the various household obligations that awaited us inside our respective homes.

"What's it like there?" Eva asked a couple of days before our departure. It was so hot, we'd taken to sitting in my backyard with our feet in a baby pool of cool water while the kids ran around, somehow immune (or at least oblivious) to the heat. "I only know the song. You know, 'Moonlight in Vermont' . . ."

I laughed and thought of the moon, of its bright light reflected on the still surface of the lake. The view from the window in the loft where I slept. I thought about the sound of the loons, that strange avian lullaby.

"It's peaceful." I sighed as Mouse ran past me squealing and tripping on my outstretched legs. "And cooler because of the lake. The children play in the woods all day and only come home when it's time for supper. It's quiet enough to think, to read even. I bet I read twenty books last summer. And if the weather's good, you can swim every day."

"I'd probably sink," Eva said, laughing. She was due in three weeks, but she looked as though she might go into labor any minute.

Suddenly an idea struck me. I couldn't believe I hadn't thought of it before. "Next summer you should come visit!" I said. "Bring the children."

"Really?" she asked.

"Oh, please, it would be so nice. They could swim. Pick blueberries. There's a tree house. Johnny would love it."

Johnny, at the moment, was bouncing on a pogo stick on the small, square patio near the back steps. Up and down, up and down. *Squeak, squeak, squeak.*

"Well, then, it's a plan!" she said, clapping her hands together.

I knew that by the time we got back from Vermont, Eva would have had her baby. And I would be four months along, nearly halfway there. Eva had convinced me that I needed to tell Frankie about it before we left. I was three months now, farther than I'd ever made it before. I'd hidden the slight swell of my belly under aprons but I wouldn't be able to pull it off much longer. Besides, I knew Frankie would be over the moon; Francesca and Mouse would finally have a baby brother or sister. And as frightened as I was, a little tentative part of me thrilled at the notion of becoming a mother again, and of having a friend to share the experience with this time. Eva and I had discussed the names we'd considered, imagined the little ones playing together as our girls did. We'd pored over pink and blue paint samples Ted brought home from the hardware store, lingered over baby layettes in the Montgomery Ward catalogue. Still, the idea of telling Frankie made my stomach do flip-flops, and so I waited. On the Thursday before we were to leave, I still hadn't told him.

I spent the entire morning packing and cleaning the house. I must have done five loads of laundry, most of it the girls'. I gathered their favorite toys, packed a bag for the train ride: cards and snacks and books. I made sure I had saltine crackers and a bottle of ginger ale for Mouse's motion sickness, hoping she would sleep most of the way. I made a freezer full of casseroles, things that Frankie could just pop in the oven and heat up throughout the month: tuna casserole, beef stew, and lasagna. He wore a uniform to work, and he knew how to operate an iron, so I was spared there. But I made sure all the towels were clean, that there were fresh linens on the beds.

Chessy and Mouse were trying to get in every last possible minute with Donna and Sally; all morning they were back and forth between the houses, clinging to the final few hours with each other. I kept reassuring them that we'd be gone only four weeks, and that when we got back, school would start and they'd see each other every day. They would be in the third and first grades, respectively. Frankie had lobbied for the Catholic school but had, due to my stubborn resistance, lost. I had no problem with him bringing them to Mass every Sunday. I didn't put up a fight when he wanted them baptized or later when they each had their first communions. But I put my foot down when it came to their schooling. Frankie must have known I wouldn't budge, because he let well enough alone after our first discussion. Besides, the Catholic school was halfway across town, and the brand-new elementary school was less than a mile away. Even he had to admit that the round building, with each classroom like a slice of pie, opening to a huge cafetorium, was pretty impressive compared to the tired, old brick monstrosity that was St. Dorothy's.

I fed the girls an early lunch, and then the older ones took off out the door again. Sally and Mouse stayed behind, lingering under my feet in the kitchen as I tried to clean up. Despite the fact that they were playing nicely, I was starting to lose my patience. "Girls, why don't you go play outside?" I said as kindly as I could. They had their baby dolls set up around the kitchen table and were feeding them imaginary sweet potatoes.

"Mama!" protested Mouse, but then they reluctantly left, cooing apologies to their baby dolls.

I stood at the kitchen sink, washing the pots and pans, looking out the window as the girls put their babies together in the toy baby carriage that Mouse had gotten for her birthday. Their tenderness was so sweet—little mommies and their small charges. I'd never played with dolls myself, so it always surprised me to see my girls exercising those precocious maternal instincts. I'd preferred climbing trees and swimming in the river when I wasn't busy reading books. Gussy was the one who played with dolls; by the time we adopted Chessy, she and her Frank already had two real babies of their own.

I'd never been *opposed* to the idea of being a mother, but I also had found it less instinctive and more like playing an elaborate game of make-believe. Chessy and Mouse were each just a couple days old when we adopted them. With Chessy I had felt like a fraud, like a big phony, when the nurse put the baby in my arms. It was as though I were, indeed, only playing dolls, and with no experience. Frankie tried to comfort me, but I spent her entire first night at home crying. But then, somehow, after only a few nights and days spent caring for her, of watching her face as it twitched in sleep, of smelling the scent of her skin when I held her close to me, I began to feel like a *mother*. Or at least like less of an imposter. By the time we adopted Mouse, it seemed that this was just the way things were supposed to be.

I tried to imagine what it would be like to have a newborn in the house again. All those hours spent feeding and diapering and cleaning. I dreamed that blue light of three a.m., the eerie solitude that belongs solely to new mothers. I wondered if I would feel differently with this baby than I had with the girls—if carrying this baby inside of me would make any difference at all. I'd been alone with both Chessy and Mouse. Alone all day while Frankie worked and then up alone with them most of the night. I imagined taking walks with Eva, each of us pushing a stroller, our babies nestled inside. This time I would have someone to share it with. Someone to talk to. A *friend*.

As I washed the dishes, I rehearsed the ways I would offer the news to Frankie, anticipated his glee.

I was drying the cast iron pot in which I'd made the spaghetti sauce when I felt the first pain. It nearly knocked me over. I set the pot down and steadied myself, pressed my hand against my chest to slow my heart. *No*.

The cramp came again, and I gripped the edge of the counter. I felt my entire body being taken over by the pain, and my temples pounded. But surprisingly, instead of thinking of the baby, instead of worrying about what was happening inside my body, my first impulse was to call Eva. Wincing, I made my way to the phone.

"Hello?" she answered. Her voice immediately calmed me.

"Eva. Can you please make sure the children don't come over here?"

"Billie, what's wrong?"

"Oh God," I said, my grip loosening on the phone. My legs gave way and I sank to the floor, watching both horrified and fascinated as a bright red flower blossomed across my apron. The tears came then, and like the miscarriage, there was nothing I could do to stop them.

Eva was at the door within seconds. She helped me into the guest bathroom and called my doctor. She sat with me in the bathroom, held a cold washrag to my face, gave me ice to suck on, talked softly to me, and stroked my hair. And later, when I was finally able to stand, she got me up the stairs. From my room, I could hear her cleaning up the bathroom.

I managed to get into the shower, where I stood, watching

the blood swirl down the drain, picking up the slippery, tattered pieces of another imagined future in my fingers. Sadness and loss overwhelmed me.

Eva knocked on the bathroom door.

"Come in," I said. I could see her shadow behind the glass.

"Are you okay?" she asked.

I let out a small cry.

Her hand pressed against the glass door of the shower; I pressed my own palm against it. The water at my feet was pink now, but the pain continued to come in thick, powerful pulses.

"I'm going to go check on the children," her silhouette said. "I'll be back in a few minutes." And then she was gone again. I squeezed my eyes shut, riding the waves of pain as though they were only water. I tried to imagine that I was swimming in the lake in Vermont. I tried to conjure *moon, loon, sky.*

I must have stood there for nearly an hour. The hot water ran out, and I was shivering. I carried the handful of everything that was left and sat down, naked, on the toilet. I didn't know what to do with the remains. I couldn't seem to bring myself to put them in the bowl.

Eva knocked on the door again. I reached for a towel with my free hand and covered myself the best I could. She came in, and I uncurled my fist and started to cry again. She took a deep breath. "Would you like me to take care of that?" she asked.

I nodded, and she took a tissue from the box behind the toilet. She waited for me, for instructions.

"Just throw it away," I said. "Please. Outside. And there are some pills. From Frankie's surgery." Frankie had had some kidney stones removed the year before. I could picture the bottle of pills in the medicine cabinet. "In the downstairs bathroom."

The pain returned as she left, and I sat on the toilet as my body expelled everything that remained. This time, I didn't look. I simply closed the lid and flushed.

When the pain subsided, I made my way to the bedroom and lay down. She returned only a few moments later.

"Do you want me to call him?" she asked softly, handing me the pill and a cold glass of water.

I shook my head. I thought of Frankie's face every other time this had happened. I couldn't do that to him again. To myself.

She nodded. "What time will he be home?"

"Six," I said. "What time is it now?"

"One thirty."

After I had fallen asleep, she took care of the children, even put together the dinner I had planned for that night. She got all of our suitcases gathered, and at five thirty she came and woke me up. "Frankie will probably be here in a little bit. Are you sure you're going to be okay to travel tomorrow?"

I nodded. "Thank you."

She sat down next to me on the bed. "I'll miss you in Vermont," she said, frowning. "Will you send me a postcard?"

"Of course," I said, sitting up, feeling woozy.

"Lie down," she said, and I obeyed.

I reached for her hand. "And you need to write me, as soon as the baby comes." The word *baby* caught in my throat and felt like a cotton ball in my mouth. My stomach cramped as if in response.

She kissed her index finger and touched it to my forehead. And something about that simple gesture made me feel soft inside, as if the pain were loosening its grip, if only for a moment. I didn't want her to leave, and I could feel that place where she had touched me long after she was gone.

The pain pill had softened the edges of things. It was just a dull ache now. I felt hollow. Emptied out. I knew I was still bleeding, would continue bleeding for a while. I also knew that Frankie would expect that we have sex that night; it would be weeks before we'd see each other again. I tried to remember the last time I'd told him I was menstruating, hoping he'd believe me again.

That night I made supper, though I could barely eat. I took another pill and sat at the dinner table feeling separated from my pain; I could still feel it, but it was not a part of me. It's as though the cramping and backache and agony were somehow outside of my body.

Frankie was accustomed to being turned away, and I expected he would deal with my rejection the way he usually did. But when I said I wasn't feeling well, mouthing *female troubles,* instead of muttering under his breath and walking away, he stayed and leaned in so close to my face that I could smell the wine on his breath, see the way it discolored his teeth.

"*Female troubles,* huh?" he hissed.

He was drunker than I had thought. Sometimes this happened; he'd seem fine and then something would shift, and I'd realize that he was actually *loaded*. Like a gun. All the chambers empty except for one. Our conversations like games of Russian roulette.

"Frankie, please," I said, forcing a smile, trying hard to keep the peace.

"Seems more like *I'm* the one with female troubles," he said, pointing his callused fingertip into my chest. I couldn't help but think of Eva, of the tender way she had kissed her finger before pressing it to my forehead. But this was not tenderness. He pushed, and his finger felt like something sharp against my sternum. "Nothing but troubles out of this one. Nothing but grief. I'll tell *you* about female troubles. You're nothing but *un pesce morto*." *A dead fish*.

I thought of the baby then, of what was left, swirling down the drain. Grief and anger overwhelmed me. His ignorance of everything that happened that day made me hate him. I knew it was illogical; he didn't even know. But his obliviousness still infuriated me. His cruelty. I even thought for a moment about telling him what had happened, making him experience at least a bit of the pain I was feeling. But instead, I just silently listened to his venomous words and, finally, his angry shuffling down the stairs. I strained to hear the sound of the cupboard door opening and closing. The slosh into the glass. I worried only a little that he'd be even drunker and angrier when he returned. After a few tumblers of wine, he had a temper and could snap. *Had* snapped. But after half a jug, he usually just fell asleep. When he came up an hour later and sat down on the bed, unable to even undo his belt, I knew I was finally safe. And within seconds, he was snoring.

But I did not sleep, could not sleep. Even with the pills. My brain felt muddy, my emotions confused. Sorrow and relief and anger and guilt all swirled together, mixing with the pain, floating above me like a storm cloud. And the tears that drenched my face, the blood that continued to seep and seep from my body, could have been simply the dampness of rain.

Gussy knew something was wrong, of course, when she picked me and the girls up the next day from the train station in Two Rivers. As we piled into Frank's station wagon, our girls climbing all over each other in the backseat, bickering over who got to sit next to the window, Gussy looked at me in that way she had: that big-sister way that made me feel both loved to death and patronized. I ached to tell her about the miscarriage, but I also dreaded revealing yet another one of my many disappointments. I wanted her compassion but not her pity.

"What happened?" she asked. "Is it Frankie? What did he do this time?"

I had the terrible habit of only talking to Gussy about Frankie after he did something stupid or hurtful. In Gussy's eyes, Frankie was a caricature, a foolish man who drank too much and whose tongue was too loose. I always had to remind myself to share not only Frankie's foibles with her but his kindness as well.

"He wasn't out stealing trees again, was he?" she asked, laughing a little, and I had to resist my own laughter.

The last time I'd had a conversation with Gussy about Frankie was when he'd come home one night with three saplings, pulled up by their roots. He'd gone out for a couple of drinks with the guys after his shift and got the bright idea on his way home that he could take some of those pretty red maples he saw growing on the side of the road near Spot Pond and plant them in our backyard. Convinced that the police weren't far behind, ready to arrest him for theft or vandalism or whatever crime pulling trees up by the roots and putting them in the back of your Studebaker constituted, he'd pulled into our driveway so fast he'd left tread marks on the pavement.

"No." I shook my head. I glanced at the girls in the backseat, who were eavesdropping on us now, and said, "We'll talk later."

"Because, Billie," she whispered, glancing in the rearview mirror at the girls. "I swear, if he does anything that stupid again, I'm going to come down there myself and talk some sense into him." If Gussy had any idea about what really happened between Frankie and me, the words he used, the things he called me, she would be horrified.

Gussy liked to consider herself my protector, even though the opposite was almost always true. I was three years younger, but when a neighbor boy down the road took Gussy's brand-new bicycle from her on the way to school and wouldn't give it back, I was the one who wrestled him to the ground, bloodied his nose, and sent him crying home to his mother. When a different boy broke Gussy's heart in the eighth grade, I was the one who left a nice, fresh cow patty from our pasture in his book bag. Now that we were grown, I simply protected her from the truth.

"No need for that, Gussy. Frankie's been a good boy."

And that was the truth, for the most part. Frankie drank too much. He could get angry, even cruel. But while he certainly raised his voice, he would never dare raise a hand to me, or to the children. His drinking usually manifested in foolish, impulsive behavior: stealing trees, setting off firecrackers in the front yard, juggling my best china in the kitchen. On the occasions when his jolly drunkenness turned into rage, I knew how to navigate the dangerous waters of his anger. First I made sure the girls were far, far away from him. Second, I knew what would make things worse and how to avoid them. I also knew that patience, above all else, was the antidote, because his storms were like tornadoes.

They brewed, they touched down, and then they were gone. If you could just hunker down and find a safe place to hide, within no time at all it would pass and the air would be calm again. I'd witnessed the same storm pattern with his sisters' husbands as well, though most of their wives hadn't figured out that it's best to stay in the eye of the storm. When his sisters visited, I watched them get berated and shoved around, and later, when they had gone back home, I worried for them and thanked my lucky stars that Frankie was, in comparison, so very tame.

"Mind if I smoke?" I asked. The scent of cigarettes, particularly my own, had been intolerable during the last few months. But now that this pregnancy, like every pregnancy, had ended, I found myself hungry for them again.

"Put your window down then," she said, rolling her eyes.

Gussy always complained when she rode with Frankie and me in the car, both of us puffing like dragons, the windows rolled up to keep out the cold, the children complaining of upset stomachs in the backseat. Gussy had never even taken a puff of a cigarette, not one puff. I lit my cigarette and rolled down the window. I took a deep drag and allowed the smoke to fill all those empty places inside of me. I imagined myself filled with vapors, the ghosts of all those babies that had once resided inside me.

The air outside was cooler than it had been at home. As we drove through Quimby and then away from town and into the woods toward the lake, I felt like everything was suddenly cleaner, brighter, greener. There is something about going home, like water always wanting to rise to its own level again. This was my level. Here was my water.

The kids opened the car doors before we even pulled to a stop. Mouse tore off her clothes, stripped down to her panties, and ran toward the lake. I smiled at her abandon, her freedom.

"Now will you tell me?" Gussy asked.

"Let's just swim," I said, tossing my cigarette into the bushes.

I followed Mouse's invisible path down to the water's edge where I took off my own shirt, leaving my shorts on, and swam. I was still bleeding, would still be bleeding off and on for the rest of our time here, but somehow being in the water, being surrounded by water, made it seem not so violent a thing.

I told her about the miscarriage later that night after the children had gone to sleep. I tried to pass it off as though it had been expected (it *had* been expected) and that I was fine. That was the pretense I have always had with my sister: that nothing could harm me, my hide as thick as an elephant's. But she knew; she always knew. And so she just held my hand as I told her what happened. For some reason, though, when she asked me later, on a lighter note, what else was new that summer, I didn't mention the Wilsons. I didn't tell her about Ted and his wide face and giant hands and big, red Cadillac. I didn't tell her about how nice it was to have a friend so close to home. And I didn't tell her about everything that Eva had done for me that day. Maybe I didn't want her to be jealous, to feel like someone was stepping on her big-sister toes. Or maybe I just didn't have the words to articulate the wonderful sense of contentment I had knowing that, despite everything, I wasn't alone anymore: that just across the street was someone warm and kind. Or maybe it was more selfish than that, and I just didn't, for once, want to share.

Gussy helped me unpack that night, lingering longer than she needed to. Finally, as the sun went down and the exhaustion of the trip, of the whole summer, descended upon me, she kissed my head and said, "I'm here. If you need anything at all. Love you, Gingersnap," and drove away, leaving us alone at the lake.

Gussy calls tonight as I am getting out of the tub. I can hear my phone vibrating in the other room, and I consider letting it go to voice mail, but know it's unfair to make her worry. I am careful not to stand up too quickly though. The last time I rose out of a hot bath for the telephone, I saw stars and almost went down, crashing into the porcelain bowl of the tub. *This is how little old ladies break hips,* I'd thought. *This is how bones crumble.* The world is a treacherous place at this age.

"Hi, Gus, what's the news?" I say.

"I just got off the phone with Johnny," she says. "He called to see if I'd convinced you to come home yet."

Feeling a little woozy, I sit down on the bed so that I don't accidentally fall to the floor. I had stupidly hoped she would just let this go. Forget about Johnny.

"Billie?"

"That's what they call me," I say, and wrap my towel around me. My hair is dripping wet and cold on my shoulders. Outside, a foghorn lows.

She sighs. "You know Ted passed away?"

I bristle at the mention of Ted. "How would I know that?"

"Suicide," she says.

This is startling to me. I would have been less surprised to hear that he'd been murdered. "How?" I ask, not really wanting the grisly details but needing an image, something to make the suicide real. To make his death real.

"I don't know," she says. "I didn't ask."

"When did he . . . ?" I say. How is it, after all this time, this news comes as a relief? As though I have been waiting for this for the last five decades?

"This summer. I think it's when Johnny really went off the deep end. He said he's struggled for years now, he's been in and out of trouble. But his father's suicide sent him into a tailspin."

"I really don't know what he expects of me," I say. And I don't. I am an eighty-year-old woman living on the other side of Johnny's world. The ties that bind us are frayed with age, weakened by time and distance. Barely a thread anymore.

Gussy coughs. "All of this is, um, more complicated than I thought."

It is my turn to sigh. I don't know why she's being so elusive. "What's going on, Gus?"

There is silence on the other end of the line, a terrifying abyss growing between us.

"Gus?"

"Please just come home," she says softly. "We can talk about it when you get here."

"Talk about what, Gus? There isn't anything you can tell me about Ted Wilson that's going to upset me. Seriously."

There is that silence again, that gulf, and when she finally speaks, there's a tumbling sense of urgency to her words. "I found a flight that gets into Burlington at three o'clock this Friday. I can pick you up and then we can have supper here, get some sleep. In the morning we can head up to the lake to see Effie and the girls. Johnny said he could come up on Sunday. Would Sunday be too soon?"

"*This* weekend?" I say, feeling suddenly too hot, my skin prickly. "I don't know. This seems crazy."

"Of course, he has to work on Monday, so it would be a short visit. I can ask Francesca about coming up too. If you stay a couple of weeks, maybe she could visit the next weekend."

I can feel a breeze come off the ocean and through the cracks of my window.

"Would chicken and dumplings be okay?"

"Chicken and dumplings?"

"For supper. When you get here."

My sister has always been the one to take control, the one to grab hold of the universe, my universe, when it begins spinning out of control. I am grateful to her. But I am also powerless when she is this determined.

"I already bought the ticket," she says. "You just need to get to the airport."

Later, as I lie in bed waiting for sleep, I try not to think of Ted and all the possible ways he might have taken his own life. I try not to think of Johnny and whatever bottom he hit after his father's death. I try not to think of that tenuous bridge between us, the deep water beneath, the memories and years below. I try only to think of seeing my sister again. It's been two years, and we may not have that many years left. Either one of us.

At the end of that summer, when the girls and I returned to Hollyville from Vermont, the entire pregnancy and miscarriage seemed far away, like a gauzy dream. Going home after being away for so long *always* felt a bit dreamlike; it would take a few days before I felt as though I was in a real place rather than on a stage, the furniture and appliances all out of proportion to the ones in my memory, the colors too bright. Frankie looked strange to me too, like an actor playing Frankie. The touch of his hand felt foreign and papery at first, though he'd just been to visit us a couple of weeks before.

Even Eva seemed like some fabrication of my mind, a story I made up to entertain myself, to pass the time. We didn't have a phone at the lake yet then, but I had sent her a postcard from Vermont, taking nearly a half hour at the Rexall in Quimby selecting one that would somehow entice her to join us there the following summer. But I hadn't heard back. And Frankie had been useless. He said he hadn't seen Eva at all while he was home, that his encounters with Ted had also been few and far between. I half expected when we pulled onto Beechtree Street that Mrs. Macadam would still be sitting on her porch, or that the FOR SALE sign might still be stuck beneath the lilac bush. But instead, there was Eva. Eva with a tiny little bundle in her arms. I felt my cheeks flush, my blood quicken in my veins. She rushed down her porch steps when she saw our car, Donna and Sally and Johnny all close behind.

I threw open the passenger door as soon as Frankie pulled the car into our driveway and hollered across the street. "Pink or blue?"

"What's that?" she hollered back.

"Girl or a boy?" I shouted again, feeling foolish.

"Why don't you go across the goddamned street instead of making such a goddamned scene!" Frankie said, opening the trunk and pulling out our suitcases.

I ran across the street, overwhelmed by a need to touch her, to confirm that she wasn't just some figment of my imagination. I put my left arm around her and squeezed, and with my right I touched the top of the baby's pink bonnet.

"This is Rose," she said.

"She's beautiful." I peered down at her small face. "May I hold her?"

"Please," she said, and carefully handed her to me. I didn't remember my own children being this small. She felt no heavier than a whisper in my arms. Her eyes were closed shut, her cheeks the blotchy pink of a newborn's. "She's wonderful," I said, feeling that empty place inside me open wide.

Eva nodded, smiling. Now that I was closer to her, I could see the fatigue in her face, the exhaustion that deepened the shadows beneath her eyes. While my own skin was freckled brown from the summer sun, Eva was pale: not sickly, exactly, but her complexion was one of someone who has been stuck inside and out of the light.

"Tell me about Vermont," she said, squeezing my hand tightly. "I got your postcard. It looks so beautiful there. I told Teddy I want to go visit you next summer. Even if it's just for a week. I thought Donna and Sally would go mad without your girls here."

It had worked! The postcard picture of the lake reflecting the fiery autumn leaves of the trees surrounding it had done its job. I was glad suddenly I hadn't opted for one with a covered bridge or a cow.

Frankie was glad to have us home, and on his best behavior that first night back. He barely drank with supper, and he even helped dry the dishes afterward. He played six games of Chinese checkers with the girls before shooing them upstairs for their baths. And then after they were tucked into bed, he raised his eyebrow and cocked his head. "Miss me?" Frankie was the eternal optimist, all his glasses half full, even this one.

And so I led the way upstairs to our room, and turned out the lights before slipping off my clothes. I hurried into the bed, and waited for him to undress as well. Under the covers, in the darkness, I felt the familiar angles of his bones, the eagerness of his hands and mouth. I tried to make him feel wanted, to return his affections with equal fervor, but I couldn't focus. My thoughts were, as always, elsewhere. I tried, God how I tried, to simply be present, to be near, but the moment Frankie touched me I felt myself slipping away. Hovering at the edges of things. So I did what I knew would hasten things, pulled out all the old familiar tricks. And like magic, they worked (they always worked), and then Frankie was rolling onto his back, sweating and breathless, staring at the ceiling. "Good to have you home, Billie."

From somewhere came the distant sound of an infant crying and for one confused moment, my heart lurched. I had put the lost baby in a closed, quiet place in my mind, a wooden box where I kept all the dangerous secrets, all the lost things. But now, the hinges of the box screeched open, and I felt my chest expand with fear and grief.

"Goddamn, that kid is loud," Frankie muttered, rolling onto his stomach.

And then I realized the cries were coming from the Wilsons' house.

The new baby had colic. Basically, this meant that unless she was sleeping, she was crying. And it was not the gentle fuss most babies use to let you know that she needs to have her diaper changed or that she wants a bottle, but rather relentless and piercing *screams*. Screams that could make even the best mother feel helpless, useless, even angry at her child.

I could hear her all the way across the street. Even with the door closed. I could hear her when I worked in the garden, when I canned blueberries in the kitchen, when Frankie and I lay down to sleep at night. I imagined that no one in the Wilson house must be getting any sleep. I certainly wasn't.

After the kids went back to school that fall, it started to rain. For the first two weeks of September there wasn't a single day that it wasn't raining. It rained all night and it rained all day. The rain barrels were overflowing. Stuck without a car, I didn't have much to do besides putter around the house, which was quiet now without the girls. I thought about visiting Eva, but I worried that ringing the doorbell, or even just knocking, might wake the baby. I had told Eva to call me if she needed anything, even if she just needed a break, but she later told me she felt uncomfortable asking for my help. As though Rose would be a cruel reminder of everything I'd lost that summer.

I pleaded with Frankie to take the train in to work so that I could have the car, but he insisted he needed it in case he "found anything." Frankie was always happening upon discarded treasures and bringing them home. Our solid mahogany dining table had been abandoned outside an apartment building in Brookline. It had a broken leg and, as though it were a wounded animal, Frankie brought it home and tended to its injury, nursing it back to life. A large, framed mirror; an oak vanity; a treadle sewing machine; and a tricycle (though both of our girls were too big for it) had all made their way from the streets of Boston and into our little house. He felt about these salvaged items the same way he felt about the stamps he sold; every damaged piece of furniture, every antique he brought home, had a story behind it. Restoration was about keeping that history alive.

And so each morning he and Ted took off to work in their respective cars, leaving Eva and me behind. Stranded.

The Hollyville library was a mile away, which wasn't far unless it was raining. But after five days, I decided to go ahead and bundle up in my slicker and plastic bonnet and just make my way.

Chessy needed a book on Marie Curie for a report, and I thought I'd look for *The Wind in the Willows* for Mouse. I'd run out of things to read as well.

Outside, I peered at the Wilsons' house and considered checking to see if Eva would like to bring Johnny and Rose along, but I knew that taking a baby and a rambunctious four-year-old out in the pouring rain was the last thing *I'd* want to do if I were her. However, when I got to the library, it seemed that every other mother with young children in Hollyville *had* decided to brave the storm; outside there were nearly a dozen cumbersome carriages and strollers lined up underneath the narrow awning. And stepping into the children's room was like stepping into a scene from *Lord of the Flies*. Babies and toddlers, frazzled mothers, and one very harried librarian were not what I had hoped for. So I quickly located the books for the girls and then escaped to the reading annex. I found *Doctor Zhivago* still sitting on the New Fiction shelf, and as the rain pounded against the tall glass windows near my overstuffed chair, I lost myself inside the pages. When I finally looked up at the clock, it was two o'clock. That would get me home just in time for me to meet the girls after the bus dropped them off.

I gathered my things and headed to the circulation desk with my books, but something in the stacks caught my eye. Sitting alone on the floor was a woman, crying softly into her hands.

I stepped back, out of her line of vision, heart pounding, and tried to process what I had just seen. I slowly peeked around the corner again and sure enough, it was Eva. Eva completely alone, weeping into a book.

"Eva?" I said softly, stepping between the stacks.

She looked up, startled. "Billie," she said, sounding strangely relieved. There were deep circles under her eyes, and her hair was disheveled. She was dressed in a faded house dress and a pair of worn ballet flats.

"Are you okay?"

She looked at me silently and nodded, though I could tell something was amiss.

I sat down across from her on one of the step stools used to get the books from the high shelves. "What are you reading?" I asked.

She rolled her eyes, sheepishly. Embarrassed. "Just a trashy novel. *Peyton Place,*" she said, showing me her book as evidence, and then wiped her runny nose on a hankie she was clutching in her hand.

"Where are Johnny and Rose?" I asked, figuring they were in the city with Ted's family. Perhaps somebody had finally given her a break.

She looked up at me, her small nose bright red, her eyes bloodshot, and I suddenly knew something was terribly, terribly wrong. "I had to get out of that house. I just wanted to sit and read a book. I just wanted a little peace and quiet. She won't stop crying."

"Johnny and Rose are alone at the house?" I asked, starting to panic.

"No, Donna is home sick today. She's watching them."

I tried to imagine the sort of mischief Johnny might get into unattended. Donna, while older, was still only nine. Images of matchsticks and flames flickered in my head.

It was as though Eva were suddenly waking from a dream. "Oh, God, you must think I'm just awful."

"Did you walk here?" I asked.

She nodded, and I noticed her drenched overcoat in a wet pile next to her. "I'm a terrible mother," she said. "A terrible, terrible mother."

"No," I said. "You're just exhausted. It's absolutely understandable. But let's get you home," I said, reaching out a hand to help her up. Trying not to sound panicked, I said, "You can use my umbrella."

We made it back to our street in only twenty minutes or so,

but we were both soaked, and bone cold. I cannot even explain the relief I felt when the Wilsons' house came into sight and there were no plumes of smoke, no charred ruins.

Inside, Donna had made peanut butter sandwiches and she and Johnny were sitting on the floor watching television with plates in front of them. Rose was asleep on the couch, covered in a blanket.

"Now let's get you dried off," I said, and started to help Eva off with her coat.

Suddenly her mood changed. The despondency I'd seen in the library and felt in every heavy breath on our way home disappeared. She pulled the blanket up over Rose's exposed arm and playfully scolded the kids. "Well, that's not a proper lunch! Let me make some tomato soup. Grilled cheese sandwiches? And Billie," she said, smiling. "We absolutely need to get together if this godawful rain ever stops."

Taken aback by this sudden shift, I simply nodded in agreement and made my way to the door.

"Have a nice afternoon," she said, her face fixed in that strange smile. But then when we were alone again on the porch, she grabbed my arm. "And thank you." Her eyes were wide and imploring. "Now you have one of my secrets to keep."

"Of course," I said.

We were conspirators from the outset, keepers of each other's darkest truths.

"It sounds like air raid sirens," Frankie said on Halloween night when the baby had been crying for hours. We were in the kitchen; I was helping the girls put the final touches on their Halloween costumes. At first I thought it was just one of the many children dressed up as a ghost, the ghoulish screams echoing in the night. But as I sent the girls off to gather the Wilson children before heading out trick-or-treating, masks affixed and candy bags at the ready, I realized it was Rose.

I left Frankie to hand out candy to the trick-or-treaters and went over to see what I could do to help.

"Where's Ted?" I asked Eva. His car hadn't been in the driveway all night.

"Business trip," she said, shrugging. In a tired housedress and tattered slippers, I barely recognized her. She wasn't wearing any makeup, and her hair was a mess.

"How long will he be gone?" I asked.

She shrugged. "Probably until the baby stops crying," she said, smiling sadly.

"Let me take her," I said. "Is the carriage in the garage?"

"You don't have to do that."

"I know that," I said. "Now go take a nice, hot bath. Put on some fresh nightclothes. I'll be back in an hour. And if she's still crying, I'll take her out again."

"Thank you," she said.

"And when the kids are done trick-or-treating you can send them over to my house. Let Frankie watch them for a little while."

"You're the best, Billie."

I smiled, felt myself blushing.

I put Rose in the carriage, and we must have walked three miles, her wailing at the top of her tiny little lungs the entire way. Luckily, the night was already filled with children's squeals, the streets thick with ghosts and robots and cowboys and witches. And even with all that noise, there was something beautiful and peaceful about the night. The harvest moon made the entire twilight sky illumine like the jack-o'-lanterns that adorned nearly every stoop. All of the trees had lost their leaves, their skeletal forms casting intricate shadows across the streets. It was remarkably warm for the end of October. And I loved the rhythmic *click-clack* the carriage wheels made against the sidewalk.

As we made our way up and down the street, in and out of side streets, Rose howled. As I pushed her stroller up and down the curbs, she keened. As I circled the parking lots of the elementary school and the Catholic church, she screeched. But then, finally, just as we were almost home, she stopped. The unexpected silence was so absolute, so complete, I thought I'd suddenly gone deaf.

I peered into the carriage, and sure enough, Rose had simply exhausted herself. I didn't know what to do now; should I keep moving? Stay still? I peered at the Wilsons' house and saw that the upstairs bathroom light was on. I imagined, hoped, that Eva had heeded my pleas, that she was neck deep in a hot bath. Maybe some Chet Baker on the hi-fi.

And so I decided to just remain still.

The trick-or-treaters had all disappeared inside their respective homes. I could see the silhouettes of my girls and the Wilson children in our bay window. I had instructed Frankie to give them each a big plate of the spaghetti I'd made for dinner. I left the carriage on the walkway and sat down on Eva's steps, afraid, even as I moved stealthily to the stoop, that Rose would wake up and begin screaming again. I was only there for about ten minutes before I heard the front door open behind me, and Eva stood in the doorway, a silhouette against the bright hallway lights behind her. I held my finger to my lips, *shhh,* and motioned for her to join me on the stoop.

She tiptoed across the porch and looked down into the carriage, sighing, relieved. She sat down next to me on the step; her hair was wet and she smelled of White Shoulders. She had put powder on her face, and though she still looked tired, she looked refreshed. She leaned her head against my shoulder. "I don't know what I'm going to do if she keeps crying like this, Billie."

"She won't. I bet she'll grow out of it in just a couple of months."

"I don't think I can *take* a couple months of this," she said softly, lifting her head.

"I can help," I said. "Anytime you need me to."

Eva nodded. "You know, I missed you when you were in Vermont," she said, smiling.

I felt myself growing warm. Frankie hadn't even said he'd missed me. At a sudden and rare loss for words, I studied the sky. "It's a nice night."

She looked up at the autumn night sky. "When Teddy and I met, I was going to art school, you know," she said.

"Really?" I asked. I had tried to imagine their lives in California but had drawn a blank. Art school certainly hadn't been in any of my imaginings.

"I knew I'd never be an artist, but I thought maybe someday I could teach." Her eyes were still fixed on something in the distance. "I was pregnant," she said.

"Well, you certainly aren't the first couple to get married because of a baby . . ." I started.

"I was pregnant when he *met* me," she said, taking a deep breath, waiting for my response.

I was stunned. Speechless.

"The father was my teacher. He was *married,*" she whispered, though there was no one but me to hear. "It was awful. I met Ted at the restaurant where I was waiting tables. He said he'd marry me and raise the baby as his own."

"Donna." I nodded.

She shook her head. "No. I lost that baby three days after the wedding." She turned to look at me, smiling sadly. "This isn't what I'd planned," she said, gesturing to the empty street before us. "It's not what I wanted."

Her admission took my breath away. It was like she'd just confessed to murder instead of simple unhappiness. It was shocking, *thrilling*.

"Me either," I said, laughing a little and nodding, admitting this to someone else for the first time in my whole life. It felt liberating. Terrifying. Dangerous.

She reached out and enclosed my hand in hers, which was

still warm from her bath. My whole body seemed to relax at her touch, and I hadn't even realized how tense I had been. I felt calm for the first time in ages. Content. *Understood.* Then, as if on cue, Rose woke up and started screaming again.

"Well, you can't unring a bell," she said, releasing my hand. She stood up, leaned over the carriage and pulled Rose out, pressed her against her chest, and cooed into her hair. "It's okay, Rosie. It's okay."

Later that night, I fell asleep to the distant sound of Rose's cries, mistaking them for a moment for the loons' lament. And I was transported, just for a moment, back to Gormlaith, back to Vermont. I had a fitful night's sleep, half dreaming about Eva. About the married man, about a whole other life: bohemian San Francisco, medicine men. I woke with a start, heart racing, and realized that it was the silence that had woken me. It was five a.m., and Rose had finally stopped crying.

I tell my friend Juan about my trip on Thursday night as I sit at the pub, drinking my solitary stout. Lou was not a drinker, and after all those years with Frankie, I sought peace in sobriety. But now I find comfort in a nightly beer. And in the company I find at the bar.

It is a quiet night, only a few other regulars. It's that strange time of night after the daytime drunks have stumbled home but before the younger crowd shows up. Chester's caters to the locals: bikers and surfers and old broads like me. Lined up at the open window like painted clown heads in an arcade game, we tend to keep the tourists away. I like to sit and watch the people go by, the colorful parade of characters who live here. It is dusk now, the sun retired for the night, the moon stepping in to do the job of illuminating the surf.

"How long's it been since you've been back east?" Juan asks, as he gathers up the empty bottles from an abandoned table.

"To Vermont? About five years. But I haven't been back to the lake since '64," I say, realizing for the first time how very long ago that was. Juan probably wasn't even born yet in 1964.

Juan is single, divorced, but girls like him. A group of women who work at the salon next door come in and flirt with him. He humors them, but that is all. He, like me, lives alone. He has a ten-year-old son who lives with his mother in Arizona. He shows me pictures on his phone sometimes, and I can see how much he misses him.

"You need a ride to the airport?" he asks.

I had thought I'd call a shuttle after I got home, one of those blue vans you always see zipping along the road. "Oh, you don't need to do that," I say.

"I'm up early anyway," he says. "What time do you need to get there?"

"Six, I think. My flight's at eight."

"I'll be at your place at five thirty," he says, and before I have time to protest, he winks and disappears behind the bar again to take someone's order.

I've been so consumed with the details of this trip that I haven't spent too much time ruminating on the conversation with Gussy, at my irritation at being coerced. I suppose I could have just said *no,* refused her aggressive generosity, but I've never been able to say no to Gussy. And so instead, I measured out my liquids into three-ounce plastic containers. I bought a new, warm jacket. I printed my boarding pass at the library, double-checked with Linda that she and the library would be okay without me for a couple of weeks. (She insisted, but still I worry.) I stopped my paper, asked the post office to hold my mail, and rescheduled a dentist appointment I'd forgotten was coming up. I let my friends and neighbors know that I'll be gone.

Gussy said that Johnny will be driving up from Boston on the Sunday morning after I get there. That means only a couple of days to settle in. It makes me uneasy, though I know it's the whole reason for the trip to begin with. I try to imagine what he looks like now, and I can't help but think of Ted. I wonder if he still looks like his father. As a child, he was his spitting image, as though Ted had made him all on his own. But sometimes children grow out of their parents' faces, leaving that influence, that impression behind.

I leave Juan a generous tip, as I always do, and wave to him from the doorway as I head out to go back to my cottage and try to get some sleep before the morning comes. "Five thirty," he hollers. "Bright and early."

I am thinking of Eva as I walk from the bar back to my cottage. She is in the swaying palm trees, in the moon, in the receding tide. I hear her voice in the tinkling wind chimes that hang from my porch, feel her touch in the breeze. It's funny—Frankie was my husband for years, we raised a family together, I saw him at his finest, and I saw him at his worst, but when I try to picture him, the physical embodiment of him, the *man,* my memory fails. I remember his outbursts, and occasionally his tenderness. But when I try to picture his face, his hands, I'm at a loss. It's as though the years have eviscerated him, leaving only the pale skeleton behind. Even Lou, who was my constant companion for nearly twenty-five years, is shadowy now. A whisper. An echo. But the picture of Eva is brilliant. Everything about her stands out in vivid relief from the blur of the rest of my past: the scent of her hair, the way her dark irises were rimmed in green. The three freckles on the back of her neck. Tonight, when I get to the cottage and put my key in the lock, for a moment I swear I smell her White Shoulders perfume, that lily of the valley, lilac scent. But it is only the hydrangea that blooms in optimistic puffs in the hedge by my front porch.

As I close my bag and set it by the door, as I check my itinerary again, I have to assure myself that I am capable of making this journey. Even without the prospect of seeing Johnny again after all these years, this would be a daunting voyage. In my old age, the simplest trips have begun to feel epic: a walk down the pier, a drive through rush-hour traffic, and now flying home. It makes me think about my daughters' Girl Scout badges, the tasks and accomplishments it took to earn them. Cooking, Animal Raising, Folk Dancing. I wonder what sort of badge I might earn for this. What the embroidered emblem would be: an airplane, a lake, a broken heart.

It was my idea to get Eva to become a Scout leader with me. I had led Francesca's troop the year before, mostly because no other mothers wanted the job. This year, Mouse was eligible to join, and I'd already promised her I'd lead again. The year before I'd had seven girls from the neighborhood who all met in my basement once a week. It had been a chaos of arts and crafts and cooking and camping. This year only three of them were flying up to Girl Scouts, and so I'd been convinced to lead a combined group of Girl Scouts and Brownies, with two new little ones joining. After a couple of months of trying to do it on my own that fall of 1960, I realized I needed help (planning the meetings, wrangling the inevitable couple of wayward Brownies, and orchestrating the annual camping trip to Rippling River Campground in the spring). And I suspected that it might be a good distraction for Eva, an excuse to get out of the house.

"I don't know," she said. "What will I do with Johnny and Rose?"

"Bring them along. We can set up a playpen in the basement. Johnny can watch TV upstairs. It's only once a week. It'll be fun!"

Eva lay on her couch, flipping through the *Brownie Scout Handbook,* the beloved Bible of scouting.

"You can help with the *Arts and Crafts,*" I said, smiling and pointing to the table of contents.

She rolled her eyes.

I still had difficulty imagining Eva's life as an art student in San Francisco. There was no evidence in their home that she had ever been anything other than a mother and wife; the only artwork adorning their walls was a Grandma Moses print of children ice skating and Wyeth's *Christina's World* above the fireplace. We had the same print ourselves, though ours was above our couch, something Frankie had snatched up at a tag sale.

"What kind of things did you paint?" I asked. "When you were in school?"

"I wasn't a painter," she said. "I was a sculptor."

"Like the Venus de Milo?" I asked, thinking of all those pale, armless ruins I'd seen only in our *Encyclopaedia Britannica*.

She shook her head. "No, not that kind of sculpture. Mobiles, mostly. Have you ever heard of George Rickey? Alexander Calder?"

I hadn't.

"Oh, Calder's wonderful, Billie," she said, her eyes brightening. She sat up and leaned forward. "He makes these enormous mobiles. They're made of metal, but they look like birds in flight, absolutely weightless. They'll take your breath away. I'll have to take you to see his work sometime."

"Why don't you make them anymore?" I asked.

Eva looked down at the Brownie handbook in her hands and shook her head. Then she brushed her hand in the air, as though dismissing the thought like a sluggish, buzzing housefly.

Eva was like this sometimes, like the bottles of homemade root beer Frankie made in the basement. She'd pop open with excitement, her entire body buzzing and fizzing, and then, just as suddenly, she'd close up again, everything gone flat.

"Let's start with spatter prints," she said. "We can use some of those pretty maple leaves. Do a nature walk and then the art project. Two birds." When she lifted her head to look at me for my approval, her eyes were glossy.

Mouse, who hated dresses and skirts, who battled with me each and every morning over what she would wear to school, *loved* her Brownie uniform. For two years she'd coveted that plain, little brown dress. She'd even loved the tiny beanie, wearing Chessy's around the house when Chessy would let her. Once she had her very own, bought at the Methodist church rummage sale, she refused to take it off. She memorized all of the songs, the salute, and the Brownie Scout Promise (*I promise to do my best to love God and my country, to help other people every day, especially those at home*) long before the first meeting. I probably could have allowed her to run the meetings and spared Eva and me the trouble.

On meeting days, Eva and I walked to the school to pick all of the girls up, and then we marched back to my house, where I had usually prepared a snack for them to eat before setting about Scout business.

Frankie refused to allow that many little girls in the main part of the house, and so we were banished to the basement. I couldn't help but feel like we were part of some sort of underground organization. Literally. Our basement was enormous, cavernous, a footprint of the entire house, though only half of it was finished. Frankie had his workshop in the basement, where he kept his tools and the salvaged furniture he was restoring as well as a healthy stash of jug wine. My washing machine was down there as well, and a tub where Frankie made homemade root beer. He'd rescued an industrial-size freezer from a restaurant that was going out of business in the North End and that is where we kept the meat I bought on sale at DeMoulas each week. The other part of the cellar, the *cold cellar,* was where I kept my canning supplies and all the vegetables from Frankie's garden that we harvested and canned. The finished part of the basement had wide pine paneling and thin, green carpet. Frankie had furnished the room with two sofas he found at the dump and a wide, low coffee table that was perfect for crafts. There was something serious and solemn about those basement meetings. In the cool, damp darkness, we all felt a bit transported from our normal lives. This was our own little Brownie world.

Eva was a big help, but she was restless. The spring camping trip wasn't until Memorial Day weekend, and she quickly grew bored with our subterranean (and mostly domestic) activities.

"We should take the girls on an adventure. I bet the Boy Scouts aren't sitting around doing cross-stitch. Shouldn't we be *scouting?*"

"What do you want to do?" I asked.

She shrugged. "I don't know. We could go apple picking or something. At least get them outside."

There was a farm just on the outskirts of town that had orchards. In the fall, you could go there for hay rides and to pick apples and pumpkins from the pumpkin patch. They had a small petting zoo as well. It was November, a little late in the season, but it had been unseasonably warm this fall, as though winter weren't right around the corner, and so we figured we'd give it a shot.

However, in order to take such a field trip, we'd need two cars. Ted refused to allow Eva to use his Cadillac (worried, I suppose, about so many girls and his expensive upholstery), and so, reluctantly, I solicited Hannah Flannigan's help. Because, despite being generally irritating and particularly rude, she had a girl in Scouts and a station wagon too. I made sure to warn Eva ahead of time about Hannah, feeling compelled to apologize for any asinine thing that came from her mouth in advance.

We loaded all of the girls into our two cars that Sunday after church and headed to the farm, but when we pulled into the dirt parking lot it was empty. Eva got out of the car and said, "I'll be right back."

Hannah and I watched her as she made her way to the entrance. There was a sign nailed to the gate, but I couldn't read it from where we were.

She came running back to my car. "They're closed," she said, and a collective groan issued forth from the gaggle of girls in the backseat.

Hannah rolled down her window. "I knew it was too late in the season," she said.

"Oh well," I offered to Eva and the girls. "Maybe next year."

"I say we go anyway," Eva said.

Hannah's eyes widened. "What do you mean?"

"I mean, who's going to care if we pick a few apples?" she said. "Girls, come on!"

The doors opened, and the girls spilled out of the cars, but Hannah remained motionless in the driver's seat of her car. "That's *trespassing*. You cannot possibly condone this," she said to me.

Francesca looked worried, but Eva was already back at the gate, climbing over the fence. She looked back at us and motioned for me to follow.

I buzzed with excitement. "Come on, Chessy. It'll be fun."

Chessy looked terribly torn, and Hannah folded her arms across her chest. For one brief moment I had the odd thought that Chessy could have been Hannah's daughter, the grim expressions on their faces so similar. Hannah's own daughter was about to get out of the car, but Hannah reached behind her and pushed the door lock down. "We'll wait right here," she said firmly. "But if the police come, don't expect me to be your getaway car."

Reluctantly Chessy followed me, and I leaned over and whispered in her ear, "It'll be fun. Don't worry."

The orchard was not far from the front gate. It *was* late in the season, and rotten apples littered the ground. The ones that remained on the trees were overripe and hanging low. There were a few Baldwins though, winter apples, that were perfect. There weren't any baskets or boxes for the fruit, so Eva told the girls to put them in their pockets and she gathered hers in a cradle made of her skirt.

The girls, even Chessy, were having so much fun, eating the apples they couldn't carry and chasing each other through the tidy rows of trees. This could have gone on all afternoon if the farmer hadn't heard the noise and come running from his house, which was only about a hundred yards from the orchard. He was fat, stuffed into a pair of overalls, and he practically toppled over as he ran toward us. "What do you think you're doing?" he demanded.

Eva stood with nearly a quarter bushel of apples in her skirt. I thought she might try to charm him, to explain. But instead she said, "Run, girls!" And all of us started to sprint toward the front gate, apples tumbling behind us as we ran. The farmer couldn't keep up and simply shook his head as we all hurdled the fence and dashed into the cars, breathless with laughter.

Hannah looked as though she might have some sort of attack as she peeled out of the parking lot. Eva and I collapsed in the front seat of my car, roaring with laughter. Even Chessy was smiling. I turned around and winked at her.

"Terrific. You've turned our Girl Scouts into common criminals," Hannah said later. "I hope you're proud of yourselves."

Life was simply more exciting with Eva around. No one could argue that, not even Chessy.

Eva's first winter in New England was everything I'd promised when she first moved in across the street, and she was (as expected) ill-prepared for the blustery wind and bitter cold. We were both grateful, I think, to have the excuse of the Scouts to spend time together when we normally would have been stuck inside our respective homes. The biggest scouting event of the year was the annual camping trip to the Rippling River Campground in May. Planning for this trip (preparing survival lessons, creating nature-related arts and crafts projects, and simply managing the logistics of a weekend sleepover with nine girls) occupied many of those dark and chilly afternoons. And while we typed up our lessons and made shopping lists, we got to know each other. Our friendship, like a hothouse flower, grew despite the bitter cold outside.

By the time spring finally came along, Rose was able to pull herself up in the playpen we set up in the basement. By then the colic had stopped as well, thank God, and she had actually become a fairly quiet child. I could see the tension that had resided in Eva's face and shoulders slowly disappearing, melting like the stubborn snow at the edges of the road.

The older girls had earned badges for First Aid, Arts at Home, and Puppets. Mouse coveted these patches, the ones I helped sew onto the Girl Scouts' sashes. She had three more years to go to her own bridging ceremony in which she would "fly up" from Brownie to Scout. For the older girls, the camping trip was their opportunity to earn the coveted Go Camping badge. Mouse was beside herself with envy.

The camping trip was scheduled for Memorial Day weekend. Ted's sister, Mary, was coming from Boston to watch Johnny and Rose for the weekend.

"He can't handle two nights without you?" I asked.

"Of course he can, he just *won't,*" Eva said.

Unlike some other women friends I had, we didn't usually talk about our husbands with each other. We didn't get together to complain or commiserate. We didn't gossip about them over coffee or cocktails. They rarely entered our conversations at all. It wasn't that we didn't have our gripes; *I* certainly did. With any other woman I might have lamented Frankie's many, many faults: the little things, like his insistence on bringing home things from the dump, the way we never had anything new. Or the big things, like his drinking and his temper: the way he could, with a single sentence, crush Francesca's or Mouse's feelings; the way he used his words like fists when he was drunk and angry. I supposed we had a lot in common when it came to this; we could have whispered the sour smell of Frankie's and Ted's breath. Their insistent hands and hips. We could have cried on each other's shoulders about the strange relief and simultaneous loneliness of the nights when Ted and Frankie went out with work buddies for drinks, the reprieve of their absence coupled with the fear of their getting in an accident on the way home. Of what would happen to us if one of them *didn't* come home. We could have consoled each other; we could have shared our sorrow like a box of donuts.

But there was something unspoken between Eva and me, a wonderful silent understanding, that our time together was time when we didn't have to think or talk about our husbands. There was something special about our friendship; it wasn't based on our mutual misery. It was independent of our husbands. Independent, even, of our children. And so instead, throughout that long, cold winter, we had talked about books, and art, and music. We shared records, making each other sit and listen to our respective collections on the hi-fi. I was partial to the schmaltzy stuff: Perry Como and Jo Stafford and Kate Smith (my *favorite*). Eva's taste tended to be more eclectic and refined. She loved jazz and rock 'n' roll. Eva was head over heels over Sam Cooke, swooned as the needle dropped. Sometimes we danced, swiveling our hips to Chubby Checker until we were sweaty and breathless. Sometimes we smoked cigarettes and listened to Chet Baker, dreaming ourselves elsewhere.

"Dance with me," she had said one blustery February afternoon. "Alone Together" playing softly on the record player. I was taller than she was, and she leaned into me, resting her cheek against my chest. Her hair smelled like lilacs.

When the record was over, she released me and flopped down into Ted's armchair. She lit a cigarette and blew three perfect smoke rings into the air. "I am so bored," she said, her eyes closed.

I felt my heart sink a little.

She opened her eyes and looked at me. What I was feeling must have shown on my face, because she reached over and grabbed my hand. "Oh, no, I didn't mean *now*. I mean, in general."

I nodded, but I still felt hurt, though I would be hard-pressed to explain why. I was bored too. Our lives were boring. But mine had become a whole lot less boring since Eva had moved in. The idea that her life was more thrilling before she met me was something I both suspected and resented.

I found myself missing her when she went home to Ted or I

went back across the street to Frankie. I found myself thinking about her as I made dinner or ironed clothes or scrubbed the toilet. I looked forward to our time together in a way I looked forward to little else. Those hours when the kids were in school and the men were at work were like perfect little islands in an otherwise vast and mostly dull sea.

And so while I'd dreaded the annual Girl Scout camping trip in the past, this year I was thrilled by the prospect: three whole days and two nights away from home. No obligations except for teaching the girls how to lash a latrine and dig trenches. How to pitch a tent and build a campfire. The only cooking we had to do was heating up beans and franks over an open fire and assembling s'mores. No house to clean, no husbands to worry over.

Finally spring came, and on the Saturday morning of Memorial Day weekend, we gathered all of our supplies together and loaded them into the Studebaker. Frankie had agreed to drive us to the campsite and drop us off. The other girls' parents were to drop them off at the same time. We wouldn't be retrieved again until Monday at noon.

The weatherman on WBZ had predicted a 40 percent chance of rain, so we made sure to pack our rain ponchos and galoshes. The girls had each made a weatherproof sit-upon to sit by the campfire at night, and our plan was for the older girls to complete the necessary tasks for their Go Camping badge during the trip.

And surprisingly, the weather was gorgeous the first day. All of the girls got new freckles except for Katherine McDowell with her milk-white skin, who wound up with a pretty bad sunburn, which we just slathered with Eva's Noxzema to cool things off a bit. We hiked through the woods, identifying the local flora and fauna using our guidebooks. Chessy and Donna were two of the oldest Brownies, and they took great pleasure in leading the little girls. Chessy had been on the trip twice and knew the rundown campsite and its surroundings well. Her memory amazed me sometimes. She was the kind of girl who only had to read something once and could recall it verbatim at the drop of a hat even months later. Frankie liked to show her the serial number on a dollar bill, tell her to remember it, and then later, in front of friends, ask her to recall it. He'd triumphantly pull that same dollar from his pocket and exclaim, "It's photographic! She's a genius!" But while Frankie saw her skills as some sort of party trick, I knew that her memory would be useful to her later. In college, I thought, she'd ace every test. She could memorize facts about anything; her mind was like a wonderful, intricate trap. Though, like a trap, it could be dangerous too. Nothing escaped her.

"Those are lady slippers," she said, pointing to a cluster of delicate pink and white flowers growing among a sea of ferns along the hiking trail.

Donna reached down.

"No!" Chessy said. "Don't pick them. They're very rare."

"They're beautiful," Eva said, crouching down next to the flowers. "It looks like a baby's ear. Like a little tiny ear!"

I wondered if she was missing Rose. This was the first time since her birth that she'd been away from her.

Mouse was less concerned with the scientific names of things and, like me, was enticed by the smells and sounds and tastes of the forest. She shimmied up trees and yelled down at us from above. She watched the sky instead of the ground as we hiked, stumbling and falling more than once. She might have been too young to earn her own badges, but she proudly bore the scratches and bloody patches of her various scrabbles with Mother Nature.

The girls had pitched their own tents. We had three girls to a large tent, three tents total, with Eva and I sharing a smaller one at the center. When the sky began to cloud over, I taught the girls how to dig a trench so that if and when the rain came they wouldn't get drenched. Eva seemed at a loss when it came to wilderness survival, but I assured her not much would happen to us at the Rippling River Campground. We hung our food in bags from the trees to keep the bears from getting it, though there were no bears here. We dug latrines, though there was a canteen only a hundred yards away with fully functioning toilets. And we made fire from flint and steel, though we lit our cigarettes with Eva's Zippo.

By sunset, the girls were exhausted from the hiking and the sun. They ate s'mores until their bellies ached and then disappeared into their tents, where they giggled for only about an hour before there was a collective silence that fell all around us.

It was too early in the season for anyone other than Scout troops to be out camping, so we had the campground to ourselves. In a month, the sites would be overrun with families from the city trying to get back to nature, but for now, it was peaceful: the only sounds the rustle of sleeping bags inside the tents, the crackle of the fire.

"Shall we?" Eva asked, pulling a bottle of Irish whiskey out of her rucksack.

"Holy cow!" I said as she popped open two of the collapsible cups we'd brought for the girls and filled them to the rim.

"Cin cin!" she whispered, giggling, and we touched the plastic cups together and drank. It was cold out, and the liquor felt great going down and even better in the belly. I was suddenly warm. And happy. My feet were tired from all the walking, and I knew I'd be sore the next day.

I pulled out the transistor radio I'd brought to see what I could get to come in. Surprisingly, I was able to get WBZ in Boston, and "Juicie Brucie" Bradley was playing Del Shannon singing "Runaway." The signal was crackly with static and came in and out, but the music was nice nevertheless.

Eva was bundled up in one of Ted's flannel shirts, though I'd never seen him wear anything other than his work clothes during the week and khakis on the weekends. It looked like someone's idea of what a man should wear in New England, that black and red hunter plaid, and Eva swam inside the enormous sleeves.

"You cold?" I asked, pushing a stick into the dwindling fire.

"Nah," she said. "Another jigger?"

"Why not?" I said, and held out my empty cup. I was feeling pleasantly tipsy when Eva suddenly stood up.

"What are you doing?"

"Going in for a swim," she said.

"Are you kidding? It's freezing."

"Chicken." She smirked.

The small pond near our campsite was probably teeming with leeches. We never took the Brownies in swimming; in addition to the leeches, it was always too cold. Especially in May.

"You're drunk," I said, laughing.

"So what?"

I shrugged. "Have fun. Don't drown."

Eva peeled off her clothes until she was wearing only her underwear and bra. I felt myself blushing and prayed that none of the girls got thirsty or scared or needed to pee. I watched her as she stumbled down to the water, worrying suddenly about how much she'd had to drink. Eva was only about a hundred pounds. I supposed it wouldn't take much to make her drunk.

She slipped into the pond like a water snake, soundlessly, and didn't emerge again for several seconds. I could feel my heart beating in my throat, nearly choking me as I waited. I stood up, worried and starting to think that I should go in after her, but just as I was beginning to panic, she bobbed up, hooting wildly.

"Shhh!" I hissed. "You'll wake the girls." But I was so relieved she hadn't drowned, I felt the momentary impulse to run into the water and hug her. Instead I shook my head, acting as though she were one of my children, and chided, "You'll get pneumonia!"

She came out of the water then, drying off, using Ted's flannel shirt as a towel, and then pulled her clothes on. I added a log to the fire and she crouched down next to it to warm up, her teeth chattering.

"I can practically hear Frankie, if he were here. *You two girls are off your onion,*" I said, doing my best Frankie imitation.

"Ted would *kill* me," she said, shivering.

And then suddenly there they were, Ted and Frankie conjured like a mistaken spell. Eva looked at the ground, all that fire snuffed out. We were quiet for a long time, the ghosts of our husbands hovering in the smoke of the dwindling campfire.

"Do you ever wonder what it would be like, if you hadn't met Ted?" I asked softly, feeling emboldened by the booze, by the quiet, by the night. I had asked myself the same question about Frankie so many times, entertaining alternate versions of my life. I had dreamed entire lifetimes without Frankie, envisaged a thousand other presents and futures, but the moment the question left my lips, I felt as though I were trespassing; these dark woods of Eva's were ones I wasn't sure I was permitted to explore.

Eva's eyes were glassy, though I couldn't tell if it was from the liquor or something else. She was quiet for a very long time, looking out across the still water of the pond.

"Sometimes, I feel like I'm in quicksand," she said suddenly, soberly. "Like I'm sinking. Like I'm disappearing." She turned away from the water and looked at me, studied me. "He's not a good man. Everyone thinks he is, but he's not."

I didn't know what to say. This is not how we talked to each other. This was *foreign* territory, a place I didn't have a compass for. A place without maps. And so I just nodded. I wasn't sure exactly what she meant, what she was insinuating. She looked so forlorn, so sad, I tried to think of a question I dared to ask, a comfort I could possibly offer. I worried that my words were useless. Nothing I could say would change anything. But I also felt a sort of strange relief. I'd spent the last decade with Frankie, going through the motions of a marriage, finding small pockets of contentment inside a vast swath of resentment. The possibility that I was not the only one in the world who held this secret shame, who felt a tremendous cavernous hole where something true and good should have been, was oddly reassuring.

"Let's go to bed," I said. "It's late, and we're drunk. And you're going to catch your death. The sleeping bags will be nice and warm." I helped her up and she obediently crawled into the tent.

I doused the fire with a bucket of water, and made sure to hide the bottle of liquor in her pack. I crawled into the tent, shining the flashlight so I wouldn't step on her, and found my sleeping bag.

I listened for the sound of her slumber, the way I listened to make sure the girls were asleep each night before I went to bed. But I couldn't hear anything, and I started to panic. It was illogical; it was the whiskey, it was the disorienting sound of the woods and the water and bears that weren't there. I lay motionless and tried to still my heart, my own ragged breaths. She moved then, and I felt her arm come around me. "I'm cold, Billie." Relief.

I took her hand and pulled her arm tighter across me. I could feel her against my back. And suddenly every nerve ending in my body was raw. Before I allowed myself to think, to question, to pull away, I rolled over so that I was facing her, but it was so dark it was as though I were looking into space, into nothingness. I was sure she could hear my heart, pounding like a steel drum, echoing in my ears, in my head.

When her lips touched mine they were wet: salty and soft. She'd been crying, and I hadn't even heard her. We stayed like this, flesh pressed to flesh, darkness to darkness, the steady pounding of my head like a warning.

And then the rain came, as promised, turning swiftly from a few tentative drops to a deluge. It pounded against the canvas tent. Pounded against the hard ground outside. And her mouth pulled away from mine, her body pulled away from mine, and it was over. As if it hadn't happened. I was numb, paralyzed.

"Billie," she said, but I couldn't answer. "The girls are waking up."

There were times when Frankie would do things or say things when he was drinking that he would later simply erase from his memory. Wine was his great elixir, able to induce total memory loss by the time he woke up the next morning. And if Frankie didn't remember, then the things he'd said and did simply hadn't happened, and he couldn't be convinced otherwise: the time he backed over the mailbox, narrowly missing the neighbor's kitty, Florence, who had been sleeping in our driveway. The time he went to my rag bag in the basement and came upstairs wearing one of my old bras, singing "When the moon hits your eye like a big pizza pie . . ." at the top of his lungs in front of Francesca and her friend Lo. The time he climbed up on the roof at midnight just to look at the stars and fell off, nearly losing an arm on the gutter. It didn't matter that his arm was bandaged, our sheets bloody. He always had a story to explain the evidence away, and the worse his transgressions, the deeper the forgetfulness and denial. The times he pounded his fists so hard even the plates on the table trembled in fear. The times he called me frigid, stupid, *aricchi du porcu. Ugly as the hair on a pig's ear.* It didn't matter that the girls heard him, that the neighbors (even Mrs. Macadam, who was deaf in one ear) heard him. In the morning, Frankie went about his day as usual. He wreaked havoc, but his path of destruction was invisible. The girls and I were the casualties of an amnesiac.

I expected that what had happened in the tent, the moment when Eva and I touched, when we kissed, would be like one of Frankie's escapades. That in the bright light of morning, in the cold reality of day, it would simply disappear, and I'd be left questioning my sanity. Eva had been drinking; we both had been drinking. We were cold. We had pressed our bodies together for warmth, and there had been a kiss. It was as chaste as the kisses we gave our children at night.

But that did not explain the way my whole body thrummed and buzzed and *continued* to hum like an electric wire. As we raced around the tents in the rain, securing the stakes and ensuring that the girls were huddled deep inside their sleeping bags to stay dry. It didn't explain the way the thunder and lightning outside seemed to echo whatever was going on inside my own body, my own mind.

I expected Eva to deny it, not with her words necessarily but with her eyes that wouldn't meet mine. Or worse, that they would, but with no glimmer, no acknowledgment of what had transpired between us.

It is for this reason that in the morning, when the rain had finally stopped its insistent pounding against the world around us, and Eva sat up from her sleeping bag, rubbing the sleep from her eyes and patting her hair down, I was startled and a little scared when she reached for my hand.

We sat there, inside the tent, the little bit of sun that had appeared making everything light up inside our canvas cave, holding hands for nearly a minute before she brought my hand to her face and pressed the back of it to her cheek, closing her eyes.

We didn't speak about it, but that simple gesture was enough. It was confirmation that I wasn't crazy, and that I was not alone in my recollections. I was not *alone*. But while this silent acknowledgment of what had happened eased my mind, it also scared the hell out of me. Sometimes, it was easier to deny things: to pretend that everything was normal, that *I* was normal. She squeezed my hand before she let it go and opened the front flap of the tent to the new day.

The rain seemed to have come and gone, and the girls were all thrilled for the stories it left them with. They chattered endlessly, obliviously, as they packed their things and recounted the details of the storm. They were filthy and exhausted by the time their parents picked them up at the campground entrance. I distributed the Go Camping badges ceremoniously, and each of the girls beamed. And after they were all gone, Eva and I sat at a picnic table with our own girls, waiting for Frankie to show up. As we waited, I was terrified to steal even a glance at her, worried that someone might be able to read whatever it was that my expression revealed.

A half hour passed, an excruciating hour, and still no Frankie. It was Sunday, which meant Mass at ten o'clock, but it was already past noon. The campground was only five miles from our house. The girls were restless. I gave them the remaining food we had: some saltine crackers smeared with peanut butter. The bruised apples that had been picked over.

"I'm going to go call him," I said, grateful for an excuse to leave. "Stay here with the girls?"

"Of course," Eva said.

I went to the campground office and knocked on the door. The woman who had checked us in was working. "Excuse me, may I use your phone to call my husband? He was supposed to be here to pick us up an hour ago."

"I wish I could help you," she said. "Storm took the phone out. The electricity too."

"Oh," I said. "Well, thank you."

"You're the one with the Scouts, right?" she said, nodding and reaching behind the counter. "Here's a little something to keep them occupied while you wait," she said, handing over some old coloring books and a coffee can of broken crayons.

"Thank you," I said.

I hoped that by the time I got back to Eva and the girls, Frankie would be pulling up. But he wasn't there. The prospect of sitting there with this secret, our secret, was too much. I knew that if I didn't move, I might crawl out of my skin.

"Okay," I said after another fifteen minutes, trying to muster some enthusiasm. "Looks like we're walking home."

I expected gripes from the girls, but instead they just heaved their rucksacks onto their tiny shoulders and followed. I was grateful for their easy compliance.

"You don't suppose there's a badge in the handbook for this?" Eva said, trying to make me laugh, probably sensing that my whole body was tied up in knots. "Walking home because your husband forgot to pick you up? What do you suppose the emblem would be?" She nudged me playfully with her shoulder.

I smiled, aware of the spot of skin on my arm that she had touched.

"Imagine if we earned badges for all the things *we* do?" she said, grabbing my arm now. I felt a surge of something rush through my entire torso.

The girls ran ahead, skipping and holding hands.

"Stay over to the left-hand side," I hollered after them. "That way the cars can see you."

"A badge for ten consecutive nights without sleep because your baby won't stop crying," she said, laughing. "A badge for cleaning up after a sick kid!"

"Or a sick husband," I said, playing along now, the words a welcome, small release of the enormous pressure building up inside me.

"Badges for making the perfect martini!"

"The perfect lasagna!"

"The perfect blow job!" she whispered into my ear, and doubled over with laughter.

"God, can you imagine that emblem?" I asked.

Just then a car came zooming up to us, my heart leapt, and I screamed again for the girls to get over to the side of the road. It was Frankie, and suddenly all that anger and frustration I'd been feeling at the campground came bubbling back to the surface, merging with everything I was feeling about Eva, and I thought for a moment that I might just combust.

"Hop on in, kiddos!" he said.

Sticking out of the back windows were two pair of cross-country skis. "Oh, dear Jesus," I said.

This was not the first time.

Of course, it wasn't. I'd be a liar if I denied feeling this way before. That what was happening between me and Eva, the way I felt about her, was some sort of anomaly, some variance from the norm. Some *deviance*. Instead, it was a longing so old and familiar, so primitive and profound, when it surfaced this time it took only a moment to recognize it for what it was: this desire, this terrible ache. It lived inside me, was part of me, but I had learned to neglect it. It was the monster in my closet, the insane and infirm aunt in the attic. It was my shame. My heartache.

Swimming. I had been swimming since my father threw me into the pond beyond our cow pastures and watched as I first sank and then surfaced, my legs and arms and lungs working hard to keep me afloat. To keep me from drowning. And soon, I was a stronger swimmer than my sister, than the neighbor boys we played with. Than my father himself. In the water, I was powerful. Certain. In the water, I knew who I was.

I used to blame the water for what happened the year I turned fifteen.

Miss Mars was fresh out of college, but she looked younger than we did, with a blond ponytail and bright blue, a *chlorinated aqueous* blue, eyes and a round baby face. She was hired to be the girls' physical education teacher at our high school. She was also recruited to coach tennis, swimming, and cross-country skiing.

I joined the swim team my freshman year and quickly proved myself to be the best female swimmer in the school. Because most other local schools did not have their own swimming pools, our competitions were typically intramural. And so eventually, I ran out of competitors and was allowed to compete against the boys. Coach Norman, the athletic director, resisted, but Miss Mars, with her bright sky eyes, fought long and hard for my chance to compete for the school's athletic records. My specialty was the butterfly, the hardest stroke but arguably the most beautiful.

Miss Mars spent extra time helping me train, subjecting me to an even more rigorous schedule than the boys. I was up with my father in the morning when he woke to milk the cows, furiously pedaling my bicycle into town to the school, where Miss Mars, who rented a room in a house near the school, would be waiting. I can still smell those chlorine mornings, feel the warm, humid air of the pool room. In the fall, my face would be raw and red from the windy bike ride. Stepping into the pool area was like stepping into the jungle. I swam for two hours before I showered and changed for school. And after school, I met Miss Mars right after the last bell and repeated the whole process again.

Miss Mars was soft spoken but tough. I wanted nothing but to please her. At that age, I found myself willfully disobeying most of my mother's demands, but with Miss Mars, I wouldn't have considered even the smallest rebellion. If she told me to do a thousand push-ups, I would drop to the cold concrete floor and do push-ups until I collapsed. If she told me to swim ten more laps, even as my legs were trembling with exhaustion, I would only nod and dive back into the pool. And while she was tough on me, *training* me as it were, I liked to think that our relationship transcended that of coach and athlete. She was closer to a contemporary of mine than any of my other teachers. She didn't look much older than I did, and, besides her job, she didn't have any of the trappings of an adult life. She was my mentor, but she was also my *friend*.

It was during those mornings that I began to appreciate my father's work. There was something peaceful and magnificent about rising before the rest of the world, of engaging in back-breaking labor while everyone else slumbered. When I disappeared into the pool, and the only sound was the water resisting my body and the distant muffled sound of Miss Mars's whistle, I understood how it was he could live his life alone, with only his labor, his breath, and the land. I would emerge after finishing my laps both more awake and more alive than I had ever felt. And Miss Mars's smiling face would come into focus through the water in my eyes.

It was also during this time that Gussy met *her* Frank. I watched her fall in love with him with both fascination and trepidation. Her sudden vulnerability scared me. She swooned, and my heart pounded with fear. As with any kind of falling, I worried that when she finally landed, she might shatter into a thousand little pieces.

I hadn't dated any boys yet. My father wouldn't allow it. Not until we were sixteen, and then only reluctantly. Besides, boys didn't swarm about me the way they did Gussy. Boys didn't know what to do with me.

I'd always swum (in creeks and rivers, lakes and ponds) and I'd always played baseball. For four years, I was the only girl on the local baseball team, something unheard of, but they'd been so desperate for a good pitcher, the coach had finally relented and let me join. I pitched our team to a nearly perfect season that first year and every year afterward. And so the neighborhood boys saw me as a teammate. And I saw them as the brothers I didn't have.

But Gussy had *suitors*. Boys were rendered stupid and doe-eyed around Gussy. While I'd inherited my father's red hair and coarse features, Gussy looked like our mother. She was soft, with sunlight-colored hair and a fine nose and chin, kind blue eyes and an equally gentle disposition. There was a new boy trying to carry her books to school almost every single day. And I watched this, mesmerized by her obliviousness to their affections. She was friendly to those lovesick boys, but she was also aloof, which made them want her all the more. Until Frank.

When Frank came along, the old Gussy began to disappear. It was not in any way that anyone but her sister would notice, but I saw it, this strange and slow disassembling. She was suddenly concerned with her clothes, her hair, her face. She fussed in the mirror. She worried over the smallest things. I watched her face shadow with concern when Frank was late for a date, and the way she lit up when the doorbell rang. Her mood, while usually cheerful, was now dictated by something outside of her rather than that terrific inner light she'd always had. I couldn't imagine ever giving myself over to someone like this, to surrendering myself in this way.

And then Miss Mars came along. And how was what I felt

about Miss Mars different than what Gussy felt about Frank? I lived to please her. I swam harder so that she would smile and pat my back with her small, soft hands. I woke early each morning, not caring that my body still ached from the prior day's session, that my eyes were still sealed shut with the debris of sleep. Wasn't it her face I imagined on those long, cold rides from the farm to school?

I was so confused and consumed by thoughts of Miss Mars, juxtaposed against thoughts of Gussy and Frank, I stayed awake at night worrying, sleep eluding me completely on the worst nights and proving fitful on the best. Miss Mars noticed. She noticed when I wasn't eating right, when my mother and I had squabbled. She could see it in my tired strokes and labored breaths in the pool. Of course she would notice if I wasn't sleeping.

One morning after practice, she asked me into her office. I had changed into my school clothes, but my hair was still wet. I had a towel around my neck to keep my shirt dry. I sat in front of her battered desk in a metal folding chair, looking at the trophies on the shelves, the certificates, her diploma. There was one framed picture of her standing with two little boys on either side. They were her brothers; she'd told me about them.

"Is everything okay?" she asked, sitting down at the edge of her desk in front of me, her hands on her knees. "You know you can tell me if something is wrong. At school? Home?"

I didn't know how to tell her. I didn't have any words for what was happening inside my head, inside my heart. I shook my head, but tears were already springing to my eyes. I was mortified by my body's betrayal of me.

"Hey," she said, leaning toward me. "Billie, are you crying?"

I could smell the dried chlorine on her body, as well as that citrus smell of her that reminded me of summertime. Her eyes were wide and concerned. She reached her hand out and touched my shoulder, and it felt like I'd run into our electric fence in the pasture.

Crying, I leaned into her touch, and before I could stop myself, I was reaching for her mouth with my mouth. When our lips touched, I let out a small gasp at my own audacity, but Miss Mars simply shook her head and pulled back.

"I'm sorry," I said.

"It's okay, Billie," she said. Her face was red, and she looked like she might cry. But her voice was calm, even as always. "You're having a rough time. You probably just need a good night's sleep."

I left her office that day feeling trampled, as though a stampede of horses had run across my back. I didn't know how I would face her again. I didn't think I'd ever be able to return to the pool. The horror of what I had done was so enormous, I didn't know how I could ever look her in the eye; I could barely confront my own reflection.

The call from Principal Hilton came that evening. I watched my mother hand my father the phone and collapse into one of the hard-backed kitchen chairs. I watched her put her face in her hands and her whole body tremble. I heard my father's words. "What do you mean, an *unnatural attachment* to Miss Mars?"

I was sent to a therapist to help me process this *unnatural attachment*. And after ten meetings, meetings where I nodded and said what it was I knew he wanted me to say, denied all the awful things I knew to be true, he declared me *cured* and sent me on my way. My parents, still not convinced, sent me to church. My mother made me sit with her each night, forgoing homework for Bible studies, the passages proving her point underlined angrily in pencil.

The principal, who despite my troubles was reluctant to give up a star athlete, paired me with Coach Norman for my early morning lessons. But Coach Norman was a football coach and didn't know the first thing about the backstroke, the butterfly. And because I had no choice, I got up each morning that winter, walked through the freezing cold to the school with Biblical admonishments echoing in my head, peered longingly at the pale yellow light in Miss Mars's house, and then disappeared into the depths of the pool.

I have always been a swimmer. But while I had been treading water for the last twelve years with Frankie, just bobbing and floating along, now I felt the familiar terrifying but irresistible pull: the soaring, sinking, stupefying feeling I'd disallowed for the last decade. The siren's song, beckoning me. But this time, the voice calling me into the water belonged not to Miss Mars but to Eva.

I try to remember the camp at Lake Gormlaith, but here my memory sometimes fails. Memory is like that sometimes, protecting us from the most painful things. But then the most beautiful things sometimes disappear as well. All of it is like water slipping though a sieve. There are pieces though, pretty shells, that are captured. That remain. I collect them. Treasure them. I think of the shells the children line up along the railings of the cottages, and I wonder if my suitcase is big enough to carry them home.

I know that I will not sleep tonight. I am nervous about the airport, about the flight. I am worried Juan will forget to pick me up, that Johnny will change his mind, or worse, that *I* will. And so instead of climbing under my covers and disappearing into sleep, I decide to swim. An eighty-year-old lady swimming alone in the ocean in the middle of the night might seem more dangerous than any sort of flight. Even Lou used to insist on accompanying me, watching from the shore, as if she could save me were I to sink. But I don't need saving. I am a swimmer. Water is where I feel most at home. It is where I go when I cannot sleep, when I cannot think, when my nerves are raw.

It is chilly out, so I only plan to go in for a quick dip. Just long enough to clear my head. I pull on my suit and walk down the stony path from the cottages to the beach, aware of my body in a way that is impossible in the light of day. I feel the ocean breeze on my bare shoulders, feel it rushing into my ears. Sea grass brushes against my ankles and then the sand is soft beneath my feet. This is what it must feel like to be blind, I think, to be enclosed in the universe. All of it touching all of you. The same might be said of swimming. This complete and blind immersion.

The water is indeed cold, but welcoming, as it always is. I wade out, letting the water circle my ankles, my knees, my hips. I ride some waves and dip under others until I am past the break, where the water is suddenly and strangely still. Here I swim, until my legs and arms are numb and fatigued. Until I've forgotten where my flesh ends and the sea begins.

It takes every ounce of my strength to pull this old body from the water. I collapse on the sand, wrapping my towel around me, and looking with wonder out at that vast nothingness before me.

And later, to my surprise, I sleep the sleep of the dead.

I expected to lose Eva too. I waited for her to retreat, to disappear. To turn into a pale yellow light behind the closed door of her house. But oddly enough, after the camping trip, our lives simply resumed. As though what had happened between us was perfectly normal. As though I hadn't stepped through Alice's looking glass into an upside-down world. We didn't speak about what happened, but there was something else between us now: a shared secret, one that belonged to *both* of us. And somehow, despite our respective silence regarding what had transpired inside that tent, I knew that things had changed.

Every afternoon, we walked together to get the girls from the bus stop, little Johnny tagging along behind, pulling Rose in her wagon. While the children played, we listened to music and folded laundry or baked cookies for bake sales or planned our Girl Scout meetings for the following year. But all those old habits and routines and chores were suddenly imbued with an added layer; the very air had a new texture to it. My senses were heightened. I clung to the scent of Eva's laundry detergent, to the husky sound of her voice, to the beautiful ghosts our cigarettes made, the separate specters merging together between us over the kitchen table. I was aware of the heat of her hand on my back as she showed me how to get a blood stain from cotton sheets. It was a time of anticipation, a time of portent. Like the electric feeling of the air before a storm. Like the smell of rain before it falls.

We didn't even need to touch.

When the first heat wave of summer came early, in June, Eva, sitting with her feet soaking in the baby pool, leaned toward me and whispered conspiratorially, "I want to go with you to the lake." And these nine words, this simple sentence, was like the first crack of thunder in my chest. A promise so big, so dangerous and thrilling, I felt my entire body pulse.

And so, like someone battening down the hatches for a coming storm, I moved quickly into action. First I called Gussy to see if it would be okay to have Eva and her children join me for two weeks of our visit. Though I knew she wouldn't say no, I was ready to argue my case, to plead if I needed to. Frankie too was easy (so easy it made me feel an articulate and vivid flash of guilt). *I'll certainly worry about you less,* he had said, *if you've got a friend there with you.* And for a brief moment, I felt overwhelmed by remorse. But like a bolt of lightning, my shame disappeared as quickly as it had appeared. I needed to focus. We still had one more person to convince.

Eva came to the house distraught one morning after Ted had gone to work.

"What's the matter?" I asked.

"He doesn't think we should be alone at the lake without a car. He's worried about what will happen if Johnny falls out of a tree or something."

"He leaves you without a car here every day!" I said, feeling desperate. Frantic. "Besides, my sister and her husband live only twenty minutes away. We have a telephone now. We have neighbors."

But Eva kept trembling, even after I handed her a cup of coffee, loaded with milk and sugar like she liked.

"What's going on, Eva?" I asked.

She shook her head. "Teddy's been saying things. He worries."

I felt my skin go cold and clammy, the blood draining from my head and pooling in my stomach and hips. "About what?" I could barely get my words out.

"Oh, I don't know," she said, dismissively, brushing her hand in front of her face.

"Eva," I said sternly. I needed to know what he was saying.

"About *other men,*" she said, rolling her eyes and grimacing. "That's why he drives to work. Why he won't leave me with a car. He'd rather pay twenty dollars a month to park his car than take a chance that I might drive off and find some other man."

"Are you kidding?" I said. "What does he think you do with Johnny and Rose while you're off having these affairs?"

She looked at me and laughed. "You know that's what every man is looking for. A woman with two little kids in tow. Very sexy," she said, giggling.

"Nothing says romance like Cheerios in your brassiere," I said, starting to howl with both relief and laughter. "What does he think you're going to do in Vermont? Find some handsome farmer to run off with?"

"I don't know," she said, her smile fading. She shook her head. "I need you and Frankie to talk to him, Billie. Convince him this will be good for the children. For me. Tell him he doesn't have anything to worry about." When she touched my hand, it was as though I'd been struck by lightning.

I had never spoken alone to Ted Wilson. I avoided Ted like I avoided most things that frightened me, especially after the camping trip. But Frankie wasn't afraid of Ted Wilson, and I would have done anything to get him to let Eva come to Vermont. And so the plan was hatched.

"You ought to take Ted to a game," I said to Frankie. "Maybe if he felt like he had a friend in the neighborhood, he wouldn't feel so alone when Eva comes to Vermont. And you know how much happier we'd be up there. The girls would have playmates. I'd have someone to keep me company." I felt my skin growing hot as I said this and had to look away.

Frankie worked with a guy who had season Sox tickets, and when he couldn't make it to a home game would offer them to us. I figured this would be a good place to start.

"I'll give it a shot," said Frankie, shrugging. And surprisingly, he came home that very afternoon with a pair of tickets for that weekend's game against the Cleveland Indians.

On Saturday morning, I watched them drive off in Ted's car, Frankie looking a little like he'd been kidnapped, and I hoped for the best.

They didn't get home until almost midnight. I was dead asleep when I heard their voices outside the window. It became clear as soon as I came out of the heavy fog of slumber that they were both thoroughly inebriated. I knew this could be either a good thing or a terrible thing. Frankie's voice echoed loudly through the neighborhood, and then I heard our garage door opening. "Oh, sweet Jesus," I thought, knowing this could only mean trouble.

I got out of bed and peered out the window at the street below, illuminated only dimly by the gas lamp streetlights. Frankie had a baseball bat in one hand, and for a moment, as he marched back across the street to the Wilsons' house, I thought he was about to beat the sense out of Ted. But then I saw Ted coming out of his own garage with a leather mitt on one hand and a baseball in the other. They met in the street, and the next thing I knew they were playing ball. At midnight, in the middle of the street.

The lights on the Bouchers' porch went on. The lights at the Bakers' lit up. And then Old Man Castillo was out on his porch and screaming bloody murder. "Take it somewhere else, you goddamned drunks!"

Frankie and Ted roared with laughter and disappeared into the field behind our house. From upstairs, I watched them play a crazy, drunken version of baseball, using some flagstones as bases, until, as expected, I heard the crack of the ball against the bat and then the crack of the ball against my dining room window. The sound of glass shattering was followed by silence and then one big "Oh shit!"

And then they were tromping through my azalea bushes and

plucking the broken pieces of glass out of the grass. I would have been livid, but it seemed like our harebrained plan had actually worked. Because then they were walking back toward the front of the house together, and Frankie was patting Ted on the back.

I don't know what Frankie said to Ted that night, and I didn't care. I only cared that one week after the girls and I arrived in Vermont that August, Ted's red Caddie pulled up into the grass driveway by the camp and he presented Eva, Donna, Sally, Johnny, and Rose on the doorstep of the camp like a gift.

That first night at the lake, the kids were all exhausted. Johnny was so tired he fell asleep in the kitchen nook, nodding off into his plate of spaghetti. Ted carried him out to the living room and laid him on the couch. The girls curled up together on cots, and I helped Eva set up the playpen for Rose. I was too afraid to even look at Eva as I bustled about. I knew that if I did, my face would give away every emotion, all that wild longing and aching and happiness that I was feeling. I was terrified that Ted would see through me.

"Time to hit the hay!" he said finally. I had given them the big bed upstairs where I usually slept and made my own bed on the porch. He motioned for Eva, who led the way up the stairs, goosing her and she giggling and slapping at his hands, as they disappeared up into the loft.

I couldn't listen. It would have killed me if I'd heard even a sigh from Eva. And so I went out to the lake and swam until I was certain that they had fallen asleep. And later in the quiet camp, I lay awake for hours, listening to the sounds of their slumber, the old iron bed creaking every time Ted rolled over. He snored, and his snores were voluminous, like an animal's. I didn't know how Eva got any sleep at all at home. Morning couldn't come quickly enough. Ted wouldn't be staying; he had to get back to Boston for work and then we'd have the place to ourselves until Frankie came two weeks later to visit, and then he would bring them back home with him.

I was the last one up the next morning, having finally been consumed by sleep in the final hours before dawn.

Eva had made blueberry pancakes for breakfast, and the kitchen smelled heavenly. She stood at the stove, flipping the next batch of pancakes on the griddle. Ted came up behind her, as if I weren't there, as if the kids weren't all piled into the kitchen nook. He stood behind her, meaty hands wrapped around her waist, thick chin resting on her shoulder. He whispered something in her ear, and I felt my skin flush. Eva shook her head, and I longed to know what he'd said to her. I felt my knees go liquid with jealousy. With fear. For one awful moment, I wondered if I'd only been entertaining some wild dream.

"You sure you'll be all right out here in the sticks?" Ted asked then, addressing the question to both of us.

"We'll be *fine,*" she said, looking at me and rolling her eyes, as if she sensed that I was feeling left out. I was so grateful for this acknowledgment I could have cried.

Rose crawled across the floor and pulled herself up, clinging to Ted's pant legs, though her presence didn't seem to register with Ted, who was still holding on to Eva. Rose was almost a year old now and just starting to walk. I'd moved everything at her eye level that might hurt her up to higher ground. I'd put tape across the outlets and made sure all of the cleaning supplies were out of her reach.

Finally noticing Rose, Ted released Eva and reached down to scoop her up. "Well, if it isn't Rosie O'Grady," he said, gently lifting her up and tossing her in the air. She squealed with delight and then he set her down, patting her diapered bottom as if to send her on her way.

Ted turned to Johnny then, who was running a Matchbox car across a mountain of pancakes and along a maple syrup road. "Johnny, you going to take care of my girls?" he asked, and Johnny nodded.

"Well, all-righty then. I'll be off," he said, to no one in particular.

"You've got the number here, right?" I asked him.

"Sure do. And maybe I'll try to pop on by for another visit. Sure is pretty here. Slept like a baby last night."

Now it was my turn to roll my eyes.

There really wasn't enough room for all of us. I knew this would be the case, but hadn't really come up with a good plan for how we would accommodate all of these bodies for two whole weeks. Finally, we decided to give the sleeping porch over to the girls, two on the daybed and two on cots. Johnny would sleep on the couch in the living room. And Eva and I would share the large bed in the loft, with Rose in a playpen.

My heart trilled like a plucked guitar string, vibrating endlessly at the thought of being so close to Eva each night, of waking up to the smell of her instead of the stink of Frankie's wine-soaked skin. I was excited and terrified, and that entire first day I felt like I was living inside of a dream. A dream inside of a dream. A dream from which I couldn't bear to wake up.

The children, of course, were in heaven as well. After a week at the lake with only each other for company, my girls were thrilled to have someone else to play with. And I was so grateful not to have to listen to their bickering anymore. Johnny, as expected, was captivated by the tree house and quickly claimed it as his own. There was also a little boy staying at a camp down the road about Johnny's age who, like a dog, sniffed out his playmate only minutes after we shooed them outside to play. That first afternoon after we sent Ted off with sandwiches and a cold beer for the ride home, Eva and I set up the lawn chairs on the front lawn, laid down a blanket covered in toys for Rosie, and collectively sighed.

"I love it here," she said, as if speaking to the lake. "I don't think I'm ever going home."

"You don't have to," I said. I meant it as a joke, but it came out sounding serious and strange. "I mean, not for a couple of weeks anyway."

"Thank you for having us," Eva said, and reached for my hand.

Every moment of the day felt somehow fraught with import. Time slowed. Every minute was imbued with the distinct possibility of something enormous. But somehow, the anticipation of whatever it was I hoped for, longed for, was almost enough. The suspense was exquisite. I could have lingered in these charged moments forever.

That night, we built a fire in the stone fire pit that Frankie had helped Gussy's Frank make a few summers before. The kids cooked hot dogs on long sticks they found in the woods behind the camp, and then toasted marshmallows. Ted and Eva had picked up some sweet corn from a farm stand on their way up, and we ate all ten ears dripping in butter and crunchy with salt. Eva and I drank cold beers we kept in a bucket of ice, and the children played. There was something so delicious about all of this. Even the air tasted sweet.

Later, when the air grew chilly and the children were ready to collapse, we tucked them all into their respective, makeshift beds and returned outside to the yard. The picnic table was still littered with dirty plates and crumpled napkins and empty soda bottles. Rose's toys lay scattered across the lawn, and the children's bikes lay like hulking metal skeletons on the grass. We each had three empty bottles of beer next to our seats.

Eva stood up and went to the picnic table. It was dark, but the moon was nearly full. It reflected brightly in the still surface of the water. Her silhouette was familiar but new in this backdrop. She was wearing a pair of red Capri slacks and a white sleeveless blouse, but she'd kicked off her shoes earlier. It was hard to believe that it had been less than a year since she'd had Rose. Her waist had returned to its tiny circumference, though her breasts remained large. Her body was everything mine was not: soft, curvy, inviting.

She started to clear the dirty plates, and I shook my head. "You don't have to do that," I said.

"Oh, I don't mind."

"No," I said, my heart swelling with something I barely recognized: a sense of defiance, of freedom. "I mean, we don't have to do any of that. Cleaning up. Washing dishes. We're on vacation. We can make up our own rules."

She looked at me suspiciously, but I nodded, feeling suddenly bold. "Rule number one: No cleaning the dinner table until morning."

She stood back and put her hands on her hips. "Okay then, rule number two: Bikes and toys should only be put away in the event of rain."

"Rule number three," I declared, my heart pounding hard, my throat thick. "Every evening must end with a swim." I was thinking about the night at the Rippling River Campground, wishing I'd joined her in that freezing water. Here was my second chance. I also wanted to remain in this place, in this twilit aching place, for just a little longer.

"I like that rule," she said, smiling at me warmly.

And so we swam.

This is what I remember about that night: the warm surface of the lake, the freezing, murky water below, the way it took my breath away, the way my heart stopped beating when I felt the cold shock of it on my legs, my hips, my waist. I remember the sharp rocks at the bottom and the way they hurt my feet, the minnows that tickled my skin. And I remember Eva. Eva like some sort of mermaid, dipping and diving and surfacing. Her hair, relieved of its chignon, running down her back like dark water. I remember the sound of our voices echoing even though we were trying so hard to be quiet. I remember feeling my body grow in strength in the water, as it always did when I was swimming; water made me feel powerful. Invincible. Sure of myself. If not for the water, if not for the welcoming embrace of the lake, I might not have done what I did.

Eva swam to me, under water, teasing. She didn't think I could see her, as her body moved stealthily beneath the dark surface. I knew she intended to surprise me, to startle me. And I couldn't see her, but strangely, I *felt* her. I knew exactly where she was. I could sense her body the way I could always sense where my girls were in the house. It was instinctual, animal.

And so when she broke the surface of the water, just inches from me, I had to feign surprise. To pretend that I hadn't known she was coming. That all of this was coming.

"Boo!" she whispered loudly. Water dripped down her face, her eyelashes were stuck together with it. Her lips were wet, parted slightly, coyly mocking me as I pretended to catch my breath.

If it hadn't been for the water, for the darkness that concealed us, for the safety I always felt when submerged, I wouldn't have dared. But we were swimming, our bodies no different from the lake. We were somehow a part of it, and so my hands reached out and grasped her waist, that tiny little waist. I could feel the small bones of her hips just beneath my grasp. She was weightless, so when I pulled, her body floated toward me without resistance.

And then her body was pressing against mine. I could feel her breasts, so much larger than my own, unfamiliar, soft and yielding, pressing against me, my arms holding on as though she might just slip through and be carried away by the water. And so I held on, and she held on, and then I was burying my face in that soft place. (I remember the smell of the lake, after all this time; I can still smell the incredible scent of the lake on her skin.) And our lips, finally, finally were touching. I was so hungry. Like a prisoner given only gruel for years and years suddenly being presented with filet mignon. And she returned my kisses with her own fierce hunger. I was crying, I think, though it could have only been the lake. And she was crying too. I could feel the shudder and tremble in her chest. Later, inside the covers of our shared bed, I dreamed we were still swimming, the soft sheets lighter than water. And the entire night I held on, like someone afraid of drowning.

★ ★ ★

The following two weeks with Eva at Lake Gormlaith passed somehow both slowly and in an instant. Normal time was suspended without the usual obligations and concerns: without men, without lunches to pack and meals to make and arguments to be had. We were breaking every single rule that usually prevailed at home in Hollyville. We were living in an upside-down world, a world of our own making. I even told my mother we wouldn't be able to visit, that we had company. I didn't want anything, or any*one,* to steal even a moment of this fleeting, floating time.

Our days were sun-dipped, Kodachrome days. When I recollect that summer now, I see only the dazzling constellations of light on the water, Eva holding her face to the sun, her body patterned by the shadow of leaves. I see the children running one by one down the old wooden dock, leaping into the water. Carefree. I see my own heart swelling inside my chest, like a buoy, holding me up.

We clung to each other in the mornings, quietly, as the children stirred in the other room. We were both afraid, though we didn't ever say it, that one of the children would hear us. We were so careful. Vigilant. And somehow, this only heightened our longing. It was like a game, how quietly we could kiss. How silently we could make love. And instead of getting up and making breakfast for the children, we gave Chessy and Donna domain in the kitchen, where they concocted children's ideas of breakfast: French toast every day, peaches gritty with sugar, giant glasses of chocolate milk. We told them that we were on vacation and wanted to sleep in. Under covers, we moved so slowly, the bed barely creaked. And we listened to their laughter, relied on their laughter, to mask the sounds that sometimes escaped us.

After breakfast, while the children played outside, we tidied up whatever mess was left from the day before and then retired to our respective chairs on the front lawn in our bathing suits. But while Eva quickly turned the golden color of a ripe peach, I simply watched as a thousand more freckles appeared like scattered constellations on my skin. At night, Eva played connect the dots with her tongue.

We watched the sun move across the sky, in and out of clouds. On the rainy days, we sent the children to the tree house and hunkered down inside.

We read. Alone and to each other. She whispered lines of E. E. Cummings and Pablo Neruda into my hair. We drank beer in the middle of the day and took naps whenever we felt sleepy. Once, we left Chessy and Donna to watch the little ones and took the boat out to the little island at the center of the lake and made love on the rocky shore beneath an enormous willow tree. It was a dangerous and breathless afternoon. But in the safety of the trees, I felt both safe and emboldened.

"Tell me about San Francisco," I said, as Eva slipped back into her dress and sat on the shore with her knees tucked under her chin, staring out at the still water. I reached out and touched an exposed part of her thigh with my finger, let it linger there. "I want to know who you were before you met Ted."

I still had such a hard time envisioning Eva without Ted, without the children. *That* Eva was like an apparition: a ghostly Eva, a shadow Eva. But I wanted to know her, everything about her. Sometimes, with Eva, I felt unsated. Even after we had made love for hours, or held each other through an entire night. It was as though I had an itch I couldn't reach to scratch; I couldn't ever seem to get enough of her. I sometimes dreamed of a terrible thirst, of drinking glass after glass of water and still feeling as though I might die, my tongue and lips and throat parched. I had a thousand questions I wanted to ask, so many things to learn.

She sighed and looked away from the water, studying my face. She twisted her loose hair into a ponytail, securing it with a band she slipped from her slender wrist. "I left Oregon when I was seventeen. I met Liam at school. I got pregnant. He had a wife. I met Ted. The end."

She didn't like to talk about Ted. Here, Ted and Frankie were no different than the characters in the novels we read. But from the fragments of information I gathered, it seemed that Ted had fallen madly and instantly in love with Eva (how could he not?), so much so that when he learned she was pregnant, and that the father had, for all intents and purposes, disappeared, he agreed to raise Eva's baby as his own if she agreed to marry him. He loved her, and promised he would take care of her and her child. He swooped in like a giant pelican to a fish and carried her away.

"What was it," I asked, "about him?" I knew it would pain me, to hear what had attracted her to him, but I still wanted to know. Needed to know.

"Ted?" She laughed. "I don't know. I guess he was just so *charming*. Always the salesman. He could sell a cage to a lion." And I thought about how Ted had cajoled her, tamed her, caged her. I promised myself I would never do that.

"We should get back to the kids," she said, shaking her head and pulling her dress down over that soft beautiful expanse of flesh.

There were other questions I wanted to ask, but now as she reached for my hand and stood up, I knew the opportunity was gone.

Eva didn't like to talk about San Francisco, but she did like to talk about her childhood in Oregon. She'd grown up in a small coastal town; her father was a fisherman, and her mother died in a car accident when she was just a little girl. She didn't have any siblings. She spent her days collecting debris she found on the beach and assembling it into sculptures. She built fairy houses out of seaweed and pebbles and twigs.

"What happened to the mobiles?" I asked.

"Oh, they're long gone now. I left most of them on the beach."

"No, I mean the ones from art school. Do you have them still?"

She shook her head.

We were sitting on the grass watching the children play in the lake. Chessy and Donna were doing handstands, their pink feet sticking up out of the water.

I wanted to see the things she had made. I thought maybe they might help me to understand her better. "Do you have any photos of them?"

"No," she said, shaking her head.

"Mommy, Mommy, look!" Sally said. She was learning how to float on her back. In the water, she bounced and bobbed like a doll.

"I see you!" Eva hollered. "Good job!"

"Can you tell me about them?" I asked softly.

"Billie," she reprimanded. The way she said my name stung. She sighed. "Ted destroyed them. All of them. An entire year's worth of work was ruined in the matter of one night. He hated Liam. He was so jealous. My artwork was just a reminder to him of my life before he met me."

I pictured Ted with his hulking body smashing her artwork to pieces, destroying all that beauty with his stupid rage. And then I started thinking about Ted's anger, his bullishness. What Eva and I had was so pure, so good. It too was something beautiful, crafted meticulously with our hands. I tried not to think about what he would do to us if he were ever to find out, the destruction he was capable of. I had to will him away from my thoughts. He didn't belong here. Not between us on the soft grass as our children played together in the lake.

"I'm sorry," I said.

And then a shadow came across Eva's face, as though she were remembering something. Her brow knit and she blinked hard, shaking her head as though she could shake the memory away.

"Eva," I said softly, remembering what she had said when we were camping, about him not being a good man. "He wouldn't ever hurt *you,* would he?"

"Mommy! Mommy!" Donna yelled. "Look what Chessy and I can do." Francesca was riding high on Donna's shoulders. Johnny was chucking rocks at the shore.

"Johnny, don't throw rocks while the girls are swimming!" Eva said. She looked at me then, and said, "No more silly questions. Okay? Rule number four."

The day that Frankie was due to arrive for his visit and then to take Eva and her kids back to Hollyville, I could barely drag myself out of bed. It was as though someone had pulled my heart out of my chest and shoved it back in. It no longer fit. It felt swollen, constricted.

Eva had risen wordlessly with the sun and started to pack her bags. I watched her from the bed as she folded her clothes and put them into the suitcase, the lid open like a mouth. She didn't speak as she tidied and packed; then she disappeared downstairs. When I finally came down from the loft she was standing at the stove with an apron on, Rose nestled against her hip. She was making eggs and bacon in a cast iron skillet. There were gutted oranges littering the counter and a pitcher of fresh-squeezed juice.

"There's coffee in the percolator," she said, motioning to the pot.

We had stayed up late, as though morning wouldn't come if we were waiting for it. *I don't want you to leave,* I had said. *I love you,* I'd whispered, fearful that my words were lost in the dark expanse of her hair. But then she had embraced me, pressing every inch of her skin against mine, and my words, like the children's voices bouncing back to them at the lake, echoed back to me. *I love you.*

And, despite the thrill of those three words, the way they repeated endlessly in my head, in my chest, in every muscle of my body, I was still able to fall asleep just as the sun was starting to illuminate the pale curtains in the loft window. But now, my sadness, coupled with fatigue, made me wonder how I could possibly get through this day. Coffee, I suspected, would be an ineffectual elixir.

Somehow, I had managed to put Frankie out of my mind for the last two weeks, or at least into a small, quiet corner of it. I had to. The idea of him appearing, in the flesh, after all that had transpired between Eva and me seemed somehow ludicrous. And terrifying. I worried that he would see what had happened in my face. That the places she had touched somehow still bore the imprint of her lips, her fingers, her tongue.

"What time will Frankie be here?" she asked as though reading my mind as she set a plate of eggs and bacon down in front of me.

"No idea," I said. "If he sees any tag sales, he'll stop. He also usually grabs a bite at the Miss Quimby Diner."

"Okay." She nodded.

We sent the kids outside to play, but Johnny complained that he wasn't feeling well.

"What's the matter, sweetie?" Eva asked, her voice strained.

"I have a headache and a stomachache, and my legs feel itchy," he said.

Eva sighed heavily. These were our last hours together before we had to return to that other life, the one we'd shrugged off two weeks ago. "Well, it sounds to me like a good old-fashioned case of the gollywobbles," she said, lifting him up onto her lap. "And do you know the treatment for the gollywobbles?"

"Pepto-Bismol?" Johnny asked, clutching his stomach. His cowlick was sticking straight up, as usual, giving him an impish look.

"No." Eva shook her head. "Guess again."

"Aspirin?" he tried, bouncing back and forth in anticipation.

"Uh-uh," she said. "Something much more potent. Something very powerful."

"Tell me!" he said, clutching his hair with both hands, his wide blue eyes imploring.

She stood up and motioned for him to follow her to the kitchen. "This way," she said.

I followed them, lingering in the doorway, and watched as she opened the cupboard door and peered inside. "Now, where did it go?" she asked, browsing the shelves, running her fingers across the canned vegetables and soup. A bag of marshmallows, a dusty box of Cream of Wheat. "Aha," she said finally, reaching behind everything and grabbing a can of Hershey's Syrup. "Did you know that the cocoa bean has healing powers?" she asked, crouching down to Johnny's level. "It is the only known cure for the gollywobbles."

"Really?" he asked, eyes widening joyfully. "Chocolate?"

"The mighty cocoa bean," she said seriously, nodding her head.

"There's a church key in the drawer," I said.

And with that, she punctured the lid and poured the syrup into a shot glass she found in the top of one of the cupboards.

"Now drink up," she said, and handed him the glass.

Gleefully he swallowed the syrup, wiping the chocolate from his lip with his sleeve. "Better?" she asked.

He nodded, amazed. She winked at me and swatted his bottom. "Now go play!"

Frankie called from Quimby at six o'clock, and said he was just sitting down to supper at the diner, that he'd be at least another hour. We were down to our final hour, the last minutes of this strange haven, this stolen piece of heaven. And as the sun slipped quietly behind Franklin Mountain, I felt all of this slipping away too.

"You're a good mother," I said, as we sat on the front lawn side by side, not touching, watching our children dart about like fireflies in the waning light. "I wish I were as patient as you are."

"Stop," she said, shaking her head, blushing.

But it was true. I was too selfish to be a good mother. All day

I had wished the children away so that these last few minutes could be spent together. It made me feel terrible.

"Look, Mama!" Mouse said, running up to me with her small, dirty hands clenched together, her eyes wide and excited.

"What is it?" I asked, suddenly feeling such tenderness toward her, and such an overwhelming sense of inadequacy. "Let me see," I said, and leaned forward to peer into her hands.

But when she opened them to show me what was inside, her face fell. In her excitement, in her eager hands, the firefly had been crushed. The luminescence smeared across her palms. My heart ached. Because I understood this clumsiness, this dangerous greed.

"I'm sorry, honey," I said, and kissed her hand. "You didn't mean to."

Juan insists on parking in the garage and walking me inside the airport, though I keep telling him that I'll be fine getting dropped off at the curb. He carries my suitcase (which is so old it doesn't even have wheels) and holds the elevator door open for me, ushering me in first.

There is a lot of noisy construction at the airport. A new parking lot, Juan says. It looks like rubble to me, as though we are in a war zone instead of America's Finest City. It is overcast today, and the air has a chill to it. I have a sweater for the flight, and I packed some snacks. My boarding pass is in my pocket, and my license is in my wallet.

"I used to love to fly," I say to Juan to fill the empty quiet between us. It is early, and the ride from my cottage to the airport was a silent one.

"Not anymore?" he asks.

I shake my head. The last flight I can remember enjoying was when I left the East Coast, bound for California. Perhaps it was because that flight had indeed been one of flight, of *fleeing*. It had purpose, intent. It signified the end of one life and the beginning of another. I remember I had felt like my heart was soaring as the engines roared and the plane taxied down the runway. All the others since then have been imbued with portent: the flight home for my mother's funeral, for Frankie's funeral, and later when Gussy's Frank got sick. Even Francesca's wedding had my stomach in knots as I soared back to Boston. I had never met her fiancé, Michael, and I spent the entire trip imagining the worst. And now Johnny.

I can't remember the last time I flew for pleasure. When you live at the edge of the world, inside a postcard picture, there seems little need for vacation. I've become happily sedentary in my old age. But now, here I am once again, flying home, feeling queasy already, even before I have checked my bags.

"You don't need to stay," I say. "I can find my gate."

"You sure?" Juan asks. His eyes look tired, and I realize that despite what he's said, he must have risen early especially for me.

"I'm fine." I smile and give him a little hug.

"Okay," he says. "Call me when you get back. I can be here in a few minutes to pick you up. We'll miss you at the bar." I watch him disappear up the escalator and through the glass doors to the walkway. I get in line to check my bag and take a deep breath. The girl in front of me has a giant backpack on her shoulders. It looks like it might weigh more than she does. She smells strongly of patchouli oil, and her hair runs down to her waist in thick, dreaded ropes. When she turns, looking for something or someone beyond me, I see she is pretty, her eyes a sparkly green. She looks a little like Mouse actually, at that age. Wild and unruly. Mouse and Francesca have always been opposites: Chessy in her tidy skirts, never a hair out of place; her clothes never got grass-stained or torn. And Mouse, who never cared how she looked, favoring fun and freedom over fashion.

When I told Francesca I was going back to the lake to speak with Johnny, she said she didn't think it was a good idea. "Why go digging up those old bones?" she said, her father's expression. I hadn't expected her to understand. "And Mom, that's a really big trip to make by yourself," as if her concern were truly only about my health and welfare.

"I'm healthy as a horse," I said. And it was true. My last doctor's visit had confirmed that, besides my blood pressure, I am in good shape. So far I've eluded all those other harbingers of old age: diabetes, osteoporosis, arthritis. I am much more like a sixty-year-old than an eighty-year-old, except for my heart. I even have my hearing, my memory, and most of my marbles, though I'm sure Francesca would argue that.

"I can't wait to see you," I said.

"You too, Mom. Have a safe flight."

I called Mouse right after I spoke with Francesca. She is living in Taos now; she's been there for nearly a year, if I am remembering correctly. She met a man, a fellow artist, and they are living together in some sort of teepee, though when she described it, it sounded relatively palatial (as far as teepees go anyway). I've learned to let go of Mouse over the years, to understand that she will always surprise me with her choices. Because despite financial instability, her decision not to get married or have a family, her meanderings all over the globe, she is the happiest person I know. And something about that makes me proud.

The girl in front of me turns and says, "Excuse me? Do you have the time?"

"I do," I say, gently tugging my cuff upward to reveal my watch. "It's six o'clock."

"Thank you," she says, smiling. "I'm going home to see my parents," she says, continuing the conversation. "It's been a whole year."

I nod and smile at her. "They must be excited."

"They don't exactly know yet. It's kind of a surprise," she says, and twists her mouth a little, a nervous tic, I gather. "Or ambush."

This makes me laugh. I hope we get seated next to each other on this flight.

Suddenly, I feel someone moving behind me, hear a voice saying, "Excuse me. So sorry. I'm with her up there."

It's another girl loaded down with a heavy backpack. This one has short dark hair and freckles across her face. "I'm so sorry," she says to me as she moves to meet the girl in front of me, whom she kisses quickly on the lips.

The other girl punches her gently in the arm. "I thought you'd ditched me."

"Never," the dark-haired girl says, cooing dreamily at my new friend.

I feel my heart swell up, tears coming to my eyes. I look away, ashamed as they kiss again. I grimace as the old man behind me clears his throat. So much has changed, I think. And so much has stayed exactly the same.

"Have a nice flight," the girl says to me after she and her girlfriend have checked their bags and, liberated of their luggage, turn to go to their gate.

"You too," I say, and then I am alone again, overwhelmed by the smell of cinnamon buns and coffee and too much perfume.

There are few undeniable perks to being an old lady. One, I learn now, is that you get to pre-board most flights. I am quickly ushered by a helpful attendant to the line where families with small children and all those needing special assistance (the man in the wheelchair with the oxygen tank at his side, the blind woman with the service dog, and another old lady like me who seems to have lost the battle with her bones and is bent at the waist, her spine at a forty-five degree angle) are all congregating. I sit down on one of these restricted seats and study my boarding pass. My driver's license. In the photo, I am only seventy-five years old. But other than a few more wrinkles across my brow, little else has changed. I still wear my hair in two braids pinned on top of my head. I still weigh a hundred and twenty pounds. I'm still five foot eight inches tall when I make the effort.

The loudspeaker announces that we're boarding, me and the other infirm, and I rise from my seat, thinking, *This is it, lady. Your last chance to back out.* To simply backtrack through the airport, maybe grab one of those cinnamon buns on the way out. Get a taxi, go back to the cottage, and just take a nap. But as I start to plan my route through the crowd of early-morning travelers, my eyes catch sight of the two girls who had been in front of me in the check-in line. They are at the gate across the way. They are sitting side by side, one resting her head on the other's shoulder. Their flight is headed to New York. And I think about how much more courage they need than I.

Returning to our normal lives after that first summer at Lake Gormlaith meant returning to a lie. Frankie told me once that when he was little, his parents didn't have enough money for Christmas presents for all the children, and so his mother had sat down and wrapped up a dozen empty boxes and put them under the tree so that when company came over it would look as though there were gifts for everyone. It was like this, and it seemed impossible to comprehend how we had lived for so long inside these pretty, empty boxes. Our days were spent simultaneously keeping up this illusion and finding ways to be together. We lived in fear of being found out but could not stomach the alternative.

We lived in a state of constant hunger; that gnawing, futile desperation of the starved. Fearful, clawing, scheming. We learned that desire, true desire, is both raw and complex. The entire world seemed to be conspiring against us, which only made us hungrier.

The children were all in school now, at least, with only little Rose at home. And Ted, with some new, odd sense of trust (perhaps that my friendship would keep Eva from straying into another man's arms—God, how little did he know), had started riding to work with Frankie each morning, leaving his car behind. The sudden mobility that Eva had was a blessing, but it also felt like a trap. I second-guessed every good thing, every blessing, waiting, always, for the other shoe to drop.

We drove. Some days, we'd get in the car and just go. No direction, no destination, just simply moving, as though momentum alone could protect us. We'd roll the windows down to the Indian summer heat and let our hair fly. We cranked the radio up as loud as it would go, and little Rose would cover her ears with two pudgy hands in the backseat as we sang. Eva drove fast, the car almost flying in her control (or *out* of it, rather). She, and Rose, particularly liked one hilly road that dipped up and down like a roller coaster. She'd accelerate on the incline so that the car was nearly airborne when we reached the summit. Those were breathless, reckless times. Hearts pounding, we knew we should be more careful but somehow could not resist.

We clung to the moments when we could be together, though Rose's naps were the only time when we were truly alone. Each morning after everyone had left, I would finish cleaning up the kitchen and put a load of wash in, and then hurry across the street, knocking softly at the door. Rose still took her morning nap (though we knew the end of these was coming soon), which gave us a blessed hour (and sometimes two) together. We disappeared into Eva and Ted's bedroom until we heard Rose's cries on the other side of the wall, and then we would spend the rest of the day together, sharing the domestic duties at each of our houses to ensure that the floors were clean and the tubs and toilets sparkling before we got in the car and flew.

It was 1961, and in other parts of the country young black students were demanding their civil rights, sitting down at "whites only" lunch counters. Their courage and audacity to demand equal rights was something I admired but did not connect, not then, with my own life. It would be a long, long time before I felt that I had a *right* to this life, to these dreams and needs. Eva, on the other hand, saw us as somehow allied with these kids, these people who only wanted to be treated fairly by the rest of the world.

"I wish," she said once as Rose napped and we lay together in her bed, "we could go somewhere."

I was touching her hair, marveling at how it was so soft, I could barely feel it in my fingers. It reminded me of the girls' skin when they were infants.

"There are places," she said, dreamily staring at the ceiling above us. "Where girls, *women* like us, don't have to pretend."

"Where?" I scoffed more loudly than I had intended. Certainly not in Hollyville, Massachusetts.

"I knew someone at school in San Francisco," she said.

I felt my throat grow thick. The idea of Eva and Ted was somehow tolerable, because I knew it wasn't real, that it was just another empty box under the tree. But the notion of her with another woman, with someone besides me, was intolerable. I felt sick. "Who?" I managed to choke out.

"Just a girl I knew. A student. She took me once to a bar where everyone was, you know . . ."

"Why did she take *you?*" I asked. And it was like a dark shadow had crossed this sunlit bed where we lay naked while the world spun endlessly, obliviously, without us.

She ignored me, the way I knew she probably dismissed Ted's jealousy, his invidious delusions. Still, I needed to know.

"Have you . . ." I started, feeling blood rushing to my ears. "Been with other girls?"

Eva tilted her head and looked at me as though gauging whether she should answer me. I hated her hesitancy. This quiet distrust.

"I mean, it doesn't matter, I'm just curious. . . ." I said, backpedaling, wishing I hadn't asked. Not really wanting to know.

"I've felt things, before," she said softly. "But I've never done anything about it. I thought the feelings would go away. With Liam. And then Ted."

"Did they?" I asked. "Go away?"

She cocked her head again. "I suppose. Until you came along."

"Do you think it's a sin?" I asked, thinking about my mother and father. About the way they thought that God could fix me. That I was somehow broken and in need of repair. I knew that Eva made weekly treks to church, that they had a family Bible on display in their living room.

"I don't know," she said, shaking her head. "Adultery is a sin. But is it adultery when you never loved the person you married?"

"You *never* loved Ted?" I asked, feeling my heart swell. "Not even before?"

She shook her head. "I made a mistake."

I thought about Frankie then. I tried not to when Eva and I were together; I felt terrible imagining how Frankie would feel if he knew what happened after he pulled out of the driveway every morning. He would *absolutely* see this, the tender morning hours Eva and I spent clinging to each other, as sinful. It would kill him. Like Ted, Frankie could be a mean drunk, but he was generally a good man, a good father. I did love him for that. But that wasn't the kind of love I meant. Not the kind of love I felt for Eva.

"We could go somewhere," she said earnestly, tracing her finger across my bare stomach. My skin trembled under her touch. "Where we wouldn't have to hide." My entire body grew feverish as I thought about this possibility. About running away.

"Where?" I asked.

"I have an idea," she said, and sat up, clapping her hands together like a child. "Let's take a trip."

I still don't know how she talked Ted into it, though convincing Frankie was easy. I simply told him that Eva and I were going to New York City to a Girl Scout leaders' convention, a national conference being held over a weekend in January. In my mind, the convention existed. I pictured a hundred other mothers in their Scout leader uniforms, learning better ways to start campfires, braid lanyards, and peddle cookies. He said that he'd keep Ted company while we were gone.

It was the aunts, ultimately, who unwittingly made it possible. Frankie's sister Theresa agreed to come help Frankie watch the girls for the long weekend. And Ted's sister, Mary, offered her babysitting services again as well. The aunts arrived on the same train in from Boston, and Ted picked them both up. Then, after we'd given our various instructions, Frankie took Eva and me to the train station and dropped us off, the changing of the guards nearly seamless. It was almost too easy.

Eva and I got on the train, carrying our Girl Scout handbooks and luggage, waved good-bye to Frankie, and then collapsed into our seats with such tremendous relief and excitement we could barely contain ourselves.

Eva's friend Dorothy (Dot), from school, lived in New York now, had since she finished school in San Francisco. She told Eva we could stay with her. Eva said she wanted to take me to the Museum of Modern Art, to Rockefeller Plaza, to Times Square. As we hurled through the frosty morning, I felt like the farm girl I was, had always been, having never traveled farther south than Massachusetts and never farther west than Niagara Falls. I had never been to New York.

Dot, a pale wisp of a woman (a painter, Eva had said), met us at Grand Central Station. I was dizzy with the traffic noise and smells and sounds of the city, feeling like a real country mouse, as we navigated our way to the subway and then six blocks to her apartment in the Village.

"Welcome to my humble abode," she said, smirking, as she unlocked the heavy iron gate leading to the basement apartment. The steps were steep and cracked, with a thin layer of treacherous ice. The windows were smudgy and small, but inside the apartment was warm and clean.

Dot made us scrambled eggs and toast for dinner that night at a tiny stove with only two burners, gave us herbal tea, and showed us where the clean towels and washcloths were.

There were canvases propped against every inch of every wall, mostly gloomy-looking portraits of women. A lot of them were nudes, only instead of women in repose, the women appeared to be in agony, grimacing, with writhing bodies curled like fists.

Dot struck me right away as one of those women who has something to prove. She asked a lot of questions about how Eva and I met, and then went into a lengthy anecdote about the first time she'd met Eva. "Well, you know she had on that blue dress," she said, reaching for Eva's arm and then looking at me, as if challenging me to remember that blue dress. Eva had a lot of blue dresses. I didn't know which one she was talking about or why it mattered.

"And of course, Liam couldn't keep his eyes off her, *none* of us could in that dress, but she just sat right down at one of the free easels and started to sketch, and it was a drawing of him. Liam O'Leary. *Nude.*"

Eva blushed and swatted at Dot's arm, giggling.

I felt my skin growing hot. I tried to imagine this Eva, this other Eva in her blue dress, this brazen Eva undressing her professor with her pencil. I also wondered if she'd ever "felt things" for Dot. If she had ever fawned over her the way I had over Miss Mars.

"We all knew then that Eva was one ballsy lady," she said, throwing her head back, laughing.

They reminisced for another fifteen minutes or so until finally Dot seemed to grow bored with us (with me anyway) and took off to meet some friends for a drink. She gave us the address of the bar where she planned to be later, and we told her we'd meet her there after we took a little rest.

Grateful to be alone again, I sat down on the edge of the Murphy bed, which Dot had pulled out of the wall like magic. The sheets were threadbare but soft. Through the basement window, I could see Dot's feet as she walked away.

"She's something else, huh?" Eva asked. I could tell she wanted me to like her, and I didn't want to seem ungrateful or judgmental of her old friend.

"She's funny," I said.

Eva nodded. "She was the only one I had to talk to when I found out I was pregnant. . . ." Again, I felt this nagging stab of jealousy. I hated myself for it.

"Come here," I said, and motioned for her to join me.

She sat down next to me on the bed, and I stroked her hair. It was as soft as corn silk in my fingers. This was what surprised me the most, I think, the contrast between Frankie and Eva. Frankie with his hard stubble of a beard at night, his callused hands and tough skin. Eva was silk, while Frankie was metal. A corrugated tin man.

Together we lay on the bed, completely alone for the first time ever. And I remember watching people's feet move across the sidewalk through the high windows in that apartment, feeling safe in this underground place: this makeshift subterranean haven.

At about eight o'clock we took a shower together, and then got ready to meet Dot. I would have been content to spend the rest of the weekend in the apartment alone with Eva, but she was excited to show me the city, and her enthusiasm was infectious.

She wore the red dress that I loved, the one that made her look like a magazine model. She painted her lips red as well, and instead of her usual White Shoulders, she wore a perfume that smelled like cinnamon. She was like one of those fireball candies that Johnny and Mouse loved. Feeling dull in comparison, I put on my best dress, the one with raglan sleeves and a pleated skirt, a dress I'd made myself from a remnant of emerald green shantung I got on sale, and a pair of heels I'd dyed to match. The last time I'd worn it was for one of Frankie's sister's weddings.

"You look so pretty," Eva said, squeezing my hand, as the taxi moved in fits and starts through the city.

The bar's entrance was in an alleyway, and it was snowing lightly as we got out of the taxi, clutching the address Dorothy had given us. Eva leaned over and handed the driver the fare, and we stood peering down the dark alley. She reached for my hand and squeezed it again. "Ready?" she asked.

I nodded.

We made our way through the dark and found the entrance, where a couple, embracing, was blocking the doorway.

"Excuse me," Eva said, and the couple pulled apart, startled. I felt my face grow hot as I realized it was two women.

Relieved to see that we were going into the bar, they resumed their groping against the brick wall next to the entrance.

Inside, the bar was smoky and loud. There was a band playing a song from Miles Davis's *Kind of Blue,* an album Eva loved, though the last time we'd listened to that record, we'd been sitting at her kitchen table, sewing Girl Scout badges onto sashes.

My heart pounded in time with the snare drum as we walked briskly across the dirty floor to Dot, who was motioning to us from the bar. The room was packed, and all of the patrons were women, though at first glance you wouldn't have known that. While half of the women were dressed like Eva and me, in dresses and stockings and heels, the other half were dressed like men: short hair slicked back into ducktails, high-waisted pleated pants and collared dress shirts. Suspenders and jackets and ties. It was only the softness of their faces and eyes that gave them away, only their hands, their long, thin fingers and manicured nails, that held on gently to bottles of beer or cocktail glasses. It was confusing, and frightening. I didn't know where we fit into this crowd, *how* we fit into this crowd. Who these people were, who we were. Who *I* was. The apprehension must have shown on my face, because Eva squeezed my hand again and leaned toward me, whispering, "It's okay. Just relax."

The band started playing Nina Simone's "Forbidden Fruit," and Dot came over to Eva from the barstool where she had been perched like an odd little bird.

"May I have this dance?" she asked, and Eva smiled, curtseying playfully. "Of course." I felt my back stiffen despite myself.

The song was a clear favorite among this crowd, and the dance floor filled quickly. From the bar, I watched Dot and Eva dance, and it took every ounce of self-control I had not to march up to her and cut in, to claim what was mine. But Eva was *not* mine. Could never be mine. The realization of this hit me in the chest like a fist. I was near tears with frustration and anger when the band started to play Coltrane's "My Shining Hour," and Eva came over to me, breathless. She collapsed against me, closing her eyes dreamily. "Dance with me, Billie?" she asked, and my heart quickened.

Frankie liked to dance. He was a terrific dancer, but he always made me feel clumsy. He knew how to lead, but I failed to follow. At our wedding, I'd felt like an oaf on the dance floor. He'd get frustrated sometimes and simply find another partner to dance with.

"If she won't, I will," Dot said, winking at Eva and looking at her in a way that made my spine tingle.

I couldn't bear the thought of Eva dancing with her, and so I relented. "I'm a really terrible dancer," I said, shaking my head apologetically. When we had danced in her living room, there was no audience, no one to see me stumble along.

"Just follow me," she said. "It's a nice, slow song. You just need to hold on." She pulled me gently by the hand to the dance floor and stopped, positioning my hands around her waist. I felt myself blushing, though no one was paying any attention to us.

She pressed her body into mine and leaned her head against my chest, humming the music into me. My entire body vibrated with the music and her breaths. I could have stayed like this, our bodies pressed together, held together by the music, forever. But the song came to an end, and there was only stillness, the cacophony of the crowd filling in the empty space the music had made. But instead of pulling apart, she looked up at me.

When she kissed me, my instinct was to pull away. Our kisses had been private things, all of them illicit, stolen. The idea of kissing her, of touching her mouth with my own, in front of all of these people was almost more than I could take.

I remember the light in the bar was a sort of green, an absinthe green, our skin painted in verdant light as though we were standing in the forest, the sunlight shining through the trees, dappling us. When she kissed me again, I pretended that we weren't in an alleyway bar in New York City in January, but rather deep in the cool woods in Vermont in June.

Dot finally left us alone after a while, finding another girl to dance with for the rest of the evening and then disappearing with her. Eva and I both drank too much that night, stumbling out of the bar at three a.m., brazenly holding hands as we navigated the slippery streets, emboldened by the acceptance we'd found inside that absinthe-colored night.

My head was spinning from the liquor and the lights. The air smelled like a thousand things. It was a carnival of sensations, and I couldn't get enough of it. Enough of her.

"We could move here," I said.

"What's that?" she asked, laughing and pulling my hand to cross the street when the light changed.

When we reached the other side, I was breathless. "We could live here. *Together.*" And the word hung between us, pulsing and humming like the neon sign for the pizzeria we stood next to. The light from inside the all-night shop was bright, and suddenly I could see that Eva's mascara had smudged under her eyes, that the hem of her dress had come down. I felt my throat grow thick. I just needed her to say yes. To share this dream with me. But she didn't speak. Instead, she took my face in her hands and kissed me. Right there on the street. In front of the couple who sat eating pizza in the pizzeria window. In front of the taxicabs and hobos and sailors on leave. And, for a moment, I knew it was possible that we *could* leave. That there was a chance for us.

I don't remember how we got back to Dot's apartment, and I barely remember changing into my pajamas and crawling into bed. I don't think I moved all night, and in the morning, we were woken by the sound of a rooster, and I was delirious, momentarily transported to my childhood bed. It turned out instead to be Dot's neighbor, a crazy man who lived three stories up from her basement apartment, who cock-a-doodle-dooed at the crack of dawn each morning and was answered with a resounding and collective *Shut up, already!* by the neighbors and anyone who might be out at this ungodly hour walking on the street.

Hungover and bleary-eyed, we got dressed and walked down the street to a small diner for breakfast. We hadn't spoken about our conversation in front of the pizza shop. I wondered if I had only dreamed it. Wished it.

The waitress brought us our food, and I peered at Eva's face, looking for confirmation that we had actually spoken those words. About running away. But instead, Eva distractedly dug through her purse for coins and said, "I need to go call Ted."

I felt like I might throw up as she put her coat back on and disappeared outside to the pay phone. I stared at the pancake I'd ordered but couldn't bring the fork to my mouth.

She came back inside smiling sadly. "Rose has a fever and has been throwing up. He wants me to come home."

"Now?" I said, feeling the earth falling out from under my unsteady feet. I'd dreamed all night about the way it felt to be held in her arms. The way the music held us together, the way she smelled. "Can't Mary take care of her?"

"She's been crying for me. Sounds like the flu. I told him we'd catch the five o'clock train."

"Fine," I said, angry at her. Angry at Ted. Angry even at Rose, for getting sick. I felt like a rotten, spoiled child who hadn't gotten her way. I felt like a fool. I blinked hard and looked away from her out the window at the quiet street, my heart broken, and hated myself for being so selfish. Her baby was sick. What was wrong with me?

"We can still go to the museum," she said, reaching across the table for my hand. A man sitting next to us in a booth glared at me, and I pulled my hand away.

I was still queasy when we finally made our way to the museum a few hours later and Eva raced up the wide marble steps. I followed behind her, almost having to run in order to keep up.

She carried a map of the museum in her hand but didn't seem to need it. Finally, we reached Eva's destination and I was breathless, bending over at the waist to catch my breath. I still felt miserably hungover.

"Look," she said, touching my arm softly, and I stood up.

All around us were the mobiles I'd only ever seen in the books Eva checked out for me at the library. Suspended from the ceiling, they hung like living, breathing things. The colors were bright, alive against the stark whiteness of the walls.

We didn't speak as we moved about the room, peering up at these incredible kinetic sculptures, like strange and beautiful birds watching over us from above. And when I looked at Eva again, she was crying. But this time, instead of hiding her tears or brushing them away, she allowed them to travel down her cheeks, smudging her makeup, making tracks through her blush.

I went to her, and suddenly I didn't care who was watching: the stuffy guard standing in the doorway; the young man with a mustache, his hands on his hips; the elderly woman and her squeaky shoes. I put my arm around her shoulders, pulled her close, and let her cry.

A half hour before the flight to Pittsburgh is set to depart, we are herded onto the plane by a cheery attendant in a crisp blue suit and heels. Her lipstick has smeared across her front tooth, and something about this makes me uneasy. Something about all of this is unsettling. She takes my boarding pass from me and asks if I need any assistance making my way down the long, fluorescent-lit jet bridge to the plane. I shake my head. "I'm fine, thank you."

I shuffle along with the other passengers, thinking again that I could still simply turn around now. Go back. I can almost feel my body pushing against the flow of other bodies, swimming upstream back to the gate and then back to my happy life at the beach. But then I am standing at the entrance of the plane, and there are two more attendants waiting with their smiles and good cheer at the doorway. One of them takes my boarding pass and gestures, grandly, I think, toward my seat, which is just beyond the wall that separates first class from coach.

The air buzzes and hums, and my hands tremble as I take the pass back and study the seat number: *7A*. And as I cross the threshold, into the airplane's galley, I realize that this is it. There are no more chances to change my mind. There's no turning back now. In a mere four hours I'll be in Pittsburgh, and then by five o'clock I'll be in Burlington. Gussy will be there waiting. We'll make the long drive from Burlington to Quimby, arriving just in time for a late supper. I can picture Gussy's kitchen, smell the chicken and dumplings. She'll have made up the bed in the guest bedroom with her sunflower sheets. She'll have bought the maple candies I like and left them on the nightstand with a stack of books she thinks I might enjoy. I will sleep well. And then we will go to the lake, and on Sunday Johnny will arrive.

I am glad to have checked my suitcase, as I watch the other travelers struggle to stuff their belongings into the tiny overhead compartments. I have only my purse to worry about, and it fits nicely in my lap. The seat next to me is vacant until the plane is nearly ready to taxi down the runway. But just as I reach to put my purse in the empty seat, to lift the armrest that juts up uncomfortably in the middle, a large young man comes rushing down the narrow corridor, huffing and puffing and heaving his bag overhead. He's got a wide, familiar face. Red and sweaty. I am afraid to look directly at him, convinced for a moment that he is who he appeared to be when I first glanced up, thinking this is like some terrible nightmare. That Ted is not dead at all and has somehow found me, *followed* me here. Perhaps he has been following me for years. But as he plops himself down into the seat, struggling to get the seat belt across his wide lap, I ignore my trembling hands and heart and steal a longer glance.

It is not Ted at all. *Of course not.* I haven't completely lost my mind. For one thing, he's probably only about twenty years old. And while he does resemble Ted, this man's eyes are a crystal blue, not the lightless black eyes of Ted Wilson. And while Ted was large and muscular, this man is soft. Overweight. He smiles at me when he is finally able to adjust the seat belt to fit him, and he says softly, "They say if you can't buckle the seat belt, you gotta pay for two tickets." He has an accent, something sweet, Southern.

"Here," I say, lifting the armrest to give him a few more inches.

"Thank you," he says, and we are suddenly coconspirators.

"I missed my alarm, barely made it to the gate in time," he says. When he smiles, his eyes crinkle a little at the corners. "Where y'all headed? Pittsburgh?"

I shake my head. "Burlington."

"Where's that at?"

"Vermont," I say.

He smells like cinnamon buns, and I'm starting to think the reason he's late is not his alarm but a stop at the Cinnabon shop.

"That the state near Washington, DC?"

I shake my head. "That's Virginia."

"That's right," he says, smacking his leg with a meaty palm. "Where the maple syrup comes from. I'm Hugh, by the way."

"Billie," I say. "And how about you? Where are you headed?"

"Going to see my girlfriend," he says.

"That's nice. You live in different states?"

"Well, we ain't never really met yet. But we been talking online for about six months now."

"Oh," I say. "That must be very exciting."

He nods and smiles. "Hey, would you mind switching seats? I'd love to be able to look out the window."

"Sure," I say. But just as he starts to unbuckle himself again, an attendant comes over and says that we need to remain seated. That the flight is about to take off in just a few moments.

"We can switch once we get up in the air," I say, and he shrugs.

"I'm fine. Soon as I can turn on my laptop, I'll show you a picture."

"Of?" I say.

"My girl," he says.

I like this kid. People in love are almost always nice to be around, and this one is head over heels. Never mind that it's all a fantasy; there's something delightful about his hope, his trust that he's on his way to meet the love of his life.

"What y'all doing in Vermont?" he asks.

And for just a quick second I imagine saying, *Do you want to hear a real love story?* And for the smallest of moments, I think I could tell him. I could share my own story with him. That it would keep him rapt, at the edge of his uncomfortable seat, for the next four hours. That he might even shed a tear at the end.

But, somehow, I know better. While some things change, most things stay exactly the same. My love story, our love story, is one most people don't want to hear. Even now, all these years later. I am not ashamed, not anymore, but it might bring all that crimson color back to his cheeks. Might even send him seeking another seat next to some other little old lady. And so instead I just fiddle with my purse and say, "I'm going to see my sister."

The engine roars, and the floor beneath my feet vibrates. I feel my heart fly to my throat, and I make an involuntary gasping sound. I smile apologetically at him.

"I haven't flown in a really long time," I say.

"Well, I ain't never flown before," he says. "So this will be a real adventure."

We came home from New York and returned to our lives, to our lies. But something had shifted while we were away. We had dipped our toes into the vast and terrifying and thrilling possibility of life without Frankie and Ted. And while they knew nothing, or seemed to know nothing, *we* did. We had felt our bodies become weightless, light, buoyed by the mere prospect of freedom. But though this realization brought with it the vague sense of hope, the reality was that while we were gone, nothing here had changed. It was winter. It was bitter cold. There were home fires to be tended, children to be fed, and husbands to be answered to and appeased.

Ted was being sent out on the road less and less. Eva told me she worried that he was losing clients, that his drinking was interfering with his work. She said he came home at night smelling as though he'd not only had a couple of cocktails with lunch but possibly several more throughout the rest of the day. Some days he skipped work altogether, opting to stay home with Eva instead.

"Isn't he worried about getting fired?" I asked.

"You'd think," she said. "But he gets his head wrapped around something and he can't let go. I think it's this weather. It makes him crazy."

"What do you mean?" I asked, though I was afraid to hear her answer. Since we had returned from New York, I felt like I was waiting for someone (Frankie, Ted, even Chessy) to unravel the fabrication. It had been too simple, too easy.

Eva shrugged.

We were at her house, sitting together in the living room folding laundry. Rose played with a shape sorter on the floor between us. As we picked through the pile of underthings, I was careful to select only Eva's and the children's, leaving Ted's shorts and undershirts to her.

"He's got these crazy ideas," she said. She plucked a pair of faded plaid boxers from the pile. She held them up, and, in doing so, conjured Ted. He hung between us, as he always did. "He's so suspicious."

"Of us?" I asked, feeling my heart rising in my throat and beating there, as though I'd swallowed a bird.

"No," she said, laughing. "Of *me*. Of the whole world."

On the days that Ted stayed home, nursing a hangover and hovering over Eva, I didn't even dare to call her. Frankie would honk his horn, his signal in case Ted needed a ride, and Eva would open their door and wave Frankie away. This was also her signal to me (she knew I was watching from the window), and with that simple gesture, I could feel the weight of winter crushing me. I knew I had to figure out a way to see her, especially if Ted was going to keep stealing entire days from us. We needed to come up with a solution, some way to be together, some excuse that wouldn't make him suspicious. Something that would buy us time alone.

And then two days later, when I was at DeMoulas shopping, and the man with the cardboard box approached me, it was as though someone had sent him with the answer. The man was grinning a wide, goofy grin. He must have known just by looking at me that I'd be an easy mark. Chessy and Mouse were with me, and they squealed giddily as they peered into the box.

"Only three left. People have been snatching them up like hotcakes," the man said. I detected an accent in his voice. Irish, maybe.

Inside there was a ratty blue blanket and three wriggling golden puppies.

"They're so *small,*" I said, my hand reaching into the box as if it had a mind of its own.

"I found them out by the creek this morning. Looks like somebody dumped them off. I can hardly believe they're alive; it's so cold out. My guess is they're only a few weeks old."

"Are they yellow labs?" I asked, bringing one puppy up to my face and smelling her sweet puppy smell, burying my nose in her warm body. I'd grown up with yellow labs, sisters named Florence and Nightingale, the only two animals allowed in our house. On a farm, animals were seen as commodities, as our livelihood, not as pets. But my father had a soft spot for dogs, and so Flo and Night slept at our hearth, curled around each other.

"Goldens, I think. Maybe mixed with something else. Pretty little things. And goldens make a good family dog," he said, nodding at the girls. "My own pup is a golden retriever. Best dog I ever had."

"Okay, okay," I said, rolling my eyes. "I know. They're good with children."

"Please, Mom?" Mouse asked, taking off her mittens and touching one puppy's tiny paws with her fingers. The paw wasn't much bigger than her thumb.

"You know Daddy can't have a dog," I said. Frankie had terrible allergies to all animals: dogs and cats and horses and rabbits. When we went to the county fair, he had to stay home because one time he nearly threw his back out sneezing in the 4-H barn. Once, Mouse brought home a stray kitten and smuggled it into her room, and his eyes swelled up so tight, he could see only enough to make his way to her room and ferret the poor kitten out. I thought it was funny that a farm girl like me had wound up with someone who couldn't be within a half mile of a horse without getting sick.

"Oh," Chessy lamented, reaching in and taking the puppy from me. I helped her cup her in her hand, and she held her close, cooing into her fur.

And then it struck me. "Maybe we could bring her to the Wilsons," I said. "That way you'd get to see her all the time. It would be like she belonged to all of us."

"Oh, please, Mom. Pretty, pretty please?" Mouse said, tugging at my shirt and the puppy's tail.

"Listen," I said, bending down to their level and whispering, making them feel, I knew, as though they were part of a very important secret. "Mr. Wilson might not be happy about this. So we're going to have to make up a little story about where we found her."

"A *lie?*" Chessy asked.

"No," I said. Francesca couldn't tolerate untruths of any sort. Little white lies might as well have been the deepest betrayals as far as she was concerned. When she learned the truth about Santa Claus, she didn't speak to us for nearly a week. And it was only after a threat of spanking that she agreed to keep the secret from her younger sister.

"Otherwise, we have to leave the puppy here," I said.

She looked as though she were weighing the options and then somewhat reluctantly said, "Okay."

Chessy was given the task of carrying the puppy home. I carried the grocery bags, and Mouse tagged along behind, skipping and playing hopscotch on the sidewalk. When we finally got back to our street, I took the puppy from Chessy and sent the girls inside.

"When do we get to play with her?" Mouse pouted.

"Be patient," I said. "And remember what I told you. *We* found the puppy down by the creek. And if we left her there, she would have died. It's too cold outside for a new puppy."

"That's almost the truth," Chessy said, comforting herself.

"It is," I said. "And this way, Mr. Wilson won't have any choice but to keep her."

The girls disappeared inside the house, and I held the puppy, warm and sleeping, inside my winter coat, against my chest, as I walked across the street. I could feel the puppy breathing in hot little bursts against the cotton of my blouse as I rang the doorbell.

"Hi," Eva said, smiling at me in that way that said a billion things without saying a single word. It took her a few moments before she realized what was peeking out through my buttons. "Oh, my goodness," she said, her eyes widening as she saw the puppy's tiny nose and tiny sleepy eyes. I unbuttoned my coat and Eva took her and held her like an infant, cradled her. "Is this for me?"

I nodded.

"What's her name, Billie?"

"Calder," I said, smiling. "Her name is Calder."

And so began our nightly walks. Every night after dinner, Eva and Calder and I would convene in the middle of the street and walk for an hour or more. We walked along the creek that ran behind our house; we walked through town, the puppy tagging along at Eva's side. We walked to the elementary school playground, vacant in the evenings. And as winter finally passed and spring arrived, the nights growing warmer, we walked for longer, sometimes arriving back at home just in time to get the children to bed. Calder, exhausted from the walk and so thirsty, drank from puddles or the dripping faucet she found at the side of our house.

We could pretend on those walks that we were alone in the world. That Frankie did not exist, that Ted was not waiting for Eva with questions and demands. Of course, we were *not* alone, not ever truly alone, as we walked through town, the illuminated rooms like eyes in the night, in sight of any of those moving silhouettes inside. But in those twilight hours, we *felt* as though we were the only two people left on earth. As we walked farther away from town, through pastures and empty parks and forests, we whispered our secrets into each other's hair, and, when twilight acquiesced to evening and only the watchful eyes of the stars peered down at us, we sometimes dared to touch. And we comforted ourselves by talking about the summer, about the lake.

If not for these nightly walks, our nightly talks, and Vermont, if not for the prospect of those two weeks together in August, I might not have made it through the rest of that winter and spring of 1962. It was the promise of the water, the moon, and Eva that sustained me. Whenever I felt like I might not be able to take another moment inside my house, inside my *life,* I had only to assure myself that soon enough we would be free again.

Then one evening in early June, when summer no longer felt quite so far away, Frankie came home with a bed frame. It was an old, iron bed frame, the kind we had at the lake. He had strapped it to the roof of the Studebaker and was busy untying it, gleeful, as though it were a Christmas tree instead of another piece of junk.

"What's that for, Frankie?" I asked. "We already have enough beds."

"It's for Theresa," he said. "She's going to be spending the summer with us."

It felt like a sinkhole had opened up underneath my feet.

"Excuse me?" I said.

Theresa was Frankie's baby sister. She'd gotten engaged on Valentine's Day; her wedding was just weeks away. We'd received the fancy invitation a month ago, with its scented paper and calligraphy.

"What happened?" I asked.

"She got a letter from Joe yesterday, says he's calling the wedding off. He took off with some other girl to Nevada or some other godforsaken place."

My first reaction should have been sympathy. Poor little Theresa. Her life, while only twenty-two years, had been a series of disappointments. Her first boyfriend was killed in a car accident. And now this. But it wasn't sympathy I felt.

"We'll set her up in the basement for now, and then she'll go up to Vermont with you in August," Frankie said. "Help her clear her head."

"No," I said, shaking my head. "There isn't any room."

"Sure there is," he said. "You can make room for Eva and her kids, you can't make room for my sister?"

"That's what I mean. When Eva and the kids come, there won't be any room." I could feel my voice breaking, my whole *body* breaking.

"Well, maybe this year the Wilsons don't come for a visit." Frankie shrugged and hoisted the headboard onto his shoulder.

Tears welled up in my eyes, and I didn't bother wiping them away. "Frankie, Eva and I have been looking forward to this." But then I realized that he didn't care about disappointing me, wasn't concerned with my plans. Desperate, I hoped he might at least care about the children's disappointment. "Chessy and Mouse have been talking about this for months. You can't take that away from them."

Frankie leaned the headboard up against the house and came back for the footboard. "Theresa is my *sister,*" he said. "Which makes her your sister too. She's coming with you to Vermont, and you can tell the Wilsons they can come another time."

With Frankie, there was no arguing. No changing his mind. He was a small man, but he was like a big brick wall when it came to things like this. Impenetrable.

That night, I refused to speak to him. I made his dinner, moving about the kitchen angrily, slamming pots and pans, having my own private temper tantrum, raging as I stirred and fried and boiled. I refused to eat as well, sitting with an empty plate before me. The girls knew something was wrong.

"Aren't you hungry, Mama?" Mouse asked. I couldn't look at her or else I knew I would break down.

"I've lost my appetite," I said.

And Frankie dealt with my anger the way he dealt with everything. He drank. And as the level of wine in the jug got lower and lower, his voice raised higher and higher. "How would you girls feel if your Auntie T comes to stay with us this summer?"

"Really?" Francesca asked, beaming. She adored Theresa. She looked up to her, more like a big sister than an aunt. "What about Joe? What about the wedding? I'm going to be a flower girl."

I waited to see how Frankie would handle this.

"Joe's an asshole," he said.

"Frankie," I admonished. It was the first word I'd spoken all night.

"Sorry," he said, though I knew he wasn't. "Joey's a *philanderer.* Do you know what that is, girls?"

"I mean it, Frankie. None of this concerns them."

But I had effectively made myself invisible, and so Frankie couldn't see me anymore. I looked down at my hands to make sure I was, indeed, present still, that I hadn't simply vanished.

"He's run off with another girl. He's a cheat. A scumbag. *Cazzaro!*" Frankie said, his face red, the wine in his glass sloshing. "Found himself a *puttana*. Broke your auntie's heart."

"Stop it, Frankie!" I said, slamming my fist down on the table.

"Don't you talk to me like that," he said, slamming his own fists against the table. "Disrespectful! I am the man in this house." Frankie stood up then, gripping the table with both hands, as though he might fall over if he didn't.

Chessy and Mouse looked terrified, and I hated him.

I hated all five feet six inches of him. I hated the way his chin jutted out; I hated his beady eyes. I hated his drunkenness; I hated his anger.

"I knew it, Daddy. I knew he was no good," Chessy started. She, like I, was always trying to assuage Frankie. Agreeing with him to quiet his rage. It killed me to see her doing exactly what she had likely seen me do a zillion times. What was I teaching her?

"Chessy . . ." I said.

"It's true. I saw him wink at the waitress at the restaurant when we went out for Auntie T's birthday."

"What do you know, Miss Ninny?" Frankie said. "Always think you're so smart? Think you're smarter than your old man, huh?" I felt all of the hairs rise on the back of my neck.

"Girls, go to your rooms, please," I said, trying to make my voice gentle.

Obediently they left the room, their plates still full of food. And Frankie barely even noticed their departure, caught up as he was in his own tantrum. His world was as small as his body, every action selfish: not a single thought of anyone but himself.

"Frankie," I said, trying, as I always tried, to mollify him. To weaken his anger. To soften him. My main job, it seemed, was keeping Frankie from boiling over. I was the one who controlled the fire beneath him. The one who made him simmer. The one who made him steam. "Listen. It's fine if Theresa comes to live with us this summer. I understand. She's family. But Vermont is important to me. And it's important to the girls. The Wilsons have already planned their summer to include a vacation with us." I knew even as I spoke that logic was likely not the right tack to take here. Logic usually stopped working about two glasses in, and Frankie had easily downed four or five at this point. He was in that dangerous place: two glasses beyond passivity and two glasses before passing out.

"Che cazzo mi frega?" he said. *What the fuck do I care?*

And in that moment, I realized he *didn't* care. He didn't care about me. He hadn't cared about me for years. I simply didn't matter. Not really, not when my own desires got in the way of his.

"I'm going for a walk," I said, standing up from the table and grabbing my sweater and purse. Frankie poured himself another glass of wine and sat down, triumphant, at the table.

I walked out the door, my whole body shaking with anger. I slammed the door behind me, regretting it as soon as I saw the girls' faces peering down at me from Chessy's window. I smiled up at them and blew a kiss. Chessy slowly lifted the sash and spoke through the screen. "Where are you going, Mama?"

"Get ready for bed. I'll be back in a little bit."

I started to walk across the street, wanting only to get as far away as possible from Frank. And as I did, the Wilsons' porch light came on. The front door opened and Eva came out, pulling a sweater around her.

"Hi," she said, running down the steps. "Are you okay? I could hear Frankie yelling all the way over here."

There was no such thing as privacy in this neighborhood, I realized, as Mrs. Baker's face appeared behind her curtains.

"Where are you going?" she asked.

"Just for a walk," I said.

"I'll get Calder."

When I told her about Theresa moving in, about Vermont, she only nodded her head and squeezed my hand, saying, "It's okay. We'll figure something out. We won't let this spoil the summer. We won't let this ruin things."

Who knew that Theresa would actually be the one to make this true?

Theresa arrived at the end of June, just as the girls were getting out of school. Frankie picked her up at the train station and brought her home, but when he opened up the trunk, he only pulled out one suitcase.

"Where are the rest of your things?" I asked her as Frankie carried it inside.

She rolled her eyes and waited until he was out of earshot before she said, "Frankie thinks I'm moving in, but this is just a *visit*. I'll be out of your hair by the end of August. I got an apartment in the city with my friend Lucy. Do *not* tell my brother."

Of all of Frankie's siblings, I liked Theresa best. And the fact that it wasn't Thea or Antoinette or, God forbid, *Andrea* living in our basement was, admittedly, a relief. Theresa was young and wide-eyed. Gullible and fun. The girls adored her because she was more like a child than a grown woman. And it didn't take long to realize that having her stay with us actually had some perks. For one thing, she was always willing to watch the girls if I needed to run an errand.

"Go, go!" she said. "It's not like I have anywhere to be. Take your time."

Eva and I made up excuses all summer long about trips we needed to take. And once in Ted's car, we were, at least for a couple of hours, free. Of course, we didn't take advantage of Theresa's hospitality too often, because leaving her with all five children—leaving *anyone* with five children (especially when one of those children was Johnny)—seemed presumptuous. But Theresa never complained; I think she liked being the fun aunt: the one who played hopscotch with Mouse, who climbed trees with Johnny, who outfitted Rose in dress-up clothes and put on plays.

Eva and I used these opportunities to drive far away from Hollyville, away from our lives, if even just for an afternoon. We went to the museums in Boston, we went strawberry picking, we just drove and parked in empty lots and kissed until our lips were swollen and bruised.

One day in July we asked Theresa to watch the kids while we went into the city (presumably to pick up some supplies for one of the Girl Scout projects we had planned for that fall) and instead drove out into the country. We had the whole day to ourselves. An *entire* day. Eva wanted to go swimming, and so I suggested Lake Cochichewick. We packed a picnic lunch, left Theresa and the kids behind.

The day was glorious: sunny, the air hot and slow. We set up underneath a shady willow away from the other beachgoers. All afternoon we alternated between swimming and lying in the cool shade, only the tips of our fingers touching.

"What are you thinking?" I asked Eva as she peered through the lacy canopy above us.

"I'm thinking that I love you," Eva whispered, the skin of her finger grazing the exposed top of my thigh, and I felt my entire body convulse with pleasure, a single touch doing to my body what Frankie had never ever been able to do.

The trip should have gone off without a hitch, but on our way home, we got a flat tire. Eva was driving, and she lurched off the side of the road into a ditch.

"Shit!" she said, her eyes widening with fear. "Did I hit something?"

"It's a flat," I said.

"Do you know how to change a tire?" she asked.

I shook my head. My father had never taught me, and Frankie wouldn't have dreamed of showing me how. He didn't even like me pumping my own gas.

Eva looked around frantically as though she could find the answer to our problem in the ditch.

"Let's go ask to borrow a phone," I said, peering down the road at a farmhouse. "I'll call Frankie."

"What will you tell him?" she asked. "We're supposed to be in Boston."

"I'll tell him we changed our mind. That we came to scope out a new camping spot at the state forest."

Eva nodded, but she still looked nervous.

A kind old woman answered the door at the farmhouse, and we both used the phone. Eva left a message with Ted's secretary, and I got in touch with Frankie, who left work early and came all the way up to North Andover to get us. We hid the picnic basket and our wet towels under the backseat and hoped that our sunburned shoulders wouldn't give us away.

"Looks like a nail," Frankie said as he rolled the flat tire into the ditch and put on the spare. (I was careful to watch exactly how he did it just in case we ever found ourselves in this sort of predicament again.) And then we followed him home.

Frankie bought the story about why we were here rather than in the city, but Ted apparently did not. Frankie had stranded him at work, so he'd had to get a ride with a coworker and then hitchhike home. His face was red when we pulled up into the Wilsons' driveway, and he grabbed Eva by the arm as soon as she got out of the car and pushed her toward the house.

"Who were you seeing?" he hissed.

"She was with me, Ted," I said.

Ted turned around, and Eva ran into the house.

"She didn't do anything wrong," I said. "Really. I was the one who decided we should go to North Andover instead. It's my fault."

Ted stepped toward me, and for a minute I thought he was going to hit me. His hands were curled into thick fists, and the muscles in his neck were straining against the collar of his shirt.

"This has nothing to do with you," he said.

I nodded; I couldn't keep my head from nodding. As though simply agreeing with him could make it so.

"*Does* it?" he said. And he looked at me, his eyes studying my face, as if everything I had done, that we had done, were written on my skin.

"Of course not," I said. "No, no, no."

Ted disappeared into the house after Eva, and I stood, paralyzed, on the sidewalk.

"You better look out, Mrs. Valentine!" came a voice from above. It sounded as though it were coming from the heavens. It was not God though; rather, Johnny perched in the high branches of their tree. "My dad is *steamin'!*" I peered up, but the sun was too bright and I couldn't see him hiding amid the leaves.

That night, when Eva did not come outside with Calder after dinner, I sat smoking on our front porch swing, listening to the muffled sounds of Ted bellowing at Eva across the street. I must have gone through half a pack of smokes out there waiting for it to stop. And later, I lay in bed, imagining what was happening inside their house. I didn't sleep the entire night, wondering what on earth he'd meant.

The next morning, as soon as the men had gone off to work, I ran across the street. Inside, Donna had made breakfast, and the children sat grimly around the table.

"Where's your mama?" I asked gently. They all looked shell shocked.

"Johnny?" I said. Johnny was sitting at the table, shoveling cereal into his mouth. He wouldn't look at me.

"Upstairs," Donna said. "She doesn't feel well."

"I told you he was mad," Johnny said.

I ran upstairs to the bedroom and found Eva still in bed, a cold cloth pressed against her eyes. I took the cloth from her and examined her face. Her eye was swollen, the skin marbled in blues and greens: fresh bruises. I recoiled, as though I'd uncovered a pile of rotting meat instead of the face I knew so well.

Anger welled up inside of me as she winced at my touch. I sat down next to her on the bed and reached for her hand, which lay like something pale and strange next to her. Like a *shell,* it struck me suddenly; her hand was like an empty shell washed up on shore. I stroked her skin with my fingertips, and she responded to my touch. "How could he do this?" I asked.

She shook her head. "I don't know."

"Did the children see?"

She wiped a tear from the corner of her battered eye. She nodded. "I know they were watching from the stairs. I don't know how to explain."

"He can't *do* this," I said. "He has no right to do this."

"Of course he does," she chortled. "I'm his *wife.*"

The word, *wife,* was something bitter tasting, its flavor like coffee grounds, detergent, orange rind. I leaned forward and kissed the damaged skin by her eye. I didn't even bother to make sure we were alone, that none of her children were peering in at me. She squeezed her eyes shut and tears streaked her cheeks. I kissed the salty tracks until her face was dry. Calder sat at my feet, her chin resting on the bed.

"Calder's worried about you too," I said.

"Don't worry. I'm okay as long as you're here," she said. Though I knew this was a lie to make me feel better. One of those lies that Chessy despised.

"He doesn't think . . . ?" I started softly, unable to say it, and fearing the worst. I didn't know how to tell her about what he'd said, and how it felt when he looked at me. I felt like I'd given our secret away without speaking a single word. Ted's suspicions were fine, were manageable, as long as they were based on his foolish assumptions. But if they were somehow grounded in the truth, in the reality of everything that was growing between us, then I knew we were no longer safe. Clearly, whatever had transpired between Eva and Ted last night was proof that we were at risk. It had been easy to dismiss his jealousy when it was based on his own vivid imagination, but if he were to actually have an inkling of what was going on between us, we were in serious danger.

"No, of course not," she said, laughing. "It wouldn't occur to him."

"Why is that?" I asked, suddenly feeling defensive, as though this were somehow an insult to me: the idea that he would never dream that Eva had fallen in love with me.

"Because," she said softly. "There's no room in his brain for such thoughts. He's too simple, and this is too complicated. And too beautiful," she added. "Ted can only see the ugly things in life."

"He can't ever do this again," I said firmly. "I swear, if he hurts you again, I'll kill him."

Ted had no control over Eva after he took off each morning. Unless he quit his job and stayed home to monitor her every move, he couldn't keep her sequestered. He stopped riding with Frankie and took his own car to work, though, and he called to check in at all times of day. If he asked what she was doing and she told him she was doing laundry and watching the soaps, he'd ask her to recount the episode's plot. If she said she was mending a pair of Johnny's pants, torn when his pant leg got caught in his tire spokes, he'd demand to hear the sound of the electric sewing machine. When he began to grill the children about the days' activities, Eva became paralyzed, terrified of being found out. He demanded the truth from Donna and Sally, from Johnny and even from Rose. There was no way we could leave the children with

Theresa anymore, because Ted would threaten them all, even Rose, with the belt if they didn't offer him exactly the proof that he needed.

And so we walked. As June bled into July, and our trip to Vermont (without Eva, without Eva) loomed, we met in the road at night and walked. I was terrified of leaving her alone with him, but powerless. We were leaving, and once again I had no say in the matter.

Though Eva had spent only two weeks at the cabin in Vermont with me the year before, the entire lake seemed haunted by her. Her absence was acute. Painful. As though she were dead instead of only distant. Her breath lingered in everything: in the mist that hovered over the lake in the morning, in the steam rising from my teakettle in the afternoon, in the smoke that rose up from the campfires we built at night.

I called her only three times that August, but I wrote her nearly every day. I knew that the mailman brought her mail at exactly one o'clock each afternoon, ensuring that she would be the only one to get the mail. It was risky; I knew this. If she forgot, if Ted stayed home "sick" one day, if the children got to the mailbox first. But there were so many things caught up inside of me, feelings that were swelling, and without Eva here, there was no release for them. I wasn't sure how I could endure an entire month of this. I felt trapped. I felt like a prisoner in some sort of bucolic paradise. All the things I'd loved about being at the lake now felt stifling. Even the scent of grass was cloying. I was overwhelmed by my own nostalgia, embarrassed by it.

The only release I found was swimming. In the water, I could pretend that Eva was with me. That it was Eva that held me up, embraced me, instead of this still body of water. But as soon as I emerged from the lake, I felt her absence in the cold chill of my skin, in the sharp pebbles beneath my bare feet, in the hole she left in my chest.

I was alone without being alone. The girls were here, Theresa was here. But even with their voices and their presence, I felt like a solitary creature moving through a vast, empty expanse. The girls felt out of sorts without the Wilson girls as well, and I knew it made Theresa, who was trying so very hard, feel awful. As if she didn't have enough to feel awful about as it was.

For most of the summer in Hollyville, Theresa had tried hard to keep her chin up. Being left at the altar, or quite nearly at the altar, had devastated but not destroyed her. Theresa, like Frankie, was surprisingly optimistic. I was amazed by her resilience, her hopefulness. Despite the fact that she was almost ten years younger than I was, there was something to be learned from her. Not that she didn't have bad days, of course. There were days early in the summer when she hadn't wanted to get out of bed (and once out of bed couldn't get much more accomplished than making herself a bowl of cereal and plopping herself down on the couch with a stack of magazines for the rest of the day). But by July, she was rising early and putting on makeup, getting dressed, and making plans. She had talked about the apartment she and Lucy were going to share, how close it was to her favorite restaurant. But our trip to Vermont seemed to make her take a step backward, as though all that progress she'd made in mending her broken heart was for naught. At the lake, she seemed similarly haunted by all that she had lost. Somehow all this beauty and peace seemed like cruel reminders of what was gone. *Joey said someday we'd get a little cabin by a lake,* she lamented. *Joey liked to fish. Joey could have swum all the way out to that island, I bet.*

"Girls, why don't you go show Theresa the blueberry patch," I offered on one particularly solemn day. Every one of us had been moping around all morning. I missed Eva. The girls missed Eva's girls. And Theresa missed Joe. It had been raining for a couple of days, which didn't help matters, and we'd already put together every puzzle in the camp. The jigsawed lighthouses and English gardens covered all of the flat surfaces. I'd made cookies and cake, and we'd stuffed ourselves with both. We'd read all the books we'd brought and most of the ones on Gussy and Frank's shelves. The idea of going to look for wild blueberries in the drizzle wasn't very enticing, I knew, but I didn't have much else left up my sleeve.

"Come on." I tried again when greeted with nothing but pouts. "I'll make a pie if we find enough."

We all walked together along the dirt road that circled the lake. The girls put on their galoshes and stomped in the mud puddles. Theresa and I walked together behind them, Theresa dragging her feet like a little girl. All of us like some sort of sad funeral procession.

The old logging road near the boat access area had a chain strung across it, which, of course, made Francesca pause. "I think it's private property," she said.

"Do you see any 'No Trespassing' signs?" I asked, irritated. It was drizzling a bit harder now, and I could feel my hair responding with its willful curls. Usually, I fought them with orange juice cans and bobby pins, taming them out into something resembling a normal head of hair, but since we'd gotten to camp I'd stopped fighting the frizz. Without Eva here, I didn't have anyone to impress.

Chessy shook her head and looked at her feet.

I lifted the chain so that everyone could scurry under, and we walked through the thickening foliage toward the spot where I knew we would find a field of blueberry bushes.

Eva and I had come here last summer.

And so there she was again: ghostly Eva in every drop of rain. The weak spittle had formed into distinct drops now, and the sky was swollen above us. When Eva and I had come, it had been raining too. We'd left the children at the camp, as we were able to do, during Rose's nap. We had given Donna and Francesca instructions for what to do when she awoke. We told them they would each earn a dollar for their efforts as well as points toward their Babysitting badge. We also promised blueberry muffins when we returned. In the middle of this same field of wild blueberries, we had found a soft patch of grass and lay together. We undressed each other under the threatening sky, touched each other gingerly, then eagerly, even when the air rumbled with impatience, with promised violence. And we held each other after, as the rain came, as it pounded down upon us, as it struck us. We had returned to the camp that afternoon, soaking wet and laughing. Holding a red bowl filled with tart blueberries. And we'd made muffins that tasted better than nearly anything I'd tasted in my whole life.

But today, Eva was only the puffs of breath that escaped our mouths. It was cold and wet, and when we finally got to the field, the girls threw up their hands, exasperated.

"They're gone!" Mouse said, running through the bushes, which seemed to have been stripped bare. By bears, I was certain. Not a single berry clung to the stems. The entire patch had been pillaged.

"Oh, shoot," Theresa said, dejected.

Francesca was looking behind us still, probably for the owner of the land and his shotgun.

"It's okay," I said, though it wasn't. This was a mother's job, I thought sometimes. Making things okay when they were not. "We'll make a pie anyway," I insisted. "I think I saw a can of cherries in Gussy's cupboard. You like cherry pie, right, Mouse?"

Mouse scowled at me. She'd grown so much in the last year, she'd nearly outgrown her name. At eight, she was almost as tall as her sister, who was nearly ten now. Her legs had stretched out from pudgy little girl limbs to the long, thin legs of a much older child.

"I promise," I said. Because this is what mothers do. "It'll be delicious."

"But it's not the same," Chessy chimed in, apparently having given up her paranoid fantasies of being arrested for trespassing.

"Nope," I said. "But it will still be fine."

But it was true; none of this was the same. We had been going to the lake since Mouse was a baby. But it was almost as if having Eva and her daughters there had somehow ruined it for us. Eva was in the steam that rose from the ceramic blackbird I put in the cherry pie. In the moonlight that shone on the water that night. In the crackle of the fire we had to build because the rain did not stop, and autumn was letting us know, here in this little corner of northeastern Vermont, that summer wouldn't be around much longer. I'd never been so happy for fall's arrival.

Eva kept every postcard. She showed me the collection later: every silly missive I scratched that summer. It was embarrassing seeing my longing on display like this: the inarticulate musings of someone so desperate and aching. Alone, each postcard was just a jigsaw piece, innocuous and elusive, but together they formed the picture of a woman so in love, of *me,* so in love, even the tips of my hair ached for Eva. I thought this would change as soon as I was able to see her again, able to be with her again, but I was wrong.

The letters Eva had sent back to me were equally fragmented. I imagined her writing them at night after Ted fell asleep, slipping them into the mailbox after he had gone to work. But while my words had been careless, meant only to relay how very much I missed her, Eva's were crafted carefully, cautiously. Her handwriting was whispery, just shivers across the paper, and beyond the words there was something I recognized as fear. I knew she was terrified that Ted might find the letters, because her words just touched the surface. Her sentences skipped like stones across the lake. The depth of those waters never touched. It was too dangerous. I worried about the things the letters didn't say.

We returned to Hollyville the Friday before Labor Day weekend, and as Frankie pulled the Studebaker into the driveway, it took every ounce of my willpower not to throw open the door and go running across the street to her. We had dropped Theresa off in the city, said our good-byes. The girls were sad to see her go, and even I was feeling melancholy. But as the Wilsons' house came into sight, my mood lifted like a rocket, and I could barely contain myself. Neither could the girls.

"Ah, go ahead," Frankie said as I offered to help unload the car. "Go say hello."

Frankie, poor oblivious Frankie, thought I'd only missed my friend: the silly chitchat, the companionship. His stupid trust killed me sometimes, made me feel like a monster.

I should have known something was amiss when I saw that the window boxes were empty. In the summer Eva usually filled them with brightly colored annuals: petunias and pansies and geraniums. In the fall, she replaced them with autumn-colored mums: red and orange and gold. She said that otherwise she'd never be able to endure the endless hours spent in that kitchen; the flowers outside her window were the beauty she needed to make her domestic life endurable.

The girls followed behind me as I crossed the street, giggling and anxious. But while I was eager to see her, I also felt rage bubbling inside of me. If Ted had so much as touched her while we were gone, I didn't know what I would do.

We stepped onto the porch, and I took several deep breaths and straightened my skirt before ringing the doorbell. Donna answered the Wilsons' door and threw herself into Chessy's arms. The two girls clung to each other. Sally was not far behind, and she simply grabbed Mouse's hand and pulled her across the threshold. I could see Johnny in the living room, parked in front of the television, and Rose was strapped into her high chair, eating Cheerios.

"Where's your mama?" I asked, forcing myself to smile when Donna and Chessy finally pulled away from each other.

Donna shrugged. "Upstairs, I think. She's sick."

"Sick?" I said. I thought first of Ted, of what he could possibly have done to her, but a little part of me hoped it was only because of my absence, that maybe she had missed me so much it had made her physically ill: that like some nineteenth-century heroine, she'd taken to bed, waiting for me to come back and revive her.

"May I go upstairs?" I asked Donna.

Donna nodded, and she and Chessy disappeared down the hall. "Hi, Johnny!" I said into the living room, and he nodded and waved without looking away from the TV.

The house was dark and musty. The bit of sun that streamed through the window at the top of the stairs illuminated a thick column of dust. The door to Ted and Eva's bedroom was closed. My throat grew thick with fearful anticipation, with pointed longing, as I knocked gently on the door.

"Billie?" she asked, her voice swimming to me like something shimmering under water, like a minnow.

I opened the door slowly, feeling my muscles pulling my lips into a smile, the joy of finally being able to see her again causing a thousand involuntary responses in my body. She was curled up in an overstuffed chair by the window, in her slip. There were books all over the floor. Her hair was down, longer than it had been when we left. Her skin was pale, and her face, without makeup, was both beautiful and unfamiliar; her eyes somehow darker, her features more fragile.

I closed the door behind me and went to her. She stood up and tucked herself into my arms, like a child, I thought.

"What has he done to you?" I asked, furiously kissing the top of her head, inhaling the scent of her. Breathing her.

She shook her head, no, no. Nothing. Nothing. Thank God. I felt the tension I'd been carrying in my shoulders suddenly release. I pulled her away from me. Her entire body was shaking under my fingertips.

"I'm sick," she said.

"I know, Donna told me. What can I get you? Some tea? Some toast? And why aren't you in bed?" I scolded. But she resisted as I started to steer her toward her unmade bed.

"Billie," she said, firmly. "While you were gone, I found something."

I had no idea what she was talking about. But she was looking at me intently, her eyes fixed on me, on my own eyes.

"The doctor says I need to have my breasts removed. That there's cancer."

I felt like the wind had been knocked out of me. Here it was: the *word,* the single word that had been missing from all of those careful epistles. The sinking stone in that white lake.

"No," I said, shaking my head, as if mere defiance and denial could make this untrue. "You need to get a second opinion."

"I have. I've seen three doctors, and they all say it's the only way. To get rid of the cancer before it can spread."

I sat down on the bed, my body so heavy my legs couldn't support it anymore. But I knew that I couldn't let on that I was terrified, that fear was blooming red, the missing mums blossoming in my chest, in my throat.

"Maybe they're wrong," I said.

She sat down next to me on the bed. She closed her eyes, tears escaping through her closed eyelids. She slipped the strap of her slip down over her shoulder, revealing her right breast. She reached for my hand and pulled it to her flesh. Her skin was hot in my hands, and I wondered if this is what cancer felt like, like a child's feverish cheek. She guided my hand across her breast, searching, and then she stopped and pressed my fingers with hers.

It felt like one of the children's marbles. And for a single, deluded moment, I pictured it, a marbled, amber cat's-eye, somehow lost beneath her skin. Misplaced. That I needed only to pluck it from her, return it to the purple velvet Crown Royal bag where Johnny kept his marble collection.

Our fingers lingered there.

"It's just the one?" I asked softly, trying to call up my rational, logical self. "If it's just the one, then why are they operating on both sides?"

"It can spread," she said. "But if they take both of them, then there is nowhere for it to go. It's preventative, I guess." She lowered her hand, but I left mine there, touching that searing skin.

And then I pulled her in close to me, kissing her, trying so hard to comfort her. To make this okay.

"What does Ted say?" I asked, his name bitter in my mouth.

She shook her head. "He won't talk about it. He doesn't say a word. He's drinking more, of course. One night he called the doctor, the first one I saw, and called him a butcher. Told him he wasn't going to let him mutilate his wife."

I laughed out loud, not because of the humor but because it was so ridiculously ironic. This man, this monster who had struck his own wife, calling a doctor, a healer, a butcher.

She laughed sadly too. And I put my chin on top of her head.

"I'm home," I said. "It's going to be okay."

The surgery was scheduled for a Tuesday morning that September. The older children were in school, and I offered to watch Rose. Ted and Eva drove together, and I could see her watching me in the side view mirror. I should have been going with her. I should have been there with her, not Ted with his silence, with his *violence*.

"Come here, Rosie," I said, scooping her up. She was crying. She only knew that her mother and father were leaving her behind, but she cried as though she knew the reason behind their departure. Her entire body convulsed with her sobbing.

"How would you like to do something really, really special today?" I asked.

She sniffed deeply, loudly, wiping her runny nose with her sleeve.

"Would you like to get your mama some apples?" I asked, and she nodded.

The next town over from Hollyville was Wilmington, where the claim to fame was the Baldwin apple. There was even a monument there on Chestnut Street, a seven-foot-tall granite slab with a perfect, granite Baldwin apple perched at the top. The orchard where we'd taken the Girl Scouts, where we'd stolen apples and been chased down by that fat farmer, had Baldwin apples. They were tart and hard and *hardy,* able to last through the entire harsh winter without spoiling, though they were more difficult to come by now, only a few orchards still growing them. They were winter apples, beautiful red apples that ripened later in the season, their best flavor coming when nothing else was growing, when the rest of the crops were dormant. I'd seen the orchards in winter, the barren, white landscape dotted with the surprising bursts of scarlet.

It was this I tried to think of as I pushed Rosie in her stroller the two miles to the farm stand where I liked to buy my eggs and vegetables. That beauty can exist even in a barren landscape.

The old woman who ran the stand was weathered and grumpy, but she had the best sweet corn in the summer and the best butternut squash in the fall. I perused the bins of gourds and the paper bags of apples, plucking a ripe nectarine from a pile and handing it to Rosie in her stroller. She bit into it, and juice dripped down her chin.

"I need some Baldwins too," I said to the woman. She was perched on a hard wooden stool, counting her money.

"No Baldwins," she said.

"Not ready yet?"

"Not till later in the season. October at the earliest."

"Oh," I said. I should have known this. Last winter Eva had made ten pies for the Girl Scout bake sale, but that had been in December. Right before Christmas. But I couldn't wait until Christmas. I needed something to give her now. Something that would be a bright spot in this dark time. Something sweet.

"I got some nice Macintosh," she said. "Some Paula Reds?" She was clearly getting impatient with me. But I was overwhelmed by disappointment. It was such a simple wish. *Apples.* Just a stupid bag of apples. I knew it was crazy, but the denial of such a small request seemed especially egregious.

We walked all the way back home without anything, and I

wept. I wept openly but soundlessly, Rosie sitting obliviously in the stroller. She finished her nectarine about halfway there, and I tossed the pit into the woods along the side of the road.

Eva was in the hospital for a whole week, but I didn't visit. I couldn't bring myself to see her in a hospital bed; I knew that my grief and worry would overwhelm me at the hospital, and this was not a chance I could take. How could I possibly explain the way the thought of losing her crippled me? How could I justify the collapse of my heart at the mere thought of her leaving? And so instead, I called her every day, and I sent flowers from our garden with Ted. Ted's sister, Mary, arrived again to take care of their children, and I waited for Eva to come home. In that single week, the weather grew cold, the leaves fell from the trees; everything died. It was as though the very earth were mourning Eva's absence along with me.

Finally, Ted pulled up one morning and rushed around to the other side of the car to open the door. Eva emerged and immediately looked over her shoulder, as if she expected me to be there, as I was, watching from my front window. It was Saturday. Everyone was home. And so while the only thing I wanted was to go to her, to hold her, to make sure she was okay, I couldn't.

At around noon, Ted appeared again outside with a rake and started cleaning up the leaves in the front yard. The children were playing outside, destroying every pile he managed to make. Calder played with them, rolling around in all that glorious muck. I took the coffee cake I'd baked, the same coffee cake I'd brought her when she first moved in, and hollered down the basement stairwell to Frankie that I'd be right back.

He was busy restoring an old oak dressing table he'd found discarded outside a house in Cambridge. He planned to give it to Francesca for her tenth birthday. The fumes from the paint thinner were strong, dizzying.

"Where are you going?" he hollered up.

"Over to the Wilsons'," I said. "Eva's home from the hospital."

Frankie and I hadn't talked much about Eva's surgery. When he asked, I'd simply told him it was female troubles, and that had sufficiently silenced him. And if he'd sensed my unease, he didn't let on. That was the good thing about Frankie's projects; they tended to consume him, blinding him to everything else going on around him: that and the stash of wine I knew he helped himself to in the basement while he was working.

The children were also oblivious. The Wilson children had been told that Eva was going to visit her father in Oregon, and so I had told my girls the same. Hannah Flannigan stepped in to help me lead the Girl Scout meetings. I offered Hannah only enough information for her to understand that I would need help while Eva recovered.

"My mother had a complete hysterectomy last year," she had said, nodding her bottle-blond head, hoping, I think, that I might confirm or deny her suspicions that Eva had undergone a similar procedure. Hannah was a terrible gossip. It was from Hannah that I had learned that our school principal was having an affair with his secretary; that the old man from down the street had once worked for the CIA; and that Lisa Miller, one of our Scouts, had a different father from the rest of her siblings. Francesca and Penny, Hannah's eldest daughter, were in the same class, but Francesca steered clear of her.

"Penny's a big fat liar," Francesca said. "She said she's getting a pony for her birthday, and that she's related to Jackie Kennedy."

I tolerated Hannah only because I truly needed her help. With five Brownies and ten Girl Scouts and without Eva, I would have taken any help I could get. I couldn't wait until Eva was well again and I could send Hannah back to where she came from.

I walked across the street to the Wilsons' house, and Ted stopped raking. "How is she?" I asked.

It was brisk out, and his face was red. He was wearing one of those hats that hunters wear, the ones with the earflaps. He didn't have any gloves on, and I noticed that his meaty hands were chapped. "She'll be fine," he said. "You shouldn't stay long though. The doctor says she needs her rest."

Ever since the day we got the flat tire, Ted hadn't been able to look me in the eye. He was always shifty, but now his avoidance of me was pronounced. He must have known that I knew what he'd done to her, that Eva had confided in me. This made me feel both satisfied and terrified. He needed to know that what he had done to her was not a precious little secret Eva would keep for him, but I also feared that he might see my knowledge as a threat and somehow keep me from seeing her, that he could, and *would,* wield his power to keep us apart. Ted was a slippery slope, and I was just trying to keep my footing.

"I brought her some cake," I said stupidly. "Is she up to eating?"

Ted shrugged and started raking again. I took this as my cue to disappear into his house.

Eva was not in her bedroom as I had expected. Instead she was sitting at the kitchen table in her nightgown, smoking a cigarette and looking at a magazine. She lifted her head when I came in, and her face crumpled when she saw me. I went to her, put the coffee cake down, and sat in the seat next to her, grasping her free hand. She snubbed the cigarette out and leaned into me.

The movie magazine was open to a picture of Brigitte Bardot. She laughed, pointing at the picture. "Liam used to say that I reminded him of her," she said. "I always thought it was so silly. Maybe before she was blond, but not now." She looked up at me, up from the photograph. In the picture, Bardot was nearly nude, lying across the empty expanse of a bed, wearing only a sheet.

Eva's nightgown was sheer, and through the bodice, I could see her bandages.

"Does it hurt much?" I asked.

"It hurts," she said, nodding, tears rolling down her cheeks.

"You're still beautiful," I said, trying so hard to make her feel better but feeling useless.

She shook her head violently. "It's not even about the way I look. It's about who I was. I look in the mirror, and I don't know this body. I feel like someone stole something from me."

It was my turn to shake my head, but my denial was futile, because it was true. She was right; it was not her body anymore. She was still beautiful. Still Eva. But it *was* as though they had removed something else, something elemental, with their scalpels.

"But they got the cancer?" I asked, the word like a tumor in my mouth.

She nodded. "They got everything."

But still, at night, I dreamed of losing Eva. I dreamed of all the ways she could be taken from me, all the ways she could be removed from my life. It was as though I knew, through this first whispery brush with possible disaster, that what we had was precarious. When I recollect that fall, all I can remember is the feeling of imminent catastrophe. Even Khrushchev and Kennedy's standoff that October, the threat of nuclear annihilation, felt only like a loud and absurd reminder that everything I had, everything I *loved,* was precious and fragile. That everything I cared about could, like the brilliant leaves outside my window, be blown away if the wind were simply to change direction.

About an hour into the flight to Pittsburgh, my eyes start to blur, losing focus on the words inside my book. Then the plane dips sharply, startling me like one of those dreams where you fall through a crack in the ice or down a steep flight of stairs. I grab for the armrest, forgetting that, because of my neighbor, it isn't there, and I get a handful of his thigh instead. I open my eyes wide, embarrassed.

"What was that?" he asks, too frightened himself to notice my accidental groping.

"I don't know," I say, lifting my hand from his leg and looking out the window as though there might be an answer out in the clouds.

As if on cue, the pilot comes over the loudspeaker. "Sorry about that, folks. We're going to be experiencing some turbulence for the next little bit. Please remain seated with your seat belts securely fastened. I'll turn off the 'Fasten Seat Belt' sign as soon as we've made it through this rough patch."

"Just bumps in the road," I say, trying to reassure myself as much as my neighbor. Still, I feel my heart beating just a bit harder in my chest. I try again to concentrate on the novel in my lap. I've brought two books for the trip, both of them library books stamped with due dates just two weeks from now, as if this somehow guarantees my return: as if the ink numbers demand it.

The first book is by Sam Mason, a local writer who comes into the library once a month or so. Not long after I started volunteering at the library we began chatting, and I learned that he and his family own a cabin at Lake Gormlaith too. He even knows Effie and her husband. We both stood shell-shocked in the nonfiction section when we made this connection. Three thousand miles away from home, and here was someone who knew that lake, loved that lake (my lake!) like I do. After eighty years I've learned not to be surprised by many things, but this genuinely surprised me. It was like some strange serendipity, and we had no choice but to become fast friends after that. I've had dinner at his house dozens of times; his wife, Mena, is a marvelous cook. They live within walking distance of my cottage, and every time I've gone over, she's sent me home with enough leftovers to last me a week. I think there's still a pan of her pastitsio in my freezer.

I actually saw Sam on my last day of work, and I promised him I'd take a little walk around the lake and check on his place while I'm there. The phone I have supposedly takes pictures, so I told him I'd try to get a photograph, though there's no cell reception at the lake as far as I know. I'll have to ask Effie.

I've read three or four of Sam's novels now. He lost his daughter a few years back, and the books he's written since her death are the most achingly beautiful of all of them. It's as though he's channeled all of his sorrow and all of his love into his writing. This is what artists do, I think. I wish sometimes that I had an outlet for all my own sorrows, that I could have transformed my own losses into something like this. Eva would have; she could turn even the sharpest sadness into something beautiful.

I try to lose myself in his words as the entire plane jerks and dips, my heart plummeting with each bump. Hugh's face is the color of milk. He reminds me less and less of Ted as time goes on, and more of Johnny. He's like a big child, this man. Impulsively, I reach for his hand, intentionally this time, and squeeze. The plane shudders violently again, and he squeezes back.

Eva and I could have gone on like this forever, I suppose: the stolen hours, the long walks. I imagine we could have found a certain happiness, a contentment, in this secret life. We could have contained it, kept it small and safe. I'm sure we would not be the first to settle for this kind of love. But right before Christmas that year, Ted finally lost his job, and this set into motion everything that followed. Of course that's only something you can understand in retrospect. At the time, it had seemed a minor inconvenience, a small wrench thrown into the cog of our quiet machine. But now, later, I can see it as the beginning of the downward spiral. It was simply the beginning of the end.

Eva said only that it was his drinking that caused him to get fired, but Frankie was able to glean the details from their driveway conversations. As he and Frankie shoveled after the first snowfall, Ted told him he'd gone to lunch with a potential client, had a few too many lunch-hour martinis, and lost his temper. Ted claimed the man had attacked him first, but I knew how Ted's rage worked. It took little to provoke him, and he was never to blame. Later, as they hung Christmas lights on our respective houses, Ted suggested that there was another agency that had already offered to snatch him up. But Christmas came and went, and Ted's car remained in the driveway each morning. Eva's phone calls were sporadic and hushed. I don't know what Ted did all day, but he almost never left the house; I pictured him standing guard and wondered even if he had somehow planned this.

If not for our nightly walks, Eva and I might never have gotten to see each other. That winter was the harshest winter in my memory, and I had grown up in Vermont, where the wind can feel like the cold blade of a knife, where most people hibernate from December to April, leaving their homes only when absolutely necessary. But each evening, Eva and I continued to meet under the muted glow of the one streetlight on our street, though sometimes even Calder, with her thick golden coat of fur, was reluctant to head out into the bitter cold. Eva told Ted that her doctor had mandated this exercise, to help in her recovery, to maintain her health. What could Ted say to this? I simply told Frankie I needed fresh air.

On the nights when Calder refused to put her paws beyond the front door, Eva and I would walk anyway, sometimes all the way into the village to get a cup of coffee or, on the weekends, see a movie. Even though Eva was young and healthy, the recovery process was a gradual one. She did not complain, but I could see the pain in her tiny winces and the occasional shudder. And so we walked slowly, me holding her elbow like an elderly woman's so that she wouldn't slip on the icy pavement. I let myself imagine sometimes growing old with her, knowing that this is how it would be. By the time we had trudged through the snow all the way into town, our feet and faces were numb, and the warmth of the theater was a welcome reprieve, the opportunity to sit down a welcome one. We also discovered that we were often alone in the dark theater, other people in town opting to stay out of the storms, which seemed to come one after another, creating the cumulative effect of an endless barrage of snow. That winter we hunkered down and watched whatever was showing: *Lawrence of Arabia* and *To Kill a Mockingbird* and *How the West Was Won*. In the uncomfortable seats, we held hands underneath the jackets on our laps. I got fat on buttered popcorn and candy. Eva also began to regain some semblance of her former self.

Because of Ted's unemployment, I knew Eva was worried about money, and so I always offered to pay. The weekly allowance Frankie gave me for groceries and other household expenses went a long way when I started to more carefully shop the sales and clip coupons. I gave up certain luxuries (the expensive shampoo I liked, the better cuts of meat at DeMoulas) in exchange for the extravagance of two hours alone in the dark with Eva, even if it meant suffering through *The Birds,* which terrified us both. Sometimes, we'd see the same movie two or three times. We could almost recite every line from *Bye-Bye Birdie.* And inside the dark theater Eva slowly healed, though it wasn't until spring that I saw her scars.

In May, Ted finally got a job interview at another insurance agency. After the kids left for school and Ted and Frankie took off that morning, I had to keep myself from running across the street. It was the first time Ted had left the house in months. Early on, he'd optimistically sent his resume off to dozens of companies, but to no avail. For the last couple of months he had spent his days drinking and listening to old records, passing out soon after dinner. This was how Eva had managed to escape for our movie dates.

I let myself into Eva's house, and Calder met me in the foyer, leaping with excitement. "I'm happy to see you too, Calder!" I exclaimed, as she stood up, her big paws pushing at my shoulders. She wasn't a puppy anymore; she had to have weighed nearly seventy pounds now. "Where's Eva?" I asked her.

She dropped back down to all fours, her ears perked up, and she looked around, confused, jerking her head around as though she were looking for her.

"That's okay, girl, I can find her. Eva?" I hollered up the stairs.

I could hear the shower running, and I took the stairs two at a time. I peeked into Rose's room and saw that she was asleep in her crib. I stood outside the bathroom door and knocked gently.

"Teddy? What are you doing back?" she said.

"It's me," I said, gently pushing the door open.

The room was steamy and smelled of her. I breathed her in, let her fill my lungs. I opened the shower door, and it took my breath away. Her back was to me; I studied the familiar curve of her waist and hips. The endless expanse of her legs. The two dimples on either side of her spine. She was so beautiful, I felt my entire body tremble and my heart fly to my throat. She turned toward me, her arms covering her chest.

I shook my head. "You don't have to hide."

She slowly, tentatively, lowered her arms, and I felt tears welling up hotly in my eyes. I blinked them away. It was so disconcerting: this obliteration, this elimination. I felt the way I had as a child when my father's farmhand, Link, lost his arm in a thresher. My mother had taken us to see him when he came home from the hospital, and I couldn't seem to make what I was seeing and what should have been coalesce: that spectral limb somehow more present in its absence. I knew I needed to touch her, to make this real for myself: to make *her* real.

She stepped out of the shower, dripping water on the linoleum. She stood before me, her skin still hot from the shower as I touched her, gingerly, tenderly, tracing the scars that ran like violent red rivers across her pale skin. We didn't speak. We didn't have to. I knew that I was the first, the only, person to have touched her like this since the surgery.

It was several more months before we were alone in this way again. But I dreamed those scars nearly every night, the shimmery red rivers on her flesh.

Ted did not get that job, or the next three he interviewed for either, and so while the winter of 1962 was harsh and long, the days of spring and early summer of 1963 passed by even more slowly, dripping like sap from a maple tree into a cold bucket. Calder started coming with us on our walks again, and so we stopped going to the movies. I couldn't wait for August, but August seemed far away, distant and unreachable. August teased us with its possibilities, its promise of freedom. Of being alone together at the lake again.

In the hazy, early summer evenings, our two families sat outside watching the children chase fireflies: Ted and Frankie drinking too much, and Eva and I always dreading the possible aftermath of these binges. Ted was a live grenade since he'd lost his job, always on the verge of explosion. And you never knew what would ignite his fuse. What little spark. I was afraid of Ted, and worried for Eva. Still, Ted and Frankie enjoyed each other's companionship, making these weekend get-togethers possible, and I would have tolerated just about anything if it meant getting to spend time with Eva. Even Ted.

On the Fourth of July, we had the Wilsons over for a barbeque. Our plan was to head into town for the fireworks after the sun went down. That summer Frankie had found a Ping-Pong table in a Dumpster and brought it home. I told him he was not allowed to put it up in the basement. There would be no room for the Girl Scouts if he did, no place for the girls to play. And so he'd reluctantly set it up in the backyard, covering it with an old tarp when it rained. Ping-Pong was not my game, but Eva was a stellar player, a match even to Frankie, whose Ping-Pong skills were remarkable.

"It's all reflexes," he said, grinning. "And I've got great reflexes."

And so Ted and I sat watching them compete.

Frankie and Ted had been drinking all afternoon, and so had Eva. I noticed that she did this sometimes when Ted was drinking. Perhaps it bolstered her, made her less afraid of him and his tirades. I watched her confidence and bravado grow with each sloe gin fizz, her need to appease him slipping away.

Before she served, she took a long sip and set her glass down. "Ready to lose?" she said to Frankie, playfully, winking.

Ted stiffened next to me. His anger was a palpable thing. It filled his body, but it also filled the air around him. It buzzed like the cicadas that had come that summer. It was electric.

"I'm ready to beat the pants off of you," Frankie joked back.

"But I'm not wearing pants, Frankie!" Eva said, swiveling her hips, her pencil skirt hugging the curves she had been able to keep.

Eva had prosthetic breasts, pads that she inserted into her bras. With clothes on, she looked exactly the way she had before the surgery. The illusion was perfect.

As she leaned forward to grab her paddle, kicking one leg up behind her, Ted stood up. "Time to go home," he said, grabbing her arm.

She turned to him, scowling. "But the sun hasn't even gone down, Teddy," she said. "What about the fireworks?"

"I said, it's time to go home." Ted's words were mushy in his mouth: oatmeal, soggy grits.

"Well, I'm busy playing a game right now," Eva said, tottering a little on her heels as she pulled away from him. She picked up the paddle and tossed the ball into the air. But Frankie wasn't watching the ball. He was watching Ted.

Ted yanked her arm back, and the ball bounced off the table and landed in the grass.

"Ow," she said, jerking away from him again, and I stood up, feeling my own sloe gin fizzes in my knees. I felt weak, dizzy, and sick.

"Stop," I said, my voice softer than I meant for it to be.

But he didn't stop. Instead he grabbed her shoulders, and as she twisted away from him, he held on. Her bra strap slipped in the struggle, and her breast, that fake breast, shifted. When she stepped back away from him, she looked deformed. Wrong.

I felt my whole body grow hot in shame. In anger. But as I was about to hurl my body at him, to start pounding my fists into that enormous chest of his, Frankie stood up.

"It's time for you to go home, Ted," he said.

"What's that, Mailman? You think I'm going to leave my wife here with *you?*"

Frankie's chest expanded. He was trying to be taller, bigger, stronger. That too filled me with white-hot shame. And then Frankie was pushing his hands against Ted's chest. "At least I've *got* a job."

"Don't, Frankie," I said, reaching for him.

"Stay out of this, Billie," Frankie warned.

The children came running around the side yard just then; they had been playing "house" out front. Rose was nearly three now, and she led the way.

The children. My first instinct was to get the children away from this. I rushed to the back porch and ushered them all through the back door and into the house. "Let's make those root beer floats I promised," I said. "Who wants a float?" Distracted, they all squealed, "Me! I do! I want one!"

"Why is Daddy pushing Mr. Wilson?" Francesca asked once we were inside the kitchen.

"They're just playing around," I said, and Chessy scowled. "Just come on," I said, handing her a corked bottle of Frankie's homemade root beer. "I need you to help me." Obediently, she nodded and grabbed the tub of vanilla ice cream from the icebox and went to the kitchen table.

From the kitchen window, I couldn't see what was happening outside. It was horrific listening to the muffled sounds, unable to make out what was going on. I could hear Ted bellowing and Frankie trying to match that voluminous voice with his own, but what really bothered me was Eva's silence. Strain as I might, I couldn't hear her at all.

Not long after I'd scooped ice cream into six tumblers and poured root beer over each one, Ted barged through the back door and said, "It's time to go home."

The children seemed to know better than to protest, and they silently gathered their things, leaving their ice cream melting in their cups.

"Where's Eva?" I managed to squeak out.

Ted either didn't hear me or chose not to acknowledge me. He ushered the kids out into our foyer toward the front door. I was staring at the back of his head.

"Ted," I said again, louder this time. "Where is Eva?"

Ted turned on his heel and growled at me. "She's not feeling well. She's gone home to get some rest."

Frankie had come in through the back door, and he was sweating. He kept slicking his hair back nervously with one hand. I knew this meant something terrible had happened outside. Something awful that he had not managed to stop.

As Ted and the children disappeared out the front door, I said to my girls, "Why don't you take your floats upstairs?"

"We aren't allowed to take food or drinks upstairs," Chessy argued.

"I said *go*."

They slipped up the stairs, and I watched as their feet disappeared through the railings. Frankie was sitting down at the table, head in his hand.

"What happened?" I said, sitting down next to him. "What was that all about?"

Frankie shook his head. "He's crazy," he said. "A worthless drunk."

"Did he hit you?" I asked, peering at Frankie's long, sad face. It didn't look as though Ted had touched him.

"Nah," he said. "But he's awful rough with that woman. A man shouldn't touch a woman like that."

I bristled. "What is he so angry about?" I asked, trying not to think about what might happen after Ted got Eva back inside their house.

Frankie laughed. "I think he thinks Eva was flirting with me."

I almost laughed too, but the laughter bubbled up in my throat and then caught short, making me lose my breath. "That's ridiculous," I said.

"I know," Frankie said. "As if she's flirting with *anyone* anymore."

My eyes widened. Frankie knew about the surgery apparently. Ted must have given him the details. And I was suddenly so filled with disgust. So angry at him, at Ted, at the world, I thought I might burst into flames.

"I'm going over there," I said. "He's going to hurt her. I need to get Eva the hell out of that house."

"You're not going anywhere," Frankie said, pounding his fist against the table, and I realized that he was just as drunk as Ted was. Not as violent maybe, not as crazy, but just as goddamned drunk. "You realize this is your fault, don't you?" he hissed.

I caught my breath and held it, waiting for the accusation. Waiting for him to say that he knew what had been going on between me and Eva, that he *knew*. I dreamed myself admitting for the first time to anyone other than myself that I was in love with Eva. That whatever the world thought, whatever my husband thought, that I wanted only one thing in the world, and that was Eva.

"If you'd just keep your mouths shut, if you girls just did as we say, then none of this would have to happen. Everyone would be happy. Everything would be fine and dandy. It used to be a woman respected her husband."

He didn't know. He wasn't talking about me and Eva. He was, as always, oblivious. And for a moment, I was actually disappointed that it hadn't finally come out into the open, that my secret was still safe, still imprisoned inside me as I was inside this house and as Eva was inside her own.

"Go to bed, Frankie," I said, sitting down, shaking my head sadly. "You've got to work in the morning."

Frankie grumbled and finished off the last swig of wine in his cup before lumbering up the stairs. After I heard the creak of the bed frame accepting his weight, I quietly went upstairs and told the girls to get on their pajamas, to brush their teeth, to get in bed.

"What about the fireworks?" Mouse asked.

"Next year," I said. "I promise. And maybe we can shoot off some of our own when we get to camp."

Vermont. It was only a month away, but it felt as far away as someone else's dream. Untouchable and private.

On my way back down the stairs, I peeked into our bedroom to confirm that Frankie had, indeed, passed out and then made my way to the front door. I sat on the porch in the porch swing, but I was too afraid to make it move, not wanting to cause any disturbance in the odd peace that had descended on the neighborhood. It was a deceptive peace though; this I knew. Because faintly, faintly, I could hear the sounds of explosions: the crackle and hiss of fireworks in the high school's football field, followed by the *oohs* and *aahs* of the crowd and behind the Wilsons' closed door, Ted's fuse hissing and curling. The loud crack of his detonation and the soft sounds of Eva, crying. Of Donna and Sally and Rose, and even little Johnny, awestruck at the display.

When the plane starts its slow descent into Pittsburgh, I realize that Hugh and I will be parting ways in just a few minutes. I think about him heading off to meet his Internet girlfriend in Hoboken. I picture her waiting for him at baggage claim, her expectancy and hope matching his as they meet for the first time. Will she be disappointed? Will he? His face is so full of boyish optimism, I could cry. At what point does this go away? This belief that the world is a good place, that love is yours for the asking? The taking?

When I met Lou, I had already lost this optimism; after Eva, I believed that love (real love) was a dangerous thing, and I wanted nothing to do with it again. But Lou was tenacious. Persistent and patient. And finally, she convinced me that love could be a quiet, easy thing. Ours was a predictable kind of love. A safe love. She was my friend first, and everything else was an afterthought. We were never secretive about our relationship, but people still assumed we were simply companions. There was never fire between us, only slow-glowing embers keeping the hearth of our home warm. I know this decision to see Johnny would pain her. It would have confirmed that even after all these years, after a lifetime, Eva still possessed me. Obsessed me. That I'd never ever truly let go.

My ears ache and my stomach plummets as the plane tilts toward the earth. I hate this part. I long for distraction.

"Chewing gum?" I ask Hugh, holding out the pack I bought at the airport.

He shakes his head.

"I hope I have time to get a bite before my next flight," he says nervously. "I'm starving. I thought they were supposed to give you snacks."

"I think that's what these are." I gesture to the packet of peanuts on my tray.

A flight attendant leans over and says, "Can you please raise your tray? We're going to be landing soon."

"Would you like my peanuts?" I ask, offering him the little foil packet and putting the plastic tray back up. I hand the flight attendant my empty plastic cup and napkin.

"Thanks," he says, and tears into them with his teeth, emptying the packet directly into his mouth with one shake.

"What's her name?" I ask him as the wheels lower loudly from the belly of the plane and we hurl, finally, toward the earth. His face is ghostly and pale; I am trying hard to distract him. Trying to distract myself.

"Who?" he asks, not looking at me, staring instead down the corridor between the seats. I can tell he's trying to see if he is the only one panicking.

"Your girl," I say, smiling and reaching for his hand.

He turns to me again at this, and color suddenly returns to his face. "Marcy," he says, smiling.

Marcy, I think. The name conjures bright blue eyes and a ponytail. A fresh-faced girl in blue jeans. Pink cheeks. I imagine she's a little pudgy. Young.

"Marcy," I say, repeating her name. I know the power of incantation to soothe. I understand the magical potency of a name. I realize that sometimes, the only thing in the world that can save the day is the recitation and repetition.

"Marcy." He nods.

Shamelessly, we hold hands as the plane touches the ground, keeps rushing forward, and finally comes to a stop at the gate. Outside the sky is a breathless blue.

"Welcome to Pittsburgh," the captain says over the loudspeaker.

"Certainly was a pleasure meeting you," Hugh says, releasing my hand, suddenly seeming a little embarrassed.

"Good luck," I say.

"You too," he says, and stands up, with a great amount of difficulty, from his seat, struggling to get his bag from the overhead bin. His sweatshirt rises, revealing the flaccid pouch of his belly. It makes me feel embarrassed for him, as though I've seen him naked. He is so vulnerable. I worry for him.

"Y'all have a nice time with your sister," he says when he finally wrestles the bag free. There are peanut crumbs all over the seat.

I nod and smile.

And then he is gone in the crowd of people, rushing toward his future, while I am falling backward, into my past.

After the Fourth of July debacle, I fully expected that Ted would forbid Eva to come to Vermont as planned. I expected that she would come to me and tell me that she would have to stay behind again this year. I mourned her loss again and imagined another stay in Vermont haunted by what should have been. But he must have felt badly about that night. He must have realized the next day when he saw the evidence of his drunken anger written all over her skin that he was in no position to deny her any happiness she might request.

I didn't see her for three days. For three whole days she didn't answer the telephone, and when I went to their front door, one of the children (usually Donna) would apologize and say that her mother wasn't feeling well and had asked not to see any visitors. At first, I feared that Ted himself had made the leap in logic that I'd wrongly suspected with Frankie. That somehow his jealous rage had turned from Frankie toward me. I lived in fear that Ted was somehow smarter than Frankie, that he had finally put two and two together. But by the third day, when Ted waved sheepishly at me as I worked in the flower bed in our front yard, those fears were dispelled.

He was dressed in a suit, wearing a hat. "Interview!" he hollered at me.

"What's that?" I asked.

"A second interview," he hollered again. Ridiculously. "At Prudential! I think they're going to offer me the job!"

"Oh," I said. I didn't know what else to say to him.

He nodded at me, and his was the face of a man filled with regret, with shame. I'd never seen him look even one bit repentant before, but his head hung low that morning, and I knew I had to see her again. It wasn't Ted keeping me away from Eva, but Eva herself.

Donna answered the door, and I said, "Hi, sweetheart, listen, I have something very important I need to talk to your mom about. It's about the cookie sales this year." I knew Girl Scout business was something that Donna could not argue against. And there was no refuting the imperative nature of the annual cookie sale, and so, despite whatever Eva had instructed her to do, she reluctantly motioned for me to go upstairs.

Eva was in her room, sitting in the window seat, reading. When she turned toward me, I was startled by what I saw. Her face looked distorted, half of it bruised, soft like rotten fruit, the skin discolored and swollen. She raised her shoulders in a shrug, as if to ask how this could have happened. As if *I* had any sort of explanation for this.

"Oh, my God, Eva," I said, dropping to my knees at her feet and resting my head in her lap. "What has he done to you?"

But I didn't really want to hear. I didn't want to envision what had transpired between them that had resulted in this. Because imagining it would somehow make this violence, this cruelty part of this world, part of reality. And I wasn't sure I could live in a world where something like this was possible.

"Ted thinks they're going to offer him the job," she said. "This is his second interview. Of course, it means a pay cut, but work is work."

"We need to leave," I said, the words ones I hadn't dared say out loud since New York. "We'll take the children and go somewhere. We'll start over."

I expected when I looked up at her that she would be smiling sadly, shaking her head at me, that she would continue rambling on about Ted's possible new job, but instead she was nodding. Her eyes were closed, dreaming our escape.

★ ★ ★

Ted did get that job, and he started the very next day. But instead of carpooling into the city with Frankie, he took the Caddie, ensuring that Eva remained trapped inside that house, quite literally immobile. And every single day, for the rest of the month, Ted arrived home at exactly five thirty, bearing an armload of flowers. The flowers were dying all over that room. Eva refused to touch them, to smell them, to look at them, or, when they died, to throw their stinking corpses away. The room smelled like fermentation, like rot.

I was so worried about leaving her for Vermont. The idea of even a couple of weeks away from her was unendurable, but Eva had promised that she and the kids would arrive in two weeks, that Ted had no choice now but to let her go; after what he had done, there was almost nothing, save her freedom, that he could deny her.

Ted and Frankie appeared to have patched up whatever tears that night had made in the fabric of their friendship as well. I suppose Ted had to have realized, probably in the hazy achy afterglow of his hangover the next morning, that he'd been insane to think that Eva was flirting with Frankie. For one thing, Frankie was fiercely loyal. Anyone who knew him for five minutes knew this. He was stubbornly faithful to his family, his friends. And he and Ted were, for all intents and purposes, *friends*. And lucky for Ted, Frankie was a forgiving man (with other men anyway). He wasn't one to hold a grudge. "Water under the bridge," he claimed. So much water. So many bridges.

Those two weeks waiting for Eva at the lake passed so slowly. I felt as though we were swimming through molasses, each day like a thousand days. Mosquitoes, grass stains, the lake. All of it was like some sort of photograph, the moment frozen, unmoving.

The girls were so independent now; they barely needed me for anything anymore. I could have spent the entire day in my nightclothes if I'd wanted. I could have stayed in bed. Chessy loved to cook, and her greatest pleasure was getting up early and making breakfast for herself and her sister. By the time I came down from the sleeping loft, my coffee would be percolating, and the kitchen would smell like vanilla and cinnamon. Something about watching her move around the kitchen like this made me terribly sad though, as if the only thing I'd managed to teach her were these domesticities, about how to reside within the four walls of a kitchen. Her happiness killed me a little bit, but what could I do? What could I say that wouldn't destroy her?

Mouse, on the other hand, couldn't wait to get outside, to get into the lake, into the woods, into trouble. At nine, she was still just a little girl, a wild little girl who didn't know how to use a spatula or an egg timer. She knew only the feeling of sun on her shoulders and the cold shock of the lake at dawn. I clung to Mouse's innocence, her beautiful refusal to fit into the world of adults. I watched her from the grassy shore of the lake and wished she could be like this forever. That it wasn't too late to save her.

I slept. To pass the time, I lay down on the daybed on the sleeping porch each afternoon after lunch and slept the hours away. Like a child waiting for Santa Claus on Christmas Eve, I relied on sleep to bring the morning faster. And I read, slipping into the worlds offered by my books and lingering there. Gussy brought me armloads from the library in Quimby and I devoured them. I couldn't get enough; I was so hungry for escape. But still, time limped.

My fuse was short and burning those last few days. Gussy came once during the final days before Eva's arrival, and found me in the kitchen yelling at the girls. I hated my own impatience with them; I hated my temper, but it was as though I had no control over my frustration. I felt more like Frankie than myself: snapping at them over the smallest things. This morning it was over a neglected syrup spill that had run off the table and onto the seat in the breakfast nook, into which I had sat. We had to wash all of our clothes by hand at camp, and hang them to dry on the clotheslines that were stretched between several trees in the backyard. I was down to my very last pair of clean shorts, and it was raining, making clean, dry clothes impossible.

Gussy pulled her car up onto the grass just as I was shooing the girls outside, despite the drizzle, cursing my sticky bottom and scrubbing at the gooey mess on my behind. The girls ran to her, clung to her, and I felt the way Frankie must sometimes feel when the girls ran to me, seeking solace from him in my arms. It felt awful to be on this end of things.

One thing I admired about Eva was her ability, despite the chaos of four children, to never lose her patience. I'd watch her clean up broken plates, wipe up spill after spill, placidly sit and somehow manage an adult conversation as Rose crawled all over her lap, tugging at her sleeves, and Johnny wreaked his usual havoc in the other room. She was a good mother, a *natural* mother. When I felt myself igniting, that crack and sizzle after something lit me on fire, I tried to think of what Eva would do. But I could never, ever seem to find the calm reserves she had: the patience. It was her best attribute with her children, though her worst when it came to Ted.

Seeing Gussy struggling with something in the trunk of the car, I gave up on the syrup, opened up the screen door, and rushed outside to help her. "Go *play!*" I said, again, to Chessy and Mouse, who were now under Gussy's feet instead of my own.

I looked at her and rolled my eyes, threw up my hands in surrender to another lost battle in this endless war of motherhood. Gussy had two daughters, Nancy and Debbie, as well, but they were older than my own. I wished sometimes that we had started our families at the same time. She always seemed to be the first to experience things in life, making her always older, always wiser than I. But I didn't want a mentor; I wanted a friend to share the experience with. I suppose this was one thing that drew me so strongly to Eva. I never felt Eva judging me, never felt her condescension. She never shook her head knowingly at me or comforted me that the kids would "grow out of it."

"Take these?" Gussy said, handing me a box overflowing with curtains I recognized from her house: red gingham ones that made me think of picnics. "I thought we could replace those tired ones in the kitchen."

I took the box, which was heavier than I expected.

"Oh, I brought some of Mom's cookbooks too. You must be sick to death of cooking the same old things every night."

There had been no cookbooks at camp: just a couple of Gussy's recipes for macaroni salad and hamburger pie handwritten on index cards and stuck with push pins into the insides of the cupboards. I used the lack of a cookbook as an excuse not to cook, making sandwiches most nights, burgers and hot dogs and grilled cheese on others. When Eva had been here before, she'd taken over the kitchen, and I had been grateful for the real food that she somehow managed to coax from thin air.

"Come in," I said. "Sorry, it's a bit of a mess. One of the girls spilled syrup all over the table."

It was always a little strange staying at camp. Gussy and Frank owned the cabin but acted like guests when they came to visit. And while I should have appreciated their efforts, I couldn't help but feel a little irritated. The idea of knocking on your own door seemed ridiculous to me, but still she knocked. This was my retreat, but it *belonged* to them. And somehow instead of feeling as though my privacy was being respected, I felt like she was calling even more attention to the fact that the camp was not mine, that it was simply on loan. Even after all these years, I always felt a little snag of irritation each time Gussy asked permission to use her own bathroom.

"I can get that," Gussy said. "Just use a little vinegar. Here, like this," she said, opening up the cupboard and grabbing a bottle of white vinegar from inside. And once again, I was the inexperienced little sister at the mercy of her much wiser, older sibling.

I sat down in the kitchen nook, exasperated, and relinquished any sense of equality I had had. The playing field had never been level between us. She would always know more, have more, be better at most things than I was.

"When do the Wilsons get here?" she asked, finishing and sitting down across from me in the nook.

"On Saturday. Frankie's bringing them up with him when he comes to visit."

The last time Eva was there, Gussy had given us even more room than normal, only coming once to visit, at my invitation. She and Eva had gotten along so well, I'd even felt a little bristle of that childhood jealousy. My friends had always looked up to Gussy, loved when she paid them any attention.

"She was sick," I said, not wanting to gossip, but also knowing that Gussy would notice. Gussy was nothing if not attentive. That's what people loved about her, what, in fact, I loved about her. She paid attention to people. She noticed the little things. She listened when you talked to her.

"With what?" she asked.

"Cancer," I said. "In her breast. She had both of them removed."

"Oh, goodness," Gussy said. "How terrible. Is she okay now?"

My mind flashed on the image of her sitting in her window, her ravaged face, the pulpy cheek that had endured Ted's wrath. I nodded, but Gussy eyed me suspiciously. She always knew when something was wrong; there was no keeping secrets from Gussy.

"Her husband drinks," I said.

"*Your* husband drinks," she said, laughing, and then as though in apology, "That's what husbands do. Even Frank drinks." This was true. Her Frank had a single highball every night after dinner. One cocktail. I'd never seen his eyes grow glassy, his voice deepen and bellow with drink. I'd never seen his knees falter. His hands shake.

I sighed. "It will be good for her to have some time away from him. I don't think she's had time to truly heal yet."

Gussy nodded and reached for my hand. "I am so glad you

have such a good friend. She's lovely. And she's lucky to have you so close."

Close. I thought about how far away I'd felt from Eva all summer. First with her sequestered in the house, and then later hiding from me. Ashamed of what her husband had done to her.

Gussy and I hung the curtains that afternoon, and I felt a small ray of optimism as the sun struggled through the ominous clouds. As the rain cleared.

"We should get these clothes out to dry while there's still sun," she said, noting the tub of wet clothes on the floor in the bathroom.

As we clipped the clothes to the clothesline, the leaves casting shadows across our faces and hands, the air smelling clean, I even felt my frustration with the children dissipating. And for one moment as we stood on opposite sides of a sheet, Gussy only a silhouette behind the fabric, I thought about telling her. About just opening up, letting the clouds of my secret part and sharing that brilliant and dangerous sun with her. But I couldn't bring myself to do it. I trusted my sister. I loved her. But I was also afraid of the advice she would give. I didn't want her to tell me that what I wanted, what I loved didn't belong to me. And never could.

The next three days waiting for Eva actually passed fairly quickly. We spent one day visiting my mother and father. While it wasn't how I would normally have chosen to spend my time, it occupied me. And the girls loved the farm: the animals and the wide open spaces to run. My mother's bitterness toward me used to sting but had grown into a dull ache. We endured each other for the children. We drank tea, and she showed me things she planned to order from the Montgomery Ward catalogue. And my father worked.

Back at the lake, I busied myself with getting the camp ready for Eva and the kids: sweeping the floors and changing the sheets on the beds. The children and I went on nature walks, collecting twigs and leaves and flowers, which we strung together and hung from the ceiling over my bed. At the end of the last day, I lay on my back, staring up at the mobile, which spun lazily in the breeze coming through the open window.

Ted's new job didn't allow him even a moment away; he was working weekends as well as during the week that summer. And so he had no choice but to allow Frankie to drive Eva and the kids up to Vermont. Frankie would stay with us only the first night, and then he would go back to the city, leaving us alone. My whole body buzzed with happy anticipation, but it was also agonizing, this thrilling, trilling feeling in my body.

All morning I paced as the girls readied the camp for their visitors as well. Mouse gathered a bouquet of wildflowers (mostly Queen Anne's lace and purple puffs of joe-pye weed) which we put in a jelly jar on the kitchen table. Chessy drew her father a WELCOME TO CAMP! sign, which we thumbtacked to one of the exposed beams in the living room.

I, on the other hand, tried to put Frankie out of my mind. Lately Frankie had seemed little more to me than an obstacle to Eva. When I stopped long enough to consider this, I was overwhelmed by guilt. But I was also quickly able to rationalize my behavior, thinking only of the drinking, the anger, the treatment I had endured for the last fourteen years. I was not some broken-down bureau that Frankie could restore. I wasn't some neglected, abandoned highboy he could rescue and then shove in a corner to look pretty. I was a woman with an intellect, with dreams, and with real desires, wants that were bigger than Frankie. Bigger than this life. He'd never once acknowledged that. He'd never once, in all the years I'd known him, considered that maybe there was more to me than what met the eye. The more I thought about it, the angrier I became, the more frustrated and intent upon pursuing all of the passions that did not include him. With good conscience. With Eva.

But, of course, following these liberating revelations was always the hard, cold hammer of reality. I was a thirty-three-year-old woman with two children, no education, and no real skills, unless you counted my pathetic forty-word-per-minute typing skills or my breaststroke. The house was in Frankie's name; the car was in Frankie's name. Even our bank account was not my own. I bristled at the thought of Frankie doling out my weekly allowance, making all of the decisions regarding purchases I made. And Eva was no better off than I, and with more children. The fantasy of running off together was just that: a fragile, fantastical mobile. We were tethered to this world, to our lives, by our husbands' strings. Flight was an illusion.

"They're here! They're here!" cried Mouse, scrambling out of the kitchen nook, where she had been worrying the flower arrangement. She was wearing blue jeans rolled up and two different-colored socks. I had learned long ago that a battle over clothing with Mouse was not one I wanted to wage. Chessy, on the other hand, had put on a clean jumper and had even polished her Buster Browns with an old sock and some shoe polish she found in one of Gussy's drawers that morning. She came bounding from the living room, dropping the book she'd been reading on the table next to me as she made her way to the back door. I pressed my palms flat against the Formica to steady myself.

Frankie was nothing if not a gentleman (during waking hours anyway, especially with other women), and he hurried out and around the car to open Eva's door: gallantly, I thought, as if he'd only been hired to deliver her to me.

Donna and Sally rushed out of the car and off into the woods with my girls, and Johnny whooping behind them, his cowboy costume replaced by an Indian headdress he'd gotten for his eighth birthday. Rose was still in the backseat, and I went to her first, afraid that if I went to Eva I would embrace her and not be able to let go.

"Rosie Posey!" I said, looking in at Rose, whose cheeks were flushed pink.

"Billie!" Rose cried, leaping into my arms. The Wilson children had stopped calling me Mrs. Valentine long ago. She buried her hot cheeks against my chest, and I breathed the baby shampoo smell of her hair.

I stood up and Eva came to me, hugging me, with Rose still in my arms, and for a brief moment, I had the feeling that *this* was my family. It was as though I had slipped into some other dimension. *The Twilight Zone.*

We pulled apart quickly, carefully, and I went to Frankie, who had his arms wide open and waiting for me. I could smell beer on his breath when he kissed me, and I glanced toward the open door of the car, and sure enough, there were three empty cans on the driver's side floor.

"I've missed you, Billie," he said. "The house sure has been empty without you."

I tried sometimes to imagine Frankie alone in that house. When I dreamed myself away from him, I couldn't help but picture what we would leave behind. What would Frankie's days be like without us? Would they be much different? I imagined him making his big breakfasts alone, sitting at the kitchen table and being able to read the newspaper without the children crawling over him, without me jabbering away in his ear. He would go off to work, as he always went off to work, and he would bring his junkyard, Dumpster treasures home without having my disapproval greeting him. He would settle in at night with his bottle of wine and his pork rinds, his *McHale's Navy* on the TV. No one would turn away from him in his bed. No one would feign sleep instead of making love to him. Would his life really be worse without me? I was starting to think that we might be doing him a big favor. And Frankie was still young. Surely, he'd find a new girl: maybe a customer who came into the post office looking for an Eleanor Roosevelt stamp. Maybe he could find another project, another fixer-upper, someone more willing to be renovated.

I had made a pan of lasagna earlier in the day; it had been more of an effort to kill time, to busy my hands, than it had been to please Frankie. But nevertheless, it was Frankie's favorite. He had given me his mother's recipe when we were first married, and I had never deviated. As it heated up in the oven, he took the kids to the beach to swim, and Eva and I stayed behind to prepare the rest of supper, though there was little to do besides toss together a salad. And so we held each other. The feeling of her in my arms never ceased to ease my mind, my worries turning soft and malleable. It was easy to hope when she was holding me.

"Let me get you some tea or something?" I asked.

"Do you have a beer?"

Normally, Eva didn't drink before nightfall, but this was vacation. I wasn't going to make a stink about it. She had been stuck in the car with Frankie and the kids all day, after all.

"Let's go sit out on the lawn," she said.

Inside the safety of the camp, we could touch each other. We were free here, if only until the kids came back from swimming. I had no idea why she would want to relinquish this delicious freedom. My heart panged in my chest like a spoon in an empty stainless steel bowl.

"Okay," I said, reaching for her hand, needing assurance that everything was okay. That nothing had changed while she was away. That she hadn't changed her mind about us. I could feel myself perspiring, sweat rolling down my sides. "It is awfully hot in here."

She smiled at me sadly, squeezed and then released my hand, and it felt as though the metal bowl had fallen to the floor. I could hear its clanging echo with every step as I followed her out the door to the yard.

I had already arranged our two chairs in the same spot on the lawn where we had sat together two years before. I had fussed over re-creating just about everything from that summer, which felt far away now.

She sat down in one chair, shielding her eyes from the sun and peering across the road and toward the lake where I could hear the sound of our children playing.

"You look good," I said, for lack of anything better to say. "Healthy." I nodded, wanting it to be true.

She studied my face, as if gauging my ability to handle what she was about to say. And then it came to me, in one horrific, clanging crash. *Cancer.* She was going to tell me they had found more cancer. I could feel my throat swelling in anticipation of the news. My whole body was trembling despite the oppressive heat. I reached for her arm.

"I'm pregnant," Eva said softly, looking down at her hands.

"What?"

She nodded, tears slipping down her cheeks; she quickly whisked them away with the back of her hand and then jutted her chin forward.

"No," I said, shaking my head.

If Eva was pregnant, that meant that she and Ted had made love. That despite the scars and Ted's aversion to them, despite his disgust, they had been intimate. That something in her had healed enough to let him inside her life again, inside her body again.

I shook my head, looked out at the lake so that I wouldn't have to look at her. "When," I said, the word slipping out of my mouth before I could stop it.

"That night, the Fourth of July, after we were at your house. The night that he"—she was struggling to get the words out—"hurt me."

I turned to look at her, willing her to lift her eyes to me. The night he had hit her? The night he had treated her like Johnny's blow-up Bozo punching bag?

"What do you mean?" I asked, though I wasn't sure I wanted to hear the words. I didn't want to picture myself inside that house, inside that madness, incapable of doing anything to help her.

"It was awful," she said.

He had raped her. Like some masked man in an alleyway at night. He had taken Eva, *my* Eva, her incisions only barely healed, her body still wounded and tender, and forced himself into her. And worst of all was that he'd left this reminder behind. A baby. Oh, dear God, another baby.

"Eva," I said. But I had no words to make this better. Nothing to make any of this better.

That night, Frankie, drunk on wine and desperate for my affections, grabbed at me, his clumsy hands squeezing and prodding and plying. His unshaven cheeks scratching my skin, his fingers demanding. Downstairs, Eva and the children slept. And under Frankie, I thought I might suffocate. That under the weight of him, I might as well be dead.

When he left the next morning, I refused to say good-bye. In my mind, he had become no different than Ted with his violence and need, his disregard, his selfish oblivion. As the children clung to him and pleaded with him to stay longer, I disappeared into the camp and busied myself so that I wouldn't scream. As he drove down the road, waving ridiculously out the open window, and the kids ran after him, making clouds of dust in their wake, I held my breath. It was only after he was gone, after the smell of him had disappeared through the windows that I opened to release him, that I could finally let go of my anger.

The day was hot and sluggish. Because of her surgery, Eva did not want to swim. The children didn't know what she had been through. She had prosthetics that she stuffed into her old bras, but a suit would have revealed the carefully constructed illusion. And so she sat alone at the shore and watched as I slipped into the cold embrace of the lake. I waved to her, splashing some water her way, but I wasn't really feeling playful. I wasn't feeling anything but a longing so deep it seemed to live inside my bones.

That night, outside the open window in the loft, the loons were keening. Eva stood in the darkness of the small room and slowly lifted her thin, cotton nightgown, revealing her body as a magician might, as if this were only a performance, as if I were only the audience to some terrifying sleight of hand. And so I sat on the edge of the bed captivated and horrified and watched, willing myself not to cry.

The fading bruises on the insides of her thighs were in the shape of Ted's hands: inky silhouettes of his anger. The blue remains of his rage. These shadow hands traveled around her hips and waist, where still they gripped and demanded. They tugged and squeezed, they damaged. They *took*. Her buttocks were like bruised fruit. And around her neck, his hands had left the imprint of a noose.

These were *new* bruises.

"Why?" was all I could ask, though the question was as absurd as that which evoked it.

She shook her head.

She came to me then, not as a lover. Not in the way she had come to me and come to me these last two years. Not with the familiar combination of hunger and fear, but rather like a lost child.

"I can't have this baby," she said, shaking her head.

In my arms, she became smaller and smaller. Alice periscoping down until she was so small I worried she might just disappear.

Below us, the gunshot rumble of Mouse's chest startled me. She had a cold, and I had rubbed menthol eucalyptus on her skin before she went to sleep. I could still smell it on my hands; it made my eyes burn.

Eva and I lay down together on the bed: the only bed we had ever been able to share in all this time. This blessed place with its worn sheets and shining moon, but tonight Ted lay with us. His fingerprints were everywhere. Her back was to me, and I pressed my body against hers until there was no space between us. I willed him away, but she winced each time I touched one of the places he had claimed.

I slowly, gently moved my hand to her stomach and cupped the soft, hot flesh I found there.

"This one will be ours," I said.

"What?"

"This baby. It doesn't belong to him. We made this. It belongs to us."

She looked at me then for the first time since she arrived, really looked at me, and I saw something soften in her face. The tension that had been worrying lines into the space between her eyes. I could do this; I could make things better for her.

Mouse coughed again, and it sounded like thunder.

"I'll be right back," I said, and extricated myself from the delicate web of arms and legs we had spun.

I slipped on my robe and went downstairs to Mouse. She was feverish, tossing and turning. "It's okay, baby," I said. "I'll get some medicine."

"What's the matter, Mama?" Chessy asked, sitting up and rubbing her eyes.

"Shhh," I said. "Go back to sleep."

After I had given Mouse some cough syrup and stroked her hair until her eyes closed, I returned to find Eva still awake. I slipped out of my robe, pressing my body against hers.

"Is she okay?" she whispered.

I nodded, and my lips found hers in the darkness. I had memorized them as I had memorized every part of her, so that when she was away from me I could summon her again. It was as though I knew even then that one day I would need this ability—to beckon her body from nothing but the impressions she left behind.

I felt as feverish, as delirious, as Mouse as I touched her. As I stroked her body with my fingertips, I was sick with both desire and fear, the bruises that patterned her skin like ink blotches reminding me with every touch of how dangerous all of this was. And her body responded with the same trembling combination of desire and terror.

Afterward, we lay naked and breathless and sweating on top of the sheets, both staring at the rafters above us. Listening as rain pattered against the roof like little feet.

We didn't hear her until the door opened.

"Mama?" Chessy stood in the doorway, just a shadow.

We both froze, as though she wouldn't be able to see us if we were still enough. But Eva quickly pulled a sheet across us both.

"Why don't you have any clothes on?" Chessy asked.

"It was so hot," I said. "We were just trying to cool off. You know how you and Mouse sometimes sleep in your panties when it's hot?"

"But it's raining," Chessy said, putting her hand on her hip. "It's not that hot."

"It's hotter upstairs. You know that," I said, starting to feel less panicked and more irritated, though my heart still felt like a hot brick in my chest.

"Chessy," Eva intoned; her voice was calm. "How would you like to take a hike up to the fire lookout tomorrow?"

Chessy loved hiking up Franklin Mountain to visit the fire warden, who lived in a cabin at the top of the mountain. He was so grateful for visitors, he kept an impressive reserve of candy for the children and allowed them to borrow his binoculars and climb to the top of the fire tower to enjoy the view.

"Okay," she said, but she didn't move.

"Why are you up?" I asked finally, hoping that whatever confusion or doubts she'd had about finding us naked would disappear if we just acted as though everything were normal.

"Mouse is really sick," she said. "She wants you."

Something about this made my heart clang with guilt. "I'll be down in a minute," I said. And then she was gone again.

Eva and I didn't speak, as though not acknowledging what had just happened would somehow make it go away. I got up quietly; went downstairs and found the vaporizer, which I filled with water and more Vicks; and made sure the girls were asleep again before I went back upstairs where, remarkably, Eva had also fallen asleep.

But I couldn't join them in their slumber. All night long, I shared Mouse's fevered dreams: of Ted laying his hands on Eva again, of this baby growing (in spite of it all) inside her. And of

Chessy, standing, scowling, in the doorway with her hands on her hips. Of what she'd seen and the fact that no matter how we explained it, no matter how oblivious she was, she wouldn't ever forget.

We dreamed ourselves free.

Though now it was with a chair pressed up against the door, locked inside that room, a prison of our own making. Between those soft sheets, in the quiet cover of trees, in whispers and glances, we schemed and conspired. We allowed ourselves to think possible the impossible; like convicts, we carefully and meticulously plotted our escape.

Somehow, the urgency of this was heightened by Chessy finding us. As though it had happened to remind us that it was only a matter of time before we were found out. If not by one of the children, then by one of our husbands.

I knew I needed to talk to Gussy. Gussy would be instrumental in our plan, the only one capable of harboring us, we fugitives from our lives. But talking to Gussy would also mean confessing, sharing a secret I had kept hidden my entire life.

I love Eva. Three words, simple yet complicated enough to turn my life inside out.

I would tell Gussy and ask her to let us come back in the spring after the baby came. Then I would find work, maybe at the library in Quimby, or maybe in a doctor's office in town. We would pay rent. We would grow a garden. We would save our money to buy a car, a house. The children would go to school in Quimby. Eva would make her art. And we would raise this baby together, this child made not from Ted's rage but from our love. We would be a new kind of family.

I love Eva, I thought; each word by itself was a beautiful thing, but strung together they became dangerous. And every time I tried to imagine saying it aloud, I knew that nothing was as simple as it seemed. That we were children playing with matches, and it would only be a matter of time before everything caught on fire.

We had four days, four days before Frankie was due to come and get us, returning Eva to Ted, and me back to that other life. We needed to feign normalcy for a while longer. Eva and I would resume our lives in Hollyville, and then, once all of the pieces were in place, I would talk to Gussy, and we would make our escape.

After the children went to sleep that night, we walked hand in hand down to the water's edge. There was a new moon, a thumbnail moon, and it was dark enough to conceal us.

"Come in with me," I said. Eva had yet to go into the water, and I had seen the longing in her eyes each time the children and I went swimming.

I watched her silhouette as she undressed by the crabapple tree. And I wished that I could have a photograph of this: the branches like lace, her body bending over to remove her sandals. Her hair falling over one shoulder. That is something I would treasure, something I could keep. But those photographs didn't (*couldn't*) exist anywhere except in my imagination.

I went into the water and waited for her. She walked hesitantly into the lake, and then came to me. And we swam. Weightless, formless, fluid. As I touched all those damaged places, it felt like a new kind of baptism, the lake washing away all that pain.

Back at the camp, exhausted and naked, we pushed the chair under the doorknob again and slipped into bed. The rain came and beat down on the roof overhead, matching our breaths with its rhythmic pattern, and we fell into our respective dreams.

As the room began to fill with early morning light, I heard a loud bang, and in my delirium, I thought it was only thunder. I sat up, my heart thudding in my chest, and I looked to Eva, whose eyes had sprung open as well. It was a car door.

I stood up, frantically looking for my robe, as I heard the back door of the camp swing open followed by quick, heavy footsteps.

I pulled back the curtains and saw the bright red Cadillac parked outside on the grass.

"Eva!" Ted bellowed.

Eva grabbed her nightgown from the floor and put it on quickly.

"Stay here," I whispered.

"No," she said. "He'll kill you."

But I didn't care. In that moment, I would have done anything in the world to keep Ted away from her. I got out of bed and affixed my robe as I heard his heavy footsteps up the stairs. I went to the door and stared at the flimsy wooden chair. It had kept the children out, but as Ted's fists pounded against the door, I knew it wouldn't take much for its legs and rails and spindles to crumble. I'd been foolish to think it could keep us safe.

"Ted?" I said, trying not to tremble as I opened the door. "What are you doing here?"

"Where's Eva?" he said. "She's not here, is she?"

"Of course she's here. We share this room. She's still sleeping. Everyone is still sleeping."

I could smell last night's drink on his breath. Clearly he'd been out the night before and had, for whatever reason, gotten the bright idea to come check up on Eva. He must have driven straight from the bar, arriving with the dawn.

Eva came out of the room, rubbing sleep from her eyes. "Teddy? Is something wrong?"

Ted looked at Eva, astonished, as though he were seeing a ghost. He must have worked himself up into a tizzy, believing that I was somehow aiding and abetting his pregnant wife's illicit love affair—that her visit to us in Vermont was somehow an elaborate conspiracy designed so that she could carry on with some other man. What a fool.

"Come downstairs. Let me make you some coffee," she said, ushering Ted down the stairs. He looked defeated now, as though he were somehow disappointed that his jealous delusions hadn't come to fruition.

I returned to the bedroom and quickly scanned the room for evidence of our lovemaking, seeing her betrayal of him in the twisted sheets, in our clothes' arms and legs tangled together in an orgy of denim and cotton. I pulled on some clothes and peered at myself in the mirror hanging over the battered old dresser. I looked for signs in my face that would give us away.

Downstairs I listened to their hushed voices and smelled the scent of strong coffee. His worries may have been appeased, but it was obvious he wasn't going to return to Hollyville without her. This I knew. And this realization, that he'd stolen our last three days here, made my blood hot, my ears red; I was more determined than ever.

Later that morning, Ted took Eva and the kids home, as I knew he would. And as the car drove down the road, Johnny's face pressed to the rear window glass, I paced. Chessy and Mouse didn't seem to know what to do. It was as though someone had come along and ripped a beloved stuffed animal out of their arms. We were at a loss without the Wilsons. We were lost without them.

As the plane from Pittsburgh to Burlington taxis slowly to the gate, I feel the patter of my heart like a child skipping rope in my chest. My hands are trembling now. I can't identify the feeling though. I can't classify it: Excitement? Fear? It's funny how emotions have become so muddy as I've grown older. The physical signs and symptoms are not always clear to read. I feel like an adolescent girl again, my body's response to the world both confused and somehow portentous.

The Burlington airport is just as small as I remember it. There is only one terminal, just a handful of gates. I think I remember where the baggage claim carousels are, and I imagine Gussy will be waiting there. But instead, as I emerge from the jet bridge I can see her standing behind the wall of glass that separates the arrivals from those waiting to greet them. She waves wildly, as though she needs to get my attention.

She doesn't look any different than she did when I last saw her two years ago. She hasn't aged in any way I can see. (She still stands her full five foot nine inches; there are no new accoutrements of old age accompanying her: no walker, no cane, no wheelchair.) Her hair is still perfectly coifed, her clothes pressed. The rouge on her cheeks and the color on her lips is exactly what I expected. My *sister*. God, how I've missed her.

"Gingersnap!" she says, delighted, her happiness unrestrained. She holds her arms out, beckoning me to come to her with her fingers that wriggle excitedly.

I feel my legs moving faster to meet her, and then I am holding her, smelling her terrific, powdery scent. *This* emotion is one that is easy to identify; I feel so happy I could burst. How could I have hesitated? How could I possibly have considered not coming? I feel like an old fool.

"You're home!" Gussy says. "I'm so excited! Let's go get your bags. How was your flight? Don't you just hate those little planes?"

I can barely get a word in edgewise. It's as though we haven't been speaking on the phone every single night since I last saw her. I think about my friend, Hugh, on the flight from Pittsburgh, what he would say when he finally got a chance to speak to his girl in person. Would it be like this? Or would they be at a loss for words?

We gather my suitcase from the baggage claim. It is one of the first ones that comes tumbling onto the carousel.

"Good Lord, how old is this thing?" Gussy asks, heaving it off the carousel for me. A gentleman standing next to her assists, and then offers her the rolling baggage cart next to him. I feel silly accepting his cart for one suitcase, but Gussy simply nods a *thank you* and loads that beastly suitcase on. We push the cart out to the garage, take the elevator up to the top, and find her car.

The sun is setting outside, and the sky is that indigo color that I have never seen anywhere but here in Vermont. Sunsets at the beach are dramatic, glitzy affairs, like the sun has something to prove, a showgirl accustomed to taking her bows before an adoring crowd every night. Twilight is more subtle here, more reserved. It couldn't compete with the autumn foliage if it tried. Though as we drive back to Quimby, it's too dark to see what I know is an amazing display of color.

"How's the foliage this year?" I ask.

"Breathtaking," she says. "Last year, it rained every day for a month. Just miserable. All the leaf peepers were disappointed. But this year, it's been amazing. Especially up to the lake."

I nod, thinking about Gormlaith, wishing that we were going straight there instead of to Quimby. I consider asking Gussy to just keep driving, to skip her house and just take me to camp.

"The chicken and dumplings should be ready just in time for us. I also rented that new Jane Eyre movie with what's-her-name and Frank's girlfriend, Judi Dench." She says this with a roll of her eyes.

Frank had a bit of a schoolboy crush on Judi Dench, so much so that when he was dying, he kept confusing all of the actresses on the hospital TV for her. *Is that Judi Dench?* he would ask hopefully. If he hadn't been so ill, I think Gussy would have smacked him.

"You haven't seen it already, have you?" I shake my head. "I thought we could stay up late, like we used to. Catch up."

"I just talked to you yesterday," I say, and then worry that it's come across as sharp.

"Well, it's amazing what can happen in a day," she says, sighing.

"What's that supposed to mean?"

"Just that I've got some surprises up my sleeve."

"I don't know if you should be springing any big surprises on this old lady. You want to kill me?"

"Oh, hush," she says, and we pull into her driveway, which is littered with fallen leaves.

Walking into Gussy's house is, in a way, like walking back into our childhoods. Because I left Vermont at eighteen and married Frankie a year later, Gussy was the one who inherited all of our parents' castaway things. And after they had both passed away, she absorbed the rest. The treasures: the cuckoo clock on the wall, the round oak table at which we both had sat for thousands of our mother's meals. The china with its tiny roses, the Blue Willow tea set, the braided rug my mother made from my father's old shirts.

I sit down on her worn sofa, picking up a copy of *Consumer Reports* from the end table. The address still bears Frank's name. Something about this makes my heart ache. Frank's been gone for ten years, but it wasn't until a couple of years ago that she finally took Frank's message off her answering machine, stashing away the little cassette tape that had captured his soft voice.

"So what's the big secret?" I ask.

Gussy has always been terrible at keeping secrets. She is what my mother called an open book; what you see is what you get with Gussy. Christmas presents, surprise parties, pregnancies—not a single bit of exciting news was safe with Gussy. Secrets boiled up inside her like water in a teakettle, busting out of her like steam in an excited whistle. The only secret she has ever been able to keep was mine. It took every ounce of courage I had to tell her about Eva. Every bit of strength and trust.

She shakes her head now, tries to change the subject. "It's nothing," she says, which clearly means something.

"Gus," I admonish.

"Let's just say Johnny has something for you," she says, exasperated, hoping to appease me with this meager offering.

"Like what?" I ask. I can't imagine what he might have held on to, what possession of Eva's he might think I'd like to have. I try to imagine Eva's things: her scuffed blue heels, her dresses. The pins she wore in her hair. What would I do with a lipstick tube, a prosthetic breast, the jaunty little Girl Scout troop leader hat?

She shrugs and turns away from me, her eyes fluttering. When she looks back at me again, she seems flustered. She's keeping something from me. "He's asked me to wait. He wants to show you himself."

I was still having such a hard time wrapping my mind around Johnny as anything other than an eight-year-old little boy slinging rubber tipped arrows from the treetops.

"Is it my letters?" I ask. I wrote hundreds of letters to Eva. I can't imagine that they still exist. Most evidence of what was between us has been lost or destroyed.

Gussy shrugs again suspiciously, and I try to imagine what thing Johnny would have that he'd beckon me all the way across the country to give me. Couldn't he have popped it in the mail? Doesn't he understand that the things that belonged to her don't matter? That the things I would want to keep wouldn't fit inside an envelope: the smell of her perfume, the feeling of her soft cheek pressed against my hand. Her laughter, like a child's. Her breath, her whispers in my ear.

"We'll just have to see, I guess," Gussy says, patting my leg, and then stands up. "Let's have some supper."

I nod. I am hungry now. But just as we are about to dig into our meal, the phone rings.

"Let the machine get it," I say, but Gussy is already rushing across the room.

"Hello?" she says. "Oh, hi, Johnny. We were just talking about you."

At the end of August, back in Hollyville, time seemed to have stood still everywhere but in my garden. It was overrun with vegetables, Frankie unable to keep up with the harvest while we were gone. He'd made an effort, but the garden looked like a jungle, a tangled mess of vines and leaves and vegetables going to rot. Untended, the garden was wild and unwieldy. I couldn't help but wonder, as I hacked my way through the six-foot-high cornstalks and the voluminous leaves, about the other ways things would fall apart after I was gone.

The first two weeks back, while the children were at school, Eva and I picked green beans and swollen tomatoes and peppers. Rose sat among the labyrinthine rows of corn and cabbage, playing in the dirt. I spent hours in the kitchen boiling and canning until my palms blistered from the lids and my face burned from all that steam. Eva, in the throes of morning sickness, couldn't bear the smell of the kitchen. I went to sleep at night dreaming of turnips and eggplant and squash, the scent seeping into my hair and my skin. No matter how many baths I took, I couldn't seem to get rid of the smell of the earth.

But with each jar I placed on the shelf in our basement, I felt a sense of accomplishment, as though the colorful glass jars were evidence of my self-sufficiency. We would have a garden. We would feed our children with the vegetables and roots we coaxed from the earth. We could survive without grocery allowances, without the men.

Rose was three now, and had given up both her morning and afternoon naps. Eva resumed her position as troop leader with me, but Hannah insisted on continuing on as a leader as well, which meant that more often than not Hannah was with us at our meetings. We were never alone.

Aching for each other, we discussed the various badges the girls hoped to earn this year: Sewing, Cooking, Wilderness Survival. We reached for each other's hands under the kitchen table as Hannah chattered on about plans for the flying up ceremony. We stole glances as we mended the girls' old uniforms, and kisses in the pantry as we perused the unsold boxes of Girl Scout cookies and Hannah's voice clattered on in the kitchen. Normally, this would have driven me mad. But now we had a *plan*. All of this was endurable, because there was an end in sight. We were only biding our time.

We knew that realistically we couldn't go anywhere until the baby came. She needed to have a doctor, but once the baby was here, we would be free. And so as Eva's belly grew, the distance between us and our future together shrank.

"I hope it's a boy," I said one day as we stood in the pantry together.

"Why?" she asked, leaning into me. Her breath skipped across my collarbone.

I shrugged. And I thought about the miscarriage. That lost baby that had first brought us together. I was certain it had been a boy. Here was our second chance.

"What would *you* like?" I asked, peering around the corner. Hannah was in the restroom freshening up. Her vanity had bought us endless stolen moments like these.

She shook her head. "Girls are easier when they're little," she said, shrugging. "But they have it so much harder later on."

"What do you mean?" I asked, putting my hands on her hips, those two perfect bones.

"I mean, a boy has a chance in this world. To be someone. To do something."

She was right. It was true. As much as I loved my girls, I feared for them. When I imagined their futures, it was not with excitement but trepidation.

Johnny was getting in trouble at school that year. It seemed like every other day Eva was getting a call from his teacher with one complaint or another about his behavior in the classroom and on the playground. He pushed, he shoved, he spat and kicked and cussed. Eva's fear, though she never said it aloud, was that he was turning into Ted. That all of Ted's rage had somehow been channeled into Johnny. That this was his inheritance, this violence.

One late September night, the kids were all outside playing kick the can or some such game. Rose was riding her tricycle up and down the sidewalk while the other children played. I checked out the window periodically, making sure that they were all staying out of the street.

I was canning the last of the beets, and my hands were stained magenta. Frankie was watching *The Ed Sullivan Show* in the other room when I heard the scream. My heart flew to my throat as I set down the tongs I'd been using to lift the jars out of the boiling water and ran to the front door. Frankie followed behind.

Rose was standing on our porch, pointing toward the street, where Johnny was standing over Mouse with his fist raised as if to strike her. I flew to him screaming, "Johnny, stop it right this instant!"

Frankie pushed me aside and went to Johnny, grabbing him hard by the elbow and dragging him onto our lawn. Johnny was nearly eight now, and tall for his age, but still clearly powerless to Frankie.

"What the hell do you think you're doing?" Frankie screamed in Johnny's face. Johnny looked terrified. For all the trouble he'd gotten into at school, I believe this was the first time he'd been challenged this way.

Ted came out of the Wilsons' house then and ran over. "Get your hands off my boy!" he said, pushing Frankie in the chest.

Frankie, startled, threw his shoulders back and then corrected his stance so that he looked like he was ready for a boxing match.

Ted towered over him.

Johnny was crying now, and snot was running down his face.

"You think it's okay to hit girls?" Frankie asked Johnny, and Johnny shrugged. "You teach him that? That it's okay to hit a girl?" Frankie demanded of Ted.

Ted pushed his chest out, and I watched as his face grew red and the muscles in his blocky neck strained. He looked at me accusingly.

I heard the Wilsons' door open again and looked up to see Eva standing in the doorway. The hallway light behind her made her an eerie silhouette. "Ted, come inside," she said weakly. But Ted was clearly not going to back down from this fight.

"What did she do?" Ted asked Johnny.

Mouse clung to my legs like she used to as a toddler. Chessy stood off to the side, her eyes wide.

"She took my bike," Johnny said. "And she wouldn't give it back."

"Is that true?" Ted said, getting his thick face close to Mouse's.

"Get away from her," I hissed.

"Sounds to me like she was just about to get what was coming to her," Ted said, laughing.

I felt anger ballooning inside of me, and all of the colors of Eva's bruises swirled behind my eyes, the color of my own rage and his mixed together.

"Sounds like somebody needs to teach that girl a lesson about her *place*."

At that, Frankie lost any composure or control he'd been trying to keep. While my fists remained at my side, Frankie's were swinging. Then, before I knew what was happening, he jumped on Ted's back like some sort of animal. He was half Ted's size, and he looked like a turtle fighting a whale.

I gathered all of the girls, including Mouse, rounding them

up like animals and herding them back to the safety of our house, their necks straining to see what was going on in the street. Johnny stood on the sidewalk, looking baffled by this display, his mouth hanging open and his eyes wide.

Inside, I sat the children around the kitchen table and found the last few remnants of some cookies in the cookie jar. I poured them each a cup of milk and as they ate, I peered anxiously through the lace curtains at the two men in the street. The sun had slipped away, and the streetlights had come on. Their hulking shadows moved soundlessly, like some sort of prehistoric beast, up and down the street. It was the slowest fight I'd ever witnessed in my life.

Then I watched Old Man Castillo come out of his house, shaking his fist, probably threatening to call the police, and he put himself between Frankie and Ted, who seemed surprised by his sudden appearance. He stood between them like a referee, arthritic hands pressed against their respective chests.

Eva had gone inside her own house as well. And I worried that Ted would lumber back into the house now and use up all his remaining fury on Eva.

"Francesca?" I said, pulling a second bottle of milk out of the refrigerator and locating a last box of Girl Scout cookies in the pantry. "Can you keep an eye on the children?"

"Why?" she asked, glancing nervously toward the window.

"I'm just going to check on Eva."

"Why?" she said again, her eyes filling with tears.

"Because I'm *worried*." And I was. That was the truth, and Chessy seemed grateful for it. Ever since Chessy walked in and found us together, it seemed like lying to her had become a nearly impossible task. She questioned everything. She longed for the untampered-with facts. I had always appreciated this about her, but now it terrified me. I worried endlessly that that image (of our bare skin on those soft sheets, of the arc of Eva's hips and my own nude body) would remain, memorized like all the other facts she stored like photographs in the album of her mind. And that someday, something would send her back to that moment, that she would pull that particular photo from the magnetic sleeve of her memory, hold it up, and suddenly understand the truth.

"Please," I said. "Just watch the kids for a minute."

"Okay," she said. And with that, she scooped Rose up onto her lap. I looked out the window; Frankie and Ted were separated now and both hunched over, their hands palming their knees, wheezing.

I ran past them toward Eva's porch, neither one seeming to notice me.

"You okay, Mrs. Valentine?" Old Man Castillo hollered after me. I turned around, tears burning in my eyes. My husband was standing in the street, oblivious, yet here was a stranger, worried about me. I nodded, feeling my entire body working not to cry.

Inside, Eva was sitting at the kitchen table, head in her hands. Calder lay at her feet. Eva's entire body visibly tensed when I knocked. And Calder began to growl.

"It's me," I said, pushing the door gently open, and both Eva and Calder looked up relieved.

"What's going on out there?" she asked.

"They're still out there, but it seems to be calming down. Mr. Castillo is playing referee. Where's Johnny?"

"I sent him to his room. I'm so sorry about Mouse. Is she okay?"

I waved my hand. "She's fine." And this was also true. Mouse, of all of the children, could fend for herself. If Frankie hadn't stepped in, I'm pretty sure Mouse would have gone swinging at Johnny herself.

Eva motioned for me to sit down at the table with her. We sat quietly, listening to the kitchen clock knocking out the seconds. "He won't hurt you if I'm here," I said, speaking what we both hoped to be true.

She looked at me, her face softening. The sharp angles of her clenched jaw releasing their grip. "I had a dream last night," she said, reaching for my hand. "That we were driving along the road to Gormlaith, that it was still summer. And it was just you and me, with the windows rolled down. You were playing that awful station you like on the radio. The sun was shining, and I kept feeling the air with my hand through the open window," she said sadly. "It didn't feel like a dream at all."

"We need to leave," I said, suddenly feeling more desperate than I ever had. "Soon." I didn't want to hear her describe waking up. I didn't want to think of her eyes opening, of her rolling over and seeing Ted's enormous body next to her. I didn't want to imagine the disappointment, the sharp edges of reality coming into focus as she woke. I knew I needed to keep that dream fresh in her mind. Keep the radio playing. I felt frantic, struggling to find a way to promise her the wind on her fingers, the sun on her shoulders.

"How?" she asked then, and it felt like an accusation. I felt myself crumbling, the music turning to static. A cloud passing over us. The car running out of gas and leaving us stranded on that dusty road. My eyes burned.

Calder stood up, stretched, and came to me, lowering her chin onto my lap, also waiting for an answer. I rubbed her soft warm ears.

"I'll talk to Gussy. We'll go, we'll just take the children and go."

Ted came through the door then, throwing it open, his face red, his hair matted with sweat. It took him a few moments before my presence registered. When he realized I was there, the color drained from his face. And he laughed. It was loud, a crackly pop of laughter, more like gunfire than joy. And that was all. He didn't speak; he only went to the cupboard where he kept his whiskey and began to pour himself a drink.

"That husband of yours is a scrappy little fella," he said.

I looked at Ted, hard. Challenging him. For a full excruciating minute I willed him to do something, to say something, to give me the excuse I was looking for to just grab Eva's hand and march out the front door. But his anger seemed to be abating. With each swig from his highball glass, his face softened.

"Maybe you'd better go check on Frankie," Eva said finally, breaking that fragile wall of glass between Ted and me. "And send the girls back over?"

I nodded, though the last thing on earth I wanted to do was to leave her here with him. As I made my way back across the street, I prayed that Ted had used up all that anger on Frankie. That tonight Frankie had taken the brunt of it. I hoped, with only the slightest bit of remorse, that he had been the one to absorb Ted's angry blows. That he was the one who was left battered and humiliated and broken. Because otherwise it would be Eva, and there wasn't a thing I could do to stop it.

That night I lay in bed and dreamed the conversation with Gussy. Sat myself down across from her and reached for her hands. "Help us," my dream self said. "Please."

"What was that about?" I ask after Gussy hangs up with Johnny. The chicken and dumplings have gone from steaming hot to lukewarm on our plates.

Gussy gathers up the dishes and pops them both in the microwave, turning her back to me, busying her hands, so she won't have to answer. "How would you feel about making a trip down to Boston?" she asks, without turning around.

"Why?"

"Johnny seems to think it might be better if we came down there to see him."

"That's ridiculous," I say. Now I am irritated. I spent five hundred dollars on a plane ticket, traveled three thousand miles, and now he can't manage to make a three-hour drive up here to talk to me?

"What about the lake?" I ask. I have been dreaming of the lake, and now that I am so close, I long for it. I don't know what I expect to find there other than an opportunity to swim in my own watery nostalgia, but I have come this far and such an abrupt change in plans feels wrong.

"I'll call Effie, see if we can go to the lake tomorrow. Then down to Boston on Sunday. After we see Johnny we can go stay with Francesca for a couple of days. The lake isn't going anywhere." The microwave beeps, and Gussy delivers the reheated chicken to me, her eyes pleading. "I'll drive."

"I don't understand any of this," I say. And for a minute I think that maybe I'll just call Johnny back myself. Tell him he's being selfish. That he can exorcise his demons some other way. I'm an old woman, and I'm tired. But I also know that he is the only true tie left to that other life, to that time, to Eva. And so I shake my head and sigh.

"Fine," I say, feeling defeated. Too tired to argue.

Almost fifty years and three thousand miles later, and Johnny once again is calling the shots.

That fall hangs in my memory like a bright red maple leaf. Clinging, cloying. Electric but also precarious. It was as though everything burned brighter that autumn. I held on. *We* held on even knowing that the threat of falling was both imminent and inevitable.

This is one other thing I know: without autumn, there is no end. Without red and gold and orange there is no finality, no conclusion. Without the sudden shift in the air, without the scent of apples and the crisp chill of morning, summer could go on forever. Without fall, summer lingers. There is a marvelous limbo where I live now, without the changing of seasons. No blazing display to signify the end of everything good. Perhaps this is what drew me to California. A place where time is suspended.

The memory of that fall in particular comes to me in brightly colored patches, a handful of leaves. Eva's hair across my pillow on a stolen afternoon. The flash of her smile as she waved to me from across the street. A sheet of rain falling outside the kitchen window where we sat drinking coffee while the children put together puzzles upstairs. There is a kaleidoscopic feeling to that fall, each recollection assembled and then reassembled, each one more beautiful than the last.

Our Girl Scout troop had been invited by the local Boy Scout troop to put on a Thanksgiving play that year, and Eva volunteered us to make the costumes. Eva had less experience with a sewing machine than I did, but in general she was more creative. Where anything beyond following a basic pattern was concerned, I relied on her. I was the worker bee, but she was the one who made the honey sweet. We made a good team.

"It'll be simple," she had said when I resisted the idea. "Just bonnets and headdresses, some buckles for the boys' shoes."

We started before Halloween, collecting fabric and feathers. Eva figured we could go ahead and make the kids' Halloween costumes while we were at it. And as much as I truly loathed sewing, it also meant an excuse to be near Eva: to have Eva in my house or to be invited into hers. We put Hannah in charge of making the programs and signs, told her we had everything else under control.

After the fight with Frankie in the street, Ted had refused to set foot in, or even *near,* our house, and I knew (though Eva wouldn't say it) that he'd demanded she stay away as well. She almost never called unless he was gone now, and came over only after he'd driven off to work, hurrying back across the street each evening long before he was due home, looking stricken once when we'd been so absorbed in sewing a row of red feathers on an Indian headdress that she didn't hear his car pulling into the driveway.

On Halloween night, she somehow managed to convince him that the Wilson children and our children (being the only kids on the street) should be allowed to go out trick-or-treating together. The older kids wanted to go ahead by themselves, but Rose was still little, so Eva and I followed behind the older children with Rose and Calder.

Rose was dressed like a ghost. Eva had offered to make her a princess costume, something sparkly like the older girls, but she'd insisted on being *scary,* and so Eva had acquiesced, finding a threadbare sheet in her linen closet and cutting out two eyeholes. Rose had also insisted on a costume for Calder, so Calder was the princess, wearing a cardboard crown and a pink satin "gown." Eva had put on a witch's hat, and I'd taken one of the finished headdresses for the play and, upon Eva's insistence, put it on. I felt ridiculous but festive. I wished sometimes I could let go and enjoy things the way that Eva did.

The night was warm and bright, the sky filled with an orange haze from the harvest moon, which shone like a jack-o'-lantern in the western sky. I resisted the impulse to hold Eva's hand as we walked down the sidewalk, stopping at each house for Rose to trick-or-treat while the older kids ran ahead, filling their pillowcases with popcorn balls and paper sacks of candy.

Eva was starting to show already, her belly like a small egg. The baby was due in the spring. She had been sick with this pregnancy, sicker than she'd been with the others, she said. She also said her chest ached, where her breasts used to be. Phantom pain. Watching Eva's belly grow was like watching an hourglass; the fuller she became, the closer we were to finally leaving. When we had discussed our plans that summer, they had felt faraway, unreal. But with each day, as her belly swelled, it was a reminder that once the baby came, all that dreaming would finally become a reality. All those fantasies would become *our* reality. It was exhilarating and terrifying.

The older kids were two houses ahead. The girls had all dressed as princesses as well, and Johnny was a cop. This was his latest obsession. Ted had bought him a costume from Woolworth's, complete with a fake gun and a shiny badge. Eva and I had cobbled together the girls' costumes with scraps from my rag bag and some of Eva's magic.

"I want to go with the big kids!" Rose said from beneath her sheet, her tiny feet stomping the pavement.

"What do you think?" Eva asked. She did this sometimes, asked my opinion regarding discipline or other issues with the children. Those moments, I could imagine us as a family, as *parents* together. She would be the fun one, the one who skipped rope with the girls and played hide-and-seek with the boys. I would be the one to lay down the law. To discipline. We would be partners. This would be our family. I had to remind myself that the decision we were making involved not only us, but six children, *seven* children. This wasn't simple. This wasn't something to be taken lightly.

"The older girls can watch her, right?" she asked.

"Why not?" I said, smiling. Rose was still only three now, but she worshipped my girls and her older sisters. She'd stay close.

I jogged ahead and caught up with the older kids. "Girls, Rose is going to come with you. Can you keep an eye on her?"

"Okay." They shrugged.

Johnny marched up ahead of the girls, pulling his gun from his holster and aiming it at imaginary bandits.

"I'll walk with her," Mouse said. After the fight over the bicycle, Mouse had refused to play anywhere near Johnny. It was with reluctance that she had agreed to come out tonight, and I noticed that she hung back as Johnny barged ahead, always the first to ring the doorbell. Watching Rose seemed like a good excuse to stay clear of him.

Delighted, Rose skipped ahead, taking Mouse's outstretched hand. Eva and I hung back with Calder, walking slowly, basking in that pumpkin-colored glow to the night. "Let's go walk by the creek," I said.

"Really?" Eva asked anxiously. She was so afraid now. Where she had once been the bold one, the daring one, she now cowered. And I hated Ted for instilling this fear in her. For making the free spirit I knew timid and weak.

"Why not?" I said. "The girls are watching Rose."

"Okay," she said, nodding as though convincing herself, and we cut across someone's lawn to the public path which led to the water. But when we got to the creek's edge, Eva asked to sit down.

"Are you okay?" I asked. Eva's pregnancy terrified me. After her surgery, I was so worried about her health. I couldn't stand the thought of anything going wrong, anything that might threaten her life.

She nodded and smiled and patted the place on the rock next

to her. She let Calder off her leash, and she sniffed along the water's edge while we sat.

I was overwhelmed then by this sense of being on the edge of things. The canopy above us, leaves clinging to their branches for dear life, the ground already scattered with their siblings. The air had the promise of winter to it, a cold whisper beneath the otherwise warm night. We were on the periphery of something enormous, teetering at the precipice. And I just wanted to hold on. I wanted to embrace all of this, to keep it close. I reached for her, and as if she were thinking the same thing, she leaned into me, clinging to me. I kissed her furiously, trying to swallow this moment, trying to put all of it inside me. If I could hold her inside me, I could keep her and the baby safe. I could protect her.

The leaves crunched beneath us as we lowered our bodies to the ground. Calder was oblivious, running along the water's edge, chasing shadows.

My hands grasped and squeezed, my hips ached and moved. I wanted to undress her. I wanted us to be together, absolutely together, under these suspended stars and moon. I couldn't stop my hands from lifting her sweater, from stroking her hair and her belly and her back. I couldn't stop any of it; it was as though every promise and hope was spilling out of me, and I was powerless to my will.

I couldn't hear anything. I was deaf to everything but Eva's soft moans as I touched her. To her heart thumping against my own. I couldn't see anything. I was blind to everything but the color of the night, the color of the leaves, the color of Eva's eyes as they peered desperately into mine. But then suddenly there was brightness, a blinding light. And a voice.

"Mom?"

I felt my heart stop. We both froze.

Johnny stood in his policeman's uniform, shining his flashlight at us. It was only a toy, but it was bright. I put my hand up to shield my eyes. And when he saw what was illuminated in that beam, he dropped the flashlight and it rolled across the grass. His eyes were filled with something between terror and wonder, and his hand flew to his mouth.

"Johnny," Eva said, pulling away from me.

I scrambled to my feet, straightening my skirt, my sweater, plucking leaves from my hair. Eva stood up as well, pulling her shirt back down, tears already starting to stream from her eyes.

"Calder!" I said weakly, running after the dog, who had settled in a patch of dead leaves and was rolling on her back. I got Calder on her leash and just held on to her, as though I might float away like a lost balloon if I were to let go.

"What were you doing, Mom?" I heard Johnny ask.

Eva shook her head silently. What was there to say to an eight-year-old little boy about this? I thought about Chessy finding us, about how simple it had been to excuse. To explain. To erase. But then we had only been lying undressed together, not even touching. There were no words in either of our vocabulary to change what Johnny had seen. No lie that would make sense.

"Nothing," she said, her head hanging to her chest as though she'd been scolded. I'd seen this same gesture when Ted got started on her too.

"Why were you and Billie *kissing?*" The word came out of his mouth like it was something poisonous. Like something bitter. It killed me that someone had seen the love between us and that it had sickened him. That it made him grimace in disgust and terror. And unable to come up with words that might make this make sense, to excuse us, to apologize, or whatever it was that he needed us to do, we could only watch as he ran. He fled back down the path, the leaves loud under his feet. The sound of all that death being trampled under his shiny shoes.

"Oh, my God," Eva said, grabbing Calder's leash from me. "Oh, my God."

Johnny had come to get us because Rose had tripped on her sheet and gotten a bloody nose. We found the entire group of kids sitting in front of the Bouchers' house, her ghost costume now balled up and made into a makeshift bandage. It was a gruesome sight. My heart was pounding so hard, the sound filled my ears and I could barely unscramble their voices, which were all speaking at once.

Eva had gathered herself together and scooped Rose up in her arms, making her tilt her head back to stop the bleeding. I swooned at the sight of all that blood, at my own blood rushing to my head with the irrefutable fact that Johnny had *seen* us, found us in each other's arms. Our secret had cracked open like flesh on pavement, and soon it would spill out, staining everything. There would be no bandage big enough to stop this awful flow. Nothing that could halt the deluge.

As soon as it was clear that Rose wouldn't need stitches, that it was just a bloody nose and nothing was broken, I left Eva there, following the path back toward our houses that Johnny had taken. I felt like a hunter, tracking him, following the scent of his confusion, certain that he would go straight to his father.

I stood outside in the street and watched as Johnny barged into the house, abandoning his candy sack on the porch. It gaped open like a mouth, pouring its contents onto the floor. I couldn't see inside, but I could imagine Ted on the couch watching TV, a sweaty glass of something at his side. I imagined Johnny telling him what had happened, painting a picture of what he had seen and waiting for his father to explain it all away.

And all the while, I stood in the middle of the street, waiting for the world to end.

Finally Eva and the other children arrived back on Beechtree Street. I sent my girls into our house, and Eva sent Donna and Sally inside as well. Rose clung to her still, and I could see the blood from her nose splattered all over Eva's shoulder.

"What do we do now?" I asked, my whole body shaking with fear.

"We go home," she said.

"He's going to kill you," I said.

But instead of denying it, instead of assuring me that everything was going to be okay, she blinked hard and shook her head, holding on tighter to Rose. She leaned toward me, and whispered calmly. "If you hear anything, please call the police." Her words were hot, palpable. And then she left me standing there and walked toward the house with Rose in her arms, like someone walking to the gallows.

I remained paralyzed in the middle of the street, watching her go, and I couldn't shake the feeling that someone was watching me. Then, when I looked up at the two upstairs windows that faced the street, I saw Johnny in the window, and his small hands were pressed against the glass.

I stayed awake all night that night, long after the sounds of older children trick-or-treating or making mischief had faded. Sleep eluded me as I lay prone in our bed, Frankie snoring as I waited for something, anything to happen across the street. But the world did not stop turning, and while sleep did not arrive, dawn, finally, did.

From the kitchen window that morning, I watched Frankie slip into the Studebaker, and, like clockwork, the Wilsons' door opened and the children poured out, followed by Ted and his briefcase. My girls left and convened with the Wilson children in the street, leaving us behind, as always. Though nothing was as always anymore.

I was bewildered. It was as though everything had only been a dream, a nightmare. But I had not been asleep. I hadn't even closed my eyes. Was it possible that Johnny had held his tongue? Was it possible he was simply too young to understand what he'd seen? Was it possible that he had dismissed it like he might dismiss a playground taunt or the bogeyman under his bed?

Eva's call came only moments after our families had departed. I dreaded what she would tell me.

"He didn't say anything," she said.

I felt the grip of anxiety on my neck and shoulders suddenly release. "What?" I asked.

"Johnny. He didn't say anything to Ted. At least I don't think he did."

"How do you know?" I asked. Though I knew exactly how she knew. If Johnny had told Ted what he had seen Eva and me doing by the creek, we wouldn't be speaking on the phone right now.

"Did you *talk* to Johnny?" I asked.

She was quiet for a long time. I could feel my heart pounding in my temples, in my shoulders, in my hand as I pressed the phone close to my head. Finally she said softly, "What would I say, Billie? How could I possibly explain?"

"Can I come over?" I asked.

"No," she said. "I've got a thousand things to do around the house."

I felt my heart plummet.

"He won't say anything," I said, but it came out like a question.

"I don't know," she said, and hung up.

And so we didn't go to each other that day; both of us were far too afraid now. Even if Johnny hadn't told Ted, our secret didn't belong to us anymore. It was an animal escaped from the zoo. It was a quiet tiger lurking in the backyard. A quiet, hungry tiger. It was best to stay inside. To hide.

The weekend came as all other weekends came. The children played together, jumping into the piles of leaves that Frankie and Ted had raked in our respective yards. Frankie and Ted had made an unspoken truce, though I knew Frankie wouldn't be inviting Ted to come over anytime soon. A line had been drawn in the sand, and that line ran down our street.

Inside the house, I felt like a puppet, going through the motions of my life, the invisible strings attached to my hands, my feet, my head, dictating my every move: laundry, dishes, floors.

Cookies for Monday's bake sale. Rolling out pasta dough, bringing jars of tomatoes up from the basement. Putting a Band-Aid on Mouse's scraped knee. Turning on the television to watch as I folded the warm, clean clothes.

I didn't know what was happening inside the Wilsons' house, but I did know I had been stuck inside my own for three days straight. I hadn't felt the autumn air on my face. The house was like a sarcophagus; if I didn't get out and take a walk soon, I might go crazy.

I knew that asking Eva to join me was dangerous, but normally we walked Calder nearly every night; wouldn't Ted suspect something if I didn't come by to get her? I couldn't live like this. Something had to give. I needed to talk to her. I needed to see her and figure out what to do next.

It took nearly every ounce of courage I had left in my body to go to the Wilsons' front door and knock. The children were playing kick the can in the street. I rushed past Donna and Sally, who were running toward the rusty can, giggling and pushing each other playfully. Mouse was hiding, and Chessy was running breathlessly a few houses down.

"Bam!" a voice said from above, startling me. I looked up through the barren branches of the giant elm in front of the house, and Johnny was pointing his Daisy rifle right at me. On any other day I would have scolded him, told him that you never, ever point a gun, even a BB gun, at someone. But I was speechless. He had a wild look in his eyes, one I recognized as his father's, and his cheeks were flushed red. "I got you," he hissed.

I scurried up onto the porch and knocked.

Eva came out with Calder already on her leash, and we descended the porch steps silently. But the entire walk down the street I could feel Johnny's eyes and aim at our backs.

The sound of the children playing faded as we walked toward the creek. We didn't touch each other, and we really didn't speak. It was as though acknowledging what had happened on Halloween night would somehow make the horror of it real. I desperately wanted her to assure me that everything was going to be okay. That we would go ahead with our plans. That, if *anything,* Johnny's discovery would hasten things. That Johnny knowing about us would only force us to expedite our departure. But we both knew that nothing was okay. That the tiger was lurking somewhere. It was only a matter of time before we turned a corner and were face-to-face with him.

By the time we got back to our street, the children were inside. It was quiet and cold outside. The cars slept in the driveways. It was peaceful. Strangely beautiful.

"Good night," she said. "I'll call you tomorrow."

I nodded, trying not to cry. I must have known that this moment of peace would be our last, that everything was about to shatter, because I hesitated before going back inside my house. I felt it in my bones. I heard the tiger's growl.

I am haunted by my memories here. And so despite being exhausted from the flight, from the long drive to Gussy's, I cannot sleep. Despite Gussy's efforts to make me feel at home (the clean sheets, the cup of tea at my bedside, the warm bath she drew), I lie wide awake in Gussy's guest room waiting for a slumber that will not come.

The room is dark save for the small yellow glow of a nightlight that shines from the guest bathroom. I press my hand to the window and feel the chill of autumn outside. At least it is warm in here; the heat comes on and shuts off intermittently, blowing in hot gusts across my face. She's taken the Windsor chimes that normally hang above the bed so they won't keep me awake, making it quiet in here. The only thing prohibiting sleep is my own thoughts: the cranking, buzzing machine of my own mind.

In the morning (if morning ever comes) we will go to the lake. Gussy called Effie, and she said they are all excited to see us. We'll spend the day with them, maybe take a nice walk around the lake to look at the foliage, and then on Sunday Gussy and I will get in the car and drive to Boston to see Johnny. I am still mystified as to why Johnny has asked us to make this trip. Gussy said that he has just gotten out of rehab, that he is in the process of making amends. In my mind I see his list, categorized by year, perhaps. *1964: Billie Valentine*. But again, what would he have to apologize for? He did nothing wrong. He was a little boy, a child; we were the adults. Johnny was an innocent bystander, only a witness to everything that happened. He might even be considered a victim. Any decent therapist could tell him this. We, the grown-ups, were the perpetrators. We were the ones at fault.

I drift off sometime just before dawn, and I awaken as though someone has rung a bell in my ear. But now as I pull myself from the murky depths of a dream that is fading fast, I realize it is only Gussy's radio playing VPR in the kitchen as she cooks soft-boiled eggs and bacon for my breakfast, as she brews a fresh pot of coffee and waits for me to join her at that big, empty kitchen table.

Today we will go to the lake, I think. We will gather fallen leaves and press them between the pages of heavy books with the children. And tomorrow, we will put coffee in a Thermos and grab a couple of bagels from that place in Quimby on our way to Boston. We will see Johnny and hear him out, let him say whatever it is he feels he needs to say. Let him offer me whatever relic it is he has to give.

I gather my robe around me and carefully make my way down the carpeted stairs. The walls are crowded with photos of our respective children: black-and-white school photos I know as well as my own wedding photo. And as I pass, I can barely return their gaze; I am that ashamed. They were only children.

The drive to Lake Gormlaith is like a drive back in time, Gussy's Subaru, with its pine-scented freshener and newly vacuumed upholstery, some strange time machine. I sit in the passenger seat as Gussy navigates the familiar roads, her seat drawn close to the wheel and her hands gripping tightly in the same way about which we used to tease our own mother on the rare occasions when she got behind the wheel.

I have not been on this road in fifty years, but somehow, I anticipate every turn, nearly every bump. Memory is funny this way; you think you have forgotten some things, but the smallest reminder suddenly delivers the past back to you. A flood. A deluge. My heart is beating in the way that terrifies me as we get closer and closer to the lake. And then thankfully, just as I fear my heart might stop, Gussy pulls into the dirt lot at Hudson's. "Effie asked if I could pick up some milk," she said. "Can I get you anything?"

I try to imagine what there could possibly be inside that little convenience store, on those dusty shelves in the smudgy glass walk-in coolers, that would take away the growing sense that I'd made a big mistake in coming here. What would that box or bag or carton look like? How much would it cost?

"I'm fine," I lie.

I sit in the idling car while Gussy makes her way inside the shop. Again, as I watch her, I see not her but our mother. Her posture, the curve of her spine. Even the back of her head, her carefully managed white curls, trick me.

Outside, the sky is a brilliant, almost alarming blue, the sun hanging like a blinding jewel nestled in its azure throat. Despite Gussy's claims otherwise, her apologies, the foliage is spectacular. *Otherworldly*. The colors of the leaves and the combinations the forests make of them are impossible, the endless landscape like a child's finger painting: a dream in crimson, violet, saffron. If I believed in God, I would see this as evidence of his existence. How else can you explain this kaleidoscope of colors?

Gussy hands me the carton of milk through my open window. "I got 2 percent," she says, shaking her head. "Maybe I should have gotten whole milk. For the children. Goodness, what do you think?"

"I'm sure it's fine," I say, thinking it is funny how Gussy, who is calm and collected during the most trying times, can worry herself into a tizzy over the smallest things. I, on the other hand, have always taken the small things in stride while the big picture finds me bumbling and fumbling.

"Ready?" she asks, sitting down, the door chiming its cheerful reminder to buckle up.

"As I'll ever be, I suppose," I say.

Three miles. Three miles that could be the network of my nerves, the very pathway made by my veins and arteries. This is how much this place is a part of me. It is my body. The breeze, my breath. This lake, as the lake comes into view, my blood. I start to feel nauseated as we round the bend where the boat access area and grassy beach appear. Unchanged. Almost preserved.

"Are you okay?" Gussy asks, reaching for my hand.

I nod, because the words are stuck somewhere inside that complicated knot of recollections. In the stones, the trees, the sinewy road before us.

"Are you sure?" she persists.

I realize I have been pressing my hand to my heart, an instinctive gesture I have adopted in the last several years. I am checking to make sure it hasn't stopped, just as I used to press my ear against Francesca's and Mouse's chests when they slept. As I did near the end when Lou was dying. But my old heart bangs hard, reassuring me under my palm.

As we pull up to the camp, I see two children playing on the broad expanse of lawn, leaping into several mountains of raked leaves. For just a moment, my heart stutters and stumbles under my fingertips. *Sally,* I think. *And Donna?* But as we pull into the drive and they come running toward the car, their dark cheeks blushed pink, I am pulled to the surface again, though it takes a moment to catch my breath.

"Gussy!" the littlest one says, opening the door and climbing into the car and nestling into Gussy's lap, throwing her arms around her neck. The older one, Zu-Zu, stands waiting patiently outside, shaking her head at her little sister, Paige, the one they call *Plum.*

How is it that these simple gestures, these nuances of the body, are passed on from one generation to the next? More so than complexion and eye color and slope of shoulder or nose, the gestures we inherit are the living ghosts. That is our mother shaking her head in this ten-year-old girl's smiling disapproval. Here is a bit of seven-year-old Gussy in the nuzzling little girl who clings to the elderly version of Gussy now.

"Okay, okay," Gussy says, finally. "Let Grammy out of the car," and Plum obliges.

Effie is in the kitchen making pancakes at the same stove where I once stood, where Eva stood all those years ago. And the girls scurry into the breakfast nook in the same manner that our own children would. How little has changed, I think. How much is exactly the same, though I don't know if this is comforting or unsettling. Effie wipes her hands on her apron and comes first to Gussy and then to me. A whisper of a thing she is; I can feel all her bones. It's like hugging a tiny bird.

Effie's hair is wound up into an enormous bun on top of that little head, secured with a pencil. She is the mobile librarian, Gussy says. Bringing books to families, to children. *We have a lot in common now*, I think. When she hugs me, I notice that despite her miniscule size, she's got strong arms that squeeze purposefully.

"It's so good to see you, Billie," she says, smiling. "I can barely remember the last time. I must have been just a kid."

I nod. She was just a teenager. If I remember correctly, she had glasses and braces then, a homely little bird. It thrills me that she has bloomed this way.

"Where's Devin?" Gussy asks, unloading some gifts she's brought for the girls as well as a dozen deviled eggs she whipped up before we left.

"He'll be here soon. He's gone into Quimby for some lumber. He's fixing the deck on the tree house."

The tree house. I can hardly believe it's still here. Suddenly I am overwhelmed by a need to see it. To climb up the ladder into the trees.

"May I go see it?" I ask.

"The tree house?" Effie asks. "Of course! But don't go up. The deck is rotted clear through. Zu-Zu almost broke her neck the last time she went up there. I had no idea how bad it had gotten."

I leave Gussy and the girls in the kitchen and make my way around the camp to the path that leads into the thick brush and trees that surround the tree house. The path is marshy, and I wish

I'd worn a pair of Gussy's galoshes. I feel as though I'm walking into an inferno as I push aside the branches of the trees. The entire forest is ablaze. I can almost feel the colors singeing me. The burning somewhere deep in my chest. At the foot of the ladder I look up, and, for just a moment, I imagine him here. Johnny in his colorful Indian headdress beating his chest and howling into that achingly blue sky. He was a child, a little boy. I've had to remind myself this a thousand times.

It was as though I were waiting for an ambush, an attack. When the phone rang again just after Ted and Frankie left for work that next morning, it could have been a bomb going off.

"Billie, Calder's really sick," Eva said. "Can you come over and help me?" The phone clicked, and there was only the static of my own breath left. The dial tone hum of my blood.

I grabbed my sweater from the back of the kitchen chair and tugged it around me as I ran out into the bright and cold November morning. I remember how startling the air felt in my breath, the way it made me almost gasp. There is something aching about the advent of winter, something beautifully cruel. The sky was turquoise, a costume jewelry sky, the sun shining like an ornament.

Inside the house, Rose was sitting on the floor watching TV, a dozen wooden blocks around her. She smiled up at me, oblivious. "Hi, Billie," she said. "I can spell my name," and sure enough, she had stacked R-O-S-E in a line in front of her.

"You are such a smart little girl," I said, and something about this made tears come to my eyes. This bright promise, this little glimmer of brilliance.

"Where's your mommy, Rosie Posey?"

"She's in the kitchen," she said. "Calder's sick."

I kissed the top of Rose's head, inhaling the strong scent of baby shampoo.

In the kitchen, everything seemed normal. The percolator sat bubbling on the counter. The breakfast dishes had been washed and stacked in their drying rack. The kitchen table had been cleared of crumbs and spills, any evidence of breakfast wiped away. But Eva wasn't in the kitchen, and the back door was wide open.

I went outside and found Eva sitting on the ground next to Calder, who was lying on the cold grass.

"What's wrong?" I asked, squatting down next to the dog and running my fingers across her warm stomach.

Eva shook her head, her eyes full. "I don't know. Ted fed her this morning before he left, while I was getting the kids off to the bus stop, and after he left, she started acting funny. Like she was drunk. She kept bumping into things, and then she came outside to the grass and now she won't get up."

I petted Calder again, peering at her face. She was panting rapidly, her barrel chest rising and falling as though she had just been running.

"Do you think she ate something bad? Could she have gotten into something?"

Eva looked up at me, choking back a sob. "I don't know."

"We have to get her to the vet," I said.

"How? We don't have a car."

"We'll borrow one," I said. "Just stay here."

I knocked on Mrs. Boucher's door, trembling as I waited for her to answer. I had only spoken to her a handful of times. She was elderly, as were the rest of the neighbors on our little dead-end road, and I was worried at first that she might not even recognize me. I knew that I had to be smart about this, if I wanted her to agree to give up her husband's Chrysler to me.

"Hello, Mrs. Boucher."

"Mrs. Valentine!" she said, her face lighting up.

"Listen, I hate to trouble you, but Eva Wilson? From across the street? Her daughter is running a very high temperature, and neither one of us has a car to take her to see Dr. Johnson. Is there any way we could borrow your car for a couple of hours? I'll be happy to fill the tank."

"Poor little baby. Have you tried an alcohol rub?"

Growing impatient, I nodded. "We've tried everything. She really just needs to see a doctor." And as I fabricated this story, I imagined Rose's skin growing hot to the touch, her eyes becoming droopy and glassy. I imagined her growing listless as her body fought off whatever germs were invading it. I almost forgot as I stood there at Mrs. Boucher's doorstep that it was Calder, and *not* Rose, who was ill. My whole life was becoming one enormous lie, and it was surprisingly easy.

I backed the Imperial up to the garage door, and we carefully lifted Calder into the back, Eva keeping an eye out to make sure Mrs. Boucher wasn't watching from the window. We loaded Rose in then, fussing over her, as if she really were sick.

At the vet's office, the doctor took Calder in right away. By the time we got there, her eyes were rolling back in her head, and Eva was weeping. She disappeared into the examination room with Calder, and I held onto Rose, trying to comfort her, but she knew that whatever was happening was bad.

After an excruciating half hour, Eva came out, her head hung, her makeup smudged. I looked up at her expectantly, and she shook her head. "They put her down. She wasn't going to make it."

My eyes filled with tears. Eva sat down next to me and I held her as she cried. "What happened?" I asked.

"The doctor says it looks like she got into some rat poison."

"*Rat poison?* How?" I knew Eva kept all of the cleaning supplies and other poisonous things on the top shelf in her pantry, far away from the children and Calder.

She shook her head, but then I felt a sucking feeling at the center of my chest, as though my whole body might just cave in.

"He knows," I said.

Eva wiped her tears. "Who?"

"Ted," I said.

Eva shook her head. "You think *Ted* did this?"

I nodded, feeling everything coming together, pieces snapping together like a jigsaw puzzle. The picture coming into focus with each click. "Think about it," I said. "She was a gift from me. So we could walk together. You said he's the one who fed her this morning."

Eva's eyes widened in disbelief, her mouth opening a little. "That's *crazy,* Billie."

"He's sending a warning," I said.

"She might have just gotten into the neighbors' garbage," Eva said, as though she could change what had happened by simply wishing it untrue. "Maybe she got into the garage somehow."

But I *knew* Johnny had told Ted, and we'd been fools to think he wouldn't. But rather than going on a rampage, rather than lashing out with his fists, Ted had laced his wife's dog's food with arsenic, put on his hat, and gone to work. Cool as a cucumber, as they used to say. And something about this realization was more threatening and terrifying than anything he had ever done to Eva's body. He was abusive and violent and filled with rage, but he was also calculating and capable of taking the life of a family pet and then whistling a little tune on his way out the door.

"I'm sure there's an explanation," Eva said as we drove Mrs. Boucher's borrowed car back to the neighborhood, but I couldn't stop trembling with both fear and a terrifying fury.

That early November night, I stood in the kitchen washing dishes and waited. I knew it was only a matter of time. I waited as I put the dishes away and mopped the floor and wiped down the countertops. I waited while Frankie tinkered with a broken toaster at the kitchen table, as the wine jug emptied, and his eyes glazed over. As I tucked the girls into their beds and as I sank into the depths of the bathtub, the water filling my ears and eyes, I waited.

The doorbell rang as I was getting out of the tub. I pulled my robe around me, and I checked my reflection in the mirror. I checked in on each of the girls to make sure they were asleep, and then I pulled their doors shut as I made my way down the upstairs hallway to the stairs.

"He said they were hugging," I heard Ted say. "They were kissing like a man and a woman. Johnny saw everything. You think my kid's a liar?" And I knew then that there was nothing to do but to go down the stairs. To enter that room and face Frankie, to face Ted, to tell the truth.

My hands were trembling, and though I was terrified, my only thought, strangely, was that Frankie deserved to know. That Ted, even, deserved the truth. And more—that I deserved to tell it. Stupidly, I also thought that now that it was out in the open, Eva and I could finally be free: that our plans would only be hastened by this sudden exposure, that revealing our secret would somehow set us free.

I walked down the stairs, and Frankie and Ted both looked at me, speechless. The absolute quiet, this horrific stillness, was excruciating.

Finally, Ted glowered, breaking the silence, but his voice was low and calm. "If you ever see my wife again, I will kill you."

Frankie's voice shook the floor beneath my feet, the walls that held the house together, my very skin. "Get out of my house."

I glanced toward the stairwell, praying that Chessy and Mouse were still asleep.

"I'll kill your whole fucking family," Ted said, pushing his finger into Frankie's chest. And then he turned and stormed out the front door, slamming it behind him.

The only thing I remember after that was feathers. A thousand red and yellow feathers flying in the air like so many autumn leaves. As Frankie knocked the kitchen table over, with all of the Thanksgiving play costumes on it, there was a storm of feathers.

Frankie's lips were gray with wine, his teeth gray as well. His breath was sour, and little flecks of spit splattered against my face as he hissed, "I should have known. All these years. You frigid bitch. You *homosexual*."

I shook my head, trying not to cry. Trying not to cower. Trying not to shatter.

"You're *sick*. Mentally ill." He tapped his head hard with his finger, and then he tapped mine. The soft pads of his finger were like bullets against my skull. And I thought of the meetings with the therapist that my parents had arranged. I remembered the hard couch, the smell of antiseptic that hinted at illness. At germs. I had thought then that they were right. I believed them. This was an *illness,* something no different than measles, than mumps, than cancer. That if I followed the doctor's instructions, I could be cured. I had even worried, for years now, that it might be something I could pass on to my own daughters. That if I touched them, if I held them too close, they would be infected by me and they would suffer the same debilitating longing for that which they could never have. It was only with Eva, only in the last few years, that I had begun to see my feelings not as those of someone afflicted, but rather of someone in love. I had believed, stupidly, that what I felt was not the symptom of a disease. It was good. Pure, even. Something beautiful. But now, here I was, feeling like I was sixteen years old again. Sixteen years old and cowering at my father's feet as he shouted at me, as he berated and accused.

"You are sick. Filthy. You are disgusting. You should not be around children. What kind of mother are you?"

What kind of mother was I? The question hit me harder than any fist.

Here is the mother I was: *barren,* my body failing me over and over and over again as I tried to bring life into this world. A mother whose own womb rejected its young progeny, expelling them before they could even begin to thrive. I was a mother who pretended that another woman's children were her own, who kept up the maternal masquerade, always afraid of being found out. I was a mother who neglected her own children, turned them away rather than infecting them with this disease that lived inside her. I was a mother who did not, could not, love her own children's father. Who could not bring herself to sleep in his arms, seeking solace instead inside another woman's embrace. I thought of all those mornings in Vermont when we left the children to their own devices so that we could linger, together, alone in the sleeping loft.

I couldn't stop shaking as he pummeled me with accusations, as his angry words, like angry blows, bruised all of the most vulnerable places inside of me.

"You're a liar, a dirty whore."

I sank down on the kitchen floor, wanting nothing more than to disappear. To simply vanish. But when Mouse came to the top of the stairs, I scrambled to my feet, ashamed that I had allowed myself to collapse like this.

"Mama?" she asked, starting to come down the stairs. "Why are you crying?"

I wiped my eyes furiously with the back of my hand and hoisted her, too old and too big to carry anymore, her legs dangling down nearly to the floor, up to my hip. I held her, embraced her, clung to her.

And as I knew he would, Frankie pried her from my arms. "Your mother is not well," he said. "Now go back up to bed."

Mouse scurried upstairs, and I could hear her feet pattering down the hallway. I thought about Chessy in her room, didn't know what I should do, *could* do or say to her if she had heard any of this.

"Who else knows?" he asked.

I shook my head. "No one."

"Liar!" His words were mushy in his mouth, softened by wine. And I wondered if he would remember this in the morning. Would this moment, like so many moments, become just a hazy, half-remembered dream to him? For once, I hoped so, as if amnesia could turn back the clock. He'd had nearly half the jug of wine that night, drowning whatever demons existed in his own mind. I prayed to a God I didn't trust that he would simply stumble away, disappear upstairs; I willed him to forget.

And then, as if by my own sheer will, Frankie stood up, and I watched as he reached for the edges of the furniture like a blind man to steady himself as he made his way to the stairwell. His pants hung loose on him, gaps in the fabric where the belt held them up. His white tank top was gray and worn, his shoulder blades sharp. He'd recently been to the barber, and there was a thick, red scab at the back of his head from a nick. All of this made me pity him. He was a child, a wounded child. I had the momentary impulse to go tuck him into bed, to put a cold cloth to his forehead and promise that everything would be better in the morning. But then he turned to me and spat one last time. "You don't deserve those children. I gave them to you, and I can take them away just as well." His words suddenly lost their softness; they were less like fists and more like knives. And I knew then that he wasn't that drunk. He would remember everything in the morning. This was the end of my life as I knew it. I could lose my *children;* he could take them away from me. For the first time since everything with Eva began, I considered the unthinkable: that my selfish needs might wind up making me lose the only other thing in the world that I loved.

This is the kind of mother I was: one who painstakingly sewed each Girl Scout badge on their sashes, who dug through the musty bins at the Salvation Army looking for a dress that I might mend and embellish for Chessy's school picture. I am the mother who made every birthday cake ever requested, defying geometry and physics, and some laws of chemistry, to do so. I was the mother who stayed up sitting next to Mouse's bed for three nights straight when she had the mumps, pressing my ear against her chest to make sure that she was still alive. I was the kind of mother who kissed bruises and bandaged cuts and colored in coloring books for hours at the kitchen table. I was the kind of mother who would have done anything to stop the suffering of either one of my daughters.

What had I done?

"Mrs. Valentine? Billie?" His voice comes to me, swims to me through the forest, where I have sat down on the rope swing suspended from underneath the tree house. It could be a voice from another time, another place. It could be only the wind. I look up and see a large man standing with a two-by-four under his arm. He is smiling, reaching out his free hand to help me up. "I'm Devin," he says. "Effie's husband."

"Oh, hello!" I say, embarrassed he's caught me indulging in such strange reverie.

"Effie tells me you used to come here back in the fifties and sixties?"

"I did," I say. "We stayed here in the summers."

"Has it changed much?" he asks.

"Yes," I say, laughing, and then shake my head. "Actually, no. Not much at all."

He is out of the blinding sunlight now, so I can see the features of his face. He sets the board down and stands with his hands in his pockets to keep them from the cold. He is twice little Effie's size. He is African American, with dark skin. Gussy told me that his sister, who came here as a Fresh Air kid in the nineties, drowned in this lake, that he and Effie met when he was renting that little house down the road. He's an artist. And despite the size of his hands, he makes intricate little shadow boxes. She has sent me newspaper clippings from the exhibits he's had. I noticed several of them in the camp when we first came in.

I remember being surprised when Gussy told me they were

getting married, amazed at how easy it was for them. If Effie had grown up when I did, she wouldn't have been safe falling in love with him. Sometimes it didn't seem possible that two living women's experiences of the world could be so very different, as if we didn't share the same planet at all. It struck me as particularly ironic that Vermont was one of the first places to permit gay marriages. There is even a bed-and-breakfast just outside of Quimby that caters exclusively to gay men and women. The old farmhouse that Eva had always dreamed of buying, the one perched at the top of a hill with a 360-degree view of the valley below, now hosts weddings exclusively for gay couples. The crumbling red barn has been repaired and painted with a colorful rainbow on one side. I can't help but feel angry sometimes, cheated and bitter and resentful. If Eva and I had simply been born later, born into *this* version of the world rather than our own, we might be together still. None of what happened would have happened. She might still be alive.

"Are you sure you're okay?" Devin asks, reaching for my hand. His skin is warm and strong, as I accept his hand and he pulls me out of the swing.

I nod, reassuring myself more than him. "Just a little tired from the trip still."

"Would you like to go up into the tree house?" he asks. "I can help you, if you'd like."

"Yes," I say. "I'd love that."

And then his little girls are running toward us, their voices like tinkling bells. And as they scurry up the ladder, their father guiding them away from the rotten boards in the deck, I study them: these gorgeous girls with their coffee skin and dark curls, with Effie's blue eyes. How could anyone ever have seen this union as anything but perfect? It makes my throat swell, close shut. There are no words for this feeling.

During the day Frankie and I pretended that everything was normal. Both of us were at a loss as to how to proceed, and so we did what we had always done. On Monday morning, Frankie even kissed me on the cheek as he always did, smelling strongly of cologne. He'd showered at least a half dozen times over the weekend, as if he could somehow scour away these new revelations. We were like robots, going through our usual routines. I made breakfast that morning, pancakes, and I combed through the tangles in Mouse's hair. I helped Chessy find her lost shoe. Frankie did not speak to me. And when they were all finally gone again in the morning, I collapsed onto my sofa and wept into my hands. I barely heard the phone ring.

Eva didn't say anything; she didn't have to. We didn't need words anymore to understand each other. She simply cried on the other end of the line.

"Eva," I said, trying hard to soothe her, like a hurt child. Like a wounded animal. "Eva."

At night Frankie and I fought. In hushed whispers and hisses. I imagine now what it must have sounded like to the children as they tried to sleep in their beds. I can almost picture Chessy, with her ear pressed to the floor, trying to decipher the words we murmured to each other across the kitchen table. I could cry when I think of Mouse curled up in her bed, clutching her Betsy Wetsy doll, trying *not* to hear.

Frankie drank, as Frankie always drank. And we went around in circles. Around and around. There was nothing I could say that could take away what had happened, was still happening between Eva and me. And there was nothing Frankie could say that could change how I felt. He accused. He pleaded. He berated and belittled and begged. And then, every night, when I thought I might not be able to take another minute, he gave up: resignation in his tired eyes and heavy sighs. When he disappeared, defeated, up the stairs, I put on my coat and walked.

I walked alone now, Eva a prisoner in her house. But I walked in her memory. I walked to remember: each crack in the sidewalk, each tree branch, each moon a vivid monument to what we had. And to what, I feared, we had lost. Every night an elegy.

And with each night, as the world grew colder and winter crept in, I began to fear the worst. As the rest of the world prepared for the holiday season, I prepared for whatever would come next. This terrible limbo, this purgatory of waiting to see what Ted would do, to Eva, to me, was like waiting for lightning. The storm was raging, and I was just waiting for the strike. Counting between claps of thunder, listening to the steady rumble and downpour.

The Scouts' Thanksgiving play was to be the Friday before Thanksgiving week, in the school cafetorium right after lunch. We had been rehearsing in the basement for weeks, but ever since Halloween, only the Wilson girls had arrived, without Eva, for our weekly meetings. They came with excuses: Rose was sick, Eva was sick, busy, tired. What I knew was that Eva was afraid. I was afraid too.

On that Friday, I gathered the costumes, which I had completed sewing on my own, and made the one-mile walk to the school by myself, lugging a laundry bag full of props and costumes over my shoulder.

Hannah met me in the cafetorium, and we taped up the butcher paper backdrops Eva had painted: the *Mayflower,* the harvest scene. I thought of her hands, carefully, meticulously painting these scenes of plenty. I had watched her as she bent over the giant pieces of paper, conjuring the first Thanksgiving with nothing but a paintbrush and paint. She was a magician and I her captive audience. My eyes filled with tears, which I quickly blinked away.

"I heard the cancer came back," Hannah said.

"What?"

"That's why Eva's been missing in action."

"No," I said. "She's fine."

"Well *you* would know, I suppose," she said, rolling her eyes.

"What's that supposed to mean?" I asked. And for the first time I considered what would happen if Hannah knew the truth about Eva and me. If our other friends and neighbors knew. I'd been so concerned with Frankie and Ted, with the logistics of how we could get away from them and be together, I had barely considered how we would actually survive in this world, this hostile place where there was no room for women like us. Where our deviation from the norm, our *deviance,* could get us sent off to a mental institution or prison even. Where our aberrations could get us *killed*.

"I'm just saying you two are so *close,*" Hannah said bitterly. "Thick as thieves."

"Shut up, Hannah," I said. Something I'd wanted to say for years. "And mind your own goddamned business for once."

She looked stunned, her face turning the same shade of red as her dress.

"Well, well, it looks like someone's having a bad day," she said haughtily, putting her hands on her hips and pursing her lips.

I shook my head and ignored her, dragging one of the cafeteria tables to center stage to act as both Plymouth Rock and the first Thanksgiving table. Mr. McNally, the janitor, was sweeping up the lunch detritus, whistling Christmas carols. He waved to me, and I waved back, unloading my sack of costumes like Santa Claus.

Only the mothers would come for the play; all of the fathers were in the city working. They would arrive in chattering gaggles with their Instamatic cameras and flashbulbs. They would huddle together in metal folding chairs, beaming with pride and waving to their children onstage. I had never, in all the time the girls had been in school, felt like I belonged to this club. These other mothers so easy in their high heels and roles. They struck me as so *content*. None of them was as restless as I was. None of them seemed to question for even a moment the tedium and pointlessness of their lives.

"I think I might need to mimeograph some more programs," Hannah said angrily. "Can you finish up?"

I nodded, grateful that she was leaving.

The Scouts were all released from their classrooms, and they rushed into the cafetorium in a flurry of nervous excitement. Alone, I fitted the girls with their bonnets, the boys with their hats or headdresses. I affixed paper buckles on their shoes. We ran through their lines once, and then we waited as the mothers filed in and took their seats, followed by the remaining students at the school.

I peered out at the crowd, looking for Eva, hoping just to catch a glimpse of her. She felt like a dream already, like some gossamer recollection. But she wasn't out there, at least not sitting where I could see her.

When everyone was settled, I pulled the makeshift curtains open, and we were suddenly aboard the *Mayflower*. The children recited their lines, carefully articulating their words and projecting their voices, as we had told them to do. When the *Mayflower* arrived, I pulled the curtains and hurried onto the stage to change the backdrop and set the table. I returned to the wings and pulled the curtains open again.

When I heard the gasp, I feared that something had happened onstage; that the harvest backdrop had fallen down, that a child had fallen or bumped their head. But the gasp was followed by a high-pitched cry and then a thousand whispers, like bees buzzing. I looked out into the crowd, and the whole audience was moving, shifting. Leaning into each other, voices growing louder and louder, followed by more women crying out.

Just then, Mr. Prine, the principal, came running up to me, as the children froze, forgetting their words onstage, distracted by the commotion in the audience.

"It's the president," he said. "He's been shot."

I felt my heart bottom out. I couldn't have heard him correctly. "What?"

"You need to stop the play," he said.

I nodded, moving quickly to the stage, where the children looked at me, bewildered. I hustled them offstage. "There's been an emergency," I said, trying to be reassuring, but my vagueness created only more chaos.

"What happened?" whispered Francesca. "Is it Daddy?"

"Oh, no," I said.

"Is there a fire?" Mouse asked, clinging to my pant leg.

"No, honey," I said, leaning down to her and hugging her.

Mouse clung to me as Mr. Prine made his way to the stage and in his best principal voice announced that President Kennedy had been shot during a motorcade in Texas, that all children would be sent home from school immediately. The official announcement was followed by one collective gasp, and the children all began to cry.

I gathered the Scouts together and held them; I didn't know what else to do. And it was then, as I ushered them down the stage steps to deliver them to their mothers, that I saw Eva.

She was sitting in the very back row, Rose asleep in her arms. Her eyes were wide, stunned, but she sat still, paralyzed. Donna and Sally went running to her, followed by Johnny, who had been watching the play in the audience. Rose woke up and started to cry. And I didn't care anymore. I went to her.

"Let's take the children home," I said.

She nodded, and together we gathered our children and began the long walk back to Beechtree Street. The sidewalks were crowded with other mothers and their children, a mass exodus from the school. As if there had been a bomb. As if the world were ending.

By the time we got back to my house and we were able to turn on the television, Walter Cronkite was explaining that JFK had just been confirmed dead. We watched, the children holding on to us in disbelief. Even Johnny, who was never still, sat motionless.

"I don't know what to do," Eva said.

I shook my head. I didn't either. What do you do when the world is starting to crumble?

"Stay," I said later as Eva gathered the children, finding their coats and hats and mittens. "Please."

She shook her head. "It's not safe."

Nothing was safe. No one was safe. Not us, not even the President of the United States.

Frankie and Ted both came home early that night, but by the time their cars pulled up, Eva had already slipped away. Because, while all the rules of the universe seemed to be somehow suspended on this day, we knew that some things remained the same.

Over the next week, a collective pall fell over our household, over all of Hollyville, and, I suspect, over all of America. The melancholy I had been feeling since Halloween seemed to have spread, like a pox, across our community. I knew in my logical mind that the two tragedies were unrelated, but the shared grief over Kennedy's assassination, the horror, was like a public expression of my most private thoughts. It was as though all of America were grieving with me.

But despite everything that had happened, to Jack Kennedy, to our nation, between Eva and me, Frankie insisted on carrying out our normal Thanksgiving tradition. Every year since Frankie and I bought the house in Hollyville, we had entertained his sisters and their families for Thanksgiving. It was a tradition I pleaded with him to break this year, but he'd insisted, swearing that if we canceled Thanksgiving they would know that something was wrong. He said that if I cared at all about the children, about our family, I would just pretend like everything was normal. His stubborn insistence struck me as desperate, childlike. However, I was in no position to argue. My sins had put me at his mercy. His will dictated nearly every breath I took. And truthfully, we all felt a bit untethered (by what had happened to the president, to our country, to our family), and I think this was his effort to restore at least a semblance of normalcy to the house.

And so on Wednesday morning, I was up (as expected) before the sun, making sweet potatoes and green bean casserole and mincemeat pies. While Frankie and the children slept, while the rest of the world slept, I made normal out of flour and sugar and salt.

Eva and I had not spoken since the twenty-second, not since we sat in shared horror and watched the rest of our world start to fall apart. I thought of her across the street, carrying out the same rituals as I was. We were like needles stuck in the deep grooves of this endless song.

Despite Frankie's optimism and insistence, I knew that having Frankie's family over, with nothing to do all day but to eat or drink, was a recipe for disaster. I imagined what the glossy picture might look like in my *Betty Crocker's Cookbook.* Ingredients: 6 Italian siblings, 6 bottles of wine, 1 angry husband, and 1 enormous secret. Combine and you will have disaster even before dessert is served.

When we were first married, I loved these gatherings. Frankie's family had been a novelty to me at the beginning: all that fabulous noise and commotion. My own family had been so reserved, so quiet. There were just the four of us: Gussy and me, our sullen father and taciturn mother. But the Valentine family was loud and funny. They swore and smoked and drank and drank and drank. While I never felt quite a part of this raucous party, I was always entertained and humored by them (though after the first few years, they stopped bothering with niceties, no longer on their best behavior).

Someone always wound up in tears at these gatherings; usually one of the sisters. And there was always an argument. Fists never flew, but insults did. By the end of most Thanksgivings, the dinner conversation had devolved into a swirling mess, and no one bothered speaking in English anymore. I always felt as though I'd been somehow transported back to Frankie's childhood dinner table, where I was an unwelcome guest: one who didn't speak the language or understand the customs.

There were so many cousins. While Frankie and I only had our girls, Frankie's sisters had, collectively, a dozen or so kids. I could barely keep them apart. While Frankie only had sisters, they all seemed to have at least two or three boys. The girls were few and far between, much to Chessy and Mouse's chagrin. The girls spent most of these holiday gatherings trying to keep the boys out of their rooms, which they ransacked and pillaged like pirates. It seemed that every year something of the girls' got broken and Frankie was making idle promises to repair or replace whatever it might be (the cracked hand mirror, the snapped jewelry box ballerina, the decapitated Tammy doll).

But all of this drama had always existed and occurred outside of our own small family. It didn't belong to *us*. While Frankie's sisters and their husbands carried on like squabbling children, we watched (at least the girls and I watched) like spectators at a dangerous circus. This year, I feared that we might not have the same immunity. I had ruined any chance of that.

Frankie's sisters were distraught over the assassination. As each of them entered the house followed by their respective husbands and gaggles of children, they clung to me, as though we had lost a family member. Many of them were dressed in black. As the first Catholic president, JFK was right up there with Jesus for the Valentine girls. And as a Boston boy, he was even bigger than

Elvis. When he'd been elected, they swooned. And when he died, they grieved.

Perhaps it was out of respect for the loss of our president that Frankie's sisters and their husbands, even the children, didn't engage in the same rambunctious display I was accustomed to. Of course they still smoked and cussed and drank. Frankie and the other men talked about Jack Ruby, and the women talked about Joann Graff, the latest victim of the Boston Strangler. She'd been killed the day after the assassination in Lawrence, Massachusetts. Frankie's sisters were terrified by the murders, and this one, on the heels of JFK's assassination, really rattled them. Occasionally the men would interject, assuring their wives that the Strangler wouldn't have anything to do with them. His victims were all either old ladies or young coeds, though this did little to appease them.

I tried to change the subject from all this grim business, attempting to engage Maria in a conversation about her new house in Lowell, but that fell flat as quickly as her husband interrupted.

"He's looking for girls like Theresa," he said knowingly, pointing across the table at Theresa, the only sister still without a husband. "I hope you girls got a deadbolt on your door."

The other sisters nodded in agreement.

Theresa looked flustered. Suddenly I wished we could get back to talking about Oswald and Ruby. That conversation seemed light and breezy in comparison to this.

Finally, while all the other sisters were occupied with their husbands, who (as predicted) had had too much to drink and were starting to bicker, and their children, who, fueled by pumpkin pie and too many pilfered mints from the candy bowl, were beginning to wreak havoc on our home, Theresa offered to lend a hand in the kitchen, and I was grateful for both her help and her company. Frankie, perhaps in an effort to keep his mouth shut, had ignored me throughout the meal, speaking to me only when the gravy boat ran dry and when we needed to grab another jar of my bread-and-butter pickles from the basement. Thankfully, everyone but Theresa disappeared into the living room. The sisters wanted to watch *The Arthur Godfrey Thanksgiving Special* on the TV, but the men insisted on the Detroit–Green Bay game. And as they bickered, the children slipped outside to jump in the rotting pile of leaves we still hadn't managed to bag up in the backyard.

"How are you?" I asked Theresa as I cleared the table and started to scrape the leftover bones and food into the trash. I had seen her only a couple of times since she came to stay with us that summer, which seemed a zillion years ago now. "How is it living in the city?"

"Okay," she said. I'd heard that she'd started seeing a new boy, somebody she met at church, but that he too had dropped her like a hot potato (though this time it was before he'd put a ring on her finger and gotten her hopes up). "I get lonely," she said.

It had been a big scandal, her leaving home and moving into an apartment with her friend. Two spinsters (at twenty-five!) living together. It had made me want to laugh and then cry when Frankie started speculating whether there was something "fishy" going on between them. But what I'd really felt was envy. When I thought about her living on her own, I couldn't help but picture how things might have been if I'd met Eva first—if she and I had not met our husbands, and had met each other instead, how easy it would be to be together: two girls who couldn't manage to find a husband, playing house in the city. As much as I loved my children, I couldn't help but feel a sense of having missed an opportunity. You could never be a single girl again after you'd made a family. That opportunity had simply passed us by.

"I'm real sad about the president," she said, drying a wet plate I had passed her.

"Me too," I said. "He seemed like a good man."

She nodded, but her shoulders shook, and she started to cry.

"Hey," I said. "What's the matter?" I dried my hands and moved to her, motioning for her to come to me. Inside my arms her entire body was shaking, quaking. It was scary, as though she were being shocked by an electric current.

She started to sob, big childlike gasps for air. I rubbed her back, trying to get her body to stop convulsing. Soothing her with my hands, because I was pretty sure I didn't have the words.

"Everybody leaves," she said. "Everybody. The second I love someone, they go away."

"That's not true," I said. "We love you. We're not going anywhere."

She shook her head. Family wasn't what she was talking about.

"What the hell is going on?" Frankie said, storming into the kitchen. He was swaying, somehow crossing the line from *drinking* to *drunk* in the last ten minutes. I could have sworn he left the room sober, but now he was clearly inebriated.

I pulled away from her as though I'd been burned.

"Don't touch my sister," he growled.

"What?" Theresa said, wiping furiously at her eyes. "You're crazy, Frankie," she said, laughing, because it was so inane.

"*I'm* crazy?" he said, listing and moving toward us. "She didn't tell you? What she is? The sick things she does with that woman across the street? She didn't tell you?"

Theresa looked completely confused. She tried to laugh it off, but I could tell that part of her was trying to process what he had just said. "Oh, just shut up, Frankie. Go back to your football game."

I could feel my own body starting to quake. "No," I said. "It's okay. If he has something to say he should say it. What is it, Frankie? What are you trying to say?" Part of me wanted more than anything for the words to cross his lips. For the accusations, the ones he'd been riddling me with every night for the last three weeks to come out, to rise to the surface like bubbles in a pan, to *burst*.

Frankie stood with his hands on his thin hips, his sharp chin jutted out defiantly, everything about his body saying he was ready for a fight. But his face was like a boy's. His bottom lip was trembling, and I noticed his eyes were wide and wet. Behind all that posturing, behind that bullying, was a man who couldn't understand how his wife could have betrayed him in such an unacceptable way. Had Eva been a man, had I loved Ted instead, Frankie would simply have gone after Ted with his gnashing teeth and striking fists. He would have been completely consumed by the rage of a cuckold. But this anger, this furiousness, was grounded in a betrayal that transcended simple adultery. It insulted every single aspect of him, including his own sex. I had rejected not only him but everything that made him a man. My heart softened, and I felt awash with guilt.

"Saffica," he hissed. *"Lesbica."*

It wasn't the cheating. Of course, it wasn't the adultery. It was that I had chosen a woman over him.

Theresa caught her breath, and when I looked at her, she looked away. Her cheeks and the tips of her ears burned red.

"I'm going to go see how the kids are doing. I promised Chessy I'd braid her hair that new way she likes," she said.

And Frankie and I were left alone, in the kitchen, alone with this chasm between us, growing like a sinkhole. We stood at the edge, peered into the vastness growing between us, and, for the first time, were rendered speechless by it.

"Come see what we've done!" Effie says, reaching for my hand. "I bet it looks a little different from when you were here, no?"

Effie gives us a tour of the camp, showing us the changes she and Devin have made since they moved in back in the mid-nineties. It feels strange to be a tourist in this museum, these ruins of my own past. As she gestures to the new wainscoting Devin installed in the bathroom, the new washer and dryer tucked into the broom closet, my eyes are drawn instead to the old scuffs on the floor. I can practically hear Johnny scraping the big armchair across the floor. I can see Eva tucking her pretty legs up underneath her, Rose crawling into her lap to have a story read. I wonder if I looked on the bookshelves I'd find that old copy of *The Wind in the Willows*. I can remember the cover's exact shade of peach, feel the cracked spine.

"This is my favorite room," Effie says happily, leading me to the sleeping porch that looks out over the lake. When Eva and I stayed here, we filled the room with cots for the girls, each of them made up with clean, white sheets and red wool blankets. Now, the room has been transformed into an office for Effie. On the walls that aren't interrupted by windows, Devin has built bookcases, which are packed with library castoffs, their shiny, plastic jackets reflecting the bright sun outside. There are books on the floor, a few Barbies, and a pair of roller skates. In the middle, facing the view of the lake, is Gussy's old desk, painted a deep forest green. This is the desk where I would sit, drafting letter after letter to Eva after she returned to Hollyville all those summers ago. I know that the drawer sticks. I can picture the faded floral drawer liners. I wonder if there is any evidence remaining inside: four-cent stamps, the parchment stationery I loved.

"We call this *the gallery,*" Effie says, smiling proudly, as she gestures to Devin's artwork that lines one whole wall in the living room: his miniature worlds captured inside crudely fashioned boxes he has made himself. I peer into each one, marveling at the beauty of his handiwork. They are like little tiny dreams. Figments. Glimpses. Effie beams as she runs her fingers along the little brass plaques affixed to each, the ones etched with the titles: *Zu-Zu's First Haircut. Loon Egg, Unbroken. Winter.* I wonder briefly if anyone ever commissions work from him, and consider what I would ask him to capture inside a box for me. What glimpse might he be able to arrest, what snapshot? And as Effie steers us through the addition and the little guest cottage Devin is building out back and then, finally, up the stairs to the loft, I think that these four walls, the camp itself, is no different than one of his shadow boxes. It is a diorama of my own sorrow. The glistening threads tying me to the past. The broken bits of glass holding sunlight only having to relinquish it at sunset. Everything that matters in the whole world is etched into the scuffs in this floor, in the faded photographs on these walls.

I stand staring at the bed where Eva and I once held each other, clung to each other like two drowning people. Of course, it is the same bed. A new mattress, I suppose, but the frame is the same: that old iron bed. I feel lightheaded.

"Billie, can I get you some water? You look pale," Effie says. She is reaching for my arm, her tiny fingers curling around my sweater. Her big eyes look at me, worried and expectant.

"I just need to sit down," I say. I don't want to scare her. Poor girl, just trying to show off her home.

"Please," she says, nodding and gesturing for me to sit on the bed. "Lie down for a minute. I'll go get some water for you."

I resist but then have no choice but to acquiesce. My heart aches in my chest. And then the soft bed yields to me, and I begin to sink.

The FOR SALE sign went up in the Wilsons' yard the Sunday after Thanksgiving. I watched Ted pounding the wooden stake into the unyielding ground, and with each strike it felt as though he were pounding the stake into my heart. He looked up and caught me watching him through the windows, but I did not retreat. What was there to run away from anymore? He *knew*. And so instead of hiding, I simply stared back at him, trying to convey in my unwavering glance that he could not do anything that would make me withdraw, that I wasn't afraid of him.

I *was* afraid of him though. I'd seen what he was capable of, and it terrified me. He'd repeatedly hurt Eva. Now he'd killed Calder. He'd murdered a living creature. I feared for the children. I feared, even, for my own life. But I would not give him the satisfaction of knowing how afraid I was. I would not give him that.

The sign was up only for one week before it was replaced with a SOLD sign.

The Monday morning afterward, when Ted and Frankie and the children had all left for work and school, I went across the street still wearing my nightgown and robe and rang the doorbell. I peered through the small window in the door and could see boxes everywhere. It looked like it had the first day I had crossed this threshold. Just three years had passed, but in those three years was my entire life, my entire world.

It was almost winter now, freezing cold, and the wind that ripped across the front porch and through the thin fabric of my nightgown felt like an assault. I rang the doorbell again and again until Eva came and opened the door.

It had only been a few weeks since Kennedy was shot and she had sat in my living room watching the news of his assassination unfold on the TV, but she looked so different. Her belly had grown exponentially, and her face was swollen as well. There were deep purple pockets underneath her eyes, and her cheeks were pale. She looked broken. Sad. It was nearly Christmas, but there was no evidence of the holidays in this empty house. No tree, no stockings hung by the hearth. No mistletoe.

I had to touch her; I had been kept away from her for too long. Every frayed nerve in my body buzzed for her. Ached. She reached for my hand and pulled me into the house, looking frantically out into the empty street behind me.

"Where's Rose?" I asked.

"Upstairs playing," she said. "I'm trying to pack, but it's so hard . . ." she started, but I didn't want her words. I wanted her mouth, her lips. I wanted to feel my body pressed against hers. I wanted to feel her chest against my chest, her hips against my hips. I wanted to smell her hair and breath and the musky scent between her legs. I wanted to swallow her and be swallowed by her.

As I kissed her, she locked the front door behind me, and pulled the curtains shut. We stumbled and tripped across the boxes that littered the floor, their lives carefully packed, all the fragile remnants protected by newspaper. I remember her hands smelled like newsprint as they found my face in the now-darkened living room.

We made love on the dusty floor. I felt my spine bruising as each vertebra made contact with the oak floorboards. But even as I winced, I knew I wanted these blue reminders to stay; I wanted that nebulous pain in my heart to manifest as something tangible: cuts, bruises, something *real,* something that could heal.

It wasn't until Rose called down from upstairs that Eva

opened her swollen eyes and rushed to her feet. She left me, breathless on the floor, and went to her.

Later we sat at the kitchen table, as Rose played with an empty moving box, and Eva told me that Ted had gotten them an apartment in the city. He told her that if she ever saw me again, he would kill her and then he would kill me.

"We can call each other," I said. "On the telephone. He can't watch you every second of every day."

"It's long distance. He'll know. Frankie will know."

"We'll write then," I said. "You'll need to go to the post office. Get a post office box. Pay for it with cash. I will send you letters there. And you can send letters to me at home."

She shook her head. "He'll know," she said.

"No," I said, squeezing her hand. "He won't. Eva, it's the only way we'll be able to stay in touch. Don't you understand?"

"I'm worried about the children," she said.

"He wouldn't hurt the children," I said, shaking my head.

"I think he would do anything to hurt me," she said definitively. "And they're the only thing I have left. You have to understand that, Billie. I cannot lose my children. It would be worse than death."

Sometimes when everything is taken away is when you realize exactly what you have left. And what I had left, the morning that the moving truck came and took the contents of the Wilsons' house away, and Ted pulled up in the red Cadillac and took Eva away, was just the empty blue sky, white snow, and a bitter cold that shimmered like something alive in my body: a bitterness that echoed and resounded against the walls of this empty place. The entire world took on a startling quality that morning. It had snowed, but the sky was a bright, bright blue, an *aching* blue, the sun so bright it made my temples throb.

This is what I had left: I had the back of the yellow school bus battered with mud driving away. I had three loads of laundry to fold, the smell of starch and coffee. Empty plates, slick with egg and grease. I had shoes all over the floor. I had socks to darn and clothes to mend. I had an empty icebox and a full Christmas shopping list with not a single item crossed off. As I sat down in the living room, among the trappings of my life (the junkyard furniture Frankie dragged home; the Douglas fir he'd insisted would fit in the bay window but that was too tall, too full with its lush arms, and crowded out the view; the faint scent of my children—the shampoo, cereal, rubber cement smell of my girls), I felt nothing but a sense of forfeiture, as though I'd just relinquished my whole life.

I drafted the first letter to Eva that morning, spilling all that loss and longing, that desperate emptiness in what, I am sure now, were pages of distraught and overwrought prose. My handwriting was that of a lunatic. I wrote until my wrist joint ached as much as my heart, conjuring with my pen every single moment of happiness she had afforded me, evoking every nuance of hers that I loved. I'd be ashamed to read that letter now; my only hope is that it did not survive these years as I have. Of course, I had no address to which to send the letter. No post office box. No street. I had no idea where Ted had taken her. He refused to tell her the address of the apartment before they left, afraid, I am sure, that she would reveal it to me and I would go to her. And I would have gone to her. I would have, had I known where she was, left all of this behind (the dirty sheets, the unscrubbed floors, the torn and tattered quotidian accoutrements of my life) if it meant one more minute with her.

Each second that the Kit-Cat clock ticked off with his rolling eyes and wagging tail was excruciating, as though time were mocking me. Each morning when the children punched out the next cardboard door on the Advent calendar, taking turns eating the stale chocolates inside, I felt like another day had been stolen from me. Each trip through the snow to the mailbox, as I waited for her words but found only grocery store flyers and bills, felt like a journey around the world. Every night as Frankie lay next to me, willing me to love him back, felt endless. Time slowed to an excruciating crawl.

I knew that I had to do something. I had to find her. Soon, it would be Christmas, and Frankie would be home from work for a whole week. Our house would be filled with company (the sisters, their husbands, my parents); I wouldn't have even a moment alone. I would be occupied with studding hams and wrapping gifts, with sewing Christmas dresses and helping the girls rehearse their Christmas carols. And my greatest fear was that without me, Eva would forget: that I would slip away from her memory, that all remembrances of me would dissolve like bath salts into so much warm water.

But then, two weeks before Christmas, the postcard came. It wasn't signed. And it wasn't dated. It said hardly anything at all, but it said everything. Two *addresses,* written in block letters, etched in handwriting I knew as well as my own. Just a P.O. box and a street address. But those numbers and words were better than any missive of love. Because the numbers were just a secret code for me to decipher; they said, *I am here.* They said, *Come to me.*

I must have fallen asleep in Effie and Devin's bed, and when I finally wake up, I am disoriented and slightly queasy. I roll over, expecting (for a fragmented, desperate moment) to see Eva's pale shoulder. But I am alone, lying in my clothes on top of the bedspread, an afghan laid across me while I slept.

The sun has gone down outside, extinguishing the fire that was blazing in the treetops earlier. It is warm and quiet. I smell the smoke from the chimney, the sweet scent of it. I can hear the sounds of the girls downstairs trying to be quiet, their loud whispers taking tremendous effort, the small reprimands from Effie each time they forget. It is dark in the room, but beams of light appear through the knotholes in the floor as I stand up. Mouse used to call them the stars in the floor.

I am embarrassed coming down the stairs, though my only shame is being an old woman who fell asleep after a long journey. Still, I walk into the living room, where everyone has gathered, and feel like I've just come late to a party. Everyone looks up at me expectantly before returning to their various tasks and amusements. Effie and Zu-Zu are playing a game of Scrabble. Gussy is on the couch with her knitting and Plum, who looks a little sleepy herself. She is rubbing her eyes and burrowing into Gussy's side. I can hear Devin in the kitchen, the music of pots and pans and boiling water. I can smell the potent smell of whatever he is making for dinner.

The sun has almost set, and the sky is an old sky, a familiar sky, freckled with stars.

"Well, good morning," Gussy says. Our mother's words for us after a nap.

"Morning," I say, the answer she expects. "What smells so good?"

Dinner is delicious, but I can barely eat. The smells of lasagna and warm artisan bread with garlic butter mock me. I push the food around my plate like a child, and Gussy shakes her head at me like a mother. But I am too nervous to eat. In the morning, we will leave this safe nest in the woods and drive to Boston to see a man who knows the most intimate secrets of my entire life. I feel sick.

"Time for a bath!" Devin says, scooping up both girls, one under each arm like footballs, and carrying them, giggling and kicking for release, to the bathroom. As he sets about getting the girls bathed and ready for bed, Gussy and I sit in the kitchen nook drinking tea, and Effie finishes up the dishes.

"Would you like to take a walk?" Effie asks sweetly as she puts away the last pot and pan. I have been watching the way she and Devin work together, the harmony of their movements. They are like two moving cogs in this domestic machine. I envy this choreography, this symmetry. There is a balance here that defies everything I have known of marriage, of running a household. Lou and I lived together for many years, but even we seemed to have separate orbits. Perhaps because we each had a lifetime behind us when we met, we were too old to fully merge our lives.

"I'd love that," I say. I feel wide awake after the long nap, my legs restless.

"I think I'll stay here with Devin and the girls," Gussy says. "You two go."

Effie grabs a large, beige barn coat from the closet, disappearing inside it.

"Was that your Grampa Frank's?" I ask.

"Ay-uh," she says, putting the accent on thick, and it is Frank

I hear. I also see Frank in her slow smile and nod. Effie and Frank were very close: *two peas,* Gussy called them. My own grandchildren have always been faraway, dreamlike: the only evidence of their growth in the myriad of photographs stuck on my refrigerator door. Because I fled to California, I never really got to know them. I've met them, of course, and when they were very small I went and stayed with Francesca to help her out every now and then. But I have never truly been a part of the fabric of their lives. No matter how many cards I've sent, no matter how many times I've called. The distance I sought when I fled the East Coast was one that did not discriminate. It separated me from Frankie, from that old life, from all those unfulfilled dreams (and all the shattered ones), but it also separated me from my own children. It is the price I had to pay. I know this makes Chessy sad. I know she blames me for a lot of things, a lot of absences and holes in her life. I am almost as nervous to see her as I am to see Johnny.

The dirt road that circles the lake is bumpy with ruts and ridges from the grader that passes through once a week. I worry a little that in the darkness I might stumble on an upturned stone. Take a tumble. But then again, a little injury might be excuse enough to cancel the trip to Boston. And then as if on cue, as if I willed it, my ankle turns. "Oopsy," I say, my body correcting and compensating, righting itself before I take a nasty spill onto the ground, and Effie reaches for me, quickly righting me. Steadying me.

"Are you okay?" she asks. I've scared her. I know she must worry about Gussy, about all of us whose bodies are stubbornly defying us.

I nod. "I'm fine. Just clumsy."

Effie takes my elbow then and helps me navigate the dark road. I am grateful for the help, even though her gesture makes me feel old.

"Which one is the Masons'?" I ask. I have told her that I know Sam and Mena.

"That one, just up ahead," she says. It is too dark to see, right now. There are no lights on inside. I'll need to come back during the day to take a picture for Sam.

"Oh, I remember that place," I say, nodding.

"What was it like, when you used to come here?" she asks.

I look out at the lake, which is still as stone tonight, just a glass mirror reflecting the moon overhead. "It was the same," I say. "Places like this don't really change. Only people do."

Effie stops and looks at me. Her big doe eyes are asking for something I'm not sure I can give. She pauses before she speaks—thinking before speaking another inheritance from her grandfather.

"Gussy told me you're here because of your girlfriend," she says.

The word makes me blush. I know this is how women refer to each other now, even women who are only friends. But when it comes to referring to female lovers, the casual use of the word, the lack of shame, never ceases to shock me. I can't help it. This word belongs to the present, while everything it refers to is an artifact of the past. A past where that word, *any* words to describe that kind of love, was hissed or spat or not spoken at all. Even Lou and I never settled on a term to define ourselves and what we had. We were just *Billie and Lou.*

We stop to watch a pair of loons glide across the surface of the water, calling out to each other in that mournful, prehistoric language I remember so well. Effie squeezes my elbow. "I hope you don't mind she said something. It really is one of the most heartbreaking stories I've ever heard. Like a novel almost. A true love story."

I feel my skin growing warm. But it isn't the fact that Gussy told Effie about Eva, about everything that happened, but rather that someone would see *beauty* in the story. The idea that someone could hear about what happened all those years ago and not be disgusted, horrified, by all the tragedies that followed, that someone could find a sliver of the goodness, the beauty, I cling to is almost more than I can handle.

"We're going to see her son tomorrow," I say. "I feel sick over it."

Effie nods quietly. "Of course you do."

I am overwhelmed with such gratitude toward this girl right now, this young woman. I know, from Gussy's stories, that she has had her own share of sorrow. She understands secrets and loss. Her college boyfriend died of a drug overdose, but Gussy says that he was better off dead. A *monster,* she calls him. Abusive. Controlling. Mad. *Like Ted,* she whispered. I think about how happy Devin and she seem. I still have trouble understanding how people survive and move on. How you can ever let the past go. If I were able to do that, I certainly wouldn't be here. And I wouldn't be going to Boston tomorrow.

"How do you feel about chocolate macaroons?" she asks.

"I feel very good about chocolate macaroons," I say.

"Well, that is excellent, because Devin made some yesterday, and the cookie jar is full of them."

But it isn't cookies I'm thinking about as we walk back to camp. It isn't even the treacherous road beneath my feet. It is, instead, how I am going to tell Gussy that I don't want to see Johnny. That instead, I'd like to spend the rest of my stay right here.

Frankie was always a sucker for Christmas, a sentimental fool over it. It was his favorite holiday, his favorite time of year. He loved everything about it, and being around him, it was nearly impossible not to catch some of the Christmas spirit. But this year, his nostalgia, his Bing Crosby *ba-ba-ba-boo,* only made me feel sorry for him. I would never fit into this world he'd worked so hard to create. He'd cobbled together this family out of thin air; he thought he could make anything. Fix anything. Even this. He seemed to think that if he could re-create a perfect Christmas, he could rewind the clock, he could bring back the Christmases before the Wilsons. He could erase the damage Eva had done. He could buff her out, put on a fresh coat of paint, and make us new again. I imagine this was his only thought as he assembled the plywood sleigh and reindeer, as he gathered the lights. He was the curator of an imaginary history, our home the museum.

He climbed the ladder despite the ice and my warnings, carrying an armload of Christmas lights he'd carefully laid out across the living room floor that morning and tested, tightening each bulb to make sure none of them shorted out the entire mess. He balanced on the steeply pitched roof, staple gun in one hand and the lights in the other. He'd also brought a Thermos up with him, and I was fairly certain, as I heard his boots pounding the shingles overhead, that it wasn't only coffee he was drinking, his cheer as contrived as everything else.

I couldn't bear to watch. And so I stirred cocoa in the kitchen and began to bake my way through the day: chocolate crinkles, oatmeal lace cookies, gingerbread. Perhaps Frankie was right. Perhaps we could lose ourselves in tradition.

He was up there for a long time. I'd hear him stomping around, stapling for awhile, and then there would be silence. I pictured him, back against the tall chimney, sipping at the steaming brew. I tried not to think about how loose his knees got when he was drunk, about how he stumbled even on level ground.

He'd fallen off the roof before; it shouldn't have surprised me when he fell again, but it did. I even thought at first that the sound was simply the Thermos rolling down the roof instead of Frankie himself. And because of the snow, I didn't hear him hitting the ground; I only heard his moaning. Both of the girls came running down the stairs, barging out the front door in their bare feet, to find their father splayed across the snow as though he were only making angels.

"Go inside, get some shoes on and get your coats," I said. And as Frankie sat up, I saw the unfortunate angle of his leg, the wrong way it lay bent at a ninety-degree angle from his knee, a pale white thing poking out through his trousers. In my mind's effort to bring normalcy to the scene, I imagined it an icicle. But when I realized it was not ice but bone, I felt my stomach turn. I ran to the side of the house and vomited quickly, quietly, kicking the powdery snow over my morning oatmeal.

I don't know how we got him into the car: I remember Chessy on one side of him and me on the other, all legs and arms and that prevailing moaning. But somehow, the two of us managed to get him into the backseat, and I sent Mouse into the house for the woolen blanket I kept over the back of the couch. Chessy insisted on sitting in the backseat with Frankie, and Mouse sat up front. Despite the circumstances, it was a rare treat for her to be in the passenger's seat. She fiddled with the glove box and the radio, almost gleeful. I slapped her hand away from the cigarette lighter when Frankie moaned again. "God, does anybody have any booze?"

The drive to the hospital was treacherous. The roads looked clear but were sheathed in a layer of black ice. If the Studebaker hadn't weighed three thousand pounds we surely would have simply skated into oncoming traffic. It was one reason Frankie had bought this car; he'd wanted to keep us safe. The irony of this struck me like an icy blow. Frankie was sprawled out in the backseat, thankfully drunk enough (numbed by the brandy and the cold) that he didn't seem to feel much of anything. He went in and out of consciousness all the way to the hospital, though I didn't know if his sleep came from the liquor or the pain. When the orderlies removed him from the car and wheeled him on a gurney through the hospital doors, I realized I hadn't been breathing. My lungs sucked in air, and my ears seemed to pop open, as though they'd been filled with water for the last half hour and were now clear. Everything was louder than it should be: the sirens; the sound of Mouse and Francesca crying; even the radio, which I'd failed to turn off, playing Christmas carols at high volume.

For four hours, the girls and I sat in the emergency waiting room, waiting for word on Frankie. Mouse finally curled up and fell asleep on one of the uncomfortable chairs; I envied her ability to nod off just about anywhere. Outside, the sky grew bluish as night fell. The days were so short now, the sun heading off to bed long before I did.

The hospital was decorated for Christmas. Hospitals at Christmas are some of the saddest places in the world. The attempts to bring joy to a place where most people are wounded or ill always ring as foolishly hopeful. The sparkly green garlands strung along the nurses' station, the artificial tree strung with blinking lights, even the fake snow sprayed in patterns on the windows struck me as stupidly optimistic. And all of it made me think of Frankie, pounding together that plywood sleigh, stringing our dingy little house with colored lights, his insistence that everything would be okay, that we could somehow get past all of this, if we simply stuck to the script.

They wheeled him out just past dusk, a foot-to-thigh cast encasing his leg. He looked defeated, even throwing his arms up over his head in surrender. "Merry Christmas," he said sadly.

"How long will you have the cast on?" I asked, fearing the answer and then immediately regretting my obvious selfish motives for asking. I should have just asked him how long he would be out of work. How long he would be stuck at home with me. How long he would be there to watch over me, to monitor my every move. How long it would be before I could slip away to Eva. I thought of the postcard I'd carefully hidden in the inside pocket of my winter coat, so that it would be with me, a reminder always close to my chest that she wasn't really so far away.

"Six weeks," he said. "At least."

My gasp must have been audible, because it made Frankie snort. "You're stuck with me through January. What, you got better things to do?"

Usually I stayed home on Christmas Eve, making the homemade raviolis that Frankie and the girls had grown to expect for Christmas dinner and wrapping gifts. But this year, Frankie had insisted that I come with them to Mass. He used his leg as an excuse, but I knew that it was that he wanted to present a united front: to show our neighbors and friends that the Valentines were just fine, despite any rumors suggesting otherwise. As far as I knew, both Frankie and Ted had kept tight lips around our little secret, but gossip about Ted and Eva's sudden departure (during Christmastime no less!) from the neighborhood had raised a few eyebrows. Hannah had called twice, leaving messages with the girls when I refused the phone. The arguments that kept us up half the night had likely awakened a few neighbors as well, though I suspect that no one would have dreamed to see either of these two things as related.

Getting to church was no small feat, considering how immobilized he was by the cast. We had rented a wheelchair from the hospital, but it was winter, and navigating the icy sidewalks proved to be quite a challenge, never mind the steps up to the church. Luckily, a couple of friends of Frankie's from the neighborhood were able to lift him, and the chair, up to the doors. He beamed like some sort of royalty as they lifted him; I think he was enjoying this. We sat in the very last pew. The church was crowded with all the Christmas and Easter Catholics. I suspected that the congregation had ballooned some after Kennedy's assassination as well, all of those lapsed Catholics making a return to the church in support of their fallen brother.

Though I had my doubts about God, I did always feel at peace inside churches. There is something undeniably calming about all that collective reverence. I could see how faith might entice people, how the promise of something better than this life could provide respite for the weary. And that Christmas Eve I allowed myself for a moment to imagine, to relinquish my stubborn disbelief (as I imagined Chessy would do later that night as she hung her Christmas stocking on the hearth). And as all of us, except for Frankie, lowered ourselves to our knees, I prayed.

I prayed for Eva. I prayed that she would be safe. I prayed that the children would not suffer: not mine and not hers. And I prayed that we would find each other, that one day we would make our way back into each other's arms. It was blasphemy; I knew this. Inside this church, these feelings were sinful and wicked. But if God was as loving and forgiving as they all said he was, then he might also be the one to recognize that the feelings I had for Eva were not filthy or wrong. The love I felt for her came not from evil but from the best places inside of me.

Christmas had always been a time of peace in our house. For whatever reason, Frankie had a set of arbitrary rules regarding his drinking on this holiday, which he adhered to religiously. On any other night, he was half in the bag before supper ended. But on Christmas Eve he didn't drink until after the children had gone to bed. He swapped his usual tumbler of wine for extra cigarettes, chain smoking to give his mouth something to do, filling his lungs rather than his gullet. The girls knew this, expected this, and they responded to him with affections they usually withheld when he was drinking. You'd think that this would have shown him that there were rewards for his abstinence, that his sobriety had positive consequences: that we all loved Frankie a little more when he wasn't soused, that everything good about him was drowned inside that bottle.

Frankie insisted on reading the Christmas story from the Bible to the girls on Christmas Eve. He never so much as read a bedtime story to them the rest of the year, but on Christmas Eve, they curled up in his lap and listened as he painted pictures of wise men, scented the air with incense and myrrh as he spoke. He was actually a pretty animated reader, bringing the words in the fragile pages of his family's Bible to life. I made cocoa and floated marshmallows on the top and hurried the girls off to bed as soon as their stockings were hung and they had set out their plate of cookies for Santa and a carrot for the reindeer. I think maybe Frankie and I both knew that this was the last year that Mouse would believe, and there was something remarkably melancholy about knowing that this illusion, like so many others, was undeniably fragile.

Like clockwork, Frankie poured his first glass of wine as soon as the sound of the girls' beds creaked with their weight overhead. And I sighed. At least this year, he wouldn't expect sex. It was physically impossible for him to make love to me with that cast. Ever since he'd found out about Eva, he'd seemed more determined than ever. Rather than moving downstairs to the couch, he insisted on sleeping next to me. To making love to me. As though he had something to prove. And I had tolerated him, tolerated it, because I did not know what else to do. It was easier to give in. It was easier to close my eyes and dream myself away from my body as he pushed and groped and clung. I'd been doing it for years anyway; I had perfected the art of disappearing. But now, I knew that for six weeks I wouldn't have to silently suffer his touch, to endure his naked flesh and hot breath. Merry Christmas to me.

I left Frankie and his wine at midnight, after filling the stockings and leaving only crumbs on Santa's plate, and climbed the stairs, feeling the exhaustion of the holiday season, of everything, traveling through my legs and hips and hands. I climbed the stairs like an old woman, feeling as though I had aged a hundred years since Eva left, as though all of my youth and joy had been packed away in one of her boxes.

And as I closed my eyes, I dreamed not of sugarplums but of Eva. And I wished. I wished and wished and wished, like a child hoping for that special doll or teddy bear, for Eva. I wished for a miracle I knew might never come.

Inside the camp, it is quiet. The girls are asleep already, and Devin and Gussy are in the living room, chatting quietly. Effie takes off her grandfather's coat and curls up in Devin's lap like a cat. "I'm sleepy," she says. "Come to bed?"

He nods, and together they stand up, Devin stretching his arms over his head. He is so tall, he nearly touches the ceiling with his fingers. A friendly giant.

"What time will you be leaving tomorrow?" Effie asks.

"Probably around six," Gussy says, putting away her knitting and stretching as well.

"I'll make sure there's coffee on early. I also have some bagels."

"I made some sandwiches for your trip," Devin says. "They're in a bag in the fridge, with some iced tea."

"You didn't need to do that," I start.

"It's a bit of a drive," Effie says, shaking her head. "You'll be happy to have something to snack on."

I think about telling Gussy that I have decided I don't want to see Johnny. That I am content just staying here, enjoying a few days with this lovely little family. I don't need to go dredging up the past. What's the point? What will it change? Eva is dead, has been dead for a very long time. There's no bringing her back now. And maybe Johnny would be better off letting those ghosts rest too.

"Well, good night ladies," Devin says. "If you need anything, just come get us. I put a nightlight on in the bathroom."

"Thank you for everything," I say. "It's so nice of you to have us."

Effie comes over and kisses me gently on the cheek. "Everything will be okay," she says. "Just get a good night's sleep." She looks at me and squeezes my hand. And for some reason, I decide not to say anything. Not yet. I'm sure I'm just tired. It was a long trip. I'll wait until morning and see how I feel then. If I still want to skip the trip to Boston, I'll tell Gussy in the morning. No need to get into an argument tonight.

Gussy and I settle into the twin beds in the guest room addition, and for a moment I am transported back to the childhood bedroom we shared. I squeeze my eyes shut and try to evoke the farmhouse, our childhood home. I remember the goose down pillows and the prickly spines that stuck out through the ticking. The chenille spreads with their bumpy ridges between my fingers. I remember the smells of the farm outside our window, the lowing of cows and lament of the bullfrogs. I begin to settle into a different sleep, not the sleep of an old woman but that of a child. And so when the phone in the kitchen rings, it pulls me suddenly not only from sleep into consciousness but from the distant past into the present.

I hear someone scrambling to get the phone, and then the muffled sound of Devin's voice. And then there is the quiet knock on our door.

"Billie? I'm sorry to wake you," Devin says. "But you have a call. It's John Wilson?"

I wrote her letters, frantic ramblings etching out the monotony of my days, sketching the empty spaces she had left behind. I was no writer, but somehow I became both prolific and poetic in these missives. As Frankie dozed in front of the television, I disappeared into the rooms he couldn't access with his crutches and scribbled my wishes, my regrets, my fears, and, most of all, my love onto page after page, which I stuffed into envelopes, sealed with my lips, and delivered via the U.S. mail, trusting that they would reach Eva. I imagined their journey, nestled and jostled among bills and advertisements, letters from soldiers and sons, from daughters and doctors, and all the other lovers. Her responses were sporadic and clearly censored by her own fear. They were quick, dashed off, I imagined, in the rare moments when she was alone. As a result, they were much more pointed, more *poignant,* the emotion behind them distilled and condensed. *I love you. I miss you. I am so very alone.*

The letters were my only solace those long weeks as Frankie hovered and healed in the house. He was unable to make the trek to the mailbox each afternoon after the postman came, and I learned quickly how to feign boredom as I brought in the stash of mail, the only correspondence that mattered safely concealed in my pockets. Sometimes it would be hours before I could steal away with them. When I was finally alone, I held them to my face and inhaled, struggling to smell the familiar scent of her fingertips.

If Frankie had known what I was doing, the other world in which I was living, I don't know what he would have done. His days were consumed by the rituals of the wounded. I think he imagined himself a warrior of sorts: the broken leg resulting not from a drunken fall from the roof but from the very real war he was waging to get his life back, his wife back. His suffering became symbolic; his scars were battle scars, and the damage was not due to his own stupidity but to my indiscretion. I was the enemy: captured, conquered. These were the spoils of war. But I was only lying in wait. If this was indeed a battle, it wasn't over yet. Frankie only thought it was.

What Frankie missed most, I knew, was his work in the workshop. His immobility had kept him from the treasure hunts, had prohibited him from collecting and gathering those things he could restore, the real things he could fix. And without this tangible proof of his ability to mend, he was lost. When I found the broken console hi-fi at the Methodist Church rummage sale right after New Year's, I knew I'd found my peace offering. My olive branch. I loaded it into the back of the car, along with the bags of winter clothing I'd found for the girls, and smiled all the way home. The best way to defeat an enemy is to make them think you're ready to surrender. If I could make Frankie think he'd won, I knew he might loosen his grip.

He was glowing as I dragged the monstrosity into the house. It was snowing out, and my bare hands were freezing, the skin chapped. I blew into my curled fists and smiled my biggest, brightest smile. "It's a Grundig Majestic. It needs some new wiring, I think. Maybe something to shine up the cabinet. But it's a real beauty, Frankie! And it will play all your old 78s, and the 45s and LPs too, of course."

I had him. It was a project he would be able to do, right there in the kitchen if he liked. I'd even stopped by Aubuchon's and gotten the tools he'd need. It would also take him a while, the way I figured. It would keep him occupied. Distracted.

The next day (I knew I had to wait a day, otherwise he'd be suspicious of my intentions), as I made his lunch in the kitchen, I said, "I have an appointment in the city tomorrow." It was a bold move, but one I had to make.

He looked up from the cabinet, which he'd been stripping with rags dipped in Minwax. "Why?" he asked.

"I've been having some pains, and I need to see a specialist." There were few things in the world that Frankie had no argument against, and my female health was one of them. And, of course, the pains were real, but I didn't need a doctor to diagnose them.

"I'll come with you," he said. "We can make a day of it. I need to stop by work anyway, check in."

I felt my heart plummet, but I didn't allow it to show on my face. I had anticipated this, after all. Frankie was predictable, if little else. "No," I said. "The doctor's office is on the third floor, and there's no elevator. I can stop by the post office for you."

"Oh," he said.

"I can also pick up some new needles for the hi-fi," I said. "Maybe go to that record shop you like in Cambridge and get some records? Is there something you'd like? I know the girls want that new Elvis album."

He looked at me, studied my face, looking for cracks in my composure, for anything that might give me and my intentions away. But I was a stone. I had rehearsed this moment, my expressions contrived but expressing nothing but fear for my health and the innocence I hoped to convey.

"You'll call me from the doctor's office," he said. "After the exam?"

"Of course," I said, nodding, willing my face to remain stoic. Not to reveal the joy, the happiness, the excitement that I could feel rushing through my body in hot waves. I couldn't believe it. It had *worked*.

★ ★ ★

Eva had written that most days Ted came home for lunch. And he always changed his lunch hour so she never quite knew when he would show up. Sometimes it was as early as eleven o'clock. Other times, he didn't arrive until nearly one thirty. But on Tuesdays, there was a mandatory sales meeting over the lunch hour that he could never escape, and so Tuesdays she knew that he would not be able to check in on her except for the phone call he made during the break, which was always at twelve fifteen.

Eva wrote that she had asked Ted's sister to watch Rose that day, that she told her she had some errands to run including a surprise for Ted and didn't want to take Rose, who had been sick with a head cold, out into the bitter cold. Ted's sister knew nothing of what had transpired in Hollyville and had happily agreed. She'd promised not to utter a word to Ted; she'd keep it a surprise for his birthday, which was just days away.

I had memorized her address, the numbers like a magical combination to the lock on a safe. I practiced them in my head like any good thief. When I left that morning, Frankie kissed my cheek and said, "It's going to be okay. I'm sure you're fine." I'd almost forgotten what he was talking about, until I remembered the imaginary doctor, the real pains, my promise to call him as soon as the exam was over. I mentally ticked off the details of my lie, like a checklist: *doctor, phone call, record store, post office.*

The train into the city after rush hour was quiet, no hustle-bustle. I had never understood how people could stand the crowds on the train. The few times I'd ridden the rush hour train I'd felt nauseated and anxious. All that cologne and perfume and breath did a number on my stomach. I was grateful today for the empty seats and the absence of the usual olfactory assault. There were a couple of other women on the train, gloved hands folded in their prim laps. I tried to imagine where they might be headed: to real doctors, I supposed. Shopping, I imagined. I was the only one headed into the city to find my lover, to make my way through the maze of streets to an apartment I'd never visited.

I smiled at a woman who sat alone near the back of my car. She was holding an infant in her arms, the tiny, pink face peeking out of the swaddling. Eva was due in April, which made her nearly six months along now. I thought of the baby growing inside her, this child we had called our own. I squeezed my eyes shut to keep the hot tears that were welling up inside them from falling.

Their apartment was on Newbury Street in the Back Bay, just a few blocks from the Copley Square subway station, and so I took the green line from North Station, feeling motion sick as the car rocked and dipped until we finally slowed and stopped. Clutching Eva's most recent letter, I got off and emerged into the bitter cold again. The walk to Newbury Street was not a long one in normal weather, but this was Boston in January, and the air had teeth. According to the thermometer outside our house that morning, it was just above zero, but with the wind that came off the Charles, it could have been ten below. My teeth felt loose in my head, rattling and chattering as I clutched my coat tightly around me and walked headfirst into the wind. By the time I got to the building that she had described, I was almost completely numb with the cold. The wind had beaten my face, and it felt as though I had been slapped. Every inch of my exposed skin stung. The tears that the wind and everything else evoked froze, matting my eyelashes together and rendering my nose hairs solid. I was sure I looked a fright, and I certainly didn't want Eva to see me like this.

I stepped into the revolving doors of the building and was unprepared for the blast of heat that awaited me when the doors spit me out into the lobby. The warmth filled my lungs and made me cough. When I held my hand to my face, it was frozen in a grimace. I took off my hat and patted at my hair, which I knew had been undone by the wind and the woolen hat. I shook the snow off the rubbers that covered my shoes and then peeled them off and stuffed them in a baggie in my purse. I stared at my reflection in the giant oak-framed mirror that hung by the elevators. I barely recognized myself anymore. I had aged in the last two months. The color that had flushed my skin from a summer spent with Eva lying along the shore of the lake was gone, replaced with a ghostly pallor. My eyes were snuffed out, the sparkle I could usually locate there gone, the irises flat, dull green circles, brown at the edges. My hair even, which usually was the color of vibrant autumn maple leaves, seemed brittle and dull. Winter had descended upon me, and I was worse for the wear. I pulled a tube of lipstick from my purse and quickly outlined my lips. Then I squirted just a little of the Evening in Paris perfume from the bottle Frankie had given me (that Frankie always gave me) for Christmas. I smiled, my mouth resisting, still frozen in a grimace, and pressed the button for the elevator.

I had not spoken to Eva on the phone. The last correspondence we had had was my confirmation that I would be here on Tuesday, today, and that I was counting the minutes until I could see her again. I could only trust that she would be waiting for me in apartment 505. The fifth floor felt as far away as outer space as the elevator began to make its slow ascent.

"Billie," she said as she opened the door. She leaned forward, looking down the dark hallway after me. "No one saw you come?"

I shook my head, and took her hand as she pulled me into the apartment.

I should have known something was wrong the moment I stepped across the threshold and into Eva's arms. But my wanting everything to be normal, whatever *normal* was between us, was so strong, my desire so palpable, that I ignored the way her body tensed instead of relaxed in my embrace. I made mental excuses for why she wouldn't look me in the eye as I cupped her face in my hands. I told myself it was just our separation that made her chest heave and tears spring to her eyes. I wouldn't let go of her until I was convinced that everything was going to be okay now. That we had made our way back to each other, that there would be a way to be together again. I whispered her name against the soft, familiar skin of her neck even as she turned her head away.

The room smelled strongly of vegetables. It almost smelled like the root cellar at home. Musky and dense. Earthy. Her house on Beechtree Street had always smelled like baked goods. Sweet and cloying. All those smells of womanhood: cookies, perfume, shampoo. But this smelled like things dying.

She shook her head, blinking hard, and forced a smile as she took my hand and led me into the apartment. The living room was beautiful but dark and dingy. The walls were papered with velvety stripes, but the paper was peeling, and there were water stains like dark clouds on the ceiling. The furniture was too large in this cramped space. The windows were covered in a grimy film, making it nearly impossible to see outside.

"It needs some work," Eva said apologetically. "It belonged to Ted's crazy old aunt."

"It's nice," I said, but it wasn't. It was horrible.

"How is Ted's job?" I asked. But I knew the moment his name escaped my lips that I had made a mistake. A shock seemed to pass through her body, no matter how hard she tried to hide the involuntary convulsion.

"What did he do, Eva? What has he done to you now?"

She sat down on the sofa and put both of her hands over her face. "If he finds out you came," she said, shaking her head, staring at the floor. "If he so much as suspects that you've been here . . ."

"I know," I said. "But he won't know. He won't find out. I promise."

"You can't ever come back," she said. "This has to be the last time."

"No," I said, feeling my grip on the world loosening. We had been in this together. Without her, without *us,* what was left? "You know you don't mean that."

"I couldn't write this to you in a letter. I needed to see you. To tell you in person." She was weeping now, not even bothering to stop the tears. Her careful makeup smeared into muddy pools beneath her eyes. I rubbed them fiercely with my thumb, my face so close to hers I could smell the chamomile scent of her tea. "He will kill me," she said. "He will kill you."

I thought of Calder, and my chest swelled with anger and loss and fear. I could feel my heart beating in my ears, the blood pounding like fists at my temples. I reached for her hand and she pulled it away from me, shaking her head. "We can't do this anymore. He's right. It's sick. It's wrong. We were just confused. I am so confused."

My eyes widened as she recited the words I was certain he had repeated like a mantra in her ears, as she minimized what had happened between us to an illness, to an accident, to a mistake.

"It's over, Billie," she said, wiping away her tears and taking a deep breath. "It has to be."

I stood up then, feeling as though I might faint. My legs seemed to have disappeared out from under me. I stumbled, no different than Frankie, but drunk on love and filled with a lethal combination of rage and despair. I backed away from her, terrified by what she had become, by what he had made her. I backed up until I was standing in that foyer again, in that damp, dark place that smelled of rot.

"He can't kill you," I said, my voice coming from somewhere so deep it felt as though my very heart were being excavated. "You're already dead."

I didn't call Frankie from the imaginary doctor's office with made-up stories about my female troubles. And I didn't go to the record store to buy *Fun in Acapulco* or to the post office to inquire about Frankie's disability benefits. I didn't get on the train and go home so that I could meet my children at the bus stop, and I didn't stop at the market along the way to buy a roast or ground beef or a ham. I didn't plan another menu in my head; I didn't think once of the laundry that needed to be washed, the cookies I'd promised to bake for the Winter Carnival at the school; I didn't think about anything but Eva. Eva and our baby. Eva in that dark prison of a home, with its dark walls with their velvet stripes like prison bars. As I walked through the blistering cold, I thought only of Eva. Eva's head resting on my lap each night in Vermont, the way I wound her hair between my fingers and the soft sounds that came from her lips as I did. As I soothed her. I thought only of the way she laughed, those big, hiccupy laughs that seemed so incongruous with her dainty doll face, her delicate lips parting in joy. I thought only of her tongue as it skipped across my body, as it pried and pleaded, as it soothed and sated. I thought only of the way it had felt that one night in New York to hold her hand as we walked down the street together, as we danced with each other in front of the whole world. For everyone to see. For that single night without the presence of shame.

Ashamed. I was ashamed that I hadn't stayed there, waiting for Ted to come home. I was ashamed at my own cowardice with Frankie, ashamed that I had bought into his dream to erase the last three years. I was ashamed that I hated my body for all the ways it had failed me: by its inability to carry a child. Its inability to want a man. Its inability to resist the pull toward Miss Mars and then Eva. I was ashamed of my shame.

The new Prudential Tower rose like a monolith on Boylston Street. It towered over everything, dwarfed everything around it. Fifty-two stories high; they said when it finally opened, you'd be able to have a panoramic view of the city from the skywalk. That you'd practically be able to see the entire world from up there. This is where Ted would be working. Ted, watching Eva, never losing sight of her. Towering over her, a force so large, a force so big and so grand, there was no escape.

I stumbled away from the tower, trudging through the wet and cold, allowing the wind to permeate me as I made my way to the footbridge that led to the esplanade. The river was choppy, the water like a moving sculpture beneath me. I watched the icy current, mesmerized and paralyzed, thinking *I could swim*. If I were to just shed my clothes and leap into the water, the river would have no choice but to embrace me, to hold me. I'd been a swimmer my whole life, and not once had water ever failed me, accused me, spurned me. In water, I was absolutely who I was supposed to be.

That was what I was thinking, it truly was, when I slipped off my shoes and started to climb over the fence that separated me from the river below: brain and heart numbed by the frigid New England winter. I was only thinking, *I could swim*. I could just *swim*.

I was the only one out here, the only one stupid enough to face this bitter cold, and I felt absolutely alone as I stood, perched as if to dive into the icy depths below. It was the way I had felt for years, before Eva came along and changed all that. And now Eva was gone, and I was alone again.

I held on to the fence behind me, felt my legs, protected only by my thin stockings, pressing against the cold, metal barrier between earth and water. The wind urged me on and then pushed me back. It whispered in my ear, beckoning. When I felt the tug at my coat, I thought it was also only the wind playing games with me.

"Lady?" a voice said, and I turned around.

Standing on the walkway behind me was a small child, a little boy. He wasn't dressed for the cold: no boots, no scarf, no mittens.

"You aren't thinking of jumpin', are ya?" he asked.

Jumping? I had only thought of swimming. Of the glorious, graceful dive into the water. Embarrassed, I shook my head.

He held out his hand, and I took it. And despite the cold, his skin was warm. He helped me climb off the fence and back down to earth. I used his shoulder to steady myself as I climbed back into my soaking wet pumps. I hadn't put the rubbers back on, and my shoes were soaked all the way through.

"You been cryin'," he said. Not a question, just a simple statement of fact.

I studied his face. His dark hair, the freckles across the bridge of his nose. He looked like Johnny. Not exactly, but there was something familiar. The same but different. And suddenly, I felt my stomach plummet. The children. God, how could I be so selfish? How could I have even considered diving into that icy water? Eva was a better person than I. A better mother. I hadn't once considered the children. Maybe Frankie was right. Maybe I didn't deserve the children. I felt overwhelmed by guilt, by this terrible failure.

"Why aren't you in school?" I asked him as he led me away from the water's edge.

"I am. I only came outside for a smoke."

"What?" I said, horrified.

"Just joshin' you, lady. I go home for lunch, but sometimes I come here instead."

"Well, let me walk you back," I said.

"You think I go to school around *here?*" He laughed. "I'm a Southie."

"What are you doing all the way up here?" Misplaced maternal anxiety ripped through my body like the cold wind that was coming off the river now. "You shouldn't be walking the streets all by yourself."

"Well, *I* ain't the one who was gonna jump into the rivah," he said, his accent as thick as Frankie's.

"Touché," I said.

"What's that mean?"

I just smiled. "Well, let me at least walk you back to the subway station," I said.

"How about I show you something instead?"

"You're not planning to go back to school at all, are you?" I asked.

"How 'bout you stop asking questions?" he said.

He led the way down Boylston Street, and I followed behind. He stopped when we got to a building that appeared to be an old fire station.

"Come on!" he said. I knew that if I didn't go inside with him, I would risk frostbite. I might lose my toes, my fingers, if I didn't get out of the cold soon. I couldn't feel my feet at all, and my face was completely immobilized by the cold. I struggled to get the door open, and even then it took every ounce of my strength to remain standing and not collapse by the information desk, where a lady with eyeglasses suspended from a beaded chain around her neck looked at us, shaking her head with disapproval.

"There's some cool stuff in here," he said. "But I gotta go, before they call the boys on me." And then he was gone, just a flash of gray disappearing through the doors just as quickly as he had earlier materialized at the river's edge. I wondered if years from now he'd remember me, the crazy lady in her stocking feet whom he saved from jumping into the Charles River. Would he tell the story to his pals at the pub, to his girl as he courted her? Would he wonder at the serendipity of his skipping school and finding me? Maybe, maybe not. I might escape his memory as quickly as these paintings and sculptures would. I might become a small smudge in his impression of this day, if he remembered the day at all. Childhood is filled with a zillion miracles we are less likely to remember than forget. But I knew that I would always remember him: the face splattered with freckles, Johnny's face, the runny nose, and warm hands. I would remember the small tug at my coat that saved my life. The gentle reminder that I was not alone in the world. I was a *mother*. I still had to take care. This day for me would not be the impressionistic blur of a childhood recollection but rather the clear photograph of the day that I'd almost given up. The day I'd let my selfish sorrows almost overwhelm me.

I sat down on one of the benches meant for the weary museum patrons, and boy, was I weary. I took a hankie out of my purse and blew my nose, which, like a frozen pipe, seemed to have burst and started running a nearly unstoppable stream. Then for some reason, rather than looking at the painting before me, a painting that surprisingly has escaped my memory now, I looked up. And when I did, I saw the mobile. The enormous, brightly colored shapes suspended as if by nothing but hope and imagination. And for the second time that day, I felt like someone was sending me a message.

I make my way slowly from the guest room to the kitchen, where Devin has set the waiting phone on the kitchen table. He's disappeared again upstairs, to give me privacy, I suppose, though I want nothing less in this moment than to be alone with that telephone. I consider simply hanging up, cutting Johnny off before he has a chance to speak, silencing him. I realize that I am terrified of what he has to say to me. I worry that he will tell me how damaged he is by what happened, how if not for Eva and me, he would have been like any other boy. If we hadn't been so selfish, so single-minded and intent, then we would have stopped to consider the children. That my own children suffered as well. I have had this conversation with Francesca a hundred times. She herself has accused me, has blamed me, has ripped my heart open with her harsh words.

I am beginning to expect less and less that he has summoned me here to apologize for revealing our secret to Ted and setting into motion everything that happened that winter. I imagine now that he will have accusations, that he will blame me. I suspect that he has called me here to finally seek retribution for his fractured childhood. And the worst part is, I know that his indictment is exactly what I deserve. I blame myself. Of course I do.

I can smell the fire in the wood stove, hear the crackle and hiss of the logs inside. Effie and Devin are sleeping, Gussy is sleeping, the girls are also fast asleep. I am completely alone in this midnight kitchen. Alone with Johnny's voice and my smoldering remorse.

I have spent nearly fifty years immersed in the memories of my time with Eva. I have relived every moment I had with her a thousand times. In my mind, I have changed history. I have contemplated every single factor, fiddled with my decisions. Tinkered with the tiniest choices I made, in an effort to prevent disaster. I have lived a life of regret. Even the life I made with Lou was overshadowed by the tragedy of Eva. It pains me to admit this, but it is true. And this realization hits me like a blow to the chest. I feel my heart beating wildly, and I start to feel dizzy. My ears fill, and stars circle my vision. I use my hands to steady myself against the kitchen table, will myself to stay conscious. Will myself to stay alive.

I stare at the pale white phone, the same old phone that has been here forever, attached to its base by a curling umbilical cord.

What do I owe this man? I ask myself as I reach for the handset through the blur of stars. *What do I owe this child?*

What do you owe to someone whose mother you killed?

I knew Eva hadn't meant it. Her pleas for me to leave her, to forget her, were spoken out of fear. Insincere. I had to trust that if I simply hung on she would come around, that patience and persistence would bring her back to me. That Ted hadn't completely brainwashed her. That there was still hope. If I hadn't held on to this fragile sliver of belief, then I would not have survived that winter.

The letters I wrote to Eva after that awful day in the city were not the same pathetic, lovesick epistles I had sent before. Instead they were carefully crafted entreaties. They were diagrams, plans. In them I outlined how I would get her and the children out of that dark, suffocating apartment, away from Ted, away from that life. And how, if we were intelligent about it, we could begin our new life together. Every day for three weeks I delivered a new letter to the mailbox while Frankie took his shower, which was thankfully nearly an hour-long process because of the cast. And then later, when the cast was removed, and he was finally able to go back to work, I slipped the letters in the mailbox after he had gone off to the city.

At first there was no response. I worried that she no longer even made the trip to the post office to collect the mail. I tried not to think about my letters piling up inside that tiny receptacle, the postman shaking his head and cramming the next missive in.

I thought of calling, but in addition to the fear of Frankie seeing a Boston number on the phone bill, we were still on a party line, and both Mrs. Boucher and Hannah were notorious for listening in to other people's conversations. I also never knew when Ted might be there, when he might pick up.

And then, on Valentine's Day, as the mailman trudged toward our house, slinging an extra heavy sack over his shoulder, as he stuffed a single envelope into the mailbox, my heart soared. I shoved my slippered feet into a pair of Frankie's old boots and ran clumsily to the mailbox. The envelope inside was large, not the letter-sized ones I'd been sending her. It was excruciating, almost more excruciating than the days (after days) when the mailbox was empty. Because here was the answer to the arsenal of questions I had been asking. Here it was, in a manila envelope, dampened by February snow.

I sat at the kitchen table, clearing a spot. I had been working on a project for the Girl Scouts, and every flat surface in the house was covered with pinecones. I slipped my finger under a loose part of the flap and gently tugged until the glue yielded. I pinched the envelope open and turned it upside down, spilling the contents onto the table. Not surprisingly, there was no letter inside. Eva had always felt self-conscious about her writing, so I wasn't surprised. But what was inside spoke louder than any words.

Lying on the Formica tabletop, it could have just been an intricate web of nearly invisible strings. It could have only been the filaments of my imagination, the tiny hearts, each no larger than my pinkie nail, just confetti. But when I pulled the one center pin, the tiny silver bar at the middle, the hearts (my heart!) took flight. Suspended from the network of thread were a thousand tiny hearts, floating in air.

I carried the mobile carefully upstairs, trying to figure out where I might be able to hide it from Frankie. I paced from room to room, looking for a spot in the house that he did not go. A place that belonged only to me. But it didn't exist. In all these rooms, there was nowhere I could truly call my own. And the realization of this was what undid me. I sat down, finally, on the bed Frankie and I had shared for the last fifteen years, and wept. The thousand hearts collapsed beside me. I knew then that I needed to call her. This was ridiculous. I just needed to hear her voice.

Surprisingly the number was not unlisted, an oversight on Ted's part I was certain. Perhaps he didn't think I'd be brazen enough to call. But I was. That's exactly what I was. I dialed the number the operator gave me, and within only a couple of agonizing moments, she answered. "Wilson residence."

"Eva," I said.

"Billie?"

All of that certainty that had been in her voice when I stood in her apartment had disappeared. All that questioning and second-guessing. All that talk of illness and moral corruption and godlessness seemed to have slipped away.

"I love you, Eva," I said. Unable and unwilling to keep any secrets anymore.

"I love you too," she said. "I feel like I am dying here."

And then I heard the crackle and static of someone picking up on the party line. Hannah, I was sure. I heard a small clicking sound, a breath.

"Wait for me," I whispered. "I promise it will be soon."

"Billie?" she said, but I knew that if I stayed on, the entire neighborhood would know about our tryst within hours. And so I hung up.

When the girls got out of school for Easter break, I told Frankie I wanted to take them to Gussy's. We'd be back in time for Easter Sunday, but the week leading up to the holiday I hoped to spend some time with my sister.

Frankie was working a lot now, trying to replenish the bank account that had, despite the disability compensation, become depleted during his long recovery. Many days he worked overtime, catching the last train back into Hollyville after work, arriving long after supper had grown cold and the girls were tucked into bed. He would barely miss us as far I was concerned. But he was reluctant. He still did not trust me, not as far as he could throw me (which wasn't far, especially after his injury). But he had a soft spot for Gussy. We all did, and I took advantage of that.

"Gussy's going through some hard times," I said. "With the girls." Gussy's daughters were older than ours by several years. Teenagers now. They were hardly trouble though; Nancy was a straight A student, and Debbie was not bright but had a terrific sense of humor and was always, as far as I could tell, surrounded by friends. But fortunately, any troubles associated with parenting teenage girls were one of the areas (like female troubles) that Frankie stayed out of.

"How are *you* going to help?" Frankie asked.

"Just an ear to lend, a shoulder to cry on. She's my *sister,* Frankie."

This too was something Frankie could understand. He had plenty of sisters, each of whom had needed both his ears and his shoulders (as well as mine) over the years.

"You'll be home Saturday night," he said. "And the girls will have new dresses for Easter Mass on Sunday morning?"

"Gussy's got a sewing machine, and I've already bought the fabric." Every year I made the girls matching Easter dresses, and despite their objections this year, Frankie had insisted. I knew both Mouse and Chessy felt like they were too old now to be dressed up like frilly twin dolls. But I also couldn't help but fear that Mouse's violent rejection of the fabric I chose, the pink dotted Swiss remnant that I'd bought at half price, was indicative of something else. I hadn't liked dresses as a girl either. I hadn't wanted ruffles or bows or anything pink. I too had eschewed girly accoutrements in favor of blue jeans and baseball caps and sneakers. I was terrified that everything that seemed to have gone wrong in my wiring was also wrong in Mouse. Even Eva had suggested that what we had, what we *felt,* was some sort of illness. And despite every effort to think in other terms, I couldn't help but wonder if I had somehow infected her, passed on this sickness. And that she, like I, would find nothing but frustration and sadness in this life.

"Fine then." Frankie finally relented.

Gussy's home. How can I describe Gussy's home? From the outside, it wasn't so very different from ours: a two-story farmhouse on a dead-end street. A wide porch with a happy, wooden porch swing, still and expectant and inviting. Our house always made me feel a bit anxious (the repairs that were neglected in favor of other projects, the mess I could never seem to contain, the lights just a bit too bright—illuminating the chaos of clutter, the smell of last night's dinner and the stink of cigarettes seeping into the curtains and carpets no matter what I did). But Gussy's home was so welcoming and warm.

Gussy was a born homemaker, and I mean that in the very sense of the word. Out of this crooked house, she had truly *made a home*. If a home is where a family lives, where love lives, then she was, indeed, a homemaker. And not only was she a homemaker, but a caretaker. She *took care*. Of these four walls and everything inside of them. It was evident in all of the details. She had taken our mother's domestic lessons to heart. While I resisted all of her teachings (on how to keep spots off glasses and silver, on how to iron shirts and make hospital corners and mend socks), Gussy had studied them, perfected the details our mother had insisted mattered. While I grimaced at the very thought of those tasks, Gussy delighted in them. And as much as I used to think otherwise, I saw there was a certain happiness and fulfillment that came from making a home. You could feel it the moment you walked through their door.

The kitchen was warm and smelled of bread, even when the oven was bone cold. Gussy made a loaf of homemade bread every single day, rising before dawn to knead the dough. There was always a hot pot of coffee on the stove, and a colorful selection of teas in a basket on the counter. She attended to everyone's needs:

sugar cubes, a honey pot, a little china pitcher of cream. Iced tea brewed in a glass jar on the sill. The table was never cluttered with the girls' homework or Frank's papers. The floors were clean, and the shelves clear of dust. And she made it all seem effortless.

Frank, like me, loved books. But while my collection consisted of piles of dime-store novels and thrift-store paperbacks stacked up in teetering towers beside my reading chair or at the side of my bed, Frank had assembled a virtual library in their home. Every room had at least two bookcases, each of them stuffed with books. Every seat had a proper lamp to read by. And most evenings, rather than retiring in front of the TV, like our family was bound to do, Frank settled in front of the fire with a book while Gussy helped the girls with their schoolwork or taught them to sew or knit or do needlepoint.

Frank had exactly one glass of bourbon each night, with plenty of ice. He never raised his voice in anger, and he certainly never pounded his fists against that dining room table. He didn't disappear into the basement of the house to drink wine by the jugful or work on whatever salvaged piece of junk he'd dragged home. Instead he was *there*. Present. Reading passages aloud when he found something interesting. Offering up tidbits of knowledge like little treasures, thrilled by each discovery. He was a gentleman. A truly gentle man. And he adored and appreciated every single thing Gussy did for him and their family. After nearly eighteen years of marriage, Gussy still blushed when he complimented her. They still held hands. And he still kissed her and said "Love you, Gus," whenever he got a chance.

Did I envy Gussy? Of course I did. Gussy's life was everything a life was supposed to be. She had found happiness in that kitchen, inside the walls of that home. She was a good mother, a patient mother, and a good wife whose husband honored and respected her. Our lives, though seemingly similar, were like two opposite sides of the same coin. She never wished her husband dead. She never fantasized about running off with the lady who lived across the street. But despite any envy I felt for the happiness Gussy had found, it was impossible to begrudge her any of her contentment. She had earned it. She deserved all of this simple joy.

She was my *sister*. And she was one of the only people in the world whom I knew would not judge me. Her kindness and openness of heart was not for show. It was exactly who she was inside. And it was with absolute certainty of this that I finally told her. That I shared the secret I'd been keeping almost my whole life.

The older girls had taken Chessy and Mouse to see a matinee of *The Pink Panther*. My girls adored Gussy's daughters, looking up to them like older sisters but without any of the rivalry of siblings. Cousins are like this, I've found. Cousins are to be adored and admired.

It was the Saturday before Easter, and the girls and I were going to catch the three o'clock train back to Hollyville. I had somehow managed to make it through an entire week without doing what I'd come to do. I'd lost myself a little in Gussy's world, enjoying the peace of it, the normalcy and comfort of it. But I also knew that I was only a train ride away from my own world, and that I could not go back to Hollyville, back to Frankie, without some sort of concrete plan rather than the hazy one I'd dreamed up and shared only in my letters to Eva.

Gussy was at the counter chopping vegetables for beef stew. Gussy almost never stopped moving; no idle hands in this house. There was a certain rhythm, a pleasing cadence to the chopping of carrots and celery. A pitter patter of purpose. But I needed her to stop if I was ever going to get it out.

"Gussy," I said, feeling my entire world rocking, shaking beneath me.

"Uh-huh?" she asked. *Chop. Chop. Choppity chop.*

"Come here a minute?" I said.

She turned to me, and, seeing my face, she set the knife down and wiped her hands on her apron. She came to the table and sat down next to me. She reached for my hands, which were shaking like something electrified. "Oh, Gingersnap," she said. "You're trembling something terrible. What's the matter?"

I lifted my head, and it felt as though I were trying to support a bowling ball on a needle. I frowned and shook my head. "You know, I've never been like you," I said.

"Of course not," she said, shaking her head. "That would be silly. You're *you*."

"No, Gus, just listen."

She nodded, always obedient, and looked me right in the eyes.

"It's Eva. Eva and I . . ." Saying our names together felt dangerous and wonderful, terrifying in the way that a simple sentence could link us, grammar bringing us together. But I didn't know how to get the words out, the ones I'd rehearsed. The technical term for what I was, for what we were doing. Suddenly, it felt all wrong. Impossible to articulate. Those words just that, nothing but words. Labels on a spice jar, having nothing to do with what was inside.

"I know," Gussy said. Her voice was firm. And I knew, suddenly, that she was not simply saying this to reassure me of whatever silly problem I was having. She *knew*.

I felt my eyes widen.

"Frankie wrote me a letter, after he found out. He wrote Mother a letter too."

"What?" I said, feeling as though a cartoon anvil had fallen across my chest.

"Here," she said, rushing to the faucet with my empty water glass.

"He wrote you a letter?" I said, feeling my voice gaining volume as my incredulity grew. "He *told* you?"

She nodded. "Listen, he was angry. He was hurt. He was scared. *Is* scared."

I stood up, feeling like I needed to escape. I had to get out of this perfect little house.

"He shouldn't have, but he did."

"He wrote to Mama?" I asked.

She nodded. I thought about the last few times I had spoken to my mother, the clipped way she had talked to me. Had I been so distracted, so consumed, that I didn't realize what had happened? "What did she say?" I asked, hitting that table, that perfect table with its cheery, cherry-littered cloth.

Gussy shook her head. "You know Mama."

I thought of our mother then, our austere mother with her cold hands and stern face. I tried to imagine that stone shattering, that composure crushed.

"Did she tell Daddy?"

She shook her head again. "She insists Frankie is a liar. You know she's never liked him. She says he's made it all up. That it's just delusions, from the drinking."

"Well, it's not!" I screamed. And for a moment I feared that raising my voice in this way was certain to shatter all of those polished glasses in Gussy's cupboards, that the walls themselves might come down at my beckoning. "It's the truth. I love Eva. I *love* her."

I felt my insides suddenly unraveling from the knots they'd been twisted into for the last week, for the last four years. Saying it aloud like this, in Gussy's kitchen no less, suddenly cut all those tangled cords that had been like a noose around my neck. And the sudden liberation, like someone pulled out of the water after nearly drowning, was exhilarating. I felt my body becoming light, filling with air like a balloon. It felt almost ticklish, and I started to laugh. Even as tears ran down my cheeks, as tears ran down Gussy's cheeks, I was laughing. And she came to me, enclosed me in her arms, as though she were relieved to find me alive. She cupped my face in her hands, looked hard into my eyes. "It's okay. It's all going to be okay."

But as much as I wanted to believe her, I knew that this was simply another area of Gussy's expertise. Gussy, the homemaker, the caretaker, the soother. I'd watched her for years bring comfort to others around her. She was always the one ready with a Band-

Aid, a hot pot of soup, kindness that could undo any cruelties that had been inflicted upon those she loved. But her consolation, while a heartfelt panacea, came from her compulsion to make me feel better, not from the very real truth that what Eva and I shared would *never* be okay, not in most people's eyes. Not in Mama's eyes, not in Frankie's, maybe not even in my own children's.

I almost didn't go back home to Hollyville. The thought of facing Frankie knowing what he had done, after he had betrayed me in such an insidious way—I didn't know how I could look at him again. He had taken the most private thing in the world and offered it up like any other piece of gossip. He was no better than Hannah. As far as I was concerned, he had betrayed me as much as I had betrayed him, and I couldn't help but wonder who else he had told. Because while his pride was enormous, clearly his rage and need for revenge were bigger. He'd told my own *mother*. But I also knew that if I was going to go through with my plan, if everything I'd talked through with Gussy that afternoon was going to come to fruition, I needed to pretend as though nothing were wrong. I needed to make Frankie believe that my indiscretion with Eva was just that, a momentary slide, and that it was over, that I had made a mistake and was atoning for it.

The girls were looking forward to Easter, despite the matching pink dresses. Every year, on the night before Easter, we dyed eggs, which, after the girls had gone to sleep, and barring any snow, Frankie and I would hide in the backyard. In the morning, each of the girls was given a basket with a solid milk chocolate rabbit nestled inside. They hunted for the eggs, and then we cracked them all open, and I used them to make French toast for breakfast. Frankie would take the girls to Mass while I prepared Easter dinner: usually a ham that Frank was given at work along with maple-soaked carrots and cabbage. We had one of the neighbors take a photo of us in front of the house. I kept these pictures, practically the only family portraits we had, in one album so we could track the girls' growth. In the earliest pictures, Frankie and I looked so young. Just kids: bright eyed and hopeful.

What was I thinking back then? I tried to recollect what was going through my mind in those early years, those years before Eva. Had I really believed that I could live like this my whole life? That I could carry this lie in my heart, that I could go through the motions for ten, twenty, thirty years? I felt sorry for my twenty-two-year-old self. I looked at her standing in front of the house, clutching the bundle with Francesca inside. I studied her flushed cheeks and misty eyes. Was it the cold weather that first Easter morning that made my eyes water and cheeks burn? Or was it something else? Why couldn't I remember what it was like to be her anymore? Who was she? And where did she go?

That night the girls and I sat at the kitchen table, the cups of colorful dyes spread out before us. Frankie had retired to his workshop basement earlier than usual, coming up only to check the score on the basketball game. I could tell he was getting really drunk, and earlier than usual. He would abstain all day on Easter, the one holiday he remained sober, and I suspected he was making up for it that night.

I imagine now he was worried that either Gussy or my mother had said something about the letter. He couldn't have thought that they would keep it a secret from me. He had to have known that it would come out eventually, that you can't just light the fuse on that kind of news without expecting an explosion.

"I miss Sally," Mouse said as she dipped her egg into a cup of bright yellow dye. "I wonder if she gets to go to Girl Scouts in Boston."

"I don't know," I said, though I did know. Ted didn't allow the children to participate in any after-school activities. They came straight home after school so that they could report back to him on their mother's activities. He had made them into tiny wardens and Eva their charge.

Chessy was quiet, dipping her egg carefully into the cups. I watched her, this little girl whose face had lost that childlike quality, whose body was also becoming softer, more like a young woman's than a girl's.

"What about you, Chess? You must miss Donna," I said.

Chessy shrugged without looking at me. This sullenness was new as well, this quiet brooding. Gussy assured me that both her girls had gone through a similar transformation at about this age as well. That hormones were to blame. But I still feared it had nothing to do with estrogen and everything to do with me.

"Can we go visit them?" Mouse asked.

"That would be nice," I said. "Maybe this summer."

My heart pounded with the knowledge of what I had planned for the summer. That Mouse's wish would, in fact, come true. That if all went as planned, our two families, minus Ted and Frankie, would be together again.

"Except Johnny. I don't care if I ever see him again," Mouse said.

Eva had written that Johnny was still having troubles at school. Getting into fights with boys who were a lot bigger and stronger than he was. I knew that Johnny would be a problem we'd have to deal with.

"When is the new baby coming?" Mouse asked, scratching her name on an egg with a waxy crayon.

"Next month," I said.

"Will it be another boy?" Mouse asked, grimacing.

"We won't know until it comes," I said. "Babies are surprising like that."

When I dreamed of the baby, of *our* baby, it was always a boy. A sweet, pudgy-cheeked boy. And in my dreams, I could smell the baby scent of his hair, feel the way his fingers tightened over mine. Eva had said she felt like she did when she was pregnant with Johnny. Always sick, never hungry. She carried all of the weight in front, like a basketball. From behind you couldn't even tell she was pregnant.

The baby was due in a few weeks. And afterward, it would be time.

The girls and I finished the eggs, and we laid out their new dresses at the foot of their beds. I polished their old white shoes with toothpaste to get the scuffs out. Mouse, who still believed in the Easter Bunny, left a carrot out, and then I tucked them in.

As I was leaning down to kiss Mouse, she whispered, "What's a *homosexual,* Mommy?"

I caught my breath. The word stung; I physically felt a sharp pang somewhere deep in my rib cage.

"Chessy says that you're a homosexual. I looked it up in my dictionary, and it said that it means you love other ladies. Chessy says it's a sin. But *I* love other girls. I love you and Chessy and Eva and Sally. Am I going to go to hell?"

I could feel all of the blood draining from my face, pooling in my shoulders, in my hands. Had they heard us fighting? Had this word, this horrible word, crept up the stairs and under their door, skipped across their pillows and into their ears? Goddamn Frankie and goddamn that church and goddamn that word. I could practically hear Frankie hissing it at me, muttering it under his breath, shouting it, the alcohol making it softer, mushier in his mouth. The same word that had found its way to my ears as I slept at night, whispered between my mother and father. The questioning, the fear. The word that came from the therapist's lips after the episode with Miss Mars, the diagnosis with the cure being to simply deny or reject my feelings.

Hot tears welled up in my eyes, and I blinked, sending them shooting down my cheeks. "I love Eva too," I said. "And some people think that's a terrible thing. A sinful thing."

"Is that why she moved away?"

I was so sick of lying, so sick of rejecting and denying. And here was my chance to make all of this okay. I was Mouse's *mother.* I was the one whom she trusted and listened to more than anyone else in the entire world. I could change the way she saw things. I had this power, if nothing else.

"It is. It's scary to Daddy and to Mr. Wilson. But it's not bad. Love is never bad."

Mouse touched her finger to my tear and said, "You're crying."

I nodded.

"I love you, Mommy."

I closed my eyes tightly and allowed her to embrace me. It was the first time since she was an infant that I had held her so close. I realized, as I felt the unfamiliar angles of her shoulders and arms, I'd been so afraid of harming her, of passing on everything that scared me, that I had denied her my affections. The overwhelming enormity of this hit me hard, turning that sharp prick in my chest into a turning corkscrew.

When I released her and looked toward the door, I could see Chessy standing in the doorway, her head hung low. I didn't know how much she had heard, though it was clearly enough. But as I stood up from the bed to go to her, she turned and ran, all the way down the stairs and then down the basement stairs to Frankie.

Alcohol and Frankie were like gasoline and a rag; it only took the smallest spark to set the whole thing on fire. The spark that night was Chessy, and while I could have killed her then, I realize now that she was only scared and confused and when forced to choose, she'd chosen her father. If she'd had any idea what he was going to do that night, and everything that would happen after, she probably would have slipped quietly back into her room. But she didn't know, couldn't know; none of us could. And by then it was too late.

Frankie came barreling up the stairs, two at a time. He had a pair of plastic goggles on his forehead, which I remember made him look a little silly. In my panic, I almost laughed.

"What are you telling our children?" he screamed at me, lunging toward me.

"What are *you* telling our children?" I asked.

"The truth," he screamed. For a small man, he still had the power to terrify me. He seemed to grow in his rage, his shoulders informed by his anger. His muscles swelling with his fury. "That you're sick. That you're a whore. A dirty, cheating whore."

Mouse stood at the top of the stairs, trembling. I motioned for her to go to her room and she ran quickly down the hall. The beam of light coming from her room disappeared as the door slammed shut.

"Go upstairs, Francesca," I said.

She shook her head.

"I said go upstairs!" My own voice startled me. It seemed to startle her as well, and she ran up the stairs, slamming her own door shut.

"I can't do this anymore, Frankie. You can't punish me forever. You can't just pretend everything is okay and still hate me. Hate what I did. Who I am."

"You're ruining their lives!" he bellowed. "Their innocence. You're selfish and sick. You should go away and never come back."

I took a deep breath and steadied myself by gripping the edge of the counter. Funny, I remember now seeing the calendar, a calendar from the post office, and remembering that it was Easter the next day. A day of atonement. When Gussy and I were little, at Easter dinner everyone at the table was asked to make an apology for something they had done. And then whoever had been wronged would grant forgiveness. It helped clear the air, though the wrongs were usually small and inconsequential.

"I'm sorry," I said, thinking of how good it felt to get those little crimes out on the table. To confess. "I don't love you, Frankie, not in the way you need me to. I love Eva. I don't know how to change that. It's not going to go away."

But instead of the quiet absolution of my mother or sister and the odd benediction of my father, Frankie seethed and then got so close to my face I could tell how many hours it had been since he had last shaved. The scent of alcohol on his breath was strong, his teeth gray from the cheap Chianti. "You disgust me."

Normally our arguments would have ended here, but this time his words were not enough. They were weak weapons. But his hands were strong, and it was his hands that lashed out next, grabbing my shoulders and shaking me so hard my teeth knocked together. He stepped back, seemingly stunned by what he had done, but there were no apologies. No excuses. Instead he just turned on his heel and walked out the back door.

And then he was raging around the backyard smashing all of the girls' eggs they had so carefully dyed and painted and decorated. Stomping his feet as though he were killing cockroaches. I could hear the fragile shells shattering underneath his wingtips. For nearly a half hour, he flung himself about the backyard, not resting until every last egg was nothing but colored dust beneath his feet.

Shaken to the white-hot center of my body, I locked myself in the bathroom, watching through the window as he waged his own private war. Only when I heard the door slam and then his drunken heavy footsteps on the stairs did I dare come out. He had disappeared upstairs, likely passed out, and I knew it was now or never.

Quietly, I went up to Mouse's room and hurried her out of her nightgown and into her clothes. I went to Francesca's room next and found her awake as well and crying. She was sitting in her window seat that overlooked the backyard. She had clearly witnessed his reign of terror over the Easter eggs.

"We're going back to Gussy's," I said, but she only stood motionless, still staring out the window.

"Francesca," I said again, but she wouldn't look at me.

My impulse was to slap her. To threaten and frighten her into action. But I didn't have to, because suddenly she turned to me, her head still hung, and stood up. And silently, she went to her chest of drawers, gathered her clothes and shoes, stuffed a hairbrush and underwear into a bag.

When she finally looked at me, her face was that of a child again. Just a little girl, her cheeks stained with tears. "I'm sorry, Mama," she said.

I felt my heart plummet, my face grow hot. I was so ashamed. How could I have blamed her for this? For any of this? I shook my head. "*No*. You have nothing to be sorry for. You didn't do anything wrong. Do you understand that?"

She shook her head.

And then I went to her and pulled her close to me. "This is not your fault. None of it."

I took Frankie's keys from the hook by the doorway, and I hurried the girls into the car. It felt wonderful to leave him stranded for once. For *him* to be the one rendered immobile, a prisoner in this house.

We drove through the night, arriving at Gussy's just as the Easter sunrise was glowing pink behind the green mountains. And in that moment I felt completely reborn, *risen*. As if I had been resurrected. I had never felt so close to God.

Gussy was clearly surprised to see me pull up in Frankie's car, but she acted as though it were the most normal thing in the world. As though this had been the plan all along.

"Well, look at you girls . . . you look hungry enough to eat a cow. Good thing I just made pancakes." She winked at me and ushered the girls inside.

I had never been so grateful for my sister's house in my entire life. Frank was sitting at the kitchen table; their girls, I imagined, were still upstairs asleep. There were two Easter baskets on the table, which Gussy lifted up; she said, "I was wondering why these baskets were on my doorstep this morning! Looks like the Easter Bunny knew you were coming."

I saw Chessy grimace, and wondered how long the memory of her father crushing those Easter eggs would stay with her. "Thank you, Gussy," Chessy said, accepting the basket. Inside each basket was a small bottle of perfume and a crème-filled egg. Her daughters' favorites.

"What about Nancy and Debbie?" Mouse asked, digging her finger into the soft filling of the egg, which she had uncovered from its foil wrapper without anyone noticing.

"I think maybe they've gotten a little too old for the Easter bunny," Gussy said. "Maybe you could save them a couple of jelly beans?"

After devouring three pancakes each, the girls went off to play in the family room. Gussy set them up with a puzzle and Frank disappeared into his study, leaving Gussy and me alone.

"What happened?" she asked.

And, without hesitation (I was finished with secrets, with lies), I told her everything.

Without uttering a single word, Gussy nodded. "Okay. Okay. So what next?"

I knew that after Frankie finally figured out what had happened, he would also figure out where we had gone. And while I was definitely trying to leave him, I also knew there was no sense in trying to elude him. I knew he'd catch the first train to Two Rivers and then thumb a ride to Gussy and Frank's. My only consolation was that it was Easter, one of Frankie's holidays from drinking. Perhaps, hungover and sober, he wouldn't be nearly as rash as he had been last night.

This was, after all, what I'd been planning to do all along: my plans were simply expedited by a few months, but still, exactly what I had hoped to do. I had left Frankie. *I had left Frankie.* The reality of our midnight departure suddenly became vivid as Gussy's kitchen filled with light. I knew the important thing now was to keep a steady head, to modify those elements of the arrangements as needed but not to panic. The one major glitch was the money. I had no money but the weekly grocery allowance Frankie had doled out to me, and I'd already spent half of it on an Easter dinner we wouldn't be eating. I knew I could borrow money from Gussy and Frank, but if this was going to work, I'd need more than that. I couldn't count on Frankie being reasonable about any of this. I would, eventually, need to find some sort of work. I'd have to get the children enrolled in school. I'd have to find a place for us to live. Suddenly, the enormity of it all was too much. I felt like I had standing underneath the Prudential Building that awful day in Boston, the world growing voluminous and scary around me. And strangely what came to me then was my father's voice, quoting someone, I don't remember whom. My father, a man whose work exceeded the number of hours in a day. *The secret to happiness is counting your blessings while others are adding up their troubles.* What an odd comfort. What strange solace.

"I need to get in touch with Eva," I said, thinking of my blessings. Counting.

"Of course," she said.

I stayed at the house while all of the girls went off with Frank and Gussy to services, and I paced. It was Easter Sunday, and Ted would be home with his family. I imagined them all dressed up for church, each of the girls with their baskets. Rose would be so big now, nearly four years old. Eva, her belly swollen with the baby, her feet and hands following suit. There was a chance, just the smallest chance, that she might stay behind.

I looked at the clock. It was ten o'clock exactly. Most Sunday services were at ten. If she was home, if she had stayed behind to make Easter dinner, while Ted took the children to church, she would be home alone. And if not, if Ted was, for some reason, in the apartment, I could just hang up. Or I could say I had a wrong number. It was that simple, right?

My hands trembled as I lifted the phone from the receiver. It seemed heavier than it should be, as though it had been weighted down with sand. I could barely dial her number, though it was ingrained in my memory.

The ring trilled through my entire body, and I found myself holding my breath. She wouldn't be home. There is no way that Ted would have left her alone without the children on Easter Sunday. This was crazy, I thought. But then I heard the phone click, and her voice, as soft as skin. As if she knew it was me on the other end of the line. As if she had been expecting me.

"Eva," I said, feeling a rush both wonderful and terrifying.

"Billie?"

I knew I didn't have a lot of time. I needed to tell her exactly what to do. "I left Frankie. I'm at Gussy's now, but we'll be at the lake. If you can get the children to the train station, I'll find a way to get you."

The last four years had been spent trying to find my way to Eva. I thought of those years like an elaborate labyrinth: twisting and turning, running into walls at every turn. And at the center was Eva, my beautiful Eva. I was so close now, just on the other side of the last wall.

"Eva?"

My heart sank, realizing that this was foolish. It was like someone trying to escape from Alcatraz. The walls were made of steel; the locks were rusted shut. The key hung from Ted's thick waist. It was a ridiculous dream, one about to be shattered with her words.

Her voice interrupted my desperate reverie.

"Thursday," she said. "I'll be there Thursday." And then she hung up.

I felt like I'd been struck by lightning. My entire body buzzed and hummed, my veins and nerves the raw, plucked strings of a guitar strung too tightly. By the time everyone came back from church, I felt like I might just explode with excitement.

"Can you drive us to the lake?" I asked.

"Of course," Gussy said.

Frank said he'd deal with Frankie if and when he showed up to retrieve us and his car. Frankie respected Frank, and so I hoped there wouldn't be any trouble. "Thank you," I said. Frank was a calming force, and if anyone could keep Frankie from going berserk, it was him. I told him to tell Frankie I just needed some time to clear my head. That I'd call him in the evening.

"Have you spoken with Eva?" Gussy asked softly as we drove through the new spring foliage toward the lake.

I looked at her, nodding. "She'll be here Thursday."

Halfway to the lake, we stopped at Hudson's for some supplies. Gussy and Frank didn't usually open up the camp until

Memorial Day; there would be nothing but dusty tins of flour and cans of beans in the cupboards. The water would be off, and the cap still firmly topping the chimney. There would be dead mice in the traps, dead flies on the sills, cobwebs in every corner. The water pump would be off, the hot water heater dormant, every inch of every surface covered with dust. Luckily, I knew that the task of readying the camp was just big enough to occupy me for the next four days. I didn't know what to do with the girls though. It was too cold to swim; there might even be patches of snow in the yard. Autumn came early at Gormlaith, and spring came late. Summer was just a quick breath between the deep sighs of spring and fall and the interminable breathlessness of winter.

I used the little bit of grocery money I had left to pick up all of the staples we would need as well as fresh produce and milk as I would have any other summer. But it wasn't summer; it was only March. And it wasn't vacation; it was my life.

I've left my husband, I thought.

As I was bringing my basket of items to the register, I stopped once again in the produce section. There was a bin filled with bright red apples: Baldwin apples, those hardy winter apples that Eva loved. My heart felt swollen in my chest. These apples had somehow survived the harsh winter, plucked and packaged and transported here, without bruising or losing their color. They were survivors, these apples. I filled the rest of my basket with them, marveling at the simple beauty of their endurance.

That afternoon after Gussy left us at the cabin, I washed the dusty mixing bowls and a pie plate, affixed the apple peeler to the counter, and handled each of those apples as though they were polished gems instead of mere fruit.

"What about school?" Chessy asked. All of this was making Chessy nervous. She liked order, *needed* order, and change of any sort made her uneasy. Change of this sort was terrifying. "We have school tomorrow."

"I'll speak to your teachers. I'll get your work, and you can do it here."

This was my quick answer for a question that plagued me. It wasn't even April yet. They still had two and a half months of school left. I could enroll them at the school in Quimby, but it didn't seem fair to thrust them into a new classroom this far into the school year. Mouse would be fine, but I knew that Chessy would struggle. I just needed for Eva to get here. She would help me sort through everything. She would help me figure it all out.

"Don't worry," I said, though I knew she would, as would I. The logistics had changed with this accelerated departure from Hollyville, from our lives. Still, I told myself, people moved all the time. And they were children, the most resilient creatures in the world. Eva and I could teach them at home this spring, and then in the fall start them off fresh at school.

"Eva will be here with the kids soon," I said, because I wanted to offer her something, and this was the only real thing I had (though it didn't feel real at all).

"Really?" she asked. And the expression on her face was of someone torn, agonizing. Frankie had convinced her that what was going on between me and Eva was wicked, but she also loved Eva. Her flushed cheeks and wide eyes belonged to a girl divided, between the childhood need to trust and adult understanding. Between relief and shame. It was an expression I would see on her face a zillion times more over the years. But now, in this moment, it made my heart ache. But it also made me more resolved in my decision to leave Frankie.

I nodded. Eva would be here, and she would know exactly what to do. And we would be together. Everything else would just fall into place. It would have to.

Frankie arrived at Gussy and Frank's on Sunday afternoon as I was sprinkling cinnamon and sugar on those apples. Apparently, he stomped around their kitchen until Frank asked him to leave and then he took the car I'd left parked cockeyed in the driveway, and took off. When I spoke to Gussy she said that while he made a big show, he also seemed to be running out of steam, defeated. He apologized to her, as though she were the one he'd shaken until her teeth rattled and head ached. The one he'd spat at, screamed at, and humiliated. Red faced, he admitted he hadn't always been the best husband, but insisted that he was a good father, that he didn't deserve to lose his girls. She also said that before he left, he handed her a check made out to me in the amount of $500. He'd told her it was for the children. That no matter how he felt about me, he loved his girls. And then he'd left, like a dog running off, tail tucked between his legs. Shamed. Ashamed.

My eyes stung. I didn't want him to put up a fight, to insist that we come home. I hadn't wanted a battle with him; I'd already been waging one for years. But his easy surrender made me suspicious. I didn't trust it. Frankie was a fighter, and his tossing in the towel seemed suspect. But I had little choice but to take his gesture, his leaving, the money, at face value. Eva was coming, and whatever resistance Frankie did or didn't offer was nothing compared with what Ted was likely to do.

"Johnny?" I say into the phone, barely recognizing my own voice.

"Billie," the man says. His voice is deep like his father's. Sonorous. Eva once said that Ted's voice was the only gentle thing about him. "Listen, I'm so sorry to call this late. I know you were planning on driving down tomorrow. But I'm afraid there's been a bit of an emergency. . . ."

For a moment, I feel flooded with relief, whatever has happened in Johnny's life becoming secondary to the possibility that I will not have to go through with this. That whatever has transpired in his world will release me from this obligation. It makes me feel selfish. Awful.

"What sort of emergency?" I ask.

"I don't want to go into it on the phone. I just need you to trust me. Is there any way you can come tonight? I think it's important that you come tonight."

"What?" I ask, feeling the blackness and stars descending again. What on earth could have happened that he would need me to rush my visit? At what point did my coming even become so critical?

"Please, Billie," he says, that warm, deep voice cracking suddenly. The man is gone, and the child I remember is on the other end of the line. "I'm sorry, this wasn't the way I had planned this. Please, if you possibly can, just meet me at Mass General, and call my cell when you get here."

I hang up and sit down in the kitchen nook, staring at the

dead phone in my hands. I could just go back to bed, I think. I could just pretend this was a terrible dream. But something snags in my chest. Something old. Something primitive. And so instead, I go back to the guest room where Gussy is still deeply asleep, and I gently touch her shoulder.

"Gus," I whisper into her white curls. "We need to go to Boston tonight."

Gussy doesn't ask questions. We both simply dress quietly in the dark, and as I make coffee for the road, Gussy drafts a note to Effie and Devin, leaving it on the kitchen table. *We've gone to Boston. John says there's some sort of emergency. We'll call in the morning. Hope to be back at the lake sometime next week. Thank you. Kiss those beautiful girls.*

"I hope they see it," she says.

"Put it under the sugar bowl. Effie takes sugar in her coffee. She'll see it. Plus they'll probably wonder where we've gone."

Gussy grabs the lunches Devin has prepared from the refrigerator and packs a makeshift breakfast for us: oranges, bagels. It seems silly; morning is still so far away.

"Do you want me to drive?" I ask. Gussy has never liked driving in the dark, and I figure that driving might be exactly the distraction I need for the next three hours.

"Do you mind?" she asks, as we quietly close the screen door and walk through the wet grass to Gussy's car.

I slide into the driver's seat as Gussy buckles herself into the passenger's seat. We put our coffee cups in the cup holders, and I clear the windshield of condensation and leaves. The sound of the blades across the glass is loud, and I worry the car will wake Effie, Devin, and the girls. I turn off the radio and back slowly out of the driveway.

I feel terrible leaving them without a proper good-bye; the girls will be disappointed, I suspect. Gussy promised to make her special pumpkin pancakes. But while I hate sneaking away like bandits in the middle of the night, I feel worse that we are leaving the lake while it is still dark out. Whenever we left camp when the kids were little, they liked to make a big show of saying their farewells to each and every landmark. I can almost hear their voices in the backseat. "Good-bye, lake! Good-bye, big rock! Good-bye, crab apple tree!" Now they would only say, "Good-bye, darkness. Good-bye, stars. Good-bye, moon." It is so dark, we could be anywhere or nowhere at all.

"What did Johnny say?" Gussy asks, lifting the steaming coffee to her lips.

"Not much. He's at the hospital."

"Did he say why?" she asks.

"I don't know. I think maybe he's sick. Maybe he's drinking again?" All of this is completely mystifying. "Maybe he's been sick all along, and he's just got something he wants to get off his chest before he goes. I have no idea." I admit, the idea of being beckoned in the middle of the night so some drunk can make amends, or whatever he needs to do, makes me a little angry. It seems like so many of my years were spent appeasing a drunken fool. But still I felt the urgency in his voice, and he is, after all, Eva's son. I owe him this.

Gussy nods quietly and drinks her coffee.

I reach for my own cup and take a quick sip before returning it to the cup holder and using both hands to steer, focusing on the dirt road ahead. It is foggy, and the headlights only illuminate a few feet in front of us. I feel my hands involuntarily clenching the wheel. Anxiety bubbles like percolating coffee somewhere in my stomach.

If it were light out, we'd have passed the last place where the lake is visible before becoming hidden by the thick tangle of trees.

"Stop!" Gussy says, startling me, pointing ahead, and I slam on the brakes.

"What?" I say.

"Look!" she says, and in the beam of my headlights is a small black bear, a baby, crossing the road. Close behind it is its mother, rushing it along. She turns to face us, and I feel my throat grow thick. I've seen bears at Gormlaith only a few times before, and it has stunned me every time. I've never been this close to one. We are only a couple of feet from them. If Gussy hadn't seen them, I would have hit the baby.

Gussy presses her hand against her chest as if to keep her heart inside. And then as quickly as they appeared, they disappear into the woods again, but my heart is racing too. "Jesus, Mary, and Joseph! We almost hit them. That could have been a terrible accident."

The word, *accident,* feels like a blade. I nod. And she looks at me, her eyes apologizing. She reaches for my hand and squeezes it. Her skin is warm from the coffee. I am grateful for this, but my heart still aches.

I drive slowly, cautiously, until we are finally out of the deep woods, and I am relieved when the dirt turns to asphalt and the fog has lifted. I feel my grip on the wheel loosening, the muscles in my shoulders relaxing. By the time we get on the interstate, I have put the bears out of my mind. *Accidents.* As Gussy peels an orange and the whole car fills with the wonderful pungent scent of citrus, I try to think only of the traffic around me, the barreling semis and the mile markers ticking off as we head to Boston.

Waiting at camp for Eva and the children was excruciating. It was like the summers she had come to stay, only worse. Every moment seemed swollen, time like a slow-moving, icy river. I cleaned the entire camp. I changed the linens on the beds, I dusted the cobwebs, swept up the dead flies, mopped the wooden floors. I split the wood that Gussy and Frank had had delivered, insisting that I was perfectly capable of splitting it; it would save me money in the long run if I split and stacked it myself. And there was something pacifying, satisfying about this little bit of self-sufficiency. As the girls studied the math sheets I'd made at the kitchen nook, I donned my winter hat and gloves and allowed the early spring air to fill my lungs as I swung the ax over and over. The crunch and crack of the logs made me feel as though I was making some sort of progress: the evidence in the growing woodpile as I stacked the wood in the shed. We had many cold nights ahead of us still, where spring would forget itself and winter would return. There might even be snow before spring finally settled in.

Inside, the bowl of remaining Baldwin apples sat on the counter as a reminder that we still had much to endure. That I needed to be patient, resilient, firm.

I didn't know how Eva planned to get to me. Ted would have the car; he never left her alone with the car anymore. I assumed she'd take the train to Two Rivers and then would call for a ride. I imagined, *hoped,* that she would call beforehand and let me know her plans as soon as she had a moment alone; by the time

Ted saw the long-distance bill, Eva would be with me. It wouldn't matter anymore. I had to assume that our thinking was the same.

But Wednesday evening (when the temperature, as expected, plummeted) I sat for hours watching the fire burning in the wood stove and the phone did not ring. I stayed awake the whole night, tending the fire, pacing the clean floors. Outside the moon disappeared behind a heavy blanket of clouds. Snow clouds. And by three a.m., snow was beginning to fall.

The girls slept, but I did not. I tried to read, but every word, every sentence was like an incantation, a prayer: every syllable somehow reminding me of Eva. I made a pot of coffee around four a.m., drinking enough to warm my body and make my hands tremble. The fire crackled, cackled. And the sky softened with light, though it kept snowing.

I'd always joked that Mouse was like a baby bear, hibernating in the winter, nearly impossible to wake on cold mornings. But Chessy was up to greet the sun: more bird than bear. And this morning was no different.

"It's *snowing?*" she said, shuffling into the kitchen where I was pouring myself another unnecessary mug of coffee.

I nodded, looking out the little window at the thermometer on the tree. It was twenty degrees out.

"It's so cold," Chessy said, sitting down next to me. "Can I have some coffee?"

I raised my eyebrow at her. "Aren't you a little young for coffee?"

She shrugged, and in that simple gesture, I saw the toll that all of this had taken on her. She was a child, but in the last year she'd aged. That delightful innocence that still clung to Mouse had slipped away from Chessy. For the first time ever I looked at her face and saw the woman she would one day become. Before my eyes in the half light of dawn, the color of her eyes deepened, her face thinned and lengthened, even her hands looked older. My little girl was disappearing, and there was nothing I could ever do to retrieve her. The enormity of this awareness nearly took my breath away. I suddenly wanted to be able to hold her, to cradle her entire body in my arms. I wanted to be able to enclose that hand in my own, have it disappear in my grasp. But those days were gone. Those days belonged to some other time, and her smallness, her reliance on me for even the simplest things, was an artifact in the museum of my recollection.

"Here," I said, pouring her a hot cup from the percolator. I topped it with a healthy dose of milk and spooned in a full spoonful of sugar. "This will warm you up."

The snow kept falling as dawn turned into morning. As Mouse finally crawled from her cave of covers, hungry for breakfast. By noon, the entire world was swaddled in a layer of white. The flowers and buds that had dared to blossom were covered in ice now, their optimistic blooms frozen.

Chessy was curled up in a chair by the fire, rereading *The Wind in the Willows*. The only books at the camp for children were the ones we'd left behind over the years. We'd fled Hollyville in such a hurry that she hadn't even been able to grab *Little Women* from her nightstand. I thought I should find a way to get her a copy, perhaps from the Athenaeum in Quimby. Mouse was busy playing a game of jacks on the floor. The rubber ball kept escaping her and rolling under Chessy's chair. Chessy, deep in her book, ignored Mouse as she wriggled underneath her.

With the girls occupied, I went to the kitchen and picked up the telephone to call Gussy and check to see if she'd heard anything from Eva, but as I pressed the receiver to my ear, there was nothing. No dial tone. I clicked the switch hook up and down, frantically. But still, nothing but silence, just my pulse throbbing in my temples.

The snow and ice had probably taken down the phone line. Eva wouldn't be able to get through. I imagined her at the train station in Two Rivers, her entire brood of children waiting for what would come next, her futile attempts to reach me, and I swooned, feeling sick. All of that coffee had put me on edge, my entire body electrified with caffeine and fear.

She knew Gussy's number. I'd seen her scratch it into her address book last summer. She would call Gussy, and Gussy and Frank would go pick her up from the train station. They would deliver her to me. The children in their hats and mittens would all go outside and make a snowman. I dreamed them rolling balls of snow, the stick arms, the carrot nose. I dreamed the stocking cap on top, the red cheeks and soggy wool socks drying by the fire.

But as the afternoon progressed, the only traffic on the road was the snowplow, its lights bright on the newly fallen snow. We were ten miles from town. I might be able to walk, but the children wouldn't. The closest neighbor was Mr. Tucker, and he had gone to North Carolina to visit his sister for the week. As the sky darkened and the snow kept falling, I felt my stomach plummeting.

What if she hadn't made the train at all? What if Ted had not gone into work that morning; if he'd been ill or sensed that she was up to something? What if Johnny had said something to him? What if he had figured it all out and forewarned him? Or worse, what if Eva had changed her mind? What if she decided that it was crazy to take her four children, and the one that was due to be born in less than a month, and leave the only stable home she had? What if she, unlike me, had come to her senses and realized the futility of it all? What if she had, finally, resigned herself to the life that she'd been given instead of the one I'd promised we could make? What if she never came? I was sick with worry and sorrow and fear. I could barely keep myself together enough to heat a can of soup and make grilled cheese sandwiches for dinner. I was rendered mute as I helped the girls wash up and brush their teeth and get ready, again, for bed. I was on the verge of hysteria, though I hid it well, as I sat alone, loading another log onto the fire, waiting for whatever would come next.

All that anxiety must have taken its toll on my body. The need for sleep, for rest, trumping everything, because when the headlights shone through the front windows, I realized I had been asleep.

My eyes flew open at the light, and I listened for the telltale sounds of the snowplow, thinking it strange that they would make two passes through in one day. But it wasn't the plow. And as it slowed in front of the cabin and pulled into the drive, I felt all the fear and trembling trepidation turn into a warm rush of relief and the quavering thrill of anticipation. They were here. *This is where my life begins,* I thought. *This is it.*

I ran to the kitchen to open the back door, not bothering to put on my shoes or my coat as I swung the door open, ready to usher the Wilsons in, ready to see Eva's face, to embrace her, to touch her, to smell her, to hear her whispers in my ear as she held me. My cheeks ached from my smile, my muscles straining with happiness. I patted down my hair, straightened my skirt, futile gestures, I knew, even as I attempted to make myself presentable.

Gussy got out of the car. My eyes were blinded by the headlights; I blinked but only saw stars. The door slammed, and then there was only the sound of her feet crunching the snow. I waited for the other doors to fly open, for the children's voices to ring out, like bells, into the night.

"Billie," Gussy said, as I blinked hard again and leaned forward to peer into the dark windows of her car. I shook my head. Why weren't they getting out?

And then Gussy's arm was around me, and she was guiding me toward the door.

"Wait!" I laughed, and brushed her off. But even as the sound of laughter rose from my chest, I felt as though I'd been shot. My chest ached. My whole body went numb. I started toward the car, looking blindly into the dark windows.

"Where are they?" I asked, as her arms found me again, as her hands steered me away from the car, out of the darkness, and into the bright kitchen.

"Oh, Billie," she said, enclosing me. I felt swallowed. I couldn't breathe. "Billie, there's been a terrible accident."

I remember the apples. The bowl of apples on the kitchen table, too red. Like a painting. Like an assault on my senses. As Gussy uttered the words that would change everything, I was blinded by the red winter apples. As I flung myself away from her, screaming, I knocked the bowl over, and the apples flew to the floor, rolled under the table, and the sound of their falling was like the sound of bodies hitting the ground.

It was Frankie who had called Gussy, Frankie who had received the news first. When Ted discovered Eva was gone, he called our house, not aware that the children and I had already left and that Frankie was there alone. He was looking for Eva. He demanded to know where she was, threatened to kill all of us if Frankie didn't tell him where she was. And so Frankie told him that I'd left him, that on Easter Sunday I'd taken the girls and gone to my sister's in Vermont. That I wasn't coming back. Ted had hung up the phone then, and Frankie worried that he would come after us. He was worried about the children, about the danger I had put them in. That was when he first called Gussy, to warn her that Ted might be coming after us. And then he went outside to start the car so that he could get to us before Ted did.

But when he came back in to get his wallet, the phone was ringing again. And this time, it was Ted's sister, Mary.

Mary told him that Eva had said that she needed to borrow her car, that she was going to take the children to Plymouth Rock for the day. Their Easter break was a week later than ours, and they were all going crazy cooped up in the apartment. And Mary had said, "Of course. Though you sure you want to be out driving in this weather?"

The late winter nor'easter that had brought all of this snow to Vermont had brought freezing rain and ice to Boston. The roads were treacherous as Eva piled all of the kids in the car and got in herself, her belly so large, she was barely able to fit behind the steering wheel now. She'd packed a picnic basket for the children:

ham salad sandwiches from the Easter leftovers. There were a half-dozen colored eggs.

Eva was always a fast driver; she liked the way it felt as though the world were disappearing beneath her when she drove fast. The times we'd driven together, I'd clutched the seat as we flew over the hills, our bottoms leaving the seat, the children squealing with delight as we flew. When I imagine that drive now, the one toward us, I try to think of the glee, the sparkle in her eye as she accelerated through Two Rivers, along the winding road that paralleled the train tracks. I dream over and over again the way she might have looked over her shoulder at Donna and Sally and Johnny and Rose all breathless with anticipation. I imagine her smiling, and saying, "Hold on!" as she rounded the bend by the river.

She was so close. We were so close.

But she was upset. She wasn't thinking straight; she wasn't being careful. And she wasn't joyful but terrified and distressed. And so when she hit a patch of black ice, Mary told Frankie, she lost control of the car. It flew, turning over three times, somersaulting through the air.

I dream this flight. I dream the car, that abstract metal box, just one of her mobiles, spinning and beautiful. But there were no strings to hold her up, nothing to tether her to the sky.

Mary told Frankie that Johnny was thrown from the car, landing like a rag doll at the river's edge, glass shattered, body broken and battered but alive. But when the car finally landed, it tumbled ten more feet down into the icy river.

"Johnny will be okay. But the girls . . . oh, God," she cried.

Frankie hung up with Mary and called Ted. He called and called, all afternoon, but it wasn't until nearly midnight that Ted finally answered the phone.

"Ted," Frankie said. "Please don't hang up. I just want to know if . . . please tell me they're okay."

"No," Ted said. "I've lost everything."

Frankie said he felt his throat closing up. That he couldn't find a single word to say to him.

"What about Eva?" he finally asked.

There was a long, terrible silence at the end of the line. Finally, Ted spoke, his voice a stone sinking to the bottom of a lake. "My wife is dead."

At four a.m., the sky is the color of a bruise as we disappear into the nearly empty garage, and I park in the first space I find. It is quiet here, quiet and cold. We sit in the car for several moments before either one of us makes a move to open our doors.

"Am I making a mistake?" I ask Gussy, without looking at her. I fear that if I look at her face, I will cry.

"No," she says, shaking her head. I can see tears welling up in her eyes. She looks like she might speak, but she just shakes her head again.

"Do you think he's angry, Gus? With me? Do you think he blames me?"

I remember the night of the accident, the night I'd nearly fallen apart. I remember the way it felt like I was unraveling; every fiber of my body seemed to be coming undone. The term they used back then was *nervous breakdown,* but it didn't feel like breaking down. It felt like breaking *apart.* Somehow, Gussy had gotten the girls to stay upstairs as I came undone. When I think of that night now, as I often do, I remember almost nothing except for Gussy's arms, holding the fragments of me together. I wonder now what would have happened if she had not been there.

Frankie came to the lake the next day and took the children back home. I stayed with Gussy at the camp until I finally could make a decision about what to do next. I barely remember the days that followed. The recollections of those days feel as though they belong to someone else: as though my life were a play and I were a character moving across the paper cutout landscape of that horrifying scene. Eva was gone. Rose, Sally, Donna, and our baby all gone with her. And without them, without Eva, nothing seemed to matter anymore. I didn't care where I went. I didn't care what I did. It was over. Everything in the world that mattered was gone. And it was all my fault.

I thought about taking my own life. I recalled that urge I'd felt at the Charles after Eva had first sent me away. I dreamed myself walking into the lake and never coming out again. I dreamed of swimming, of sinking, of allowing the water to fill my eyes, my nose, my lungs.

It was Gussy who finally pulled me out of the murky depths of despair. For three days during which I could not even get out of bed, she took care of me. She fed me as though I were an invalid, pressing the cold, metal spoon against my lips. She held a cool, wet cloth to my fevered forehead. She slept next to me, her arms keeping me afloat. But on the fourth day, she came into the room with freshly pressed clothes in her arms and said sternly, "It's time to get up. Your children need you."

She drove me all the way back down to Hollyville. I think I knew then that I would never go back to the lake. I whispered quietly, "Good-bye, tree house, good-bye, lilacs and bees, good-bye, lake."

In Hollyville, she stayed for another two days to help me get settled back into my old life. The girls went back to school. Frankie never stopped working. Everyone else went on, business as usual. It was as though only my world had gone on without me, running its parallel life, and was waiting for me to simply step back into it.

Frankie was surprisingly forgiving. He didn't even drink for the first week I was back. Despite everything, he understood the power of this grief. And above all, he seemed relieved to have me home, though I wasn't myself anymore.

"Did you go to the funeral?" I asked him one night as we lay in our old bed.

He shook his head. "Of course not."

The idea that Eva and her girls had been laid to rest without me there had nearly killed me. But I knew that as much as I wanted to be there, needed to be there, it would only be inviting catastrophe. I could only imagine what the accident had done to Ted, how his rage might manifest now. I worried that he would come to Hollyville to punish me. To make me pay for first stealing his wife and then stealing her life. But I also half welcomed the idea. *Let him come,* I thought.

"Have you spoken to Ted?" I asked.

Frankie clearly did not want to talk about it anymore. His eyes burned red, and his hands shook. "I sent a card."

I felt my insides churning, burning. I tried to picture Frankie at Woolworth's picking out a sympathy card to send to Ted: some pastel disaster with meaningless passages of calligraphic scripture that was supposed to somehow express his regret that his wife had single-handedly brought about the death of his wife, three daughters, and their unborn child.

"What did you say?" I asked. "In the card?" My whole body was quaking, and he could feel the seismic repercussions of my grief in the mattress beneath us.

"What was I supposed to say, Billie?" he said angrily. "Sorry my wife tried to steal your wife? Sorry she killed her and your children?"

A blow to my jaw, a bone-crushing fist to my chest, would have hurt less.

He got out of bed then, and like a boxer who had just thrown the knockout punch, he looked somehow both triumphant and stunned.

Downstairs, I could hear him pulling the jug of wine from the cupboard. I could hear him drinking, the radio blaring a baseball game. I could feel the whole house trembling with his anger. Here was my old Frankie: the angry, frustrated man I remembered. And I welcomed him back, this monster. I needed him here to remind me what it was about him that disgusted me, that filled me with anger and self-loathing. But even as all the familiar feelings, of being trapped, of fear and rage and disappointment, mounted, I realized that it didn't matter anymore. I had nowhere to run. There was nothing for me to run to. No one. Eva was dead. And he was right, I had killed her.

"Do you have Johnny's cell phone number?" I ask Gussy.

She nods and reaches into her purse, pulling out her address book. She undoes the various rubber bands she has wound around the book to keep it together and flips to the *W* section. She reads the numbers to me, and I punch them into my cell phone. I hesitate for only a moment, my finger hovering over the Call button.

He answers on the first ring.

"Johnny," I say. "It's Billie Valentine. I'm here. In the parking garage."

Gussy and I make our way through the cavernous garage to the elevators. I think stupidly that we should have brought something: flowers, a coffee cake. But we don't know why we are here, and so our arms are empty as we ride the elevator to the third-floor breezeway and then make our way into the hospital.

I have always hated hospitals, always loathed the minty green walls and antiseptic scent, the cheerful faces of nurses and all the closed doors behind which people were sick and dying. Lou died in a hospital, attached to a thousand machines pumping life into her. It nearly killed me to see her there. When I finally go, my one wish is that I die in my sleep. That my heart stops suddenly and irrevocably while I am lying in my own bed. Or maybe during my morning swim; let the water take me. The sharks and fishes.

"Down this way, I think," Gussy says, pointing to a brass sign on the wall that says 301–313.

We turn the corner and head down the long hallway, our

shoes squeaking on the linoleum. There is a waiting area next to the nurses' station. A man stands up from one of the chairs there and faces us, lifting his arm as if to wave.

"Is that Johnny? He doesn't look sick to me," I say.

As we get closer, the man looks so much like Ted it nearly takes my breath away. My mind spins wildly, out of control. I have one foot in the present and one in the past. And for a moment, I am consumed by fear. He has finally come for me, I think. Ted has finally come to punish me for everything that happened with Eva. And I think as my heart accelerates, the engine of my body burning hot and fast, that my wish might not come true. My heart might just stop here in this awful hospital. But when we get closer, and he holds out his hand, I can see it isn't Ted (of course it isn't Ted). It is Johnny. Johnny, Eva's Johnny.

He is in his fifties now, but his face remains the same as that child I knew so long ago. The freckled face, the dark hair and wide eyes. His forearms are covered with tattoos, the inky pictures blurred in blue rivers underneath a mess of black hair. He is large, muscular. His jaw set firmly, his eyes sad and tired.

"Billie," he says, and he holds my hand, studies me as if looking for the woman he knew in my wrinkled face, in my wild silver hair. "Thank you so much for coming."

"Why are we here?" I say. I feel tricked. Cheated. We have just driven three and a half hours through the night, and Johnny is not on his deathbed. As far as I can tell he's as healthy as can be. "I thought you were dying."

Johnny shakes his head and smiles sadly, motioning for us to sit in a couple of chairs in the waiting area. Gussy sits down and immediately pulls her knitting from her purse. This is what she does when she doesn't know what to do with her hands. I envy her this mindless task, this busyness.

I sit down, readying myself for whatever it is that Johnny plans to say, and he sits across from me. He takes both of my hands, and looks at me intently. He smiles.

"I remember your face," he says. "It's the same. Your eyes."

I nod. I don't want to interrupt him, but I'm also hoping he'll tell me what's going on.

"Can I get you some coffee?" he asks. "Tea?"

I shake my head. "Why did you ask me here?" I ask.

"Gussy might have told you about my troubles," he says.

"Yes," I say. "She said you've had some problems with drinking."

"That's putting it mildly," he says, laughing a little. "I spent a lot of years trying to erase what happened that day with booze and pills and other shit. Excuse my language." He blushes.

My eyes sting. But really, what did I expect? I brace myself for his accusations.

"Losing them felt like the end of the world."

I nod, trying hard not to let those pictures in, the ones of water. The ones of them trapped. My heart is racing.

"But it *wasn't* the end of the world. I grew up. I became a man anyway. I got married anyway. I had children, houses, jobs."

I know he intends for this to make me feel better, but there is little consolation here, because I suspect he may have lost all those things as well. I can read it in his weathered face, his rheumy eyes.

"I'm not sure how you think I can help," I say.

"I didn't see you afterward. I had no way of talking to you . . ."

"I couldn't go to the funeral, you know that, right? Your father would have murdered me with his own hands. I had no choice. . . ." I feel myself coming undone again. I was reassembled that night, as Gussy held the pieces of me in her hands. But these fissures have made me weak, fragile. I worry that I am about to shatter again. I look at him, and know that he probably wants to hear my apologies, to hear that I am sorry for what I did. That little boy needs me. He needs me, and finally, here I am.

"I am sorry," I say, feeling all that sadness and remorse rising to the surface. I feel like I am swallowing sorrow, gallons and gallons of sadness filling my throat and chest. My voice breaks around the deluge. "God, Johnny, I am so sorry."

"Billie," he says, squeezing my hands and willing me to look into his eyes. "You don't understand. That's not why I asked you to come. That's not what this is about."

I look at him, peer into his face, seeing nothing but his heartache, the anguish I caused.

"You didn't say anything?" he says suddenly to Gussy, who doesn't look at us, only shakes her head.

"Gus?" I say.

Johnny clears his throat. "I need to tell you something, and I'm not sure how to say it. I've practiced this a half a million times," he says. "But there's no good way. No way to make it okay. No way to undo it. To change things."

"What are you talking about?" I say. I am aware suddenly of how bright the hospital is. Outside the sun is only now beginning its watercolor undoing of the night, the light bleeding through darkness.

Johnny's hands are trembling. "It's about my mother," he says.

I nod. Of course it is about Eva. Eva is why I am here.

"Donna and Sally and Rose all died in the accident. They were trapped in the car when it went into the river." His voice is cracking.

"I know," I say, shaking my head. This feels cruel already. "I know that."

"But my mother . . . Billie, oh, Jesus . . ." Johnny is starting to cry now, and my first impulse is to hold him, to comfort him. He could be an eight-year-old child again. But he isn't; he is a grown man. He takes a deep breath and squeezes my hand again.

"Billie, my mother and I were both thrown from the car before it went into the water."

The fluorescent hospital lights are blinding. My head pounds, and my heart pounds, and I squeeze my eyes shut. On the back of my eyes is the image of the river, the car, the children and Eva stuck inside.

"No," I say. "She and the girls were all in the car. They drowned." The air seems suddenly thinner. "Frankie told me. Your aunt explained everything that happened. Frankie talked to your father." I feel vertiginous. All of the blood is rushing from my face to my hands. Everything is numb and tingly.

"Billie, listen to me," Johnny says, willing me back. Pulling my hands to him as if he can save me now. "Mary had to tell you that. She had to tell you my mother was gone. My father made her. Don't you understand? It was the only way for him to finally put an end to it."

I hold on to the edge of the plastic seat, and Gussy's arm finds me, ready to catch me.

"It was a lie, Billie," he says, his eyes filling with tears.

"Gus?" I say, waiting for an answer.

Gussy reaches for me, her eyes wet. "Billie, I didn't know. When Johnny told me, I couldn't believe it," she says. She squeezes my hand. She looks frail now; her hands are trembling and her voice is shivery. Like a child. I feel lost in time. I feel lost. "You have to know I had no idea. Frankie either. If we'd had any idea, we would have told you. I would have taken you to her myself."

"Why am I here?" I ask them both, feeling as though I am drowning. My head held under the cold, cold water.

"She's sick," Johnny says. "She's dying. And she's been asking for you."

I am a swimmer. My whole life I have relied on the properties of water. I have trusted it to tell the truth. But water is no different than memory; I know this now.

In my memory that accident is as vivid and real as though I were standing there myself, watching as the car tumbled with Eva and the girls bouncing inside like popcorn in a pan. I can recall the smell of spring mud, frozen under new snow. The sound of the river rushing in its icy current. The taste of snow on my tongue as I opened my mouth to scream. I *watched* them drown.

But water, like memory, is more devious than it appears, becoming exactly what you need for it to be: liquid or solid. Yielding or firm. It capitulates, or resists. And sometimes, it just evaporates. It simply disappears into thin air, steam rising to the heavens and only a screaming teapot left behind.

I struggle for the memories of the conversations with Frankie, with those days after we returned home. But I can't trust any of them now; they bob and dip and then disappear. The truths are submerged.

"But I would have known," I say, shaking my head, still denying this new truth, this violent rip in the seamless expanse of my recollection. "If she were alive."

Johnny shakes his head. "She almost died. She was in the hospital for nearly a month after the accident. She broke both of her legs. Her wrists. One of her lungs was collapsed. And then, when she finally came home, it was like she wasn't really home at all. She blamed herself for the accident. She . . ."

"What about the baby?" I ask.

Johnny shakes his head.

"But why didn't she find me? Why didn't she call? She would have called me." I realize then that I am being selfish, a child. She must have blamed me too. If I hadn't asked her to leave Ted, she wouldn't have been out driving in the storm; her children would not have died. "Did she know what Ted told us?"

Johnny shook his head. "I don't know. She was only home for about a month when she took the pills. They were the painkillers the doctors had given her. My father had her sent to Danvers, you know Danvers?"

God, I thought. The mental hospital. The one that looked like a castle, a castle in nightmares.

"How long was she there?" I ask.

"Three years," he says, and I feel like I can't breathe. All those years, she was locked away only fifteen miles away from me, and I had no idea.

It is as though I am listening to a story about someone else, a made-up story. This, the supposed truth, is so far from my own. So far from what I have lived with for the last forty-eight years. I cannot reconcile any of this with what my heart knows, what my body knows.

"No," I say, wishing it away, willing it away. I can't decide which truth suits me. If it is what I knew to be true, that she died in the river that day, then it explains away the last forty-eight desperate years. It justifies the grief that has settled in my marrow, that pumps through my heart with every beat, that lives in my lungs. But this other story, this strange upended version of events, negates it all. If Eva survived, she would have found me. But she *was* alive, and she did not reach out to me, did not try to find me. I am not sure I can take this.

"She was destroyed, Billie," he says as if I have spoken out loud, by way of explanation. "She was trapped. By her guilt. By my father. There was nothing she could do. She just gave up, Billie. She had no choice."

I am crying now, tears that have lived inside my eyes for decades. They feel ancient and primitive as they emerge, as they stain my cheeks. I have stored this salty water, this ocean of sorrow inside of me for nearly fifty years. I have spent nearly half a century, half of my *life,* wishing I could unwind the years, unravel the knots, backtrack and undo. Knowing that it all began with me. That I was the one who pushed her to leave Ted. Who left Frankie too soon. That I was the one who asked her to drive through the storm to me that night. That my anger, my impatience, my foolish and selfish desire for something I could never ever have, that maybe I didn't even deserve, were what drove her and the girls into the river. Sorrow swells in my throat. "I'm sorry. I am so sorry."

"It was an accident," Gussy says, reaching for my hand. "It wasn't your fault."

"Billie," Johnny says, making me look at him. Making me look into his little boy's eyes. See the little boy's pain in that ravaged face. "For a long time, I blamed you. I did. But she didn't. My mother never blamed you."

I look at him, at his eyes that are also filling with tears. And I ask the one question only he can answer. "Then why didn't she find me?"

"Don't you understand?" Johnny says. "That is why I asked you to come here. That's why you're sitting here right now. She asked *me* to look for you. She *has* found you."

Eva is in this building. Eva is on the other side of the door we have been looking at across the hall. I can barely make sense of this. I am gripping Gussy's arm, to stay tethered to the earth. What is waiting for me on the other side of that door? Who is she now?

I try to imagine her inside Danvers. Ted had threatened her before; women could be sent there for nearly any reason back then. Defiance, depression. And Eva was guilty of both. Imprisoned for simply wanting independence. Detained for her despair.

Treated like an animal instead of a woman, like a lunatic. Danvers was the stuff of childhood nightmares, a place most people went to and never came back.

"They stayed married?" I ask Johnny. "She and Ted?"

"Yes," he says. "If you can call what they had a marriage. He never forgave her. And she never forgave herself. After I left home, they stopped bothering to keep up appearances. He had girlfriends. He disappeared for weeks, months at a time."

"Why didn't she leave?" I say.

"I don't know," Johnny says. "I was so caught up in my own troubles, I barely had room for hers, for theirs."

There are more people in the waiting room now. It is morning, and the orderlies are pushing carts with silver-lidded breakfast trays down the hallways. The eleven-to-seven shift ends, and the morning nurses come in.

"Can I see her?" I ask, my throat swollen and aching.

"Of course," Johnny says, almost laughing. "That's why you're here."

It takes every bit of my strength to stand and take Johnny's arm, which he offers to me. It is as if the past forty-eight years have finally taken their toll. I can feel every joint protest, every bone, every muscle resist. It is as though I am asking my body to make a thousand-mile journey instead of a simple walk down a hospital corridor.

"I'll stay here," Gussy says.

Johnny opens the door slowly. "Mama?" he says, leading the way into the dark room with his head first. I wait like a child behind him.

There is no answer, and for one horrifying second I fear the worst. That she has passed while I was sitting on the other side of this door.

"She's sleeping," he says, and I stop moving. "It's okay. Come in, and we'll wait for her to wake up."

We walk into the double room, past an empty bed. There is a pale curtain dividing the room in two. The only light is a dim overhead that gives everything an eerie glow.

Johnny gently pulls the curtain back and motions for me to come with him to the other side, where Eva lies sleeping in the hospital bed.

I dreamed her back alive again. For years after her first death, I summoned her every single night. I pulled her from the shallow depths of that dream river. I saved her again and again.

She was with me when I fought with Frankie, touching my tensed shoulders as he and I fought, the same argument repeated: a skipping record, a stutter, a stammer, an endlessly repeating tic. She whispered in my ear as I lay down next to him each night, calming me, soothing me with promises that this would not last forever. And I conjured her. I conjured June, the June that never came. The summer that never was. The summer after she arrived safely at camp with her children. The summer we lived together for the first time, not as a secret, in shame, but as a real family. The nights when Frankie tossed and turned, exorcising demons, exorcising Eva, I invoked her. I invited her into our bed. I let her sleep between us.

She was with me as the girls grew older, as I grew older.

She sat on top of the dryer Frankie salvaged from a Laundromat that closed down, the one he offered to me as though an appliance could provide some recompense for everything I'd lost. Her legs dangled off the edge of the dryer, as she watched me do laundry and iron Frankie's uniform. She was with me in the kitchen as I baked casseroles and cookies and coffee cakes. She sat on the edge of the bathtub at night, as I tried to soak away the sorrow, imagined it swirling in the soapy water down the drain. She wiped away a million tears with the soft pad of her thumb.

She was there at Chessy's graduation from high school, with

me as I drove home after dropping her off at college. I'm fairly sure she took the wheel that night, because I barely remember driving home.

She was the warmth of the sun, the brightness of the moon, the hopefulness of wishing stars.

She was there when Mouse ran away from home the first time, waiting with me as I paced, a dead phone in my hand after calling everyone who might know where she was. She was with me when Mouse came home with a red hickey on her neck and pine needles in her hair and whiskey on her breath and Frankie got drunk and angry and accused her of being just like her mother. When he smelled her fingers and demanded to know who her girlfriend was. When he called her a *dyke,* a *whore*. Together, Eva and I held Mouse in our arms and whispered our apologies into her ears.

She was with me every time I almost left but didn't.

And she was with me a year later, after Mouse had left for good and Frankie and I were alone: when I woke up one morning and decided I couldn't live like this for another minute. She was the one who told me that I didn't have to make his coffee, iron his shirts, endure his hateful glances or his pathetic pleas for another moment. She packed my bags for me, and she was the one who turned the key in the ignition. She rolled down the window, turned up the radio, and I remember (*I swear I remember*), she said, "Faster, Billie! Let's fly!" as her hair blew out the window.

I watch her sleep, just as I have watched her sleep a hundred times before. I have memorized her breaths, the shivers of her shoulders and her sighs. Her hair is spread across the stiff, white pillow. It is silver now, but still as long and thick as it always was. Her face is still that quiet dreamy white of youth, though the years are etched in the lines in her forehead and mouth. Her long neck is exposed, the little hollow at her throat. Something about this makes her seem vulnerable, and I have the sudden urge to protect her.

"Please, sit down," Johnny says, motioning to a chair next to the bed. It looks as though he has been sleeping here. There is a blanket and a pillow he removes to make room for me. He squeezes my arm. "I'll be out in the waiting room if you need me. Thank you for coming, Billie."

I nod, never taking my eyes off of Eva.

I reach for her hand. It rests at her side like a sleeping bird. An IV is taped to the back of it, and veins, like rivers, run across the surface of her skin.

Her eyes open at my touch, and she turns toward me, expecting Johnny, I imagine.

"Eva," I say. Her name feels like something forbidden in my mouth.

Her eyes are unfocused, but slowly, they widen in disbelief. "Billie?" she says.

"I'm here," I say. I don't have any other words. Words are clumsy things, inept things.

"I was driving too fast," she says. "I was so upset. I just wanted to get to you."

Tears are coming down her cheeks, fat, slow tears. And I feel something so old, so primitive, it's as though it were the very first feeling anyone, anywhere, ever had. I reach, instinctively, to stop the tumbling teardrop with my thumb, returning the favor, I suppose.

"Well, you finally made it," I say, feeling warmth spreading into her cold hand.

"I did," she says, nodding. "I promised I would."

Gussy returns to Vermont, but I stay in Cambridge at Chessy's house. She greets me at her door and lingers when I hug her. When she finally pulls away, her eyes are wet with tears. "Please, come in."

Her house, like Gussy's house, is warm and light and filled with books. She and her husband are both biology professors, though her husband, Michael, retired last year. He watches birds now, and he's in Nova Scotia this week, tracking puffins. I can imagine her in front of a classroom full of students; she was always, always a leader. She is humble about her accomplishments, but Michael has kept me updated over the years on the awards she has won, the articles she has had published. I am swollen with pride for her and all that she has become, despite everything, *because* of it.

There are photos hung on every wall, snapshots and more artful black-and-white photographs that document and preserve her children's lives as well as her own. After I left Frankie, she staked claim to all of the photo albums, rescuing those artifacts I left behind. Chessy, like her father, is a historian of sorts, and she salvaged these treasures from the wreckage of our family's life. Frankie had destroyed all of the photos I had of Eva in a fit of rage, and the others, the ones that remained, were too painful for me to look at. When I left, I took only one photograph. It was one Eva had taken of me and the girls at the camping trip to Rippling River. I look so young in the photo, the girls grubby and smiling.

When I called to tell her about Eva, she had only said, "Oh, my God. Oh, Mom." Now, over tea and my mother's coffee cake (which Chessy has perfected), we talk. She holds my hands across the kitchen table and listens intently. One thing I have noticed about Chessy in the last few years is that she has become a good listener. Perhaps it is motherhood that has made her this way. She never interrupts, and she has lost that look in her eye that she used to have as a child, the one that seemed to suggest she was constantly assessing, judging, what was being said and who was saying it.

This is the first time we have talked about Eva in years. About running away from Frankie that Easter Sunday. About what happened to Eva and her girls.

"How is she?" she asks me, and I feel as though someone has uncorked me. My throat opens, and my heart spills.

"She's very sick. She's had three bouts with cancer since the mastectomy all those years ago. She stopped treatment last month."

Chessy squeezes my hands.

The cake is sweet.

"Do you remember," she says, "the time we went apple picking? With the Scouts?"

I start to laugh, remembering Eva running away from the farmer who had caught us poaching his apples. I remember her looking over her shoulder, her dress hiked up, cradling all those stolen apples as she ran. I remember Mouse jogging happily along beside her, and Chessy standing behind, terrified and clutching my hand.

"I remember thinking that she was magical," Chessy says, her face breaking into a smile. "I was always such a scaredy-cat. I remember wishing that when I grew up I could be just like her."

I blink hard to keep my tears from falling.

"Me too," I say, my words catching in my throat.

"I have something for you," she says, standing up. "A little surprise."

"I don't think I can take any more surprises," I say, half expecting Frankie to jump out from behind the kitchen counter, though he's been dead now for a decade. "Please."

"Stay right here," she says.

When she comes back, she hands me two packages. Both of them are beautifully, meticulously wrapped. "Just open one. The other one is for Eva."

I carefully undo the ribbon and slip my finger under the tape to reveal what's inside. It's a frame, I can see, and my heart pounds as I turn it over.

The photograph is of Eva and me standing together at the boat access area at Gormlaith. It was taken that first summer, before Eva got sick, and she's wearing her blue bathing suit. We have our arms around each other and are mugging for the camera. We look so young, so beautiful, so happy. For one brief moment I am transported. I can feel the cold water around my ankles, almost taste the breeze. I can hear the sound of a biplane that has flown overhead. This photo was taken only a moment before it flew across the sky, and we all looked up, shielding our eyes from the bright sun. I can smell her skin, feel her hand on my hip.

"Where did you get this?" I ask, my throat swollen.

"After Daddy burned all the pictures, I found the negatives and hid them. There were only a couple of pictures of Eva. But I like this one. Do you remember the biplane?"

I nod, smiling.

"Eva said someday she'd like to ride in one of those. Feel the clouds in her hair, that's what she said," Chessy says, laughing.

"I remember," I say. "Thank you."

Every day for a week, I go to the hospital and visit Eva. I bring her little gifts to make her happy: the photograph from Chessy, maple candies, lilac hand lotion, magazines. I sit next to her and hold her hand as I read from the books we used to love.

When she sleeps, I spend time with Johnny. He's a good man, and he's trying so hard to get better. His father's suicide has tested him, has pushed him to examine himself. To examine his life.

"How is Mouse?" he asks one afternoon as we eat lunch in the hospital cafeteria. "God, I was such a rotten little shit to her."

"Mouse is terrific," I say. "She lives in New Mexico. In a teepee."

He slaps his knee and laughs so hard. I think of him and Mouse tearing around the neighborhood in the Indian head-dresses Eva and I made, their war cries. Their whooping laughter.

"I'm going to stop in New Mexico and see her on my way home," I say.

"Well, please tell her hello," he says.

Eva knows I am here, though sometimes she doesn't know who I am. When this happens, I am rendered speechless and paralyzed until her memory comes back; it's like the moon, waxing and waning as she grows sicker. Sometimes she confuses the stories we read with real life.

"Tell me that story," she says softly one morning. It is cold out now; winter is coming.

"What story?" I ask.

"The love story," she says.

"*Ethan Frome*?" I ask. We've just finished this one; it's sitting next to her on the nightstand next to a blue plastic pitcher of water.

She shakes her head; her eyes are glistening. "No, the one about the artist. The artist and the swimmer. That swimmer with the beautiful long legs."

I nod, and I lean over and whisper in her ear. "A long, long time ago, there was a very lonely woman who thought she'd never fall in love . . . until the beautiful artist moved into the empty house across the street."

Eva closes her eyes, and I think she has fallen asleep. I lean over and kiss the fragile skin at her temple, feel her pulse beating underneath with my lips.

Her voice is just a whisper.

"I want to go to the lake, Billie. Will you please take me to the lake?"

Gussy drives us to the lake, and I sit in the backseat with Eva. We hold hands, sharing a quilt that Chessy sent along with us to keep Eva warm. The air is brittle outside, but the sky is bright. The few remaining leaves cling to their branches, and the road is carpeted with them. When the lake comes into sight, Eva squeezes my hand and I look down at our intertwined fingers. After all this time, I still recognize every bone in her hand. I have traced every tendon and vein with my fingertips as though they were a map leading home.

Effie and the girls are waiting for us outside. Plum is swinging in the swing under the tree house, and Zu-Zu is doing cartwheels on the lawn. Effie waves excitedly, and runs to the car as we pull into the driveway.

"Welcome, welcome!!" she says as we get out of the car. And we both help Eva out of the backseat. Effie takes Eva inside, and Gussy starts unloading the trunk, all of the baskets and bags. On the way up from Boston we drove past a farm stand, and Eva had asked if we could stop. Gussy pulled over, and Eva insisted on getting out of the car. She went straight to the bins that were overflowing with apples.

"Look," she said, reaching for me. "Winter apples."

"Devin and I have a surprise for you," Effie says after we have settled Eva on the daybed on the sleeping porch. She takes my hand and leads me out to the back, where Devin has been working on the guest cottage. It looks like something from a fairy tale: gingerbread trim, a miniature porch, a Dutch doorway.

"It's almost finished," she says.

"It's still a little rustic," Devin says, opening the top Dutch door. "But there's a working bathroom. I've got it wired now too, and there's a nice space heater to keep you warm. Come on in." He opens the bottom half of the door and takes my hand.

I follow him into the little cottage, my heart pounding hard and certain in my chest. Inside, the walls are made of cedar; it smells like the forest. There is a double bed, covered with pillows and quilts, a tiny writing desk, and bookcases filled with library books.

"I asked Gussy what your favorites were. The Athenaeum gave them to me on permanent loan," Effie says.

I run my fingers across the spines.

"And look!" she says, her eyes bright. "We found these in the old shed before we tore it down. I don't know why I held on to them, but I did."

On one of these shelves there are twenty or thirty record albums. I pick up the first one and smile. Sam Cooke. "This is Eva's favorite," I say, my eyes filling with tears.

"There's a record player here. I bought a brand-new needle."

"Thank you," I say. "This is all so thoughtful."

Later that night, after Gussy has left for home and we have moved our things into the guest cottage, Devin and Effie disappear into the camp, leaving us alone. I can hear the sound of their girls' laughter, and it makes me smile.

Eva is tired, I know. This has been a long trip, and I can hear her labored breath as she moves to the bookshelves and picks up the record. She slips it from its sleeve and runs her fingers across the label. She bends over to put the record on the record player and then lowers the needle into the groove, and that old crackle and hiss overwhelms me.

"Dance with me, Billie?" she says.

I move to her and she leans her head into my chest. The music fills the cottage, and my feet remember. My hands remember. My whole body recollects.

We slip gently into the past, like two bodies into water, but when we emerge it is not into the past, not into that place where we never belonged. But instead, we surface into a new future, the future we should have had, the one we were denied. The one stolen from us.

"Remember?" I ask as she peers up at me.

And she looks at me with her eyes as bright and wild and beautiful as they ever were and nods.

"I remember, Billie. I remember everything."

Memory is the same as water. It is a still lake bathed in moonlight, a vast ocean, a violent river ready to carry you away. It can calm you or it can harm you; it is both more powerful and weaker than you'd think. It is a paradox.

Back at home, I seek solace in the water: in the steaming hot showers that pummel my tired shoulders, in the cool water I drink to stay alive. I find all the necessary comfort in the ocean, in its crashing waves singing me to sleep and in its enormous embrace.

It is winter now, though you wouldn't know it. All of the tourists are gone, and the beach belongs to me and the other locals. It is good to be home again. Linda is glad to have me back at the library. Robert decided to go back to school for the second semester, and while this is good, I know she needs me to help fill the space he has left behind. Juan too is happy to have me back. He expects me each night, and we watch the sun set together in the nearly empty bar before I make my way home. The girls at Daybreak chat and smile as they make my coffee the way I like it, and my refrigerator is full of good things that Mena has made and Sam has delivered. I am taken care of here. I am not alone.

And so each morning I rise, as I always rise, as soon as the sun taps my shoulders and I click off the twinkling lights on my porch to let Pete know that all is well. Then I slip on my suit and make my way down the stone steps to the beach.

The water is cold, but it makes me feel alive. *Reminds* me that I am alive.

"You are a swimmer," it says in its thunderous voice. It is right, I think. I am a swimmer; that is what I have always been. And from my place in the ocean, I glance at the shore to look for her. For Eva, though I know she is really gone now. I was there, this time, to say good-bye.

But sometimes, when the light is right, I still find her standing there. She wears the bright blue suit she always wore, and her legs are long and strong. Her lips are red, and her hair tumbles freely down her pale back. She waves a big, happy wave to me from her place on the shore. And she cups her hands to her mouth to holler something out to me, but the music of the ocean is too loud, and I can't hear her anymore. And so I just smile back at her, put my head and arms into the water. And I swim.

Acknowledgments

Stories are always gifts.

Most of the time, they arrive simply as offerings from my own imagination. But other times, they are bestowed by others, presented tentatively, wrapped in beautiful paper and tied up with complicated little bows. *Bodies of Water* was such a gift.

In the summer of 2011, Hurricane Irene devastated much of my home state of Vermont. The deluge carried away old barns, homes, and bridges. We had just left our summer camp on Newark Pond in the Northeast Kingdom, where we spend every August, and were staying with family on our way home. Because I was driving, and because of the storm that was pummeling the entire East Coast, our hosts graciously asked us to stay another night. And something about the storm, something about being trapped inside, hunkered down together for one more night, seemed to open all of us up, and, because I come from a family of storytellers, we started to share stories. But it was *this* story, this beautiful love story, that kept me awake all night long. As the rain and wind pounded against the windows, I could almost feel the ribbons in my fingers as I slowly began to unwrap this gift.

This novel is absolutely fiction, but the seed of truth planted that night, nurtured by all that wild rain, was where it began. And so first I thank you, Irene, you miserable witch; here is proof that at least one good thing came out of your fury.

Thank you to my cousins (*second* or *once removed* or whatever you are), Angela and Carlene Riccelli, who shared and shared and shared. Who trusted and then shared even more. This is for you both.

Thank you to my mother, Cyndy Greenwood, for being there and encouraging me to tell this story. And to my father and sister who, for some reason, continue to be my biggest fans. To Esther Stewart for her early read, as well.

To Patrick for helping when things get rough.

To Mikaela and Esmée for reminding me again and again of why I do what I do.

To Rich Farrell for your honest and meticulous reading every single time.

To Miranda Beverly-Whittemore for your friendship, for the perfect title, and for your crazy talent.

To Henry Dunow for your wild and beautiful enthusiasm. It always comes just when I need it the most.

And to Peter Senftleben (as always) for helping me to part the clouds.

A READING GROUP GUIDE

Bodies of Water

T. Greenwood

The following discussion questions and playlist are included to enhance your group's reading of *Bodies of Water*.

Discussion Questions

1. This is a love story, but it is also the story of an affair, an infidelity. Discuss how that impacts your reading of the characters and empathy to their situations.

2. Billie's insecurities about herself as a mother run deep. Are they warranted? Is she a good mother? Why or why not?

3. What does Eva represent to Billie? Do you think Eva was in love with her specifically or with the notion of her? Do you think she would have stayed with Billie had she made it to Vermont?

4. Each woman has a different motive for getting involved in this relationship. What are these motives? What does each woman gain from the other's love and companionship?

5. Billie has made a life for herself in California. Do you think she is truly happy? Why or why not? How about at the end of the novel, once she knows what really happened to Eva?

6. Billie alludes to another relationship, but she says, "Even Lou, who was my constant companion for nearly twenty-five years, is shadowy now. A whisper. An echo. But the picture of Eva is brilliant." What do you think this says about her relationship with Lou? Discuss your impressions of Lou.

7. Discuss each of the marriages (Ted and Eva, Billie and Frankie). How would you characterize these men? How are they similar? How are they different?

8. What do you think motivates Johnny to orchestrate the reunion between Eva and Billie? Why did he not do it sooner? Discuss what his relationship with Ted might have been like growing up.

9. What does Billie sacrifice in order to move on with her life? Are there any other victims here?

10. This novel returns to the fictional Lake Gormlaith found in many of T. Greenwood's novels. Discuss what the lake setting provides for Billie and Eva.

11. Do you think that Gussy knew what was transpiring between Eva and Billie? Was she complicit in the affair? Do you think she knew that Eva survived the crash? If so, why would she not tell Billie?

12. In the end, Johnny tells Billie that Ted lied to end the affair, and told Frankie that Billie was dead. Do you think Frankie would have told Billie the truth if he knew it?

13. How might the love story between Billie and Eva have played out if they had met in 2013 instead of the 1960s? Would their romance really have been easier, more accepted? Why or why not? Discuss how the social and cultural restrictions of the 1960s shaped their affair and what the differences would be today.

14. Early on, older Billie observes patrons of the library: "I've seen how lost people get on the Internet, tapping away frantically. Teenagers lined up in a row not speaking to each other, but rather clicking away on their Facebook pages, sending e-mails, instant messaging, ignoring one another in favor of their virtual friends. Watching them makes me feel strangely lonely." Explore the theme of loneliness in *Bodies of Water*. How and when is Billie lonely? When is she not?

15. Reread the opening paragraphs to the first and last chapters. Has the concept of memory evolved over the course of the novel? If so, how? If not, discuss the consistencies. Talk about the importance of memory in the book and in the way you experience your own lives and loves.

The *Bodies of Water* Playlist

Music is significant in setting the tone and time period in *Bodies of Water*. Below are the songs and artists mentioned in the novel; listening to them might set the mood for your reading group meeting.

"A Change Is Gonna Come"
This song by Sam Cooke isn't used in the novel, but if there were a soundtrack, this would be on it, its theme song.

"Moonlight in Vermont"
A jazz standard that has been covered by hundreds of singers, but the most notable versions that Eva would know are by Ella Fitzgerald and Louis Armstrong, Sarah Vaughan, Billie Holiday, Ray Charles, Frank Sinatra, and, again, Sam Cooke.

Chet Baker
By the time Billie helps Eva take a soothing bath away from the kids in 1960, Chet Baker had released over a dozen records. She most likely would have had *Chet Baker Sings* or *Embraceable You* to put on the hi-fi.

Perry Como, Jo Stafford, and Kate Smith
Billie's preferred musical taste, with Kate Smith being her favorite. I imagine she used to watch *The Kate Smith Show* when Frankie was drinking his wine.

Chubby Checker and Sam Cooke
Eva liked to listen to jazz and rock 'n' roll more than Billie did, but they would sometimes dance to Chubby Checker.

"Alone Together"
The version Billie and Eva dance to in February 1961 was most

likely recorded by Peggy Lee but could have been performed by Judy Garland or Chet Baker.

"Runaway" by Del Shannon
Billie picks up a fuzzy signal on the radio while camping with the Girl Scouts and they listen to this number one hit from 1961.

Kind of Blue by Miles Davis
The song being played by a band when Billie and Eva first enter a New York City bar with Dot is off of one of Eva's favorite records, the Miles Davis classic *Kind of Blue*.

"Forbidden Fruit" by Nina Simone
Another song the band plays in the bar, which seems appropriate.

"My Shining Hour" by John Coltrane
Eva and Billie dance to this song in the bar before sharing their first public kiss.

The Hollies
When Billie goes to Boston, she offers to stop at a record store and pick up the new Elvis album, *Fun in Acapulco,* for Chessy and Mouse.

Have you read all of T. Greenwood's critically acclaimed novels?
Available in trade paperback and as e-books.

BREATHING WATER

Three years after leaving Lake Gormlaith, Vermont, Effie Greer is coming home. The unspoiled lake, surrounded by dense woods and patches of wild blueberries, is the place where she spent idyllic childhood summers at her grandparents' cottage. And it's where Effie's tempestuous relationship with her college boyfriend, Max, culminated in a tragedy she can never forget.

Effie had hoped to save Max from his troubled past, and in the process became his victim. Since then, she's wandered from one city to another, living like a fugitive. But now Max is gone, and as Effie paints and restores the ramshackle cottage, she forms new bonds—with an old school friend, with her widowed grandmother, and with Devin, an artist and carpenter summering nearby. Slowly, she's discovering a resilience and tenderness she didn't know she possessed, and—buoyed by the lake's cool, forgiving waters—she may even learn to save herself.

Wrenching yet ultimately uplifting, here is a novel of survival, hope, and absolution, from a writer of extraordinary insight and depth.

GRACE

T. Greenwood's extraordinary novels deftly combine lyrical prose with heartrending subject matter. Now she explores one year in a family poised to implode, and the imperfect love that may be its only salvation.

Every family photograph hides a story. Some are suffused with warmth and joy, others reflect the dull ache of disappointed dreams. For thirteen-year-old Trevor Kennedy, taking photos helps make sense of his fractured world. His father, Kurt, struggles to keep a business going while also caring for Trevor's aging grandfather, whose hoarding has reached dangerous levels. Trevor's mother, Elsbeth, all but ignores her son while doting on his five-year-old sister, Gracy, and pilfering useless drugstore items.

Trevor knows he can count on little Gracy's unconditional love and his art teacher's encouragement. None of that compensates for the bullying he has endured at school for as long as he can remember. But where Trevor once silently tolerated the jabs and name-calling, now anger surges through him in ways he's powerless to control.

Only Crystal, a store clerk dealing with her own loss, sees the deep fissures in the Kennedy family—in the haunting photographs Trevor brings to be developed, and in the palpable distance between Elsbeth and her son. And as their lives become more intertwined, each will be pushed to the breaking point, with shattering, unforeseeable consequences.

NEARER THAN THE SKY

In this mesmerizing novel, T. Greenwood draws readers into the fascinating and frightening world of Munchausen syndrome by proxy—and into one woman's search for healing.

When Indie Brown was four years old, she was struck by lightning. In the oft-told version of the story, Indie's life was heroically saved by her mother. But Indie's own recollection of the event, while hazy, is very different.

Most of Indie's childhood memories are like this—tinged with vague, unsettling images and suspicions. Her mother, Judy, fussed over her pretty youngest daughter, Lily, as much as she ignored Indie. That neglect, coupled with the death of her beloved older brother, is the reason Indie now lives far away in rural Maine. It's why her relationship with Lily is filled with tension, and why she dreads the thought of flying back to Arizona. But she has no choice. Judy is gravely ill, and Lily, struggling with a challenge of her own, needs her help.

In Arizona, faced with Lily's hysteria and their mother's instability, Indie slowly begins to confront the truth about her half-remembered past and the legacy that still haunts her family. And as she revisits her childhood, with its nightmares and lost innocence, she finds she must reevaluate the choices of her adulthood—including her most precious relationships.

THIS GLITTERING WORLD

Acclaimed author T. Greenwood crafts a moving, lyrical story of loss, atonement, and promises kept.

One November morning, Ben Bailey walks out of his Flagstaff, Arizona, home to retrieve the paper. Instead, he finds Ricky Begay, a young Navajo man, beaten and dying in the newly fallen snow.

Unable to forget the incident, especially once he meets Ricky's sister, Shadi, Ben begins to question everything, from his job as a part-time history professor to his fiancée, Sara. When Ben first met Sara, he was mesmerized by her optimism and easy confidence. These days, their relationship only reinforces a loneliness that stretches back to his fractured childhood.

Ben decides to discover the truth about Ricky's death, both for Shadi's sake and in hopes of filling in the cracks in his own life. Yet the answers leave him torn—between responsibility and happiness, between his once-certain future and the choices that could liberate him from a delicate web of lies he has spun.

UNDRESSING THE MOON

Dark and compassionate, graceful yet raw, Undressing the Moon *explores the seams between childhood and adulthood, between love and loss . . .*

At thirty, Piper Kincaid feels too young to be dying. Cancer has eaten away her strength; she'd be alone but for a childhood friend who's come home by chance. Yet with all the questions of her future before her, she's adrift in the past, remembering the fateful summer she turned fourteen and her life changed forever.

Her nervous father's job search seemed stalled for good, as he hung around the house watching her mother's every move. What he and Piper had both dreaded at last came to pass: Her restless, artistic mother, who smelled of lilacs and showed Piper beauty, finally left.

With no one to rely on, Piper struggled to hold on to what was important. She had a brother who loved her and a teacher enthralled with her potential. But her mother's absence, her father's distance, and a volatile secret threatened her delicate balance.

Now Piper is once again left with the jagged pieces of a shattered life. If she is ever going to put herself back together, she'll have to begin with the summer that broke them all. . . .

THE HUNGRY SEASON

It's been five years since the Mason family vacationed at the lakeside cottage in northeastern Vermont, close to where prize-winning novelist Samuel Mason grew up. The summers that Sam, his wife, Mena, and their twins Franny and Finn spent at Lake Gormlaith were noisy, chaotic, and nearly perfect. But since Franny's death, the Masons have been flailing, one step away from falling apart. Lake Gormlaith is Sam's last, best hope of rescuing his son from a destructive path and salvaging what's left of his family.

As Sam struggles with grief, writer's block, and a looming deadline, Mena tries to repair the marital bond she once thought was unbreakable. But even in this secluded place, the unexpected—in the form of an over-zealous fan, a surprising friendship, and a second chance—can change everything.

From the acclaimed author of *Two Rivers* comes a compelling and beautifully told story of hope, family, and above all, hunger—for food, sex, love, and success—and for a way back to wholeness when a part of oneself has been lost forever.

TWO RIVERS

Two Rivers is a powerful, haunting tale of enduring love, destructive secrets, and opportunities that arrive in disguise . . .

In Two Rivers, Vermont, Harper Montgomery is living a life overshadowed by grief and guilt. Since the death of his wife, Betsy, twelve years earlier, Harper has narrowed his world to working at the local railroad and raising his daughter, Shelly, the best way he knows how. Still wracked with sorrow over the loss of his lifelong love and plagued by his role in a brutal, long-ago crime, he wants only to make amends for his past mistakes.

Then one fall day, a train derails in Two Rivers, and amid the wreckage Harper finds an unexpected chance at atonement. One of the survivors, a pregnant fifteen-year-old girl with mismatched eyes and skin the color of blackberries, needs a place to stay. Though filled with misgivings, Harper offers to take Maggie in. But it isn't long before he begins to suspect that Maggie's appearance in Two Rivers is not the simple case of happenstance it first appeared to be.